P9-DKF-295

THE

GIRL

FROM

EVERYWHERE

THE

GIRL

FROM

EVERYWHERE

HEIDI HEILIG

Greenwillow Books, *An Imprint of* HarperCollins*Publishers*

The Girl from Everywhere
Copyright © 2016 by Heidi Heilig

The text of this book is set in Simoncini Garamond.
Book design by Sylvie Le Floc'h

Library of Congress Cataloging-in-Publication Data is available.

ISBN 978-0-06-238075-3 (hardback)

16 17 18 19 20 PC/RRDH 10 9 8 7 6 5 4 3 2 1
First Edition
 Greenwillow Books

To Bret,

for whom I first wanted to go back

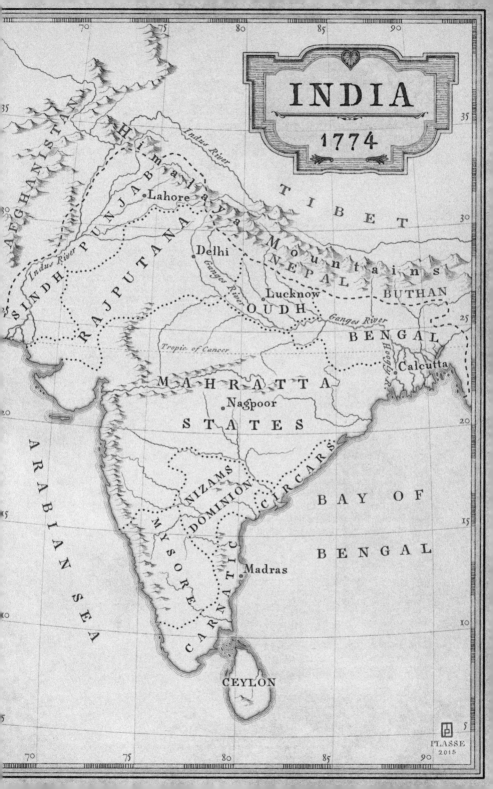

CHAPTER ONE

I t was the kind of August day that hinted at monsoons, and the year was 1774, though not for very much longer. I was in the crowded bazaar of a nearly historical version of Calcutta, where my father had abandoned me.

He hadn't abandoned me for good—not yet. He'd only gone back to the ship to make ready for the next leg of the journey: twentieth-century New York City. It was at our final destination, however, where he hoped to unmake the mistakes of his past.

Mistakes like me, perhaps.

He never said as much, but his willingness to leave me behind was plain: here I was, alone, haggling for a caladrius with a pitiful amount of silver in my palm. Part of me wondered whether he'd care if I returned at all, as long as the mythological bird was delivered to the ship.

No, he would care, at least for *now*. After all, I was the one to plot our way through the centuries and the maps, the one who helped him through his dark times, the one who could, say, identify fantastical animals from twenty paces *and* negotiate with their sellers. Then again, once we reached 1868 Honolulu, he would have no need for navigating or negotiation. I was a means to an end, and the end was looming, closer every day.

But he never worried about that. I tried not to either; I tried desperately hard. Worrying did me no good, especially now, with the bird seller peering at me, as bright-eyed as any of his wares.

"Very rare, this bird!" The merchant spoke louder than the distance between us warranted; we were nose to nose across a stack of cages, but I couldn't step back or I'd be swept up in the scrum of shoppers. "The caladrius will cure any illness, just by looking a patient in the eye—"

"I know, I know." I'd read the myth in an old book of fables: the caladrius could take disease on its wings and burn it away by flying near the sun. The legend also said if your illness was incurable, the bird would refuse to look at you; of course the merchant hadn't mentioned that part.

He crossed his arms over his chest. "Good health is priceless, girl."

"I know that too." I wiped my brow. The sun was panting in the sky, and the heat curdled the perfume of jasmine above the odor of sweat. I had to get back to the ship, if only for some air. "Please. It's for my mother. She'll die without it." Normally I wasn't above using a sob story to haggle, but it felt different when the story was true. In fact, she had already died without it, sixteen years ago. "My father would never, ever recover."

The man's eyes softened, but then the crowd crushed against my back, making space around a fat British officer; locals didn't dare jostle the Company Raj. Distracted, the bird seller glared at the Englishman. "Please," I said again, slightly louder, trying to add the gleam of charity to the tarnished rupees in my hand.

He sucked his teeth, wavering. "A bird like this is worth her weight in gold to a prince."

"But the princes of India don't have any more gold," I said. "The British took it all, and they don't believe in the myth of the caladrius."

As soon as the words were out of my mouth, I knew it was the wrong thing to say. The man's face hardened. Awkward, awkward. I scrambled for a way to backpedal. Between us, his wares beat their wings against the bamboo bars, singing for freedom like Orpheus in Hades. A hand touched my shoulder and I spun, ready to take out my vexation on this bold stranger, but I bit back the words. Kashmir had appeared like an oasis. "Hello, *amira*."

"Let me guess," I said. "The captain sent you here to rush me." Under his careless hair, there was not a drop of sweat on his brow.

"To help you." He gave me his most charming smile, then turned it on the bird seller as he poured gold into the man's palm. "This should be more than enough," Kashmir said, reaching over to pluck up the bamboo cage. Then he slipped his arm into mine and steered me away from the wide-eyed merchant. "Come, Nix. We have to go."

I was more surprised than the bird seller. "Where did you get so much gold?"

"Oh, you know," he said. "Around."

We were halfway back to the docks when the shouting started.

Kashmir handed me the birdcage. "Don't run," he told me. Then he took off.

"Thief!" The Englishman was barreling toward us. "Thief!" Kashmir had left a swirling wake in the crowd; I set off after him.

The treacherous street threw obstacles underfoot: baskets of locusts and pails of yogurt and blankets laid with ripe rambutan. I dodged past women in rags and women in silks, men in loincloths and men in uniforms. The birdcage swung from my fist and sweat stung my eyes. Kashmir was far ahead of me—or rather, I was falling behind.

I racked my brain for a solution from the stories I knew. Unfortunately, most of those stories were myths, so most of the miraculous escapes came about by the pursued being turned into a tree or a star or a bird or the like. I looked back over my shoulder; the Englishman was gaining. I clutched the birdcage to my chest and tried to summon more speed.

I broke free of the market, careening around a corner and bouncing off a donkey. Kashmir was standing on the wharf, waving me toward the ship. I skidded to a stop in front of him, and he took my shoulders, steadying me. "Why did you run, *amira*?"

"Why did *you* run?" I returned, breathless.

"So he would chase me! *Yalla. Vite!* Get aboard and go!" He pushed me along and I stumbled down the quay.

My father was helping Bee rig the sails, but when he heard the Englishman's cries, he stopped and stared. Then he redoubled his efforts, calling out to Rotgut to cast off the lines as the Englishman loped nearer. Locals scattered, but Kashmir waited until I'd cleared the gangplank. When he started to run, it was too late.

The Englishman grabbed him by the collar of his thin linen shirt, his muttonchops quivering in rage. "You half-caste thatch gallows!" He drew a pistol out of his belt and pressed the barrel against Kashmir's cheek. "Give me back my coin and I won't shoot you where you stand!"

Kash didn't bother responding; he made a chopping motion toward the ship, but we were already slipping the berth. I looked at my father in disbelief, but he met my stare with his ice-blue eyes. "He can take care of himself."

Despite the heat, I shivered; if Kash had kept the caladrius, would I be the one left behind on the wharf? I set the birdcage on the deck and gripped the rail, gauging the distance to the pier, but then Kash shoved the Englishman's gun upward. The man squeezed the trigger, and the bullet flew wide. He'd kept his grip on Kashmir's collar, but not on Kashmir, who tore his shirt down the front as he pivoted on one foot and threw his arms back out of the sleeves. He left the man reeling backward with the linen rag in his hand and a bewildered expression on his face.

I ran to get a rope, but when I came back to the bulwark,

Kashmir was nowhere to be seen and the Englishman was screaming from the edge of the pier, fumbling with his gun. I followed his outraged eyes to the stern of the ship, where Kash was swinging his leg over the rail.

"Stop the ship! Stop at once!" the Englishman said, appealing to my father as he tried to reload. "Your coolie is a thief!"

Kashmir put his hand to his chest in a gesture of injured innocence: Kashmir, who would make you laugh to steal the fillings from your molars. Then he ducked as the Englishman fired again, the bullet crunching into the oak of our mizzenmast. I stared, stunned for a moment, then dropped to the deck beside the birdcage, my breath ruffling the caladrius's feathers.

The *Temptation* was a fast ship, so we were out of range by the time the Englishman had loaded a third shot. I clambered to my feet, my hair plastered to my cheeks and my ears ringing. Kashmir was no worse for wear, despite his lost shirt. His golden skin shone, flushed with exertion, and, I suppose, victory. He caught my eye, and I turned away.

"You're blushing," he said.

I heard the amusement in his voice. "It's the heat."

"What a rush!" My father passed the wheel off to Bee and came trotting down the stairs to the main deck. He picked up the cage, peering inside. "My God, she's beautiful," he said, grinning. "Thanks, kiddo!"

"Thanks?" I yanked my shirt straight. "You should be thanking him."

Slate popped a thumb up. "Thanks, Kashmir!"

I stared at him as he cooed at the bird. "You risked his life for that thing."

"Thanks *a lot*, Kashmir."

"He was nearly shot, Dad!"

He shrugged. "He wasn't, though."

"But he could have been!"

His energy faltered for a moment, like a candle burning low. Absently, he rolled up one of the sleeves on his loose cotton shirt, exposing the blue ink crawling up his arms; unless you knew where they were, the tracks were very hard to see beneath his indigo tattoos. Then his grin returned as he nodded to the cage in his hand. "Good thing we have a cure-all, then. Come on, let's fill those sails! Where are we going next, Nixie?"

I wanted to tell him exactly where he could go next, but I bit back the retort. This was nothing new; my father wasn't one to reflect long on his transgressions. He left that to me. "New York, 1981," I said. "I laid the map out this morning.

On your table. Didn't you bother to look?"

He ignored my question. "But . . . every twentieth-century map I've ever seen was off a printing press."

"It's a hobbyist's map. Hand drawn." I drew myself up taller. "I bought it myself last time we were there."

He didn't look impressed. "Fine, great. But are you sure it will work?"

"Making it work is *your* job, Captain," I said. "Until you teach me how to Navigate, of course."

Although he made no answer, he stared at me a while longer before he spun on his heel and went to his cabin. Suddenly I was aware of the eyes of the crew, but when I turned around, Bee seemed very interested in the river ahead, and Rotgut was studiously cleaning his fingernails. Only Kashmir caught my eye. "And *you*," I said.

"Me? What did I do, *amira*?"

"I was this close to getting the bird seller to take my price," I said, but his grin widened; I wasn't fooling him.

"Even if that's true, you said it yourself. The English took all the gold. I was just doing a little redistribution."

"It's still wrong to steal, Kashmir."

"What else should I have done?"

"Maybe leave the bird?"

He looked at me sideways with a twinkle in his eye. "Come, *amira*. You were thrilled when I put it in your hands."

"That's because cure-alls are rare in mythology, outside of healing springs. Not because I think we'll actually get to use it."

"The captain thinks we will. And you know how he is."

"And how is that?"

Kashmir pursed his lips. "Very difficult to refuse."

I folded my arms across my chest. "No argument there," I said softly, staring at the water of the Hooghly. It was the color of bile. "Is the cargo secure?"

"You mean the tigers?" There was a lilt in his voice.

"Yes, the tigers, in all their fearful symmetry." The big cats had been delivered to the ship in flimsy bamboo cages; Kash and Bee had been the ones brave enough to wrestle the cages into the hold. I actually was impressed, but with Kashmir it was usually best not to let it show.

"Last I checked, they were sleeping like kittens," he said, reaching into his pocket and pulling out a gold watch to check the time. Then he tilted it; water ran out from under the face. "Well. They should be fine all the way to New York."

"Where did you get that?"

"Ah. This?" He looked at me from under his brows; if I hadn't known better, I'd have said he was embarrassed. "He shouldn't have called me a half-caste."

I gritted my teeth. "You can't blame that on the captain's orders."

"No, I can't. This was just for me."

"You know, if I had your morals, I could solve all my problems."

He shrugged one shoulder and slipped the watch back into his pocket. "If I had your problems, I could afford to have better morals. I'm going to get another shirt. You have ten seconds to stop me. No?"

He went below, leaving me at the bow. We sailed past the tumbled ruin of Fort William, where the East India Company claimed a hundred English prisoners had perished due to Indian savagery in the dungeon called the Black Hole of Calcutta. Downstream of the city, fishermen pulled *illish* from the turgid river and children swam naked at the *ghats*. I piled my hair atop my head in an effort to cool down, but the breeze licked the back of my neck, hot as a giant's breath.

Kashmir was right about the captain; when he wanted something, he did not stop until he had it. No matter what it cost. No matter who it hurt.

And what he wanted more than anything was to return

to Honolulu, 1868. That's why he needed the map now on offer at Christie's auction house, and the money to win it.

The captain had never bothered investing in stocks, or betting on sports, or even opening a checking account. Slate spent much more time thinking about the past than the future, and it was always a scramble for money whenever he remembered it was useful.

So I'd plotted a route, pulling the maps from his collection. Cash for tigers was not the simplest course I might have charted, but I'd wanted to see as much as I could before the auction. After all, if Slate was right about the map of Hawaii, I might never go anywhere else again.

My mind skittered away from the thought. It was pointless—no, foolish—to worry; none of his Honolulu maps had ever worked. Better to concentrate on the task— and the journey—at hand.

As it was, I planned to exchange our cargo for U.S. currency when we reached our next destination, where the leader of a Chinese gang had a soft spot in his heart—and cold hard cash in his pocket—for the big cats. According to the newspaper clippings I'd read, he'd been known for using them to dispose of rivals.

After that, Slate could easily bring us to the auction in

2016; fifty-one years prior, the captain had been born in New York, and his erstwhile home awaited him just beyond the edge of every map he Navigated. The year 2016 was long after the gang leader had been killed in a shoot-out, but with the map from 1981, it should have been a simple matter for the captain to steer the *Temptation* through two centuries, from the Bay of Bengal to the waters of the Atlantic off the coast of Long Island. After all, though he wouldn't call it home, he knew the city well.

Which is why it surprised me when the map of 1981 failed.

We were sailing toward the edge of the map of Calcutta under a sky so starry it looked sugared; the night would never be as beautiful after the Industrial Revolution.

Those stars dimmed as we slipped into the Margins of the map, the slender threshold between one place and the next, where India in 1774 ran out and the next shore appeared. Mist rose around us like the souls of drowned sailors, and the only sound was the muted hollow music of waves moving along the hull. Everything seemed calm, but the seas in the Margins were unpredictable—the currents mercurial and the winds erratic—and passage was always rougher the farther afield we traveled. And, very rarely, there were ghost ships in the fog, captained by those who had found the way in, but not the way out. I rubbed some warmth into my bare arms.

"Are you all right, *amira*?"

I made a face and nodded toward the mist. "The Margins always reminds me of purgatory. The place between worlds."

Kashmir's brow wrinkled. "Isn't purgatory supposed to be hotter?"

"That's St. Augustine's version. This is more like the Asphodel Meadows in Homer. Although with fewer bloodthirsty ghosts."

Kashmir laughed. "Ah, yes, of course. I must catch up on my reading."

"Well, I'm sure you know where my books are if you ever want to steal them." I grinned as I turned back to the helm; just as quickly, the smile fell away. Slate had taken the wheel to steer us toward the far-off shore only he could see . . . but his face was full of frustration. He swung his head back and forth, he gripped the wheel, he leaned forward as if to get a closer look—but it was clear he couldn't see our destination.

The ship rolled on the swells, and bronze light flickered in the fog, followed by the low grumble of thunder. Rain pelted the sails, and the mist writhed in a sudden gust. In the crow's nest above our heads, Rotgut cursed; he must have been swaying like a metronome.

New York should not have been difficult, not like this. "What's wrong, Captain?"

"I don't know!" Slate wrenched the wheel starboard, trying to take us around, but the waves were pushing hard to port. Near the prow, Bee tensioned the halyard on the jib, the bell at her waist swinging as she moved.

The *Temptation* groaned, and the ship shuddered as a swell hit, followed by another high enough to send spray over the rail. Kashmir caught my arm and pulled me close to the mast. I held on, keeping clear of the boom; my fingers found the rough splinters of the bullet hole. A breaker washed the deck, the cold sea soaking my feet.

"Slow down," Slate said. "I need more time!"

Kashmir sprang into action, racing up the stairs to the quarterdeck and grabbing the sea anchor. I followed on his heels and helped heave it off the stern. As the canvas caught our wake and dragged, another swell hit broadside and jolted us hard enough to rattle my teeth. This time Kashmir stumbled; I took his hand and grabbed the rail, bracing for the next wave, but it never came. The sea stilled once more as we ran right off the edge of the map.

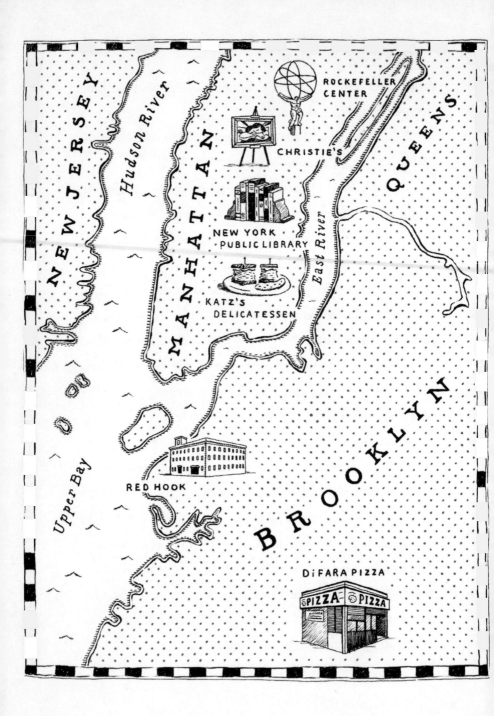

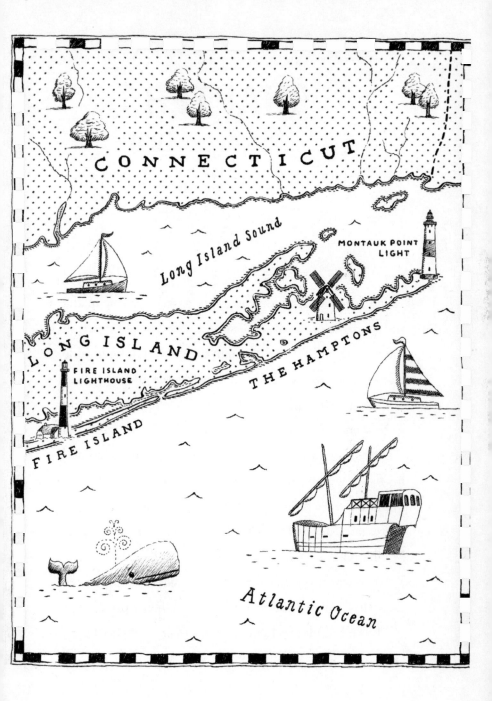

CHAPTER
TWO

The black water faded to blue, and I blinked in the sudden light of dawn—no, sunset. A breeze snapped in the netting and swirled through the mist, pulling it aside like a curtain to reveal, in the distance, the glittering glass skyline of New York City. The Twin Towers were nowhere to be seen—this was not the eighties, but I didn't need to see the shore to know it. The captain swore and slammed his fist down on the wheel, stalking away and back, pacing like a tiger himself. This was Slate's native time and place: late May 2016, within sight of the southern tip of Manhattan.

This was also where the auction would be held, in three days' time, whether or not we had the money to win it.

Little bubbles of hope, like sea foam in my stomach.

If we missed the auction because he failed to Navigate, it would be his fault, not mine. And I would be safe, at least for a little while longer.

The dark sea had calmed, and we floated like a leaf on a pond. I peeled my fingers off the rail, and off Kashmir's wrist. He glanced at me, but I spread my hands. "The map looked fine to me," I said, my voice soft, but the captain whirled around as though I had shouted an accusation.

"Maybe you didn't look hard enough," he said.

I met his eyes. "Hand drawn. Good detail. Dated. And new to us," I said, ticking the four points off on my fingers. No matter how detailed a map, once we'd visited, we couldn't go back, and Slate didn't always remember where he'd been or what he'd done. Still, I'd only just bought the map, so I knew for certain he'd never used it.

"And yet it's a dead ender!"

"So what went wrong?"

He snorted. "Nice try, Nixie."

I threw my hand in the air. "Figure it out yourself, then."

"You sure you don't have any ideas?" the captain said, taking a slow step toward me, then another. "I know you've been nervous about going to Honolulu."

His doubt stung. I knew my worth lay in my abilities, my

knowledge, the way I could chart a course. Without that, I was little more than ballast. I felt my face redden; out of the corner of my eye, I saw Bee and Kashmir watching. "Don't blame me for your failures, Slate."

He glared at me another moment, then returned to the wheel, gritting his teeth and squeezing with white knuckles as though willing us into the right decade. But to no avail. The fog did not rise, the wind did not drop, and the shoreline stayed stubbornly constant.

Bee approached me so I could hear her soft question; sweat or sea spray gleamed on her scarred brow. "If 1981 won't work, do you know another map to try? One where we can trade tigers for dollars?"

I pressed my fingers to my temple, trying to call up everything I'd ever read; not an easy task. "I suppose . . . someone in Rome might buy them for the Colosseum, but even if the captain could go back that far, we'd probably lose money overall."

Slate threw me a disapproving look. "On top of it being inhumane."

"As opposed to selling them to the yakuza in Chinatown?" Kashmir said with a grin.

"If a man kills a tiger, that's inhumane," Slate muttered.

"If a tiger kills a man, that's just inhuman."

"The gang was the White Tigers, actually," I said. "The yakuza are Japanese."

"What's the currency in ancient Rome, *amira*? Is it gold?"

"Not most of it," I said. "But the coins themselves are quite valuable."

"We'd have to find a new buyer," Slate reminded me. "My coin guy died two years ago."

"How hard could that be?" I said.

"The auction's on my timeline," the captain said. "We've only got three days."

"Two now," Kashmir corrected him.

"Then you think of something!" I glared at them both.

A roar drifted up from the hold; it was a curious sound, like whale song. The captain swore again and left the helm, jogging down the stairs from the quarterdeck and into his cabin, slamming the door behind him. I ran my hands through my hair. As first mate, Bee took his place, but for a moment, my fingers itched to take the wheel. Could I do what the captain had not?

"You didn't do anything?" Kashmir said to me.

"What?"

"To the map."

I blinked. "No! If I had a mind to sabotage a map, there are better candidates."

"Ah." He leaned against the rail, tilting his head to study me. "So," he said. "What makes you nervous about Honolulu?"

Turning to face the water, I frowned at the waves. "It's complicated."

"I haven't got anywhere else to be."

My fingers tapped an idle beat on the metal rail; the brass was cool under my palms. Kashmir was the only person aboard the ship who did not know every detail of the circumstances of my birth, and I was reluctant to surrender the strange, small bliss I had in his ignorance. Kash was the most confident person I knew; would he even understand how scared I was? Or worse—might he fear for me, too? Still, at this juncture, even if I didn't tell him, he would know soon enough. But how to explain? I'd never told the story before.

"Oi!"

Startled by Rotgut's shout from the crow's nest, I followed his skinny finger to the lights in the distance; a sleek white boat on the water, far off, but coming toward us.

"What is it?" I called up.

"Coast Guard!"

I stared at the boat for a long moment, trying to convince myself it wasn't headed our way—until another roar echoed in the hold. Then I ran to knock on the captain's door, hard, though I counted to ten before opening it.

Even so, Slate looked surprised to see me. I met his eyes, deliberately not glancing at the box in his hands, the box he normally kept under his bed. It wasn't worth telling him to hide it; if we were boarded, it would be harder to explain the tigers than to explain his stash of opium. "We need you on the radio," I told him.

His fingers tightened on the box. "It might help the map to work."

"*Now*, Captain." I shut the door behind me, harder than I had to.

Back on deck, Bee was taking the ship around while Kash raised the sails. We were moving again, plowing the waves, heading east along the southern coast of Long Island. I grabbed the halyard, helping Kash with the sail as I watched the lights of the boat off our stern, closer now and gaining.

According to Slate, the Coast Guard in New York had always been a pain, but much worse, of course, since 2001, far nosier and almost impossible to bribe. Nothing like the eighties, in the uncivilized city of my father's youth. To make it worse, the Coast Guard was full of people who loved boats, and they couldn't keep their hands off the *Temptation*.

She was a striking caravel, her black hull copper clad below the waterline to keep out worms (and worse, depending on what waters we traveled). She rode on a keel fashioned from what looked like the rib of a leviathan, carved with labyrinthine runes from stem to stern, and at the prow, a red-haired mermaid bared her breasts to calm the sea.

Even if the Coast Guard wasn't inclined to search us, they would take any chance to stand on the deck and spin the wheel and tell Slate how they played pirates when they were children. Of course, once on deck they were bound to hear the tigers roaring. I gritted my teeth and waited for the captain as below, our illicit cargo growled in their rickety cages.

Just as I was about to knock again, Slate emerged from his cabin with the radio hissing, but he stared at the Coast Guard ship for a long time, blinking slowly in the fading glow of sunset. My heart sank; his pupils were the size of dimes. "Captain?"

My voice startled him to action. He lifted the microphone. "New York Coast Guard, New York Coast Guard,

New York Coast Guard, this is the ship *Temptation*, *Temptation*, *Temptation*, over."

A brief crackle of static, and then a hiss as we waited. Bee gnawed her finger. "Did he find another map?"

I shook my head. "He can't Navigate now, not with them watching."

"Can't or won't?" Bee said.

"Shouldn't," I said. "People will report it. Or film it and put it on YouTube."

"Privacy is important," Bee said. "You get little of it in prison."

"New York Coast Guard, New York Coast Guard." Slate bounced the microphone impatiently in his hand. "This is the ship *Temptation*, over."

The lights off the stern were getting closer; another roar reverberated through my feet. "What do we do if they don't answer?"

Kashmir made a face. "We could throw them overboard."

"The drugs?"

"The tigers."

"New York Coast Guard," Slate repeated. His brow shone with sweat. "This is the ship *Temptation*, over."

No answer, and the lights grew closer still. "Captain—"

Slate swore and dropped the radio to the deck, striding toward the helm. "Bring me a map, Nix!"

"What map?"

"Any map!"

"But—"

"Nix!"

The speaker crackled then; we both froze. "The *Temptation*, this is the New York Coast Guard, please switch to channel sixty-six, over."

Kashmir scooped the radio off the deck and handed it to the captain. "New York Coast Guard, this is the *Temptation*, switching to channel sixty-six, over." Slate did so, the speaker still hissing softly.

"The *Temptation*, this is the New York Coast Guard." The accent was pure Brooklyn. "Slate?"

"Yes." It was almost a sigh of relief. "This is Slate. Is this Bruce? Over."

"This is Bruce. We got a call reporting suspicious activity." Bruce gave a bark of a laugh, making the speaker crackle. "Thought it might be you, over."

"A black pirate ship always scares the yachters, Bruce. Never thought she'd worry the Coast Guard."

"Worried? Nah, they just want to visit with you," Bruce said.

"The *Eagle*'s got our newest cadet on board. My nephew. Never been on a tall ship. Would you mind showing him the ropes?"

"Ah." Slate took a breath, his eyes roaming across the deck, over the sea, to the boat approaching. "I'd love to, Bruce, but, uh—" His eyes fell on me. "But we're a little busy. It's my daughter's birthday. We're having a party and everything. Over."

My eyebrows went up. "My birthday?"

"Oh, man, your daughter? What is she now, fourteen?"

I shook my head, but he wasn't paying attention.

Slate's brow furrowed. "Yeah . . . ?"

Kashmir snorted. "Dangerous age, Captain."

"Hey, don't let me interrupt the festivities," Bruce continued. "Say happy birthday for me. I'll tell the boy he's gotta wait. Probably for the best, he's a handsome kid. Welcome home, over."

"Bruce, thanks, over and out."

"Yeah, thanks, Bruce," I said under my breath.

Slate shut off the radio. It was only another few seconds before the ship behind us slowed and changed course. I pushed my hair out of my face and watched their lights fade. Slate dropped the radio on the deck and dragged his hands down his jaw.

"Finally a bit of luck, *amira*," Kashmir said with a half grin.

I grimaced. "Only a bit, though."

"Yes, too bad about the handsome nephew."

"Why?" I said. "You were hoping for a pretty niece?"

He winked at me, but not even teasing Kashmir could lift my mood. We were nearing the Hamptons now, and no closer to our destination. In fact, the tigers prevented us from getting into the harbor at all; Bruce, who Slate never failed to bribe with good liquor when he got the chance, might be able to call off the Coast Guard, but the harbormasters would notice the roaring as soon as we tied up to the dock.

"Nixie."

I turned. Slate had retaken the wheel, and he hadn't relaxed. "What?" I said, although I knew what he was going to say.

"I need you." His voice was soft, pleading. "I need your help. I can't miss that auction. I have to have that map. Please."

I kept my face stony, but the guilt in me was rising like a tide. I'd chosen the wrong map, I'd plotted the wrong course: mistake after mistake after mistake, all the way back to the start. "I'll check again. Maybe there's something I missed the first time."

"Not likely," Kashmir said, winding his pocket watch.

"I appreciate your confidence," I said in a flat tone. "Wait a minute." I grabbed for the watch and missed. He was much quicker than me. "Let me see that."

Once I asked, he handed it over without a fuss. The watch was three inches across, a triple-case gold repoussé design of Adam and Eve in paradise, and it was heavier than it looked. On the back there was the signature, even a serial number—and of course, it was in exceptional condition for its age, in spite of its dunking. I pressed my lips together. After scolding him for taking it, the hypocrisy stung . . . but it was worth twice what I would have gotten for the tigers.

Kashmir inclined his head; he understood. "What's mine is yours, *amira*."

I leaned into him, resting my temple on his shoulder in a gesture of thanks. Then I straightened. "Captain?"

"What?"

I tossed the watch to Slate, who caught it and held it up to the light. "I'm sixteen."

"Right," he said absently, studying the watch. Then his eyes widened. "Oh!" He closed his fingers around the watch and kissed it. His knees sagged and he leaned against the wheel, laughing.

"Easy come, easy go," Kashmir said. Another indignant roar drifted up from below; he rolled his eyes. "Well, most of the time."

"Why are the tigers so restless?" I nodded toward the captain, who was opening and closing the watch case, delighted. "I know for a fact we're not out of opium."

"No, *amira*, but we're out of meat. I've fed them every last scrap on the ship."

Rotgut's head whipped around, the thin braid of his beard flying in the wind. "You gave them everything in the galley?"

"*And* the bag of jerky from under your mattress."

"Thief!" Rotgut scowled.

Kashmir grinned at him. "Glutton."

Rotgut swore in Chinese. Kash responded in Persian— and Bee interrupted with a jangle of the bell she wore. "Settle down," she said in her quiet whisper, her brown eyes sparkling. "You're both right."

"So," Kash said to me. "Where can we leave the tigers?"

"Leave them?" Rotgut straightened up. "Why leave them?"

I cocked my head. "What else do you want to do with them?"

"Kash just said we're out of meat."

I couldn't help but laugh at his joke. At least, I hoped it was a joke.

"We're not eating them," Slate said. "Christ." He turned the wheel and pointed us toward the dark shoreline. "We'll drop them off ashore."

"What? Just—just drop them off? Where?"

He grinned at me. "That is an excellent question!"

"Fine." I stared upward, trying to think. No stars here; the sky was the flat navy of a city night. "Okay. Just a minute." I jogged below to my cabin. My cell phone was still in the back pocket of the jeans I'd worn the last time we were in New York. I'd prepaid for twenty dollars' worth of data then, definitely enough for a few Google searches. I powered it on as I returned topside. "Rotgut?"

"Eh?"

"Can you get a line in the water? And Kash, we should run dark for this. Will you take in the lanterns?"

"And what will you be doing?" Kashmir nudged me as he sauntered past, toward the bow.

"I'm looking up the local donor list for the Friends of the Bronx Zoo."

CHAPTER
THREE

We left the tigers in the Hamptons an hour past midnight, on a private dock behind a hulking mansion belonging to a philanthropic wildlife lover. Rotgut had landed a few bluefish and released them reluctantly to Kashmir, who used them to slip the tigers enough opium to calm them. Then we sailed away at speed. About an hour later, helicopters flew over us as we were passing Fire Island, but they didn't stop.

The next morning began blue and clear, and we sailed into the harbor with a day to spare before the auction. Slate watched the approaching shore with a look on his face like he had never known disappointment, nor ever would. He kept grinning at me, giving me credit for his joy—better, at least, than taking responsibility for his sorrow.

My own mood had improved as well. Part of it was the

season; when Slate had told Bruce it was my birthday, it was only partially a lie. I was sixteen or so, that much was true, although no one knew exactly. Not Bee nor Rotgut, who had been on the *Temptation* longer than I had, and certainly not Kashmir, who'd only come to the ship a couple of years ago. You'd think the captain would know—when he bothered to think about anything but himself—but it was a mystery to him as well. After all, he was away at sea when I was born, and my mother was gone when he returned, although to a very different place.

I'd spent the first months of my life in the opium den where my parents had met, cared for by the proprietor, a woman named Auntie Joss. After he had mourned the only way he knew how, Slate had barged in, wrapped me in a quilt, and taken me away. He hadn't bothered asking Joss for details, so my birth date was hard to pinpoint. Instead, the crew generally celebrated my theft day sometime in early summer, whenever we spent a few days in a place where it was early summer. Though there were no signs pointing to an actual party, my father's mention of one had lifted my spirits. He didn't always remember.

The bigger part of it was that the captain had waved me over to the helm for the last leg up the Hudson, through the Narrows. He stood over my shoulder, and my route was bounded on all sides by banks and buoys, but my heart beat faster as the ship surged forward under my watchful eyes, the brass wheel warming to my steady hands. For a moment, I could pretend I was captain of my own fate.

The city unfurled to port and starboard: busy, crowded, full of strange people and stranger sights. Nowhere else in modern-day America was so much variety crammed into so little space. People from all over the world lived side by side—and stacked atop—each other, like the maps in our collection. Libraries and museums displayed the debris and plunder of kingdoms long gone and times far past. Being in New York was like being able to Navigate on dry land.

The *Temptation* joined the parade of oddities and curiosities. Some passengers on the Staten Island Ferry pointed as we sailed toward the dock in Red Hook, but they didn't stare for long. Tall ships were a rare sight in this era, but New Yorkers had seen it all before.

Even so, New York was no longer the city of my father's youth; the only signs left of the urban decay he'd tried to escape were on his person. Tall, tattooed, and painfully thin, the captain would have fit right in sleeping on a bench in a bygone Tompkins Square. The hard edge was authentic. But when he had to, Slate could fake it.

As soon as we were moored at Red Hook, he put on a pair of pressed slacks and covered his ink with a fine suit jacket in preparation to meet his dealers—his antique dealers. Dressed that way, he looked almost like any other New Yorker. It was only the nervous shifting of his eyes that hinted at discomfort, but not with the city, nor with being on land. With his own skin. No matter where we went, he never felt at home.

I recognized that feeling. I'd inherited it.

He took the pocket watch and left us at the dock with a list of chores to finish before we left port, including repairing the spar that had snapped in the storm and filling the bullet hole with epoxy. It was a rapid reversal for me—from captain to boatswain—but Kashmir only teased me a little, and we worked hard, side by side, cutting, shaping, sanding, staining, until we had a new spar and the bullet hole was gone. For a few hours, I focused on the wood of the mast, trying not to think of the auction, memorizing the grain as though it was a map to a distant shore.

The captain returned that evening with a heavy briefcase and a buoyant air, while Kash and I were still only between the first and second coat of varnish. Slate dropped the briefcase on the deck and ran up to us, palms up, grinning.

"What do you want?"

"High fives," he said, as though it was obvious. Kashmir started laughing. I glanced down at my fingers, stained black and sticky, and then back up at Slate's clean hands. Then he winked at me, and I couldn't help but return his smile. Slate clapped Kashmir on the back and put his other hand on my shoulder, warm and firm. "Good work on the pocket watch! You couldn't have planned it better."

I made a face. "I didn't plan it at all."

"Well, you know what they say! Chance favors the prepared mind, and there's no mind more prepared than yours." He leaned in to kiss the top of my head.

"Dad!"

"And fortune favors the bold," he added as he sauntered backward, pointing at Kashmir. "They say that too." He raised his hands again, tilting his head to gaze at the heavens. "The stars are aligning for us!"

I followed his eyes upward and laughed. "There are no stars."

"Yeah? Then what's that?"

"Jupiter."

"Well, there are still stars," he said. "You just can't see them. If you could, they'd be aligned, trust me." He picked up his briefcase and turned to his cabin. "It's fate. This is all meant to be. I guarantee you, by tomorrow night we'll be back in paradise."

The smile wilted on my face. "So what time is the auction tomorrow, Captain?"

He stopped in his tracks, and it was a moment before he answered. "Early." Then he opened the door and vanished behind it.

I stared after him. It was never a good sign when he wouldn't give me a direct answer, but I wanted to be there tomorrow to see the map, to know what I was facing. Forewarned, forearmed, as Cervantes had said.

Kashmir was watching me. He quirked an eyebrow, but I pretended not to notice. "I never thanked you for the watch," I said, dipping my brush into the varnish and running it along the black spar. "I should have thought of something like that instead of bothering with the tigers."

"It was more fun this way."

I gave him a pointed look. "Maybe for you."

"*Mais non, amira*, come on." He wiped his cheek with his shoulder. "We brought two Bengal tigers into the twenty-first century, where Bengal tigers are a rare and precious resource."

"Not as precious as a pocket watch."

"Not as pricey, perhaps. Who said it was thieves who know the price of everything and the value of nothing?"

"Oscar Wilde," I said. "And it's cynics, not thieves."

"Ah! That explains it, then."

I stuck out my tongue at him. Then I looked down at the brush marks in the tacky varnish. "Think we'll finish tonight?"

"This coat needs time to dry. We can finish in the morning." Kashmir regarded me for a moment. "Early."

We woke before dawn to put the final coat on the mast. After we'd finished, Kashmir found the thinner and wiped his hands with meticulous care; I did a more cursory job, leaving the half-moons under my nails as black as rotten teeth. Kash took a nap in my hammock while we waited, but I stood by the rail until Slate appeared on deck, sharply dressed and vibrating like a plucked string. He stopped in his tracks when he saw me there.

"You're coming with me?"

"I thought I could help," I said, but he just stared at me.

"Give you a second pair of eyes? In case it's a forgery or a copy or something."

His face darkened. "It's not a forgery."

I tried to laugh, but it came out like a cough. "I've seen your other 1868s, Slate. Some of them were practically drawn in crayon."

"Christie's doesn't sell fakes."

"They did a couple years ago, actually. A painting called *Odalisque*. Big scandal."

He opened his mouth, shut it again, then ran his hand over his scalp, tousling his carefully combed hair. "I'm going to be late."

"Then let's go."

I shook Kashmir awake, and the three of us took the subway from Brooklyn to Rockefeller Center, emerging into a sea of sundry New Yorkers, both permanent and temporary: texters looking down and tourists looking up, and crowds of girls my age waiting to scream for some celebrity outside NBC Studios. Christie's auction house was a large limestone building located at the south side of the plaza, where flags in all colors from all nations snapped in the summer air.

Kash and I accompanied the captain as far as the lobby, where the security guard put down his newspaper and asked for government-issued ID as he eyeballed Kashmir, who wore his white linen shirt in his typical fashion, unbuttoned nearly to his waist, and me, with my black nails and my tattered hoodie. Slate was the only one with a valid card.

The guard made a call from the phone behind his desk, staring at Kashmir the whole time. When he hung up, he shook his head and apologized in a way that made it clear that he had no regrets; Slate spread his hands and started toward the elevators. "Sorry, kiddo. I'll be back in a bit."

"But Dad—"

He turned back to take my hands in his. "Everything's going to be fine, Nixie. Trust me." Then he threw me a hopeful grin over his shoulder, leaving so quickly the elevator doors closed before I could respond.

But what good would a response have done? There was no argument that would change his mind. I'd tried them all before, the last time he'd found a map from 1868. I watched the elevator lights glowing and fading like fish in the deep sea; there was a pressure in my chest as though I were a hundred feet underwater. In a gallery several floors above me, the map dangled like the sword of Damocles.

I started when the security guard picked up his paper with a rustle and a flourish, flashing the front-page story:

WHOA THERE, TIGER! The big cats in the photo were familiar; they lay tranquilized in the rear of a police van. Kashmir caught my eye and winked. With a confidence that I could never emulate, he strolled right up to the commissioned mural on the long wall, inspecting it so closely as to be breathing on the paint.

I nibbled my thumbnail until I tasted varnish. What was happening up there? Had the auction begun? Were others bidding, and if so, how high? I pulled out my cell phone and blinked at the screen—only eight minutes had passed. For something to do, I began to clear my inbox of all the emails I'd received since we'd last been here and now, but it depressed me to scan and delete all the events gone by, all the talks I'd never hear. I put the phone back in my pocket and watched the security guard, who had laid down the paper on his desk and was glaring at Kash with his jaw clenched. No matter the era, cops never liked Kashmir.

Kashmir strolled the length of the painting at a distance of three inches not once, but twice, pausing at the end to read the title aloud (*"Wall Drawing Number Eight Ninety-Six,"* he said with a sniff. "I much preferred number five thirty-two, didn't you, *amira*?") and commenting on the color ("So intense, almost . . . vulgar?") as well as the texture ("The glossy finish, it appears . . . moist . . ."), his voice echoing all the way to the top of the triple-height lobby. The security guard sighed audibly.

After nearly an hour of this, during which I checked the time, on average, every seven minutes, I finally took Kashmir's arm and steered him toward the glass-and-bronze doors. "I need some air."

"Just a moment, *amira*." He slipped out of my grasp to trot back to the guard, leaning in over the desk. "Alas, *ya sidi*, it seems she's not an art lover!" Then he jogged toward me and whisked me through the doors.

"I didn't know you were such a connoisseur yourself," I said out on the sidewalk.

He tugged my hood over my eyes, laughing at my expression. "I've never stolen art. But it's always good to be prepared, in case the opportunity should arise. Did I embarrass you?"

"Yes. And you know it. *'Ya sidi'*?"

"I was just having fun. Let me make it up to you. I saw a cupcake place a block away."

"I haven't got any American dollars."

"So?"

"*No*, Kashmir. We've had enough people chasing us this

week. Did you see the picture on the front page?"

"I most certainly did." He pulled a folded copy of the *Daily News* out of the waistband of his pants and opened it to page two. "It's a good photo but their headlines are such drivel."

"Is that—"

"It *was*."

"Kashmir!"

"Newspapers are like umbrellas. If you put one down, someone else will pick it up. Besides, his lips were moving while he read. And I knew you'd want it."

I grabbed the paper—if only to stop him from waving it around, in case the guard came out after us—and shoved it under my hoodie. After a moment, I took it back out and scanned the story: the tigers had been handed over safely to the zoo's veterinarian.

"Thanks." I folded the paper and put it in my bag.

"Of course, *amira*." Something in the tone of his voice caught me. It dawned on me then: he hadn't been putting on the act to irritate the security guard, but to entertain me.

"Thanks," I said again, softly.

He shrugged. "It passes the time. Speaking of which, the other day you were about to tell me something complicated."

He was quiet; so was I. Then he pushed my hood back gently, his fingers grazing my ear. "Come on, *amira*. What's in Honolulu that the captain needs so badly?"

I bit my lip, glancing back toward Christie's, then down at the pavement under my shoes. The mica in the concrete glimmered in the sunlight. "My mother. She died there in 1868, the day I was born."

CHAPTER
FOUR

I couldn't look at Kashmir; I feared seeing pity in his eyes. Instead, I leaned against the wall, my arms crossed, watching the people passing by. "Slate got to Hawaii on an old map by Augustus Mitchell—1866, 'The Sandwich Isles.' He still has it in the box he keeps under his bed."

"I didn't know you were part Hawaiian."

I shook my head. "Half Chinese. Lot of immigrants worked on the sugar plantations. Slate met my mother in an opium den."

"Ah."

"Not like that! Well, not her. Lin worked there. She never touched it except to make up pipes. Made sure he stopped too. I wish I knew how she'd done it." I tried to smile, but it came out twisted. "I suppose if he has his way, I'll be able to ask her."

"So that's why he wanted the bird."

"The bird is strong medicine, but she died from an infection. Penicillin would likely have worked just as well."

Kashmir's brow was furrowed, and behind his eyes, questions were forming. "Then why didn't he bring her some?"

"Slate was at sea. He didn't even know she was expecting." I sighed. I'd had to ask Rotgut to tell me the whole story; Slate refused to talk about it. "He needed money so they could get married and live happily ever after in paradise. And he had a map of Hong Kong in 1850, and the next edition of the Honolulu map from 1869. So he went to China to smuggle back some opium to sell. He sailed out in early 1868, and by the time he came back in 1869, I was there and . . . my mother was not."

"And so he's looking for a map of 1868 to save her." Kashmir had his hand on his chin, and his eyes were far away. "But can he actually change the past?"

"We do it every time we Navigate," I said. "The watch you took. Or the tigers."

"A pocket watch is not a person, *amira*." He searched my face for answers. "If he succeeds, what happens to the years between then and now?"

"I don't know, Kash, that's the trouble! Some people

think that reality would split into two versions, or that it already has split and I just don't know it. But others think that if the past is changed, I might just . . ." I spread my hands, and we both considered the empty space between them.

"What people? Other Navigators?"

"Ha, no. Physicists. I've never met another Navigator aside from Slate, and he won't tell me anything."

Kashmir leaned against the wall next to me, and we watched the yellow cabs crawl by. Finally he shook his head. "No. He won't do it. He may dream about seeing her again, but he would never actually risk it."

"You think so well of him." In spite of myself, I attempted a smile. "This isn't the first map he's tried."

Kash stared at me. I'd never seen him so nonplussed. "When?"

"More often when I was younger." I shrugged, trying to hide my fear, swallowing down the terror clawing up my throat. "Most of the maps he'd found were worthless. One was even run off a Xerox. But the last time was almost three years ago. Maybe six months before you came aboard. It was an Asher and Adams map he bought from a collector in Tahiti. He was so excited. I tried to ask him exactly what would happen to me if the map worked, but he only said to trust him. I tried to, but . . ." How to explain the doubts, the maddening uncertainty of those terrible hours? The memory was a jumble of dark, disconnected moments like flotsam in a vast sea of dread, and the words turned to sand in my mouth.

Thank God the map had failed. But despair had lifted off my shoulders and settled, like a vulture, onto Slate's. We'd spent months in the doldrums of my father's depression, drifting in the Pacific where the ocean was thick with whales and white sharks. I'd leave trays of food outside his door, which was where Slate left them as well. Eventually he had emerged from the room, thin and pale as a bone under his tattoos, dark blue bruises under his eyes and in the crooks of his arms. He had devoured a huge plate of food, vomited over the rail, and fallen asleep on a pile of rope rigging. When he woke up the next day, he took the wheel again and never said a word about any of it.

Which was fine by me. There is something terrifying about seeing someone strong standing on the edge of the abyss, like a ship on the lip of a whirlpool where the whole sea plunges into the maw of Charybdis. There is that moment when they reach out—like a drowning man will—and if you're within reach, they will pull you down with them. I didn't want to stand there beside him. I didn't want to be dragged down.

In the three years since, I'd let myself hope we'd run out of maps from the era, that I was safe, that the captain had finally put the past behind him. But here we were again, and Slate wasn't even trying to swim against the current. In fact . . .

"But what?"

I looked up at Kash, tasting copper; I'd been chewing my lip. "He doesn't have any idea what will happen to me, and I don't think it matters to him either way."

"*Amira* . . ." His expression was mixed—sympathy and disgust—and I couldn't bear it. I was almost relieved when the captain emerged from the auction house. He started toward us, but Kashmir gripped my arm, whispering fiercely in my ear. "Why do you help him?"

I watched my father swinging his briefcase and grinning ear to ear, his joy visible, so rare, and effervescent as fine champagne. "How can I say no, Kash?" I murmured. "She's dead because of me."

And then Slate was there, clapping his hands together, the color high in his cheeks, and for a moment I glimpsed what my mother must have when she fell in love. Slate was as picturesque as any ruin.

"*You* look happy," I said. I couldn't help it; like an old wound, it itched.

"Oh, yes, Nixie, yes, I am, indeed! I am not disappointed. I never am, when I come to New York. I love New York!" he shouted, spreading his arms wide. Passersby watched, bemused; Kashmir watched him too, his face troubled.

"Me too." My eyes went to the briefcase. "Is it in there?"

"Oh, no. No, no, no. They'll put it in a padded box and deliver it to the ship in—pardon me," he said, turning to a woman and lifting her wrist before she could protest. "May I see your watch? Thank you. Four hours." He released the woman, who jerked back her arm and hurried away. "Four hours!" He tossed down his briefcase and wrapped his arms around my and Kashmir's shoulders. "I can hardly wait!"

He released us but made no move to pick up the briefcase. I nudged it with my foot. "It's empty, then? You bid everything you had?"

"Nixie," he said, with mock disappointment. "Nixie, Nixie, Nixie! Did you think I wouldn't be able to keep a little something back?" He knelt before the briefcase, flipped open the latches, and revealed a thick stack of bundled twenties. "See? Your mother taught me how to haggle!" He was in a very good mood, then, to mention my mother. His eyes were bright with manic excitement. How long would it last?

"Jesus, Dad," I said as people stared. "Someone will rob you."

The captain laughed. "Yeah." He jerked his chin toward Kash. "Him." He grabbed the wad of bills and split off a handful. "You know what? Here. This is for you, this is for you. . . ." He stuffed twenties into our fists without counting them. "And the rest is for Bee and Rotgut."

I held the money in both hands. It must have been nearly five hundred dollars. "Does this mean we have shore leave?"

Slate stopped in the process of unknotting his tie. "Shore leave? What for?"

"To spend this." I grinned at Kash. It was only a brief reprieve, but it was something. "There's an exhibit opening this weekend at the Met about the Book of the Dead. Or a talk tomorrow night about pre-Christianity in Armenia that—"

"Oh, Nixie, no." The captain shook his head and threw his tie into the briefcase. "There's no time for all that. We're leaving in the morning."

"Well, how about a bookstore, then? Just for the afternoon."

"We've still got to manage the deliveries. But if you see something quick between here and the ship—"

I stared at him, the money crumpling in my clenched fist, although it wasn't about the money, really; the one thing I could never buy was more time. "Forget it," I said, shoving the worthless bills into my bag. The newspaper Kash had given me was more valuable. "Let's just go."

The euphoria in his eyes dimmed, but only for a moment. "Eager to be under way? That's my girl!" The cheer in his voice was forced, but he hugged me, with both arms, and lifted me up off the ground.

"Dad!" But I let myself hold him too, as tightly as I could.

He let me down, staring at me for a moment, his eyes brimming. Then he made a beeline over to a man selling roasted nuts out of a cart. He bought half a dozen bags, dumping one into his mouth and chewing fiercely while stuffing the others into the pockets of his suit.

Christie's sent the map to the ship by car. When the sleek Lincoln rolled up to the docks that evening, Slate, who had been pacing on deck like a cat in a cage, went entirely still. Bee signed the release form, and she and Kashmir carried the crate up to his cabin, all while Slate watched, nothing moving but his eyes. Only when they set it down outside the door did he spring into motion and tug the crate inside, letting the door swing shut behind him.

I winced when the door slammed, but the silence of his absence seemed louder still. It shouldn't have; since our embrace on the sidewalk I'd seen him slipping away into his head, into his plans for tomorrow and all the rest of the future, grand dreams of what might come from his newest treasure map. But perhaps naive hope runs in my blood. Bee cleared her throat; I'd been staring at the closed door.

She came over to stand beside me as I leaned on the rail, and side by side we watched the western sun wash the towers of Manhattan. "This is the better view," she said. Her voice was soft, a raspy whisper because of the scar that lay like a noose around her throat.

"Agreed." The city shone across the river, a temptation all its own, but it might as well have been an ocean away. "I just wish we had more time here."

"Us too. Ayen loves the lights," she said. "But I love the bull."

"The brass bull? On Wall Street?"

"Yes. He reminds me of my song bull, although he grazes on a different green." I laughed, and she tapped the cowbell at her belt. "Sometimes I miss my herd."

"Does Ayen?"

Bee grinned, and the scars on her cheeks—like rows of pearls—curved with particular mischief. "She misses the dancing. She says there's a warehouse party in Red Hook tonight. House music. What is house music? She tried to explain, but I've never heard anyone play a house." Bee shook her head dramatically, but she winked at me.

I couldn't help but smile back. Bee was Na'ath, from a tribe in Northern Africa where cattle were both kith and currency. Ayen was her wife who'd been killed years ago, before Bee had come to the ship. But in accordance with their beliefs about death, Ayen was still with her, doing those little annoying things ghost wives do, like make you drop your breakfast or trip over a coil of rope. Or bother you about going to warehouse parties in Brooklyn. "Admit it, you would take her to the party if we weren't sailing at dawn."

"The worst part is, she already knows it."

"Well. There's not much dancing on the ship, I suppose."

My eyes returned to the captain's door. "Do you wish you could go back?"

"Back where?"

"To Sudan. To before Ayen died."

"Such an odd idea. We were already there." She stroked the necklace of her scar. "He does not think before he acts. Would you like me to burn it?"

"To—*what*?"

"The map. I should have done it with the last one, but the idea came to me too late. Ach." She flicked her hand over her shoulder as though a fly had buzzed her ear. "Yes, yes. To be honest, it was Ayen's idea. But I would gladly do it."

"Burn it?" For a moment my heart leaped at the idea, and I was shocked I hadn't thought of it before. It would be so easy. Then I bit my cheek, ashamed. I had already taken her away from him once. "No. No, but thank you. I . . . thank you. I'm certain the map won't work," I lied. "None of them have."

"Ah, well, good. Otherwise, I imagine you might worry."

Downtown, a glass monolith seemed to blaze, catching the slanting sun as it crept toward the sea. She waited for a response, but I made none. Finally Bee dropped her hand onto my shoulder for a moment, then let it fall away. "I'm going to go organize the deliveries. You come too."

Bee recommended hard work as a cure for any emotional turmoil. I followed her down into the hold, which still smelled of tigers, although the cages had been replaced by a handful of boxes scattered haphazardly. Instant coffee; my father lived on the stuff. A crate of toilet paper. Aspirin and iodine and antibiotics. Bleach and bamboo toothbrushes and toothpaste with fluoride.

We broke down the cardboard boxes and repacked their contents in the wooden chests we kept for the purpose. Then we piled all the crates against one wall and scrubbed the hold till the teak gleamed. Bee was polishing the floor with beeswax when a box of vitamins tumbled down from the top of the pile; she scolded Ayen under her breath. The faint smell of honey filled the air. By the time we finished, I did feel better. And hungry.

"Must be nearly dinner." I pushed my fists into the small of my back; the hatch framed a sky tinged with pink.

"Or past it," she said. "It gets dark late here in summer." At the mention of summer, she smiled like she couldn't help it.

"What did you do?" I asked, but I didn't bother to wait

for her answer. She followed after me as I raced upstairs to the deck.

Kash and Rotgut had been just as busy as we had. A table was laid on the deck, and on the table, all the culinary delights New York had to offer: pungent halal chicken and rice doused in hot sauce, pork dumplings in Styrofoam clamshells, a cardboard box marked DI FARA'S PIZZA, pastrami sandwiches thick as dictionaries, creamy cheesecake covered with glistening scarlet strawberries.

Kashmir flung his arms wide. "Happy theft day!"

"Glad we stole you," Rotgut added, raising a bottle of Brooklyn Lager in his bony fist.

I cast my eyes about, but it was only the four of us on deck. I lifted my chin as Kashmir patted the seat beside him—the one with its back toward the captain's cabin. We dined like New Yorkers on the deck while Manhattan's skyline shimmered in the water like the Milky Way and my father shut himself in the map room, conspicuous by his absence.

CHAPTER FIVE

After the party, Bee watched while I made up an extra plate of food, but she didn't say anything. There was no answer when I knocked on the captain's door, but it was unlocked, so I let myself in.

The light was dim—he'd thrown bits of fabric over the lamps—and the room was stuffy, the heat raising the vanillin scent of old paper from the maps spilling from the shelves and cupboards lining the walls. Slate hoarded maps like a dragon hoards treasure: maps of every shape and shore, in parchment and paper, birch bark and Nile linen, kangaroo leather and sharkskin. There were maps punched in copper, painted on urns, and one scratched into the surface of a shelf mushroom. He even had Robert Peary's 1906 map of Crockerland, a continent that enjoyed a scant seven years of existence before being judged a fata morgana; after 1914, it no longer existed on any map, nor anywhere else at all.

I needed air. I set the plate on the table and crossed the room, stumbling on a pile of books, to open the aft deadlights. The breeze ruffled the edges of the black curtains of the sleeping alcove. The captain dozed behind them, his newest map resting on his chest like a blanket. I clenched my fists to keep from snatching it away.

Instead, I went to the drafting table, where the map of 1981 lay, pinned down by half-empty coffee cups. I took the cloth off the lamp above the desk and leaned over the page, looking closely at the lines. The cartographer's focus had been delineating New York neighborhoods, with each shaded in different watercolor and detailed down to major landmarks. I drummed my fingers on the table. Still, to my eye, there were no hints this map wouldn't work.

Frustrated, I rolled up the map and shoved it into the cupboard with all the other dead enders. The rest of his Hawaii 1868 maps were there. There was no reason for me to worry that the new map would be different. I licked my lips and tasted salt.

No reason at all.

I closed the cupboard more noisily than necessary, but

the captain didn't even move. Since I'd started cleaning, I kept going. I picked up the books—myths, legends, history—scattered around the room like confetti, and returned them to their shelves. The dirty clothes I threw in the empty hamper. The caladrius's cage was on the trunk; I filled a cup with water for her.

The bedsheets had spilled into a tangled pile on the floor. When I picked them up, I uncovered the box, lying open, displaying Slate's most precious things: a block of black tar, a stained pipe and fresh needles, a bottle of pills, all nestled beside the map of 1866, the map of the time before I came along and everything went wrong.

I kicked the whole mess back under the bed, hard enough it hit the wall.

My palms were damp. I wiped my hands on the bundle of bedding and let it drop back to the floor. Then I took a deep breath to clear my head. The breeze off the ocean, cooler now the sun was down, had swept away the musty smell in the room, but Slate still hadn't stirred except for the gentle rise and fall of his chest under the 1868 map. I could no longer contain myself; I took one corner between my thumb and forefinger, lifting it gently away, and he started awake, his hands closing reflexively on the edges.

"I'm going to put it on the table," I said. His eyes focused on mine, and he released the map, trading it for the plate I'd brought. I glanced at the page, and my heart sank.

It was nothing like the others. Inked, faded, signed, dated. A. SUTFIN, the drafter, had printed in neat block letters and drawn in a very precise hand. And the map was original. But even that was no guarantee it would work. Suddenly I was absurdly grateful for the inexplicable failure of the 1981 New York.

"It's a good map, isn't it?"

I looked up at him; Slate was balancing the plate, untouched, on his knees, waiting for me to agree. I dropped my eyes back to the page and chewed my lip. "I hope it's worth what it cost."

"It is *priceless*, Nix."

"Right." Not a crease, nor even a crinkle. Someone had preserved this map quite well.

"Thank you," Slate said then.

That gave me pause. "For what?"

"For the map." He picked up the fork. "And for dinner."

I pursed my lips. Why had I been surprised? He could afford to be kind now he had what he wanted. "Of course, Captain." My voice was vague as I studied the map. It was only the island of Oahu, and in fine detail. Beautiful lines.

His duty done, he stabbed a dumpling with the fork. "This is good."

"Good." My eyes roved over the contours on the page, seeking flaws and finding none. The mapmaker had even labeled Honolulu's main streets—Nu'uanu, Beretania, King—as well as the post office and the major churches. The city was centered around Iolani Palace, the seat of the King of Hawaii; there, just a few blocks northwest, was Chinatown. I ground my teeth.

"You know," he said, his mouth full. "The last time I had a pastrami sandwich from Katz's was when I was your age. This is from Katz's, isn't it?"

"Yeah."

"Why so quiet?"

But then his face fell and his fork paused in midair. For a long time, neither of us spoke. He put down his fork and squeezed his eyes shut. "There was a party."

I shrugged as if I didn't care. "It's fine."

"I'm sorry, Nixie."

"I don't want to talk about it, Captain."

"Kashmir told me, but I forgot."

"I can see that."

"I said I was sorry!" He threw his hands up, suddenly defensive. Then he clenched his fist and brought it in front of his mouth. "And I am," he added quickly. "I was distracted, is all. The map is very distracting." He set the plate aside and smiled hopefully. "But it's beautiful, isn't it? And it's almost like a gift."

"A gift?"

"To you."

I couldn't help it; my lips twisted like a juiced lime and the response was too bitter not to spit out. "To *me*?"

"Well . . . don't you want to meet your mother?"

His question seemed designed to induce guilt, and it cut deep enough to reveal a splinter of cruelty, hard as bone. "My mother's gone, Slate." I put the map down on the drafting table, smoothing it with my palm. "On the map I came from, she's dead."

Slate blanched, but he answered evenly. "That's why we've got a new map."

"A new map . . . a new version." I traced the line of the Tropic of Cancer. "A new wife?"

"What are you talking about?"

"I've been thinking about it. The map where you met is the map where she died. A different map means a different version of her." And of me, but I did not bother saying it. I doubted it would matter to him.

He stood, arms crossed, drumming the fingers of his right hand on his left arm. "It's the exact same place."

"So?" I opened one of the cupboards—the fairy-tale maps—and unrolled one at random. "Greece with gods on Mount Olympus, Slate. And here." I pulled out the map right beneath it. "Two hundred years later, the next cartographer replaced Zeus with Jupiter. And then we have"—I opened another cupboard, the less-fanciful histories, and pawed through them—"Mount Olympus during the Ottoman Empire, where you'll find brigands and highway robbers and no gods at all." I let the map roll itself up. "Going back to the same place doesn't mean you'll find the same thing."

"It does if it's the same time!"

I smiled grimly as he started to pace. A perverse part of me was enjoying myself. "Remember where we found Kashmir? That French map of Persia in 1740, in the Vaadi Al-Maas, but here, a historical map of Nader Shah's empire, 1740, look," I said, pointing. "Same place, same time, but there's no such city. The shoreline's different. Do you think Kashmir exists there, somewhere in the middle of the Persian Gulf?"

"Those are two completely different mapmakers. You can't compare some Frenchman's fantasy of Arabia to—"

"Mitchell and Sutfin are two different mapmakers."

"But they were mapping the same version of Hawaii."

"Which version? My history? Or your fairy tale?"

"It is *not* a fairy tale!"

The volume of his voice brought me up short. His eyes were wild; I could see the whites all the way around, and suddenly none of it was amusing. "And if you succeed?" I said softly. "Then what?"

"What do you mean, then what?"

I opened my mouth, then closed it. In Sanskrit mythos, they say breath is life, and I didn't want to give life to my fears; I didn't want to say it aloud. *Then what will happen to me?*

After our shouting, the silence rang in my ears. He took a deep breath, then another. "Then we all live happily ever after," he said finally, calm once more. "You've done a lot of studying, Nix, and you know the maps, but I know what I believe, and that's all that really matters."

My breath hitched in my throat to hear it stated so plainly. "Good to know how insignificant my thoughts are to you," I said bitterly.

"That's not what I meant." He reached out an uncertain hand, as though I was a bird in the bush. But he let the hand fall back to his lap and cupped it in the other, squeezing until his knuckles cracked. "If I tell you a secret, will you feel better?"

I rolled my eyes. "I'm not twelve, Captain—"

"It's about Navigation."

That brought me up short, and my anger dissipated like mist under the sun. I had asked so many times; why now? Was it gratitude? Or guilt? Certainly it was the only gift I wanted from him. But it didn't matter—I wasn't about to question it. I found my voice. "What? What is it?"

He turned back to his bed and stared for a moment at the plate he'd left there. Then he broke a piece of bread off the sandwich and put it into the caladrius's cage. She cocked her head shyly on her slender neck before dipping it down, delicate and precise, to eat from his hand. A winch in my gut wound tighter, but I was afraid if I asked again, he'd change his mind. "Navigation is not just about the maps," he said finally, as though to the bird. "Part of it is belief."

"Belief?" My mind was racing. "What do you mean?"

He brushed the crumbs from his palms and sat back down on his bed. "I've never been able to get to a place I didn't believe existed. Doubt can stop a map from working."

The edge of the Sutfin had started to curl; I ran my finger down the side. "So . . . you believe this map will work. That's no secret."

"If belief affects whether a map works, I'd think belief also affects what you find there."

"You *think*, or you *know*?"

"Fine, I *know*." He scrubbed his hands through his hair. "I know she'll be there, and I know everything will work out."

"How can you be sure?"

"It's fate." He looked at me—no, through me, as though just behind me was his future. "It's inevitable."

I ground my teeth, feeling tricked. "This isn't about Navigation, it's about delusion." Disappointment was bitter on my tongue, but he didn't flinch in the face of my scorn. Another breeze purled through the room, and I shivered. "I suppose if you're going to see Lin again, we might as well throw all that overboard." I flicked my hand toward the box under the bed. "You know she would hate to see it."

His eyes refocused, and he met my stare with a steady gaze, but the silence stretched between us like a rope about to snap. Was that doubt? I turned my face so he wouldn't see my expression, but when my eyes fell on the Sutfin map, my smug smile wilted. I wanted the map to fail, but why take joy in tormenting him? At heart, all he wanted was an escape, and that I understood—only too well. "Tell me more about Navigating," I said then, too eagerly, breathless at the thought of freedom.

Slate laughed a little. "Why should I?"

"Because . . . because I asked." He laughed again, louder, and I stiffened. "Please?"

He did not answer me. He was so quiet I couldn't even hear him breathing. Finally I faced him; he was watching me and his expression was serious. "Why, Nixie?" he asked again, but it was clear he already knew.

Still, I did not answer. If I told him the truth—that I would leave him behind and never look back, that I longed to go anywhere and everywhere he was not—he would argue; worse, if I confirmed it, he would never teach me. "Because I helped you," I said at last.

He made a face. "We don't strike bargains, Nixie, not between you and me. We don't haggle over things."

I clenched my jaw. "I'll try to remember that the next time you ask for money to buy a map."

"This is a good map, Nixie," he said, stabbing another dumpling. "There won't be a next time."

CHAPTER
SIX

I went back outside, leaving Slate to his dinner. There was no sign now of the party; the deck was clear for tomorrow. I leaned on the rail, staring without seeing at the cars moving along the Brooklyn-Queens Expressway. The warmth of the day had long faded, and the night air was quite cool; the haze gave the headlights halos.

I pressed my thumb between my brows. I already regretted arguing with the captain. What had been the point? He was certain—he said he was—and nothing I could say would turn him from his tack.

At least I'd gotten something out of it. It was a small thing—one bright minnow in a school—but the captain had always been tight-lipped about Navigation. Now I knew why. Had he finally discovered the map I'd taken? No . . . he could have guessed I'd want to strike out on my own someday. Besides, he didn't know his collection well enough to notice one map missing.

I'd tucked it away in my cabin, at the bottom of my sea chest, along with my entire life savings: six hundred and forty-two dollars, after today. The map was small, fragile, the color of tea: Carthage during Roman rule, 165 A.D. There, white salt, so cheap in modern America, could be traded for gold, or jewels. Or a small, fast ship of my own.

Slate had so many maps of his past; why shouldn't I have a map of my future? I couldn't spend my life stuck on my father's ship, tossed by his tempestuous moods, waiting for the day when he managed to steer us directly onto the rocky shore where his siren sang. I wanted my freedom, even though it likely meant never seeing the rest of the crew again. Once I knew how to Navigate, nothing could keep me aboard the *Temptation*.

Then I heard bare feet on the deck behind me, and the silver sound of tiny ankle bells. "I like it when you don't try to sneak up on me."

"I know," Kash said, coming to stand beside me. "You're up late."

"It's my watch."

"Ah, well, then you won't mind if I borrow your

hammock?" He held up the bundled canvas and raised an eyebrow.

I had a room, of course, belowdecks; we all did. There was plenty of room on the *Temptation* that on any other ship would be taken up by a larger crew, or a motor, or any number of things in any number of eras. Still, I preferred to sleep on deck on nice nights. My room was too empty to lend itself to easy dreams. This was in sharp contrast to the rest of the crew, who filled their rooms to bursting with relics or reminders of their lives before they'd come aboard: locks of hair and curved bull horns, baskets, bells, begging bowls. I hadn't really had a life to bring with me.

We strung the hammock between the mast and the rail. Kashmir bowed graciously. "After you?" He waited till I'd settled in, cross-legged, before climbing in to sit facing me. The hammock barely swung; he was a natural acrobat. The Englishman in Calcutta had never stood a chance of catching him.

He must have seen it in my face—the admiration—and he put his hands behind his head, feigning a stretch, giving me a smug look. I rolled my eyes. "You're blocking the view."

"I *am* the view, *amira*," he said, framing himself with his hands—his crisp linen shirt, his careless hair—then laughed. After a moment, though, his humor faded a bit, as did mine. "I'm sorry you'll miss your talk about Armenia."

"Well, thanks to you, I did have a chance to learn something interesting." I pulled a newspaper clipping out of my pocket, an article from the paper he'd stolen for me. "ISLAND UNDISCOVERED. Sandy Island . . . a little dot we have on an 1850s whaling map of Australia. Up until the other day, you could see it on Google maps too, but it didn't come up on satellite view. A bunch of scientists tried to visit and they couldn't find it, so Google erased it."

He frowned. "What happened to it?"

"It might have been an atoll, finally covered by the sea. Or maybe it was a myth in someone's cosmology. Either way, it's gone now."

"Ah, well. Nothing lasts forever."

I kicked him, making the hammock sway. "That's very glib. We have shelves full of maps of places that only *used* to exist. Everything unique is vanishing."

"The age of exploration is long over, *amira*. Now it's the age of globalization. And once everyone agrees something is one way, all the other ways it could have been disappear."

I folded the slip of paper back into a neat little square, the ink smudging my fingers. "I wish we didn't all have to agree."

"We don't. You yourself are very disagreeable," he said, still grinning. "Don't worry, I still love you. Which reminds me—" He reached into his shirt pocket and drew out a slender silver chain upon which dangled a black pearl set like a bud between two leaves of filigreed silver. He held it up before my eyes like a hypnotist's pendulum.

"Oh, no."

"Oh, yes. Did you think your only gift from me would be a secondhand newspaper?"

"It's not like you paid for either of them."

"How do you know? I had all that money from the captain."

"Because I wasn't born yesterday."

"Doesn't that depend on the map?" I made a face, and he laughed. "Come, *amira*! Yesterday you were glad I was a thief."

I folded my arms. "I know, but still."

"A compelling retort. Then again, if I weren't a thief, we'd never have met."

"Good point," I said, finally smiling. "Although maybe more for my side than yours."

Kashmir had come running to the *Temptation*, a skinny stowaway from a fantastical city in the Vaadi Al-Maas, where snakes the size of the mainmast slithered through a carpet of diamonds the size of plums. I'd been on watch the night he'd clambered aboard and pressed behind the bulwark; he'd only had enough time to meet my eyes and put his finger to his lips before a troop of guards came trotting down the street in stiff formation, their shamshir glinting in the light of the sickle-shaped moon. When the captain of the guard glanced my way, I pointed down the street.

I should have guessed Kashmir would become a nuisance. And a bad influence. But most importantly, a friend.

And all in the last two years, in times and places I'd never have visited had my history been different. Slate himself had warned me, a few days after he'd learned about our newest crew member: "He wasn't always here, and he won't be here forever." I swallowed, my throat suddenly dry at the memory. My father only had two years with Lin. Would it be worse to lose Kashmir, or never to have known him? For a moment, I pitied Slate as much as I resented him.

The necklace blurred in my vision and I blinked rapidly. Then I held out my hand, and Kashmir dropped the pearl into it, the chain pooling like mercury in my palm. Who had he stolen it from? Did she know it'd been taken, or did she think it was only lost? It would soon join the rest of my growing collection: a gold bracelet, ruby earrings, even a thick platinum band too big to fit any of my fingers. I never wore the stuff, but Kash took any excuse to give me stolen jewelry. He didn't seem to care that I didn't enjoy acquiring it half so well as he did, and it tickled him to take theft day literally. "Thanks, Kash."

He waved my words away. "It's nothing. Besides," he added with a grimace and a nod toward the captain's cabin. "I can see you've already got a seagull around your neck."

"The saying is 'albatross.'" I sighed. "And this particular albatross is an inheritance from my mother. A family heirloom."

"Heavy burden to bear. Makes me glad I never had a family."

The breeze ran its fingers through my hair. I twisted my curls together and knotted them at the nape of my neck. "You didn't leave anyone behind when you ran?"

A secret smile in his eyes didn't reach his lips. "No one who would miss me. Not like you, if you go."

I snorted. "You give the captain more credit than he deserves."

Now the smile appeared. "I wasn't talking about him." He winked outrageously; I laughed. Then Kash reached over to tuck an errant strand of hair behind my ear; the hammock swayed gently, or was it the ship? Behind us, the city sparkled with lights, reflected in the black water. "You've never been a little curious?" he said. "About where you're from?"

"I'm not from Hawaii. I was just born there. And even if I was curious, I wouldn't want to be stuck there forever. There are so many other places to see."

"Well," he said then, straightening. "Seeing as how you're saving up to run away, shall I take that trinket to your room and throw it on the pile?" He held out his hand.

His joke hit too close to home. "Who said anything about me running away?" But I thought again of my map of Rome and my little stack of bills, hidden at the bottom of my trunk—the first place anyone would look. I glared at him. "I wish you'd stay out of my room."

"That's a funny joke, princess, when you're talking to a thief."

I passed the necklace over. "Not a very good one, if you give away all your loot."

"I enjoy it too much to stop."

"Stealing jewelry from people in port?"

"Bringing you treasures you care nothing for." He spoke lightly, but his words were too flippant and behind his eyes was something I recognized: loneliness. The moment stretched.

"I do," I said finally. "I do care." I looked at the necklace, glimmering in his palm, and saw it with new eyes: in all our scrambling for money, I'd never once considered selling off the jewelry he'd stolen for me. "Here." I bowed my head and lifted my hair out of the way. Kashmir hesitated before he leaned in, his nimble hands darting around my throat and attaching the clasp at the nape of my neck. His breath smelled of cloves, and his fingers were warm.

I bit my lip, trying to remember the Persian phrase I'd found in an Iranian guidebook and tucked away in my head for a moment like this. *"Takashor."*

He laughed, showing his white teeth. *"Tashakor,"* he repeated.

"That's what I said."

"No, it's not."

I pursed my lips. "All right. Let me try again. Thank you, my friend," I reiterated, this time in my own language. I put my hand to the pearl. "It's beautiful."

"As are you, *amira*," he said, putting his hand over mine, and we both smiled like it didn't mean anything.

The next morning, we left the harbor and returned down the Upper Bay, our sails glowing like paper lanterns in the sun. We passed the buoys at the mouth of the river and skimmed the foamy waves of the green Atlantic as my fears approached and circled like sharks.

Not a cloud marred the sky and the horizon was clear; soon the coast of Long Island was a distant rim on a bowl of mazarine blue. Bee had her hand lightly on the wheel, and Rotgut sat in the crow's nest, his feet swinging like a child's in a big chair. I leaned over the rail at the bow, tugging at the pearl of my necklace. The captain was still in his cabin, but Kashmir was trimming the sails.

"A little help, *amira*?"

Side by side, we cleared the deck, as we did before any Navigation . . . or attempted Navigation. As I worked, it was easy to forget, but after we finished securing the boom, we had nothing left to do but wait.

I stood in the meager shade of the mast. The wind from the south toyed with my hair and made the sea shimmer. It was foolish to worry, I told myself. The map wouldn't work. No matter *what* my father believed.

Then the door to the captain's cabin creaked open, and he emerged. I stood up straight as Bee stepped aside and Slate took the wheel, staring out over the bow. I stared too, watching for fog and seeing none. My hand returned to the pearl at my throat.

Kashmir elbowed me, and I choked out a sound like a laugh. I elbowed him back, so glad he was near. Because in the back of my mind, I did not doubt the map, after all.

"So, what do you think? *Combien de temps jusqu'a ce qu'il renonce?*" Kash said, glancing at Slate. "How long until he gives up?" Kashmir had come to the ship with a solid grasp of a handful of languages; I had taught him how to read, and in return, he'd taught me French, so he could make private jokes in public. *"Des jours? Des semaines?"*

"Oh, weeks, definitely," I answered with forced levity.

"He'll stare at the horizon until he drops, then wake up and try again tomorrow. We're in for a long wait."

"Ah, well." Kash folded his arms and looked over the rail into the water; it was a deep jade, a shade darker than his eyes. "Rotgut tells me you can catch lobsters here."

"He told me too. He's very excited."

"He's always excited when it comes to food," Kash said.

"Can you blame him? He was a monk before he was a cook."

"Speaking of food, are you hungry for breakfast? There's cold pizza in the galley. Unless Rotgut's eaten it all."

I laughed. "Not yet, but I'm glad we're stocked up in case he has us drifting for . . ." I turned to point my chin at the captain, and saw his eyes. They were faraway and focused on something else, something on the horizon, something the rest of us couldn't see.

The words lodged in my throat as I followed his gaze. The fog had come just off the bow, pale and shimmering like organza. Behind us, New York's hazy coast had evaporated like dew. For a moment, the whole world was still and my blood rushed loud in my ears. Then the wind picked up again, in a different direction, twisting my curls past my face and bringing a new scent, sweet as milk after the briny breeze that raced along the shores of Long Island. The mist was melting away as quickly as it had appeared, revealing a wide sea the color of cobalt.

The map had worked.

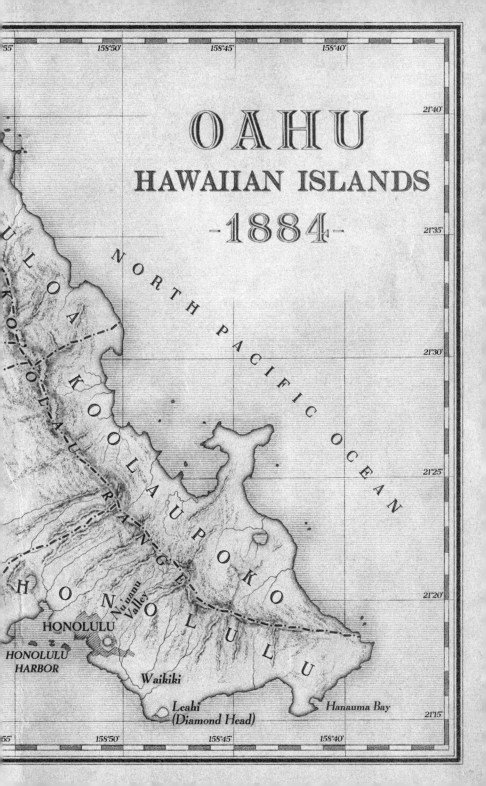

CHAPTER
SEVEN

My thoughts scattered like chipped ice, and my vision blackened at the edges, as though I was staring through a spyglass. For a moment, I thought the Pacific Ocean would be the last thing I ever saw. Then warm hands gripped my arms, and I sagged against Kashmir's chest, my breath burning in my lungs.

"Amira?" He lifted my chin and I focused on his eyes, seeing fear there for the first time since the day he'd come aboard.

"I'm fine." I locked my knees and pushed against him, trying to find my footing. Then I ran my hands over my arms, as if to reassure myself I was still here. "I'm fine."

"Land to starboard!" Rotgut called from his perch. "Steamer aways aft."

I dragged in a gulp of air and shaded my eyes. I could

barely make out a smudge of lead gray that would, within a few hours, resolve itself into a string of islands, as Rotgut had said, away off starboard: the one place and time in the world I didn't want to visit.

It had been so easy. Almost as if we were welcome here.

"Make ready!" Bee reminded us as she hauled at the halyard, raising our sails. The *Temptation* creaked as she swung around and caught the following wind.

"Right," I said aloud, as much to shake myself into action as to answer her. "Nineteenth century, nineteenth century, ah, running lights." The thoughts were coming slow, but they were coming. By 1850, both the United States and the United Kingdom had mandated colored signal lamps aboard ships. We were along a major shipping route, after all; the steamship puffing away south and east of our position was not the only other ship we'd see today.

I lurched into motion, my legs like wood, fetching the lamps we'd removed for our trip to Calcutta—too modern for that era—the red and green glass for port and starboard sides, as well as the clear white lamps for the top of the mainmast and the tip of the bowsprit.

I handed three of the four off to Kash, who climbed the mast and ran the lanterns out to the ends of the yards. I took the one for the prow, clipped it to the rope, and hoisted it out over the water, where it led the way to the island where I was born . . . or would be born, or would have been born, depending, of course, on the map.

As we approached, Oahu opened her arms as if to crush the vessels gathered before her into an embrace: schooners and trawlers, cargo ships wallowing in the water, American gunners sullen as threats, and canoes darting among them like swallows. Above the waterline, volcanic peaks caught the clouds in their black teeth, their sides riven by emerald valleys sewn with silver waterfalls. In the east, the crater of Diamond Head blazed scarlet in the sun.

What would we find? Was Lin waiting for Slate's return, scarcely half a year gone by, while he had journeyed, longer than Ulysses had, to come back home? Was this the end of my father's odyssey? And if it was, where did that leave me?

Cast adrift? Set free? Or dragged below the water?

But our arrival hadn't erased me. It might be possible for two versions of the same person to coexist: one who knew the thrill of adventure, and another who knew only the comfort of home. Briefly, incongruously, my mind conjured up an idea I hadn't envisioned in a long time: a mother. I imagined her arms around me, cool and soft, the opposite of my father's fierce embraces. She was his harbor; could she be mine as well? I shook my head. Of all the tales I believed, this was somehow the most implausible.

I would be a stranger to Lin. How would Slate even introduce me, at sixteen, to her, still pregnant and barely half again my age? And how would he explain the long years he'd lived without her, mapped so clearly on his face?

Although now, within sight of paradise, some of that time had fallen away. Glowing with anticipation, Slate handed off the wheel to Bee and bounded to the prow. His eager eyes roved the shore, as if for a glimpse of Lin herself, but then . . .

But then . . .

Within half a mile of the harbor, his hope crumbled, his face fell, and my own treacherous heart rose. He flung himself back from the rail, his hand over his face as though blinded, or weeping.

As we approached the island, the captain brought the birdcage out on deck. He removed the hood, and the caladrius blinked, her eyes black as polished pebbles. My protests rose and then died in my throat as the captain lifted the bird gently toward the sky. She cocked her head, taking in the water, the land before us, even my face, but she did not look at the captain before she beat her white wings and leaped into the air. He watched until she was a bright speck against the emerald isle, before he turned away once more.

I reached for his arm, but he shook me off like I was a stranger in the street and went back to his cabin. The locks clicked into place behind him.

Pity mingled with relief and made me feel seasick. I picked up the empty birdcage and crushed it into sticks, tossing it piece by piece into the waves as I scanned the shore.

What had he seen from so far away? Was it the steamships in the harbor? No, they'd been in Hawaii since the 1830s. The town by the beach? Or, there, the steeple of Kawa'iahao Church—but no, the church was finished in 1842.

"Qu'est-ce que c'est?" Kashmir asked. "What are you staring at?"

I half raised my hand as I studied the scene, trying to see through my father's eyes. There were flags on Iolani Palace, flying at half-mast—was there anyone Slate might have known enough about to match their deaths to a date? Then I let my hand fall. It wasn't the black flags flying over the palace that he'd noticed, but the palace itself.

"Iolani Palace didn't exist in 1868," I said. "We're quite late."

In spite of my relief, the idea was galling. How was it possible? A date was the most basic anchor on a map. All good maps had anchors, something setting the map in the right place and the right time. Iolani Palace, for example.

I remembered it now, labeled on the page, but I hadn't really *seen* it. I had been too focused on the date. I could have saved myself the worry if I'd only checked more closely.

But who drew a map and misdated it?

Kashmir shook his head. "So is the map broken, or the captain?"

I blinked. "That's a very good question." I crossed my arms. Slate wouldn't give me any answers, but A. Sutfin must live here. Perhaps he could shed some light on the dates, if I could track him down.

My thoughts were interrupted by the sound of a cowbell. Bee let the bell fall back to her belt and gestured at the mainsail: the edge was luffing. Kash and I moved to trim the sheet.

"Could be worse," Rotgut said as he came down from the crow's nest. "I'd enjoy a nice tropical vacation. Has the mai tai been invented yet? Maybe I'll invent it."

"Depending on how long we're here, you could open a tiki bar," I said, taking hold of the halyard. "Although I don't know how you'd pay for it."

"The captain should have some money at the bank," he said. I dropped the slack rope in a tangle on the deck; Kashmir tripped and shot me a look.

"Money? In a *bank*? Like with an actual account and everything?"

Rotgut shrugged. "He opened it for Lin when he sailed. When he returned, he was . . . too distracted to bother closing it."

"I see."

"But let's not forget the most important thing," Rotgut said. "The fishing here is *incredible*." He waggled his eyebrows. "And maybe Bee's admirer is still around."

"Ehhh." Bee waved her hand dismissively.

"What's this?" Kash asked.

"A local man sniffed around the ship for weeks. Handsome fellow. I didn't have the heart to tell him she was already married." Rotgut leaned close to fake a whisper and pointed at Bee behind his hand. "But she pushed him over the rail and into the bay."

"That was Ayen, not me!"

I laughed along with them, but it was odd to consider how much history they had here, in this home I'd never known. Of course, I knew the *Temptation* had been docked here for almost two years. But to hear their stories, told as casually as one might open an old book to a dog-eared page . . . it was unsettling. Kashmir and I were the only ones aboard who'd never lived in Hawaii.

We sailed between the coral reefs along a meandering route of deep indigo, past Quarantine Island, the little sandbar at the edge of the bay from which clouds of sulfur smoke spewed from giant fumigating ovens. The green furze beyond the gold band of the shore resolved itself into broad-leaved bananas alongside coconut palms as stately as standards, spreading breadfruit trees, and falling, tumbling masses of bougainvillea.

Rotgut called out to a pilot ship approaching, flying the snappy flag of the Kingdom of Hawaii. The harbormaster hailed us as we approached, and came alongside. His broad brown face was bisected by a thick mustache, which was very much in style in the late nineteenth century, and he introduced himself as Colonel Iaukea, collector of the port.

He seemed suspicious at first when Bee hailed him from the captain's place at the wheel. Was it her skin color he questioned, or her sex? Then again, it could have been the ship herself; it wouldn't be the first time the *Temptation* had raised eyebrows.

Whatever Colonel Iaukea thought, it didn't matter much; he was nothing like the New York Coast Guard. I introduced us as a survey ship commissioned by a company in San Francisco. Then Kashmir brushed by the man; he half turned, and I raised my voice to regain his attention. "Uh, interested in building a fish cannery along the eastern side of Oahu! Or, ah, possibly the western side," I extemporized. Kashmir moved away, and I relaxed. "Depending, of course, on local conditions."

The colonel took my claim at face value. In fact, after Kashmir palmed the silver he'd taken from the colonel's coin purse and gave him a hearty handshake, the harbormaster was quite diplomatic, claiming it was in the interest of beating the setting sun that he didn't bother making even a cursory search.

We were greeted by a small crowd at the dock; Chinese porters with tonsured heads, graceful native women with baskets of tropical fruit and shining masses of black hair, a wrinkled man bent under a huge piece of coral. Almost everyone—young, old, local, or foreign—was bedecked with blossoms, strung in leis thrown around their necks or tucked behind one ear.

One particular young man—my age, with blond hair and bright spots of pink on his pale cheeks—stood squinting at the ship and writing furiously in a booklet. But why? He was too young to be a reporter. Then his eyes, roving over the ship, met mine, and he grinned. I lifted the corners of my lips tentatively, and he tipped his straw cap in my direction. Suddenly shy, I went to help roll the sails. What was it like, on the other side? Watching the ships come and go, instead of watching the ports appear and recede?

When they saw our ship lacked interesting news or cargo—or more likely, lacked hordes of sailors willing to spend their pay on trinkets—the impromptu dockside market dispersed, the boy along with them, as the sun set and the gas lamps in the streets of Honolulu began to shine. Before they went, Kash bought a dozen ripe mangoes—his favorite—and a copy of the *Evening Bulletin* for me, which gave us the exact date: October 24, 1884, even later than I'd thought. In fact, this was the time and place I'd be living, had Slate never stolen me away.

The harbor had become a winter forest of bare masts, lit by smoky torches that made the water sparkle like a scattering of black diamonds. The sounds of drunken laughter and someone pounding a piano out of tune drifted from the sandy town road to the dock. Sailors made their way toward the watering holes downtown;

later that night, they'd stumble back, singing off-color shanties off-key.

The crew of the *Temptation* stayed aboard and made a simple meal out of Rotgut's catch, a couple of snapper, and our bottomless pitcher of wine, taken from a mythical map of Greece. I'd brought my paper to the table. The headline—MOURNING CONTINUES FOR PRINCESS PAUAHI!— explained the half-mast flags, and the article described the start of the second week of lamentation for the princess. Victorians were so in love with the rituals of death. Apparently, she'd left "a large estate earmarked to support the declining population of native children. The untimely death of the princess is another blow to the royal lineage, which has not been spared the high mortality afflicting their race—"

"So. 1884," Rotgut said. "At first I thought he'd done it."

"So did he," I said under my breath.

"Do you know what went wrong?" Bee asked

"Well, I do have some theories," I said, putting my finger on the page to keep my place. "I could test them out if you'd let me take the helm."

"Ask your father," Bee said, flashing her teeth.

"Come on, Bee. What's the worst that could happen?"

Bee laughed then, a sound like a rasp. "I have some theories. But let's *not* test them."

Her answer wasn't unexpected; this wasn't the first time we'd had this exchange. I went back to my paper. "Mortality afflicting their race . . ." Ah, here. "The princess lies in state under black feather *kahilis* made from the glossy plumage of the o'o bird—"

"Nixiiiieeeee!"

The captain's voice was harsh and braying. We all froze, Kashmir with a piece of fish halfway to his mouth.

"Nix!" The slurred voice was muffled behind the thick mahogany of the door.

I stood, but Bee raised her hand. "Let me." She walked over to the closed door and knocked. "Captain?"

Only silence. Rotgut took another swig of wine. She knocked again, louder. "Captain, are you all right?"

"Where's my daughter?" came the shout, but the door didn't open. Another silence, Several ships away, someone was playing the harmonica with more bravery than skill.

"Nix?" His voice came again, soft, pleading. I strode over, my feet landing hard on the decking. Kash tried to grab my arm, but I shrugged him off.

"What do you want?" I shouted through the door.

There was a long pause. "I see her."

"Who?"

Silence.

"Captain?" I knocked with my fist. "Captain!"

Nothing.

Fine. *Fine.* I kicked the door; thinking it was still locked. But it flew open, and there was Slate, staring up at me from the floor. Lank hair was plastered to his forehead; his eyes were rimmed in red, and the blue of the irises were a slim halo around the black holes of his pupils. The heavy odor of sweat crawled into my nostrils. Beside him on the floor was the box. My fingers itched to grab the whole mess, to hurl it into the sea: the things he loved best, gone in an instant. Instead I tightened my grip on the doorknob. "Go to sleep, Slate."

He blinked slowly at me and sat up, crossing his legs. "Come in," he said, almost politely.

"I am in." I spread my hands, standing there on the threshold.

"No, come here. I want to show you something." He opened the box, and the implements gleamed in the low light. My lip curled.

"Slate, I don't want—" I was stepping back out the door, but he had pulled out the map of 1866.

"You should." He unfolded the paper with excruciating care, his face intent, and laid it across his lap. "You should see."

I hesitated. I'd never actually seen the old map, he was so protective of that box. Stepping slowly back into the room, I closed the door, but only halfway. "What is it?"

"It is . . . what was." The map was faded at the creases, almost torn in places from being folded and unfolded so many times. "Here," he said, stroking the page with one finger.

I took a step closer to see.

"We took out a flat a block away from Chinatown. You could smell the ocean, and there was a little garden in the back. Your mother ripped up the rose bushes and planted bitter greens. The landlord was pissed, but the roses had been dying anyway. The air was too salty for them."

The boards beneath me creaked as I shifted on my feet. He never, ever spoke about her.

"I can see her now." His eyes slid shut, and he smiled crookedly. "God, she was beautiful. And she knew it too."

I only stared at him. He had no pictures of her, of course. I used to look in the mirror when I was younger, picking apart my own face—trying to recognize what was his, so I could discover what might have been hers.

"I offered her anything," he went on. "Do you know that? I told her I could take her anywhere, give her whatever she wanted. She only ever asked for one thing." His eyes snapped open and cut to the box beside him. With sudden violence, he grabbed it and threw it across the room—it hit the wall and I jumped back, my shoulders hitting the door as the contents scattered. A syringe rolled under the bed; the steel spoon clattered on the floorboards. I groped behind me for the doorknob, but the captain hung his head, slumping, all the fire gone out. "I was a better person with her."

My heart fluttered in my throat like a bird, but my feet were rooted to the floor. He focused on the map again, tracing a road from the harbor to the mountains with one callused finger. "I wanted to buy her a house. That's why I left. Somewhere up in Nu'uanu Valley. Something expensive, with a big garden and room for kids." He didn't look at me when he said it, but I felt the implication—for me. He left because of me.

He put the map aside and lay back, staring up at the ceiling in a fragile silence. It took all of my willpower not to take the map myself, to try to see what he had seen, but I didn't move—I barely breathed—afraid he wouldn't say any more.

"I thought this was it, Nixie," he said finally. "I really

did. I hadn't been this close to her in fifteen years."

Neither have I. Still, I said nothing.

His head lolled to the side. "You would have loved your other life," he said, and in that moment, I believed him. I could almost see it, the place he'd described, as clear as if he'd drawn me a map.

"You were right, you know," he went on. "It was a fairy tale. A beautiful country, a faraway kingdom, true love." He closed his eyes to better see the past. "A world in a grain of sand, and a heaven in . . . in . . . what's that line?"

"A wild flower," I said, my voice hoarse.

"Yes." He sighed. "And I had infinity in the palm of my hand." He was quiet again; soon, his breathing evened out. Still I lingered, hopeful, but he said nothing else, and so I shifted, slowly, carefully. The doorknob clicked as it turned, and he stirred. "I wish I could show you." His breath made the corner of the map tremble. "I wish you could see what it was like."

I stepped quickly across the threshold and took a deep draft of the cool night air, trying to relieve the sudden ache in my chest. Then I eased the door shut behind me, and as the latch clicked, I whispered so softly even I barely heard it: "Me too."

CHAPTER
EIGHT

There was something charming about waking to the sound of a rooster.

Even if that rooster was so ancient he creaked more than crowed. And even if it came before the dawn was more than a twinkle in the horizon's eye.

The air was mild and I was comfortable, still half in a dream I couldn't remember, but did not want to leave. I shut my eyes again and listened to the world awaken.

"*Cock-a-daaaaaaaack! Cock-a-daaaaaaaack!*"

First the rooster, along with the quiet chime, rhythmic and close by, of metal against metal, maybe the wind moving a rope with a brass clip back and forth. Then pots clanging against pans: someone had started breakfast in the galley of the frigate beside ours. The far-off sound of a horse's hooves, and the rattling of a cart coming down the road with early morning deliveries. And, sudden and loud over the water, a shouted curse from someone in the schooner on our other side.

I rubbed the sleep out of my eyes and sat up, making my hammock sway. Farmers may rise to roosters, but sailors rise to swearing.

The sun was rising too, turning the clouds in the east the color of cream. The ship felt quiet. I didn't think anyone else was awake yet. Last night Kash had snuck ashore, and he hadn't come back by the time I'd fallen asleep. I'd heard Bee and Rotgut murmuring over their worn game board into the early hours, playing Go and taking each other's stones. And of course the captain wouldn't be awake, not for some time—not after last night.

The rocking of my hammock stilled. I raised my eyes from the harbor, over the town to the valleys above: deep wrinkles in the thick green velvet of the mountains. Which one hid the house with the big garden and the many rooms?

I shook the thought out of my head. It was a good time to do chores; the day was still cool, and I needed busy work so I didn't start imagining memories I'd never had.

"*Cockadaaaaaack!*"

I slid out of my hammock on bare feet and stopped in

my tracks. It hadn't been a rooster after all; there, perched on the rail, sat the caladrius, peering at me with its pebble-black eyes.

A quick check of my pockets yielded a linty piece of hardtack. I tossed the biscuit toward the bird. She cocked her head, skeptical at first, but my offering was accepted when I stood out of reach. I was pleased to see her eat; it was good to know she was safe.

But she wasn't the only hungry creature aboard. Giving the bird wide berth, I went belowdecks and grabbed the jar of bee pollen I'd bought at Whole Foods. Starting at the hold, I visited each lantern on the ship to feed the sky herring swimming inside. The shining little fish were straight out of a Nordic myth explaining the aurora borealis, and their mouths opened and closed like winking eyes as I sprinkled pollen into the smoked-glass globes.

We'd caught them during a wintery week in a mytho-logical version of Scandinavia—Scandia, it was called on the map—sailing under the shimmering lights of the flashing fish schooling in the sky. Slate and I had flown two kites in tandem, with a net strung between them. It had been the first and only time I'd ever flown a kite with my father, and his laughing eyes had been luminous under the northern lights.

It had also been the first map I'd ever pulled for the captain. He hadn't known anything about Scandia—I don't think he'd even known he had it in his collection—but I'd been studying the maps since before I could read and I knew the legends of that mythical country. I told him all about it and asked him to take us there, and he had actually listened to me. Moments like that, I'd felt like I could go anywhere I wanted.

And occasionally, we had. With the maps, my growing expertise, and the captain at the helm, we'd managed to fit out the ship with a handful of mythological conveniences. Not only the sky herring; we had some fire salamanders from 1800s French folklore in the cookstove. We also had a bottomless bag from seventeenth-century Wales, which came in very handy despite all the trouble we took to get it.

That map had been the oldest Slate had ever been able to use, and the Irish Sea had fought us like we were intruders, sending sharp gusts to rip at our sails and icy waves that clawed at the deck. I had been trying to shorten the mainsail against the ferocious wind when the mast split and the boom fell, and I was trapped facedown beneath it. I'd nearly drowned in an inch of water and ended up with a broken arm . . . but we'd found the bag.

I grinned at the memory; I'd worn my sling like a winner's sash. I had really wanted that bag. Bailing the bilge had always been my least favorite chore.

The only convenience I hadn't figured out was fresh water. Water was tricky, bulky to store, of course, but sometimes dangerous to pick up in port. There was a myth about a cauldron with an endless supply of stew, and of course there was the pitcher of wine that never ran dry, but nothing so simple for water.

Still, I'd tried my best. My first attempt was a Mayan Chaac ax, known to split the clouds when thrown, but that only worked the once; it might have been more useful if it had been a boomerang. There was Tiddalik, the aboriginal water frog who held a river's worth of water in his belly and could be induced, with some prodding, to release it—all of it—which completely swamped the bilge with frog water. The bottomless bag was extremely helpful that day.

And I made the mistake of telling Kashmir about the Paparuda, a Roman rain dance, where a girl would traipse through the streets—or in this case, the ship—stopping at each cabin so the resident could pour water on her head. For three weeks he was begging me to try it and keeping a pitcher of water ready for the day I came dancing by. There was just no replacing our rather prosaic distiller.

Still, everywhere on the ship, there were souvenirs of all the places I'd been. I even had something from Honolulu, though it wasn't anything special; just the old tattered quilt my father had wrapped me in when he'd taken me from Joss's opium den. It was on the floor in my cabin. I didn't know why I still had it. I suppose I simply hadn't gotten around to throwing it away.

I laughed at myself under my breath. Perhaps if I'd said that to a stranger, they might almost have believed me.

I dusted pollen over the fish in the last lantern, the one on the bowsprit, and wiped my fingers on my trousers. It was still early, the sun barely clearing the mountains, gilding their peaks and washing the island with soft golden light. No one would be looking for me, not for a few hours at least, and my other chores weren't pressing.

By the time I admitted to myself I was going ashore, I was already heading below for a change of clothes.

My cabin was the first one at the forecastle, the narrow wedge of space behind the bow, where you'd be most likely to be bounced and jostled in bad weather. I used to have a bigger room—the one Kashmir lived in now—but I'd given it to him when he'd come aboard. I was happy with my hammock; all I owned were clothes and books, scattered haphazardly on the floor. I cleaned my father's cabin more often than I cleaned mine.

I kicked a path through a pile of dirty laundry and opened the large cedar chest in the corner, the one that held my map of Carthage and all of my clean things. I pawed through the trunk, pushing aside a beaded cape, cotton petticoats, a Renaissance sack gown, an I ♥ NY T-shirt. We only had a few rules when Navigating, but one of them was proper dress. When I was younger and we visited the nineteenth century, I used to tuck my hair up in a cap and let everyone believe I was a boy, but that disguise had become less believable in the past few years. Since we'd stayed near the dock, I'd been able to get away with trousers in Calcutta, but if I dressed too poorly when visiting shops here, I'd likely get kicked out. . . or propositioned.

I unearthed a black dress with a white lace collar; it was the right era, but it was wool. I thought back to the small crowd at the docks: light colors, loose dresses, no corsets or jackets. This was the tropics. I dropped the dress and shook out a striped cotton pinafore I hadn't remembered owning. It was three inches too short and so tight across the chest

I had to leave it open in the back; still, after Calcutta, I'd rather be messy than sweaty.

In for a penny, in for a pound. I passed over my black Victorian boots in favor of shapeless leather flats, comfortable and hideous. They still had yellow mud from India in the seams. Then I scrutinized my reflection in the big mirror tacked to the wall. Everything was a little off.

I was more tan than the fashion for the era, but being out on the water, that was unavoidable. My hair—coffee streaked with copper and whipped into waves by the wind and the salt—was never properly Victorian, but in this era, my mixed heritage stood out more than anything else. Although perhaps less so in Hawaii. Whenever we visited nineteenth-century England, though, I got sideways looks when I was out with Slate. Then again, so did he.

However, there was much I had inherited that I couldn't change. Nothing gave me away outright, and I was fairly comfortable in the vernacular of the era; that was another rule, of course, one should never speak to the franca unless you used their lingua. I did, however, throw a shawl around my shoulders, which didn't match, but it hid the open back of my pinafore. I slapped a brooch on it in a futile attempt to pull the outfit together. Then I gave up. It would have to do.

The caladrius had flown the ship. I was about to do the same when a voice stopped me.

"Nice shoes. *Tres belle.*"

"Dammit, Kash." He was in my hammock, grinning like a rake. I narrowed my eyes. "You aren't looking too flash yourself. Is that the same shirt you were wearing last night?"

"God, I hope so." He extended his foot lazily to push off against the rail. The hammock rocked gently. "Where are you going?"

"Out. Like you."

He raised an eyebrow, but he didn't press for more information. "One should always make one's own mistakes, instead of the mistakes of others, *amira.*"

"Out like me, then."

"Dressed like that?"

"And what's wrong with it?"

"It looks like you chose the pieces by throwing darts. And you are terrible at darts. Besides, it's much too short." He pointed vaguely toward my ankles and winked. "The whole world can see the top of your foot. You look like a hussy."

I grabbed my skirt and flashed him my knees. He pretended to swoon. "Don't worry. This is late Victorian, not early. More permissive."

"If you say so. Just try to steer clear of the saloons and the dens of iniquity. I can tell you where they all are if you want to plan your route."

I laughed. "More fun to find them myself."

He called me back as I was halfway down the gangplank. "Amira!"

"What?" I turned to face him; something was coming at me. I grabbed for it and wobbled on the slender board, only barely catching my balance as my fingers closed around the leather bag. It clinked, and I swore.

"*Khahesh mikonam,*" he said, giving me a little salute.

"I didn't say thank you."

"Bad manners. You're welcome anyway."

"Didn't we just have this argument?"

"I won that money fair and square. Or do you disapprove of gambling too?"

I weighed the purse in my hand. "Yes . . . but not enough to give it back."

His laughter followed me onto the wooden timbers of the dock. The streets ahead were empty in the thin light of morning. I stood there on the wharf between ship and shore; the mermaid at the prow leaned in like a conspirator, encouraging me.

This was old Honolulu, before tourism began in earnest, before skyscrapers and seaside hotels. There would still be locals speaking the native tongue, telling native stories; their culture was fading but not yet gone. Waikiki would still be a swamp, and there was nothing taller than three stories downtown, except, here and there, the steeples of churches, rising above the bars and brothels.

This is where I would have lived, if my mother hadn't died.

I stepped off the dock and onto the packed earthen road.

CHAPTER
NINE

Only halfway up the short street between the dock and the town proper, the smell of fish and coal was overpowered by the scent of "spirituous liquors," both new and used. Nu'uanu Avenue, or FID STREET, as some sailor had scratched into a wooden signpost, was aptly lined with grog shops. There were puddles in the street, although it hadn't rained yesterday, and the rats barely bothered to get out of my way. I made a face as I stepped over a pile of manure. Paradise indeed.

Still, I kept my eyes wide open, waiting, hoping to find . . . something. Anything. Although I'd never walked this path, the memory of the map was clear in my mind's eye, and the story my father had told me echoed between my temples. These were the streets where my parents had walked, arm in arm; perhaps even now I was passing by the front door of their flat. When I reached King Street, the wide avenue running past the palace along the curve of the harbor, I took a left into Chinatown without even making the decision.

A mere block from the stately stone and stucco of downtown Honolulu, it was as though I'd wandered into another city. Here, a multitude of shops and shanties lined the street, mostly wooden and roughly built, each one squeezed against the next, with additional stories and extensions built out from the original structures, as tightly packed as a colony of oysters. It was very clear why the fire coming in 1886 would destroy it so completely.

The streets weren't empty here. On a corner, a woman sat on blanket along with her wares: a dozen coconut half shells filled with fresh butter. A skinny boy walked by, carrying an impossibly large basket of greens down an alley, right past a pile of rotting wood from under which a mother cat glared at me, nursing her kittens. I stepped carefully over a foul gutter, already red with blood; halfway up the block I heard the shocked mutter of chickens as the butchers did their work. Farther down the street, two men in battered straw caps were unloading bags of flour from a mule cart and in through a doorway. The hand-painted sign above the wide street-front counter featured beautiful Chinese calligraphy, and, unsteadily, in English, MR. YOUNG'S BAKERY.

I dodged around the delivery men and pressed against the counter, breathing deep the smell of sugar glaze and butter. Steamed buns marked with lucky red dye sat warm and plump in baskets next to rows of moon cakes stamped with the symbol for fortune. The baker was old and his eyes were kind; had he ever smiled at my mother as she stood in his shop, inhaling? I opened the purse and was careful not to gasp in front of Mr. Young; Kashmir had given me much more than I'd expected.

Wandering north with two pork buns in my hands, I saw a sleepy little beagle who raised her head from the dirt as I approached. "I bet you'd like a bun." The dog answered by giving the street a lazy thump with her tail, and I tossed her a pinch of dough that disappeared in a single sniff. I crouched down briefly beside the creature and patted the brown-and-white flank, raising a puff of dust into the air. When I stood, the beagle did too. "Rooooo!" she said. "Roooooooo!"

I threw down the rest of the bun and hurried away, and the beagle, mollified, declined to follow.

The watery sunlight crept along the tops of the buildings as I nibbled the second bun. It was delicious . . . but no more or less than any other. What had I been expecting to find, or to feel? As I walked the streets of my birth, there was no sense of terroir, of groundedness. I didn't belong here more than I belonged anywhere else.

Was that a relief or a disappointment? Perhaps it was still too early to tell.

Sweat began to prickle on the back of my neck; I lifted the shawl to get some air. Thank all the gods I hadn't worn the wool.

"Excuse me?"

The voice came along with a soft touch on my shoulder; I whirled around, wrapping the shawl tight.

It was the young man I'd seen scribbling away yesterday, blond hair and straw hat with the black ribbon around the side band. His wide blue eyes gave him a startled appearance, or perhaps he really was startled; he stepped back abruptly, nearly treading on the hooves of the chocolate-brown mare he held by the reins. I'd never seen such fair skin in a tropical climate; it was pale as cream.

"Beg pardon," he said. "I didn't mean to alarm you, but you dropped this. Back by Billie. The dog." He held out his hand; in it was the heavy purse of coins Kashmir had given me.

I slipped the half-eaten bun into my pocket and swallowed hard, the dough like glue in my mouth. "Thank you. Thank you so much."

"A pleasure, miss." He gave me a little bow, looking modestly down at his very shiny boots. "She's a good dog, though she's quite a beggar."

"More of an extortionist." My voice sounded odd in my ears as I tried to duplicate the rhythm of his speech; there was a hint of an unfamiliar accent, something musical in the cadence. "Is she yours?"

"Oh, no. Best I can tell, she spends most of her time near the harbor, watching the ships."

"You two have that in common."

"Well!" One corner of his mouth quirked up shyly. "I couldn't very well miss the arrival of a pirate ship in Hawaii."

I laughed. "We aren't pirates."

"Thank goodness," he said with mock relief. "Though I suppose that's why you're lost in Chinatown rather than looting the palace."

"I'm not lost."

"Then you're braver than most tourists. They find Chinatown too unsavory, so they hide in more salubrious environs."

I couldn't help but grin. The language of the Victorian era was quite charming. Or maybe it had just been a long time since I'd had a conversation with anyone but the crew. "If you think Chinatown is unsavory, you should try a port. Besides, I was born here."

"Were you? But . . ." He tapped a finger against his chin. "Where have you been since then?"

I hesitated, then gave the simplest answer. "At sea."

"Ah! That explains it."

"Why we've never met?"

"Why you seem out of place."

I pursed my lips as he stood there with his shiny shoes and his pressed linen suit in the middle of the ramshackle block between the bars of Fid Street and the open sewer of Nu'uanu Stream. "Appearances can be deceiving."

He laughed and followed my eyes down to his boots. "Very fair. Though I might claim to be braver than most *haoles*—whites," he explained at my quizzical look. "Chinatown can be as picturesque as the rest of the island, if you know how to look at it. Don't laugh. There's always at least one good sketch to be done here." He put his hand over his heart—no, over the book in his breast pocket; the outline of it was visible under his linen jacket. His fingers were dark, smudged with ink.

"You're an artist, then?"

"Only when my father isn't watching."

I shrugged one shoulder. "The best artists had family who disapproved."

"That's true. Then again, very likely so did the worst."

I snorted, then covered my mouth; he grinned back at me. "Well, now of course I'm curious."

It took a moment, but he reached into his jacket and pulled out the booklet. It was clearly homemade, a sheaf of paper folded in half and bound with ribbon. I opened it to the beginning. On one page, moonlight pooling on a secret bay, seen from under the feathery fronds of palm leaves; on the next, a village of grass houses huddled close in a clearing, and here—

"A map?"

"Ah, yes. On one of our rides through Ka'a'awa Valley, we discovered a trail leading to an ancient temple, back behind the abandoned sugar mill. I've sketched it on the next page. They say human sacrifices were made there. At the temple, not the sugar mill."

It was gorgeous work, if gruesome—both art and cartography. The lines were thick and dramatic, with drips and drabs of ink like the spatter of blood. "You have other maps here," I said, turning the pages eagerly; the next one was bordered with delicate seashells.

"That one is a path to a hidden beach, and"—he reached over and flipped a few more pages—"that is a partial map of the tunnels in Kaneana Cave. No one has ever fully explored them. Yet." He gave me that shy smile again, and for some reason I found myself blushing.

I dropped my eyes and turned another page; the image gave me pause. Black ink slashed the paper like the stroke of a cutlass: a ship as sleek as a shark, bound tightly to the pier. I could almost hear the creak of the rope as she strained at her bonds. At the prow, the mere suggestion of a solitary figure, as ephemeral as a wisp of smoke. It must have been me. "This is beautiful," I said, but the word fell short. "It is . . . true."

"You're too kind," he said, looking up at me through his lashes; they were long enough they nearly brushed his cheeks when he blinked. "She makes a lovely subject."

I glanced up from the page, suspicious, but his expression was earnest. The next page was blank. I handed back the book with a sigh. "I can see why you'd call me a tourist."

He laughed. "Should you need recommendations, there are few requests I cannot fill." He tucked the book back in his pocket and made a shallow bow, removing his hat to do so. "Blake Hart, at your service."

"Perhaps another time," I said with regret. Then a thought occurred to me. "Although . . . do you know an A. Sutfin, by any chance?"

"Sutfin? Sutfin . . ."

"He's a cartographer. No? Then . . . how about a public library?"

"Not many people visit Hawaii to go to a library. Probably partly because there is no library, but I'm guessing that's not the main reason."

"You aren't making good on your claim."

"Well!" he said, but he grinned back at me. "I do apologize. You are posing hitherto unfamiliar challenges."

"Don't trouble yourself over it," I said. "There are always other tourists."

"But none I'd so like to impress."

My God. He *was* flirting. "I . . . uh . . ." My face burned as my fickle words scattered like a school of fish in the deep water of his blue eyes. The moment stretched like a rack and I writhed upon it. Where was the banter I found so effortless with Kashmir?

"I apologize," he said again, finally saving me from the

silence. He spun his hat in his hands. "I am . . . not usually so bold. If you hadn't dropped your purse, I likely never would have spoken to you. Isn't it funny, what can happen by merest chance?"

"Indeed it is. Thank you—" I cleared my throat; something was sticking in it. "Thank you again, Mr. Hart."

He stepped back slightly and made another little bow, suddenly formal again. "A pleasure, miss. Good day." He put his hat on his head and tipped it. "I hope to see you again. Perhaps by merest chance." Then he continued down the road. I watched him go, but he didn't look back.

Of course, then it came to me, the reply I should have made. "None I'd so like to impress," he'd said, and then I should have said "You certainly left your mark." And I would have patted the coins he'd returned to me. Clever, you see, because an impression is a mark, and a mark is another word for coin. At least, it is in Germany . . . no, not till 1920; before that it was the Thaler. Hmm. Maybe it was best I'd said nothing.

He disappeared into a shop, one of a number of people coming and going through Chinatown, just as I was, though he knew every step of the way, and I was a stranger in paradise. I strolled down the street, wistful, looking at everything and everyone without knowing what I was looking for. Here, the Lotus Leaf restaurant, accepting a delivery of eggs, there, Wing's Laundry, filled with steam, across the street, Joss Happy House Apothecary, a *fenghuang* painted on the sign. Farther down the block, a man in stained canvas trousers took a barrow full of plaster through an open doorway. There was a cat curled in the shade of a barrel, and a girl selling ugly Kona oranges out of her apron.

I was almost to the river when I realized what I'd read.

Joss Happy House.

I spun on my heel and practically ran back to the apothecary.

CHAPTER
TEN

I peered in through the dirty window. It was dim inside, most of the light coming in through the open doors in the front and rear of the narrow shop. There were no customers. I hesitated outside in the street, but only for a moment.

The air in the shop was cool and sharp, scented with turmeric and dried leaves, and another smell, distantly familiar, that tickled my nose. The rear of the shop was a mess of barrels and boxes in haphazard stacks, nearly obscuring a cramped spiral stairwell leading down to a basement below. A scarred wooden counter stood to my right, and behind it, a plump woman with iron-gray hair and eyes cloudy with cataracts. She squinted when I came in, her tanned skin creasing like crepe.

"Zao an," she said. "Good morning."

"Good morning."

"Ah. How can I help you?"

The walls were lined with rough wooden shelves, and those shelves with containers of all shapes and sizes—glass jars and bamboo baskets, lacquered boxes and paper envelopes holding all manner of ingredients: powders and seeds and roots and fungus, clear liquids and oils and organic shapes suspended in spirits, even a giant jar, displayed prominently on the front counter, containing a glittering golden serpent coiled in amber liquid. It did indeed seem to be an apothecary. Was this Auntie Joss, the woman who'd introduced my parents in an opium den? I had no idea how to ask.

"What is your ailment?" She reached out and took my hand in hers, running her fingers over my wrist bones, my thumb, my knuckles; she must have been nearly blind. "You're thin. You have lost appetite? Low spirits? I have something for you."

"Are you Auntie Joss?"

Her fingers paused in their exploration of my palm, and then she released my hand. "Everyone from Hawaii knows Auntie Joss."

"I'm not from here."

"Oh?"

"Are you . . . Did you . . ." I couldn't figure out the words. "I do need a cure," I said at last.

She reached under the counter and drew out a lava-rock mortar and pestle, setting it on the counter with a heavy thud. "What's the illness?" she said, running her hands over the jars.

"Addiction."

She dropped her chin and smiled like she had a secret, showing the tips of teeth the color of old ivory. "You do know Auntie Joss."

"Only from a story."

"An old story. Didn't you know that selling opium is illegal these days?" She rubbed her thumb, almost absently, along the lip of the stone bowl. "The king has passed many new laws since your father left."

My throat tightened. How had she guessed? Or had I said something obvious? But it wasn't important—that wasn't why I was here. I pressed myself against the rickety counter. The liquid in the glass jar sloshed gently, the snake's coils rocking in the fluid. "You knew my mother." My mouth had gone so dry, it was barely a whisper.

"Don't ask me what she was like," she said, bending to

put the mortar back on its shelf. "The last time I saw her was years ago."

What to ask, then? My palms were slick against the rough wood. "Do you have any stories about her?"

"Her stories are not mine to tell."

I tugged at the pearl pendant on my necklace. "Then . . . do you happen to have anything belonging to her? A trinket or an heirloom? Something to remember her by? Of course I would pay you its face value—"

"I do, in fact," she said, and I regretted mentioning money as she gestured to the large glass vessel on the counter.

"I'm sorry," I said dubiously. "She kept a dead snake in a jar?"

"You mean Swag?" She tapped her thick fingernail hard on the glass. "He's not dead!"

I didn't know if she was eccentric or making a cruel joke. Or addled from the opium she used to sell. I changed the topic. "Is there anyone else who knew her? Friends or family?"

"No. Other than me, she was all alone. Your father promised he'd take her away from all of it," she said with a hoarse chuckle. "And he did, after all. Not as he expected to, but for any problem there are many treatments and few cures. Why don't you ask him what she was like?"

I didn't bother answering that, and I don't think she expected me to try.

"I wish I could say you resemble her," she continued. "But even if I could see your face, I cannot quite remember hers. Tell me again your name."

I sighed. "My name is Nix. It's the name of a water sprite from legend."

"Nix? N-I-X? But another meaning is nothing."

"So I've heard. Many times."

"But did you know, if you spell it backward, X-I-N, it is 'happy' in Chinese?"

I paused. "No, I didn't know."

"Quite an interesting name. Both lucky and unlucky all at once. Five must be your number."

"Five?"

"*Wu.* Meaning is 'me' and also 'not.' Me and not me. Nix and Xin. Happiness and nothingness. Would you like me to draw your charts?" She gestured vaguely to a numerology table decorated with phoenixes cavorting up the sides. "I can tell your future for half a dollar," she offered, her blind eyes staring into the space above my head. "Who you will marry. How you will die."

"I'd rather not know."

"Your mother didn't want to know either," she said, shaking her head. "Her number was four."

"Four?" I said, my voice eager. "What does that mean?"

She held out her hand and waited patiently; it took me half a minute to decide to place a half dollar on her wrinkled palm. She rubbed the coin between her thumb and forefinger before tucking it into her thick cotton belt. Her hands found a stack of thin rice paper on one of the shelves; she peeled up one sheet and laid it on the counter. Then she picked up a bamboo brush and a pot of watery ink with a flourish.

"I will write it down for you, so you will not forget." I rolled my eyes, but at least I was getting a show for my money. "This is five. Your number." She stroked the brush across the page, slow and deliberate. Her eyes were half closed; she must have been working by feel. "*Wu.* And this is for your mother. Four—*si*," she whispered as she drew the Chinese character, leaning in closer. "Death."

"Death?" I waited, but nothing more was forthcoming. I gritted my teeth, then, feeling tricked. "That's nothing I didn't already know."

"Ah?" She lay down the brush and threw sand on the

ink. "Well, it is not difficult to tell the future of a woman who only has a past. I told your father's future once. He is seven, that's the number for togetherness. And for ghosts. Have you changed your mind about learning your own? Perhaps it shall be a tall stranger and a long journey."

"No, thank you." I didn't bother to keep the disgust out of my voice.

A smile crossed her lips and died in her eyes. "You don't believe?" She slid the paper over to me. Her writing was choppy and ungraceful. "Odd, considering your father's profession."

I gasped. Never before had I met a stranger who'd known about Navigation; my father had always insisted on secrecy. "I suppose I'm considering *your* profession."

"Apothecary?"

"Charlatan. Although I suspect it's better than opium dealer."

"Auntie Joss is a dealer of many things," she said. "Exotic wares. Special cures. Rare spices. Information. Is there nothing else you seek?"

"No." I slapped my hand down on the paper and slid it off the counter. "Not from you." I rolled it up and started for the door, and then, from the corner of my eye,

I saw the serpent was still moving, and not from the natural rocking of the liquid in the jar.

Out of the center of the ring of golden coils, a scaly head lifted above the waterline, blinking its emerald eyes. The creature had tiny backswept horns and short whiskers on its chin; it wasn't a snake at all. I'd only seen a sea dragon twice before—once at the edge of a mythic map of Thailand, and once frolicking in a fjord in the eighteenth-century Baltic Sea. I leaned in close, my breath fogging the jar.

A forked pink tongue tasted the air, once, twice, and then the animal moved urgently toward me, sliding up and down inside the container, as if trying to find a weak spot. Tiny pearlescent claws scrabbled against the glass.

"I told you he wasn't dead," Auntie Joss said. She lifted the lid, and the dragon rocketed upward to clutch the rim of the jar, the water dripping off his scales. He cocked his head and peered at me.

I forgot my anger. "He was my mother's?"

"For a time."

Wonderingly, I reached out my hand; he leaped onto my wrist and scrambled up my arm, tiny claws pricking my skin through the fabric of my dress. Before I could stop him, the creature went straight for my neck and closed his jaws around the pearl at my throat.

"Oi!" I tugged hard on the necklace; it popped free of the dragon's jaws. He strained toward it, but I closed my hand around the gem.

"What have you got there?" Auntie Joss said, leaning in. "What is that? Are you wearing pearls?"

"Just one." The pink tongue tickled my fingers, exploring for weakness.

"He must be hungry," she said. "I can't afford to stuff him, price of pearls being what it is." She held her hand out again.

The dragon settled around my neck, nestling into my shawl, his nose wedged into the O formed by my forefinger and thumb—still wrapped tight around the pendant—and his tail draped down my collarbone. He was as smooth as a snake, but unlike those cold-blooded creatures, he was warmer than my skin. I tucked the roll of paper under my arm and dug my hand into the purse for some coins, pressing them into her palm without counting them.

She rubbed her fingers over the coins. "I forgive you for calling me a charlatan. His name is Swag. It has no meaning in Chinese. Good-bye."

I almost left without another word, but I paused in the doorway. "I am looking for something else. Maps, if you have any to sell. Or if you know anyone who does."

Her eyes were wide and entirely disingenuous. "Maps of what?"

I clenched my jaw. "You know what sort of maps. I'll pay for good information."

She nodded like she'd won. "I'll send to the ship for your consideration. I may have something for you."

The way she said it made me uncertain whether I should have asked. But I pulled the shawl tight and left the shop, very aware of the smooth weight of the little creature around my neck, and by the time I'd gotten safely back to the *Temptation*, I'd forgotten to wonder about what she might send my way.

CHAPTER
ELEVEN

"**R**otgut, I need a big pot."

"Of what?"

"Just a pot."

He was standing over a pan where pork belly and pancakes popped and sizzled. The heat in the galley was hellish, and he was wearing only his orange *du bi ki*, the loincloth rag he'd made out of one of his old pure-cloth saffron robes. It was covered in grease stains, and his arms were spattered with tiny dark scars from frying oil. He was so skinny it was hard to imagine he'd ever eaten before.

As if to help me picture it, he grabbed a piece of bacon and tossed it, still sizzling, into his mouth. "Just a pot, hmm? Let's see."

He clanged through his collection, some hanging from hooks, some stacked haphazardly on shelves, some shoved in the corner behind the barrel of oil. He scooped a stack of coconut bowls out of a large cast-iron pot and handed it over.

"This'll rust."

"You need it to hold water?" He put the cast iron back on the shelf and ran his fingers down the row to a beaten copper kettle.

"Saltwater."

"Saltwater! Just a pot, you say. You need glass." He passed me a bowl.

"Too small."

His hands fell to his sides. Rotgut was usually quite patient, but there were limits; he'd left his monastery for a reason. "What," he said, very deliberately, "do you need it for?"

Gently, using one hand, I lifted my shawl away from my neck, revealing the golden dragon sleeping on my shoulders.

When I'd returned to the ship, I'd rushed to my room to raid my jewelry box. Swag had decided to help; he'd pushed his nose through the jewelry, snuffling and digging. I caught a glimpse of the long strand of pearls Kashmir had given me last year, likely stolen from a flapper or a society girl, before it began disappearing down Swag's throat. I tugged back, worried he'd swallow the string, and the strand burst, scattering pearls across the floor. The little dragon rampaged through the room, claws clattering on the decking, chasing them down. Once he'd had his fill he wobbled onto my shoulders, his stomach so distended it threw him off-balance.

He couldn't stay up there forever, though. Sea dragons needed water, and so I needed a pot.

"Look at this!" Rotgut exclaimed, his eyes full of joy. "You know, your mother had one like—"

"Exactly like this," I said. "I met Auntie Joss today."

Some of the joy fell from his face. "That old pusher? I'm surprised she isn't dead."

"She seems like a survivor to me."

"That's true. How did you find her?"

"By—by merest chance, really," I said. "I was walking through Chinatown and I noticed her sign."

"Really? Out in the open?"

"She's an apothecary now."

"Ah." He leaned against the doorframe. "Makes sense. Even the last time we were here, they were making it illegal to sell opium without an expensive license."

"Who was?"

Rotgut shrugged. "Probably people who wanted to keep their monopoly on opium."

I snorted and Swag startled, then dropped his head back to my chest. Rotgut chucked the little beast under the chin. "We had one, you know. In the river behind the temple. Bigger than this, of course, but only three claws, not five. Why were you in Chinatown anyway?"

"Just . . . looking around."

"Did you find what you were looking for?"

"You know, I could probably use a bucket."

He found me a wooden pail with a brass handle; I'd be able to tie a rope to it and dip up fresh seawater whenever Swag needed it, which is what I did. Then I lugged the bucket to my room and eased the dragon off my neck and into the water. He barely batted an eye as he sank beneath the surface and curled up on the bottom, his nose almost directly under his fat belly.

I'd never had a pet before. I'd seen ships with cats and dogs and parrots and, once, an ancient tortoise, but we'd never kept animals on board, aside from the sky herring, or that aboriginal water toad, ugh. With a little luck, I wouldn't accidentally kill Swag. Although if he'd lived through sixteen years of neglect after my mother's death, he had to be tough.

Sitting there, gazing at the little creature, my eyes began to sting.

I put the remaining pearls in a dish nearby. Then I ran back to the kitchen for another small bowl full of fresh water, just in case. I put it beside the pearls; then, as nervous as a new mother, I moved both of the dishes closer to the bucket, then away a bit, in case he knocked into them getting out.

As I was worrying over the arrangement, a voice drifted in. "Hallooooo! Halloo, the *Temptation*!"

I listened, but no one else answered. Of course not; it was Slate's watch. I left off my fussing and headed topside.

"Halloo, the ship!"

I went to the rail and peered down. A man in his early forties stood on the dock below me, dressed in slim-cut black trousers and a fine frock coat, all of it wool, and though the sun was still quite high, he didn't appear to notice the heat. "Who are you?"

He squinted up at me, making a moue behind his dark blond French-forked beard. "Good day. I've a message for the captain of the ship."

I narrowed my eyes; he hadn't answered my question. "From who?"

"I represent a group of persons interested in arranging a business transaction," he said, as easily as a lawyer.

"And *who* are these persons?" I reiterated slowly.

"I am not at liberty to say," he responded, as though he found that disappointing. "May I come up and speak with him?"

Bee leaned over the rail beside me. I gave the man credit; he didn't so much as blink when he saw her. "Go on," she said to me, putting her hand on the holster at her hip.

"Pardon?" Her voice hadn't carried to the man's ears.

"I'm coming down," I shouted.

I made my way down the gangplank and stood before him on the deck. He was a full head taller than I was; I had to shade my eyes as I looked up at him. Had the man purposely positioned himself so the sun would be over his shoulder? "I'm the captain's daughter. What can I do for you?"

The curve of the man's smile was half a degree from condescending. "A pleasure to meet you. When might the captain be available?"

"It's impossible to say," I said as sweetly as I could. "Until I know what he is making himself available for."

"I see." The smile was still there, but the mirth had gone. "Then you may tell him I was sent by a mutual friend."

"The captain doesn't have any friends here."

"On the contrary, he has many friends! He has not yet met them all, but I am eager to make the introduction. I've heard so much about him." His voice was deceptively light.

"Quite extraordinary, the stories of his exploits. Almost . . . unbelievable."

The skin behind my ears prickled. What did he know? "Well," I said, trying to match his tone. "I wouldn't make a habit of believing every bit of gossip I heard."

"Oh, I don't." He let his eyes rove over the *Temptation*: the carved keel, the brazen figurehead. He nodded toward the mermaid. "The things she must have seen, eh?"

I swallowed the sudden tightness in my throat. "If there's nothing more—"

"Just one thing. Please do tell him we will reward him generously for his help."

"We don't need money." I turned to leave.

"I'm not offering money."

I paused with one foot on the gangplank, unwilling to ask. He told me anyway.

"We have in our possession a treasure map." He steepled his fingers in front of his lips. "And the treasure is one only your captain can claim, because he's the one who lost it, back in 1868."

Damn everything.

A mutual friend. I gritted my teeth. She'd said it, even before I'd asked her for maps—a tall stranger and a long journey—but this was not Adelphi and she was no oracle. It wasn't hard to see the future when you were the one planning it. She must have been ready for Slate's return, as patient as a spider on a web. But I was the one caught, unable to escape the threads of my past.

Then I had an odd thought, a ray of hope. "The map. Is the drafter's name Sutfin?"

"No," he said, with a smile that was practically a twinkle. "It is not."

I felt like Ulysses myself then, between Scylla and Charybdis, the beast and the abyss. I closed my eyes, struggling for composure. "Come back tomorrow."

The man took his leave, strolling merrily away, while I climbed the gangplank with heavy steps. Bee was shaking her head. "Never trust a man with a beard. They're always hiding something."

"And not just his chin. He wouldn't tell me his name or his business."

Bee rolled her shoulders. "Might be best if he never does."

I grimaced. "He doesn't strike me as the type to give up easily."

"I could take us out to sea," she offered. "The gentleman won't be swimming in that suit."

"And the next time we're in New York, the map will be waiting for us at Christie's for twice the price. I can't escape it, Bee." I started toward the captain's door.

"Then fight it."

"That doesn't work."

"That's because you've been fighting *with* him." She sighed, the air rasping in her throat. "You don't have to help him. You're not responsible. It isn't your fault your mother's gone."

My breath hitched in my throat, and she reached out with unusual tenderness and put her thumb on my chin. Then she clapped my shoulder.

"But if you still want to escape, take the afternoon. Waking him up, it's not going to be pretty."

I bit my lip. "I . . . I took leave this morning."

"I won't tell on you." Bee walked over to my hammock and kicked the lowermost curve. "Kashmir!"

He flipped himself out of the sling and onto his feet, his eyes wide and his hair mussed. "What?"

"Budge yourself and take this girl ashore. She's getting underfoot."

He blinked twice and then saluted. "Aye, Captain!" With little effort, he swept me up and hoisted me over his shoulder, knocking the air out of me. "Shore leave!" he shouted as he trotted down the gangplank.

"Kashmir!"

"Ah!" he said as I pounded him on the back. "That was my kidney!"

"Put me down," I said breathlessly, "or I'll take out the other one!"

"You should know, *amira*," he said, emphasizing the Persian accent he often kept hidden. "We don't negotiate with terrorists!"

I smacked his rear as he trotted ashore. On deck, Bee was shouting. "Ayen, pull back his blankets. Rotgut! Start some broth! And get a bucket of cold water!" I thought again of Ulysses, and of the sirens. Would Bee tie the captain to the mast until he was himself?

Kashmir set me down on the dock and put his hands on the small of his back. "I know one of our options on leave is brawling, but usually that's later, *after* the drinking and the gambling."

I straightened my skirt, staring toward the ship, wanting to run back, wanting to run away. "Do you think they'll be all right?"

"I have an idea," Kashmir said, pulling at my sleeve. "Let's find you some new clothes."

"You can't distract me with shopping," I said. "I hate shopping."

"And it shows! I'm not trying to distract you, I'm trying to help you."

I knew what he was doing, but I gave in anyway. "I'm only helping you look good by comparison."

"I don't need any help to look good. All you're doing is making it seem like I keep unfashionable company."

He jumped back before I could swat him.

The street was much livelier than this morning. Wharf rats milled around the Esplanade, ready to dive deep after a penny tossed into the ocean, and fishmongers were selling shellfish out of bushels on their backs. Riders cantered regularly down the dirt roads, men and women alike riding astride rather than sidesaddle, with long hair and garlands of flowers streaming behind them. Nearby were the distinctive sounds of a ukulele being played; I scanned the street and found the shop, wedged between a bar and a feed seller. An old man was smiling and strumming, smiling and strumming, while inside the shop, his sons bent their heads over their saws.

This time, we turned away from Chinatown and toward fashionable downtown. Merchant Street was graveled to keep mud off lacy hems and shiny leather shoes. Discreet shingles offered the services of lawyers and bankers, factors and financiers, giving way on Fort Street to more ornate and fanciful signs advertising milliners and engravers, jewelers and dressmakers. Kashmir paused in front of a lovely shop with a bay window shaded by a fragrant jasmine vine, and on the scent rode an incongruous memory of racing through the hot streets of Calcutta.

He took a moment to finger comb his hair and button his jacket; even creased from long wear, it was still quite debonair. "Let me do the talking," he said then. "I'm afraid if you make any decisions, you'll end up with a whiskey barrel and a pair of galoshes." Then he breezed in through the door.

Putting on airs in the most typically outrageous fashion, he ran his hands over every bit of lace in the shop, demanded tea in a perfect imitation of a posh English accent, and then announced I needed a new set of clothes immediately.

"We've just arrived from London, where she had an entirely new wardrobe made, and look, look how she grows! What is this, burlap?" He rubbed a piece of cotton between his fingers. "We need a finer weave. Her parents feed her too much. I swear, a girl at liberty to eat what she likes is at liberty to grow as tall as she likes! But do they listen to me? I am only the tutor, they say, they do not hire me to know anything. No, not Chinese silk, it's too inconsistent. Do you have any from Piedmont?"

The Tutor was a persona he took on sometimes, often in the eighteenth and nineteenth centuries, whenever he and I were alone together in front of others. It was bossy, superior, and very entertaining. Kashmir picked words out of people's mouths as easily as he did the coins from their pockets, but I had no idea where he'd ever met such a supercilious personality. He was pulling out all the stops. He flounced onto a couch and shook back his curls as the two women hid their laughter behind their hands. The sign outside proclaimed them the Mercier Sisters, Fine Dresses, and I learned their names were Nan and Emily.

Measurements were taken, and much was made of how this lavender trim set off my eyes, or the green would complement my hair. Then, of course, Nan noticed my muddy sandals.

"Simpleminded girl," Kashmir said, shaking his head and tut-tutting. "She had a lovely silk pair when we left California, but she was battling a touch of mal de mer and an old salt convinced her the cure was to drink tea out of her right shoe."

Nan, the older sister, shook with laughter, but Emily's eyes were round. "And what happened to the left?"

"We served biscuits in it, of course," Kashmir answered.

"Only the lowest sort has tea without biscuits. Can you make up a new pair to match?"

We left the shop with the promise of a dimity cotton skirt and an embroidered jacket, a white-and-pink–striped silk dress with a "modified bustle" of some description, and a new pair of silk shoes, all to be ready next week. We also had a drastically lighter coin purse, although Kashmir had only put down a deposit, with the balance to be paid on delivery. Once we'd left the shop I shook my head and whistled.

"Don't worry," Kash said. "Money is best spent quickly. You never know when someone might pick your pocket."

"I never knew you had such a fine eye for fabrics," I said as we continued up the street. "You should have been a tailor instead of a thief."

"I have a fine eye for all things, *amira*, which is why I'm a thief and not a tailor."

I laughed in spite of myself. "I just hope I do those fine fabrics justice."

He looked at me then, with one eyebrow up, and said something under his breath in what sounded like Persian.

"I didn't understand that."

"You weren't meant to."

His expression—a peculiar half smile—embarrassed

me, so I turned toward the shops on the other side of the street and pretended to be interested in the hats in a window. They were fantastically styled, with swooping brims and showy feathers.

"You don't want those," Kashmir said. "They've used albatross."

"Ugh, really?"

"To a landsman, they're very fashionable."

"How did you learn so much about clothes, anyway?"

"Necessity. Clothes have always told most of my lies for me."

"Ah." We were both quiet for a moment, staring at the window. I could see his shadowy reflection outlined in the glass. "This isn't what you usually do on shore leave."

He shrugged one shoulder. "I can't deny it."

"So what do you actually do for fun?"

A slow smile spread across his face. "I told you before."

"Dens of iniquity?"

"Drinking, brawling, gambling. Think carefully, *amira*. You may regret it."

"I'm counting on it."

CHAPTER
TWELVE

From the milliners, I followed Kash to Fid Street, where we fortified ourselves with a dinner of potpies and watery beer at the koa-wood bar of the Anchor Saloon. When the cheering started next door, he drained his glass and stood. "Hurry up and get your drinking done, or we'll miss the brawling."

The Commissioner's Saloon advertised boxing matches between sailors, only a nickel to watch. Kashmir elbowed me. "What do you think, *amira*? If we fight, we get in free."

I dug out ten pennies, but only after pretending to give it careful consideration.

The next match was between a massive harpooner and a scrappy coalman. We placed our bets, Kashmir for the one, and I for the other, and I looked to be winning until the coalman ducked a swing and the harpooner hit a cook in the crowd. Kashmir pulled me outside and we watched through the window as the ensuing brawl broke two tables, five chairs, and half a dozen noses.

"That's more than a nickel's worth," I said, a bit breathless.

"Only the best for you!"

We found a more genteel atmosphere at the Royal Saloon, where the laughter spilling into the street was hearty but not raucous. We split another pint—the beer here was dark and strong—and sat at a tiny table in a dark corner, catching our breath and listening to a fat man tell a bawdy joke.

He roared at his own punch line, and so did the cadre of men around him. The bartender delivered another beer; the big man drained the rest of his glass and made a sizable dent on the next, wiping the foam from his thick mustache on the sleeve of his jacket. It was a fine jacket, with gold braid and epaulets on the shoulder above the thick black mourning band . . . an awful lot of epaulets.

Suddenly thrilled, I grabbed Kash's wrist. "Kashmir—"

"I know. They say he comes here almost every night."

We watched the last King of Hawaii drink with his

people. The jokes and the beer kept flowing, and about an hour in, Kalakaua bought a round for the entire bar in honor of his cousin, the late Princess Pauahi. Under the merriment was something familiar as he stared into his fourth empty glass, and my thrill faded like an old photo.

"He dies of it," I said under my breath. "The addiction." I sighed. "Do you know . . . most people think his last words were 'Tell my people I tried,' but that was a novelist's invention."

"What were they really?"

"'I'm a very sick man.'" I pushed aside my own mug, no longer thirsty. "We should get back to the ship."

A shadow crossed our table. Kashmir sighed. "I wish you'd said that ten minutes ago."

I looked up into a pair of angry, blackened eyes. The sailor looming over us wasn't tall, but he was broad; his shoulders were twice the width of my own, and they moved under his shirt like a python constricting. The man was a stranger to me, but apparently not to Kashmir. "Where's my money, darkie?"

I choked, but Kashmir barely raised an eyebrow. "Do I know you?"

"You got rich off my match last night at Commissioner's."

"Oh, was that you? I didn't recognize you without blood all over your face."

The man ran his tongue over his split lip. "That was me," he said, speaking with the deliberate precision of a drunkard. "You bet against me. I threw the match." The sailor leaned heavily on the table with his fists; his knuckles were raw. "I get a cut, that's the deal."

"We never made a deal."

"Just give him the money, Kash."

"Your mulatto's talking sense." He was nose to nose with Kashmir, and his breath was brandy fumes.

"It's not his, *amira*."

"It's not worth a broken jaw," I said through my teeth.

"No, but it was worth the dresses I spent it on earlier." Kash placed his hands primly on the edge of the table. "Look, sir, I'm sure we can settle this like gentlemen—" Without changing his expression, Kashmir lifted our side of the table. The sailor went down, smacking his forehead against the wooden tabletop. He collapsed in a heap, covered in beer, and we leaped over him; Kash didn't tell me not to run this time.

We had half a minute's lead before the sailor stumbled out of the bar and into the muddy street, screaming obscenities, blood pouring from his nose. Kashmir looked back over his shoulder and laughed. "*Now* I recognize you!"

Another thirty seconds, and patrons came tearing out after the sailor, including two members of the Honolulu police force, hastily shoving their red caps onto their heads. Kashmir and I splashed down a crooked alley, cut through the yard behind a laundry, and finally hid down a basement stairwell across from the Royal Hawaiian Opera House. We pressed into the shadows against a thick wooden door, trying to hear footsteps over the sound of our pounding hearts. Something wet started wicking up my skirt, and I hoped it was only water.

It had been quiet for a good five minutes before my shoulders started shaking.

"*Amira* . . . are you laughing or crying?"

"Both?"

He wrapped his arm around me and pulled me close, my back against his chest. "Shh, shh, shh. *Negaran nabash, cher. Negaran nabash.* Shh."

Whatever he said, I knew what he meant, and his tone was soothing. I took a deep, shuddering breath and wiped my nose on my sleeve. "I don't know how you stay so calm."

"I did warn you, *amira*," he said, reaching into his pocket for a handkerchief. "But I've seen much worse."

I dabbed my eyes with the square of silk and tried to steady my voice. "I didn't realize how seriously you took your shore leave."

"This was years ago. Before I came to the ship. Our friend back there wasn't half as menacing as the Sofoor. The Street Cleaners."

"Street Cleaners?" I refolded the handkerchief; it was monogrammed B. L. I traced the initials and wondered whose they were. "Not the type with brooms, then?"

"They swept you up like trash. If they caught you sleeping, you'd wake up in the refuse pits outside the city, with the dead dogs and the dung and all the other waste." His chest rose and fell against my back. "We used to argue about it—what we would do if it happened to us. You could live a very long time down there. There was plenty to eat."

For a while I had no words. In the silence, the incongruous sound of laughter floated from a nearby bar. "That's . . . horrifying."

"There were many who praised the shah," he said softly. "Indeed, the city had never been cleaner." He shrugged. "See? It could always be worse. For example, we could have been facing the winner of the fight."

The mirth stole back into his voice, but I couldn't let go of the images of the pits, the waste of it all. I shuddered. "I'm glad you're with us now."

He laughed a little, then rested his chin on my shoulder. "Me too, *amira*. For many reasons." His breath was warm on my neck, and I shivered again, but not from fear. For a moment, all I wanted in the world was to turn around, like Lot's wife, like Eurydice, to see what was in his eyes, but before I could gather the courage, he gave me another squeeze and dropped his arms. I sighed with regret, and with relief. "Let me take a look. Count to sixty. If I don't swear and start running, you can come out."

"And if you do swear and start running?"

He flashed me his teeth. "Then wait ten seconds and start running in the opposite direction."

He didn't swear, and neither of us ran. We returned to the ship as dawn was breaking, and as we passed under a thick banyan tree, I learned that on land, the first sign of a new day is not sunlight but birdsong.

I climbed the gangplank with my eyes half closed, but I stopped dead at the top. The captain was sitting stooped on my hammock. Suddenly I was wide awake.

His hands were wrapped around a mug of his vile

instant brew, and his eyes were so hollow as to seem blackened. They cut from me, to Kashmir, then back, taking in my flushed face and my dirty dress. "You smell like beer."

"And you look like hell."

Something—a shrug or a laugh, I couldn't tell which—made the hammock swing. "Where have you been?"

"Exploring paradise."

Slate raised an eyebrow, and Kashmir drew himself up. "We went to a pub for dinner, Captain."

"And stayed for breakfast?"

Kashmir grinned easily. "The food was good."

"Hmm." Slate tasted his coffee and made a face. Then he jerked his chin toward the hatch. "Better get some rest."

"Aye." But Kashmir hesitated; I shook my head just a fraction of an inch, and he left. Slate stared after him for a long time. At last he spoke.

"You and him?"

"What? No." I kept my voice casual, but he narrowed his eyes and searched my face.

"Best not to get too attached," he said finally, hunching his shoulders over his coffee and staring at the water.

I rolled my eyes. "You're one to talk."

He didn't rise to the bait. I shifted my weight on tired

feet, but he only sat there, blowing air over his coffee. He always brewed it hot to make it bitter, but he never drank it till it was cold.

"What do you want, Slate?" I said, my voice loud in the night air.

He looked up at me suddenly, like he'd forgotten I was there. "Tell me about the man who came yesterday."

"What do you want to know?"

"Everything!"

"Didn't Bee tell you?"

"She didn't say much."

"Neither did he," I said. "But he *knew*."

Slate didn't need to ask me what I meant. He stood and started pacing. "So he could ask for anything. Literally anything."

"Maybe he's just an opium smuggler," I said, wanting it to be true. "Joss sent him, after all."

He stopped in his tracks, then swiveled on his heel. "He said that?"

I bit my lip. "Not exactly. I—I met her yesterday."

"Where?"

"In her apothecary! Christ. What are you afraid of? She might expose me to opium?" I ran my fingers through my hair; they stuck in the tangles. Exasperated, I dropped my hands to my sides. "Don't meet with him, then. When he comes back, we'll send him away."

Slate stared at me. "You know I need that map, Nixie."

"You haven't even seen it. What if it's another dead ender?"

"If it's good, I'll need it."

I just shook my head; it was starting to throb. "Can I go to sleep now?"

He chewed his lower lip, staring at the lightening sky. "Fine, but only a couple of hours. He'll be back soon."

"So?"

"So I need you at the meeting to figure out how to get him what he wants. Don't look at me like that, Nixie. You know I can't plan a route without you."

I crossed my arms. "If you want me there, teach me to Navigate."

The desperate smile faded. "I'm serious."

"So am I."

"I'm not *asking*, Nixie."

"Good," I said, light-headed with exhaustion and beer and this new feeling, rebellion. "Because I'm not either. That's the deal. Take it or leave it."

"I am your father," he said; I only laughed. "I am your captain!" His shout echoed in the harbor.

"So what are you going to do?" I jutted out my chin; victory was within my grasp. "Keelhaul me? Hang me from the yardarm? Leave me in the next port?"

"No!" Slate threw down the pewter mug. It bounced and tumbled to the bulwark; coffee splashed across the deck. Somewhere on shore, a dog started barking. "No," he said again, quietly this time, and the coldness in his voice froze the laugh in my throat. "Not *you*."

"Who, then?" I asked, but his eyes flickered to the hatch where Kashmir had just gone, and I gasped.

He folded his arms and stared at me. "I warned you not to get too close."

"No." It was barely a whisper; I don't even know if he heard.

"I told you he might not be around forever."

"You're disgusting." For a moment, I couldn't move, turned to stone by the ugliness of the implication. I pushed my way past—I couldn't get away from him fast enough—but he grabbed my arm.

"Now you understand," he said, his eyes bright. "The pain of losing someone you love."

My mouth twisted. "Oh, I've understood for a while, Captain," I said, spitting the words out like broken teeth. "But you always come back when you want something. Maybe one day I'll lose you for good."

He released my arm, and for a moment, neither of us moved. Finally he dropped his eyes, ashamed, but not enough. "I'm going to try to catch some sleep," he said, picking up the coffee mug. "I'll see you in a few hours."

For once, I went to my cabin. Wide awake, I dug out my map from my trunk and traced the lines of Carthage: the scoop of the bay, the wide main street leading up from the harbor, the market where I would make my fortune and buy my own ship and cast off this anchor dragging me down.

CHAPTER
THIRTEEN

After my argument with Slate, there was no chance of sleep—and no chance I would miss the meeting—so by the time the sun was fully risen, I was waiting on deck for the man to arrive.

I had even tidied up the captain's cabin, perhaps more forcefully than necessary. I'd had to work around Slate, and more than once, I caught him watching me out of the corner of his eye, though neither of us dared speak.

Around ten, the man called up from the pier, and I showed him aboard with a thin veneer of civility. He gave Slate a self-assured nod as he entered the captain's quarters and took the chair I offered. Then he smoothed the lapels of his frock coat. "Captain Slate. At last. And your daughter, is she Miss Slate, or Miss Song?"

Any pretense of cordiality fell away from Slate's face.

"If you know her mother's name, I'm sure you know we never had the chance to marry. What do I call you?"

The man's smile only widened; perhaps he had noticed, as I had, that the captain had not asked his name. "You may call me Mr. D."

Slate wasted no more time. "*Miss Song* tells me you have a business proposition for us."

"Ah, yes." Mr. D folded his hands neatly and waited. After a few moments of silence, he shifted slightly. "It is for your ears only."

"I never hide anything from her," Slate lied.

"Unusual," Mr. D said. "Although perhaps the unusual should not be unexpected. As it is vital to the gentlemen I represent that everything be done in utmost confidence, let me impress upon the both of you the importance of confidentiality, by showing what's at stake."

He took a thick square of paper from his breast pocket and unfolded it with excruciating slowness. "This is a copy of a map of Honolulu, showing the downtown area and the harbor."

"A copy?" Slate said.

"I did not think it wise to take the original out into the world. What if I had been waylaid? By brigands?" Mr. D was smiling, but I caught his meaning. "On it are marked several locations of note," he continued. "Including the more interesting, ah . . ." His eyes flickered up to me, then back down. "The more interesting bars, brothels, and opium dens. It was inked in November of 1868."

"Let me see it." And there it was, the energy of the strummed string, the coiling of the great cat before the spring. Slate remained in his chair, but barely.

"Of course." Mr. D laid the paper on the desk between them, smoothing it with a graceful motion.

The captain stood, stooping over the desk, exploring the page. "It's not dated," he said immediately.

"I can assure you it's authentic."

Without lifting his head, Slate glanced up at him, letting his smile show.

"The date can be inferred from the depiction of the city. You'll note that a popular place for tourists and locals alike had, very temporarily, a change of name. Joss's shop had become . . ." He placed one delicate finger down on a point on the map; Slate's eyes followed, and his breath caught in his throat.

"Hapai Hale?"

"Apparently there was a woman working there whose

condition was quite the talk among the regulars." By the look on Slate's face, Mr. D must have been talking about my mother. "You know how the locals are, always jabbering. Shortly after, tourists started calling it the Happy House, not knowing the meaning of the word *hapai*. It's quaint, but the natives are charming about such things."

I looked from Mr. D to Slate. I didn't know the meaning of *hapai* either. Slate pressed his fist to his mouth, as if kissing the tattoos on his knuckles. "It is . . . suspiciously specific," he said after a long pause. "Where did you acquire it?"

"It belongs to one of my colleagues," Mr. D said. "His brother was the artist."

"I'd like to speak with the brother."

"Tragically, he passed away years ago."

"Oh?"

"Drowned in the bay. Drunk, I believe. The black sheep of his family. You may imagine, a man who would map the dens of vice would frequent them as well. I was the executor of his will, and it was in the performance of that duty that I noticed the map, and of course our mutual friend told me you would want the original."

"How fortuitous," Slate said.

Mr. D spread his hands and then clasped them. "Who

can say what force throws us all together? But we are now bound by a mutual interest, which is what brings me here today."

"Yes." Slate narrowed his eyes. "Your price." He gazed at the map; the longing was plain on his face. "Name it."

Mr. D nodded, as though he had never expected any other answer. "It's quite reasonable, I assure you. My colleagues and I, in exchange for this map, all we want is . . . well . . . money."

The word turned Slate's head. "Money?"

I frowned. I'd been worried after Mr. D's mention of unusual skills and extraordinary tales, but money? Money was . . . well, not *easy*. But maybe Slate already had enough at Bishop Bank. Perhaps my father's fears—and his threats—had been for nothing. The captain returned to his chair. "How much?"

"I must remind you, this must be kept in complete confidence, or—"

"Yeah. Yes." Slate took a deep breath. "We are already in agreement."

Mr. D laced his fingers. "For this map, my colleagues and I require nine hundred thousand dollars."

My jaw dropped, and Slate raised one eyebrow. "Nine

hundred thousand?" he said, his voice so steady even I could barely hear the shock. "That's a—a princely sum."

"Almost kingly," Mr. D said with a smug look.

"Obviously there won't be any deal without me seeing the real map first," Slate said.

"Certainly, sir," Mr. D replied. "I wouldn't expect any different from you."

"Nine hundred thousand." Slate glanced at me, his expectation clear: it would be my job to gather Mr. D's ransom. I gritted my teeth, my mind racing. It was an outrageous amount.

We'd have to stay on the island; we couldn't leave and come back, not without another map. Although if we had another map—could we find another map we knew would work? One that would bring us to a time after we'd made the deal? It would have to be inked tomorrow or later, that was the real trick of it; but not too much later, or Mr. D might grow impatient.

"And how long before you expect payment?" Slate said, but I was only half listening. Why did they want nine hundred thousand dollars in the first place? As Slate had said, it was a princely sum, especially for the era. That kind of money could change history.

"We aren't unreasonable. Say, before the year is out?"

"Well," Slate said. "I despise haggling. Bring me the map—the original. If it's good, you'll have your money."

Mr. D lifted his hand, palm out. "Ah, one moment, Captain. Unfortunately, sir, it's not that simple."

"And why not? Has the price gone higher in the last few moments? If the map is authentic, you can have a million."

I swallowed. Damn his pride.

"The price is unchanged, and the map is authentic. I am a very honest man." Mr. D smiled. "The only quibble is, we want that money to come from a very specific place."

"And where is that?" the captain asked, biting into each word.

"From the vault at Ali'iolani Hale. The Royal Hawaiian Treasury."

I gasped audibly, but Mr. D didn't seem to notice; his eyes were locked on the captain's. I swallowed again as the words sunk in. Nearly a million dollars from the treasury.

"Treason," Slate said at last.

"You are not a subject, sir. It is merely piracy."

"Merely," Slate repeated, and laughed. "I wasn't talking about myself."

The genteel charm dropped from Mr. D's face. "I have offended you," he said, his voice clipped. "I will remove myself from your presence." And he plucked the map from the desk and crumpled it in his fist.

"No! No . . . sit, please," the captain said, trying to soothe Mr. D, or perhaps to soothe himself. "I'm not offended, just . . . surprised. I'm not usually involved in politics."

"Ah." Mr. D settled back into the chair so readily I suspected he hadn't intended to leave in the first place. "Would that I could say the same! Unfortunately, circumstances have forced my hand. Politics are always complicated, sir, but even you can understand that Hawaii needs a strong leader."

"I would think the king would be weakened with an empty treasury," Slate said, his tone cautious.

"I said a strong leader, sir," Mr. D said, passing the ball of paper back and forth in his hands. "Not a strong king."

I went cold, but Slate only stared for a moment, then nodded once. "One thing I would like to know," he said. "What part does our mutual friend have in all this?"

Mr. D laughed. "Ah, well, she is a businesswoman! All she wants is to be paid."

I raised a finger. "One more question, sir." Slate shook his head, but I pretended not to see it. "Why us?"

"Why? Well!" Mr. D said with a small laugh. "I was

under the impression you'd want the map."

I dropped my hand to my lap. So it was not our strengths that brought him here, but our weaknesses. Who else would consider doing something like this for a scrap of paper?

Slate rubbed his hands over his head. "Before I give you an answer, I'll need to see it. The map. The real one."

"Very well."

"Meet me tomorrow?"

"Ah, tomorrow is Sunday, I will be at church."

Slate stared at him. "Of course you will."

"An idea occurs to me," Mr. D said smoothly. "In a week's time, on the night of the full moon, the owner of the map—the artist's brother—is hosting a soiree at his home. Perhaps you'd like to attend? You can meet my colleagues face-to-face. You can assure yourself of the map's authenticity. And you can give us your answer."

Slate chewed his cheek. "Yeah, fine. That's fine."

"I'll ensure an invitation is delivered tomorrow. And I'll send a carriage for you." Mr. D stood. "I look forward to your attendance—and your answer—at the ball."

Slate, lost in thought, did not respond. "As do we," I lied for him, for I had a sinking feeling I already knew what the answer would be.

CHAPTER
FOURTEEN

With Slate trailing behind us, I escorted Mr. D out of the room. Though the distance from cabin to gangplank wasn't more than twenty feet, I was protective of the ship. Slate had told me from a very young age not to talk to strangers about Navigation. Obviously he hadn't always followed his own advice.

Once safely ashore, Mr. D paused for a moment at the edge of the dock, still holding the wadded copy of the map. The man made sure to meet Slate's eye before he smiled brightly and tossed the ball of paper into the sea. Then he gave us a nod and stepped into his coach. Slate watched the street long after the carriage was out of sight.

"Captain?" I said, and he startled. I took a breath, trying to sound firm. "The answer will be no, right?"

Slate blinked, slowly, as if he'd been dreaming. "I can't answer that until I see the map."

I stared at him. "We're not going to steal that money. We can't participate in this."

"We'll do what we have to." Slate pushed off from the rail and walked toward his cabin.

"You may," I said, calling after him. "Leave me out of this one."

He stopped in his tracks and then swiveled slowly on his heel. "Did you forget our conversation last night? I told you, Nixie, I need your help."

I met his eyes dead on. "Not as much as you need Kashmir's."

Slate stared at me, his face turning red, before going to his cabin and slamming the door.

I slid down against the bulwark and stared up at the clouds, pulling the pearl of my necklace back and forth along the chain.

"What does he need my help for, *amira*?" Kash was peering at me over the lip of my hammock. "What did the fine gentleman want?"

I sighed. "The contents of the treasury."

"*Khodaye man!*" His eyes were round as coins. "What

did the captain say? No, that's a silly question. Of course he said yes."

"Technically he's still thinking about it," I said. "We're supposed to take a look at the map at some party next week."

"How much money is it?"

"In the treasury? Nine hundred thousand dollars."

He whistled low. "In all my life I haven't stolen a tenth so much."

I looked sideways at him. "There's no reason to sound happy about it."

"I shouldn't take pride in my work?"

"Not when it's wrong."

"Robbing a king?" He gave me a crooked smile. "Even I've read Robin Hood."

"The treasury doesn't belong to the king, it belongs to the people."

"I've tried that one before. It didn't work. If you can get arrested for taking something, it's not yours."

"That's what I'm saying. It's wrong."

"It's *illegal*," he corrected. "There are a lot of things that are illegal but not wrong. And probably more that are wrong, and still legal."

"There has to be a line, Kashmir," I said angrily. "A person can't do just anything for love."

He shrugged one shoulder. "I would."

"Yeah, well, you're a thief. Your relative morality is already suspect."

"Ah," he said then, standing. "Well. I'll leave the morality for those that like the taste of it. I always preferred bread."

"Kashmir, wait!" But he didn't. Instead he slipped down through the hatch. I waited to hear him slam his cabin door, but he did not oblige.

Left alone with my frustration, I went through my chores with a distracted energy, sweeping the deck, feeding the sky herring, even filling the big copper vat with water and tossing in one of the fire salamanders, followed by my dirty laundry. After the water was good and hot, I plucked the little creature out with a pair of bamboo tongs; his flat-mouthed expression was one of mild offense.

By the time I was hanging my clothes out to dry, I was calm enough to feel ashamed. Kashmir wasn't the one I was mad at. I hung my last shirt on the line and went downstairs to knock on his door.

"Come."

I opened the door a crack and peeked in. He was lying

there on his back in the pile of ratty silk pillows he used for a bed, reading. He didn't look up from his book.

I cleared my throat. "I'm sorry about calling you a thief."

"Don't be," he said quietly, turning a page delicately with his finger. "It's the truth, after all."

"Only part of it. And not the most important part."

"Well." Then he put his book on his chest and smiled up at me, waggling his eyebrows. "What is the most important part?"

I kicked a pillow at him; he caught it. "Save it for the next time we're at Commissioner's," he said, throwing it back at my head.

I sprawled down on one of the bigger cushions, sending up a puff of air. "Speaking of shore leave, there's a ball coming up and I'll need a handsome date. But you'll have to do."

"Only if I can wear my steel-toed shoes." He arched one brow. "I've seen how you dance. So. You're going after all?"

I frowned. "I need to take a look at the map. If it's fake, the whole issue is moot."

He propped himself up on one elbow. The book fell away from his hands, open on the pillows. "What if it's not?"

I had no answer, so I picked up the book and closed it.

It was well worn, with large print, the bright colors starting to fade. A version for children, like most of the books he owned. "*The Jungle Book*?"

"One of my favorites. I used to feel like Mowgli."

"Feral?" I said pointedly.

His face stayed serious. "The laws of the jungle remind me of the laws of the street. When I came aboard, I had to learn a different set of laws. Everywhere we go there is a different set of laws. Most of them unwritten."

"I really am sorry about calling you—"

"It's all right. Really. What I meant is, I wasn't at home right away." He reached out to play with the tattered edge of one of the cushions. Kashmir, like me, had come to the ship with no belongings, but now the room was full of riches and reminders. The pillows were sewn from scraps of silk, and scattered around the room were wooden statues and stone bowls and bone knives and strings of seeds, tiny treasures that could be slipped into a pocket. On the walls were pages torn from books; as I leaned closer, I saw they were poems.

All I had collected were dust and costumes. I sighed. "Do you feel at home now?"

He met my eyes. "You help me to."

"Oh. Good," I said, nonplussed. I leaned back, gazing

down at the book in my hands, trying desperately to think of something to say. "You know, Kipling was a horrible racist." Oh, for God's sake. I threw the book aside.

But it made him laugh; I was relieved. "Well, I stole the book, so he wasn't paid. Besides, that version was published in the 1960s. He was long dead by then."

"He's out there now, though. He and Mr. D would get along."

"This is the age of empire. There are a lot of people who share their views."

"And a lot of people being ground down under their feet."

"Maybe at the bottom of it, it's all just the law of the jungle." He sat up and wrapped his arms around his knees. "While you were doing your laundry, Slate called me in to talk."

My breath hitched in my throat. "And?"

"I'm sure you can imagine the general idea. Why are you making that face? The captain has been good to me. He didn't have to take me in. And he doesn't have to let me stay."

My cheeks went hot, and my skin felt too tight. "You heard him last night."

"And I'm glad for the chance to earn my keep. I never

learned to beg." He shrugged. "Besides, like you said, it's for love."

"Love?" The word was bitter as hemlock. "It's just another addiction."

He sighed, but he didn't protest. We both sat under the heavy blanket of silence until a breeze stole in and rustled the pages on the walls. I stared at his stolen trinkets. "Kashmir. You're a good thief."

"Good at thieving? Or good and a thief?"

"Don't fish. We both know you're good enough to think you can steal a million dollars in gold and silver."

"Or foolish enough." He grinned.

"So . . . you shouldn't have any trouble with a single roll of paper?"

"Ah," he said, but his smile faded. "Clever."

"Of course . . . the captain wouldn't like it."

"That depends," he said cautiously.

"On?"

"On whether or not we succeed."

"Do you doubt whether we can?"

"No," he said, tilting his head. "But I do wonder why we should. I thought you were done helping him."

"Well, it's less dangerous than trying to steal the gold."

Kashmir let the silence stretch, studying me. "And?" he said at last.

I sighed. "And . . . if he's willing to do anything for the map, I'd rather he negotiate with us than them."

He gave me an appraising look. "You do understand the law of the jungle."

Hope rose in my throat. "You'll do it?"

"For you?" I blinked, unsure how to respond, aware of how unfair it was to ask, but Kashmir did not wait for an answer. "I'll try."

"Thank you!" I threw my arms around him and he laughed—or maybe it was a grunt.

"Can't breathe!"

"Sorry!" I rocked back on my heels, buzzing with energy. "So. How are we going to do it?"

"So eager now, Miss Relative Morality!"

"Stealing a map versus robbing a kingdom? I'll throw myself on the mercy of the law."

"Mercy? You've never really dealt with the law, have you? Ow," he added, even though I hadn't hit him that hard. "Well," he went on. "I don't know just yet, but I'll figure it out. And I think the best time to do that is at the ball. I heard you needed a date?"

CHAPTER
FIFTEEN

I woke the next morning with Kashmir's breath tickling my ear.

We'd talked late into the night, and I had only meant to rest my eyes for a minute, but it had been so warm in the nest of silk beside him. He'd tossed his arm over me as we'd slept; in those first moments of wakefulness, I didn't have the willpower to throw it off. My eyes drifted open and focused on his hand, inches from my nose. His fingers were curved into a soft, relaxed shape as he slept. I stared at them, memorizing the lines in the skin, the rounding of the knuckles, the little white scars.

A small part of me was ashamed at enjoying the closeness I never would have accepted had we both been fully awake, but I tried to ignore it, tried to let sleep steal back. Time passed as it does in a dream, until the sound of heavy footsteps on the deck above roused me. It must have been the captain, pacing by overhead, toward the cabin—or the hatch.

I was bolt upright half a second before he opened the door.

"Get up, Kash, it's long past—" Slate stopped on the threshold, his mouth still open. Kashmir's body went rigid, his eyes snapping open, but the captain was staring at me. With all my might, I resisted the urge to explain. I'd be damned if I'd make it his business.

Slate took a deep breath, dropped his eyes, then shifted on his feet, looking everywhere but at me. "Fifteen minutes, Kashmir." When he shut the door, he didn't even slam it.

I laughed a little, incredulous, triumphant, but Kash clambered to his feet, his hand on his forehead. "What's wrong?" I asked. "That could have been much worse."

"It also could have been better," he said, pulling off his shirt and throwing it into the corner.

"So what? He needs you."

"I'm not worried about *me*," Kash said, rifling through his closet. "I'd hate to see you in trouble."

"In trouble? For this? Nothing even happened. And he has no moral high ground, even if it did." I watched Kashmir slide a shirt off a hanger, put it on, button it up. The silence felt loud. "Which it didn't."

"I know." He glanced back over his shoulder and gave me a wink. "I was there."

My cheeks started to burn. "So where are you two going, anyway?"

He pinned his cuffs. "I'm sure you can guess."

"Creeping around the treasury?"

"Reconnoiter is a nicer word."

I made a face. "Don't get caught. The last thing we need is for you to go to jail."

"For treason?" he said, running a comb through his tousled hair. "We wouldn't go to jail."

"Really?"

"We'd be shot."

"You always know just what to say."

"I try to look on the bright side." He hooked his thumbs into the waistband of his pants. "Now, unless you have regrets about what didn't happen—"

His laughter followed me out into the hall; my ears were still ringing with it when I got up abovedecks.

It was a beautiful day, the blue sky paling beside the sapphire sea. Half a mile out, rollers were combing the sandbar in long lines of cloud-white foam, and past them, fishermen in canoes clustered around the coral reefs. The air was cool, and as the balmy breeze ruffled the water of the bay, the sun changed the surface of the sea into a Milky Way of sparkling stars.

Bee and Rotgut were stooped over a swath of netting, making repairs. When Bee glanced up at me, Rotgut smiled hugely. "Ooohhhh!"

Bee swatted at him. "Go make lunch."

"It's not even midmorning!"

"Make something that takes a long time."

Rotgut rolled his eyes, and when he passed me on the way to the hatch, he gave me a big thumbs-up.

The netting was spread out on the planks under the clothesline. I was careful not to step in it. "Word travels fast," I said to Bee as I gathered my clothes; they were warm with sunlight.

"It didn't have far to go." Bee tied off a knot. "That boy. You know he has no cattle."

"So?"

"So, I paid thirteen head to marry Ayen although the price was only ten, but if you had seen her dance, oh, the way she moved—"

"No, I know," I said, cutting her off before she went

through the entire story. "But Kashmir and I are just friends."
She pursed her lips at me, but I only shrugged. "Besides, I'm
a terrible dancer."

"Hmm. Maybe *you* should find some cattle."

"Where would I even keep them?"

"Cattle are only a metaphorical representation of worth,
Nix."

I laughed then. "Of course. Sorry."

"At least until you settle somewhere with grass."

I stopped in my work, my arms full of laundry. "Who
says I'm going to settle?"

She shrugged. "Most people do."

"You don't."

"I did. But I have no cattle left now, metaphorical or
otherwise. How would I marry? Besides, Ayen gets jealous," she said with a wink. Then she pulled another knot
tight, and the rope snapped in her hand. "Ach! Ayen!
See?"

"Right, well, as for me . . . ," I said. "There's no need for
cattle, because there isn't going to be any settling."

She snorted.

"Don't laugh at me."

"I'm not laughing at you. Ayen is laughing at you."

I yanked the last dress off the line. "Ayen should stop causing trouble."

"I told her that, but does she listen?" Bee shook her head. "No one listens to Bee. Maybe you should ask your mother."

I swallowed. "She doesn't speak to me like Ayen speaks to you."

"I'll tell the captain to ask her, then."

"I don't think she speaks to him, either."

"I think she probably does." Bee made another firm knot in the net.

"Then maybe he also doesn't listen."

Just then Kashmir came up through the hatch, looking very dapper. Both Bee and I watched as he crossed the deck and knocked on the captain's door. After a moment, it opened; he went in, and both of us stopped breathing as we listened for shouting, but nothing came. Bee nodded. "Good thing he doesn't mind."

I glared at her. "There's nothing to mind."

"As you say."

I went below and dumped the laundry in my room. From the clean pile, I picked out a yellow cotton dress with a tiny floral print that fit much better than the pinafore. I yanked it over my head, still fuming. I didn't know why her assumptions annoyed me; it was only to be expected. I had spent the night in Kashmir's room. From the crew's perspective, the meaning there was clear, even if Kashmir and I had never so much as kissed.

Though for a moment last night, we might have. He was making a joke about something, something silly, I couldn't even remember what it was, because I had turned my head to reply when I found myself staring directly into his eyes, and he into mine.

And in that moment, I saw the horizon unbounded and I reeled with the vastness of it. What new shores would I discover if I could only travel those few inches? A storm—a tempest in the pit of my stomach—but I was the skiff tossed on the waves, and my father's lesson like thunder in my ears: don't get too close. Still, the temptation was there. Kash must have realized it a second after I did; his eyes widened, but he did not lean in, nor did he turn away. He left it to me.

Bee and Ayen had nothing to laugh at.

I was debating folding my laundry or finding some breakfast when there came a familiar howl through the porthole: "Roo! Rooooo!" I ran to the galley and found one forlorn chunk of sweetbread to bring topside. I leaned over the rail, ready to toss Billie the crust, and was surprised to see she wasn't alone. There, on the pier, were the boy and his chocolate mare.

"Hello," he said, doffing his hat. "Oh, wait—"

The dog was already halfway up the gangplank by the time Blake Hart dismounted. He ran up after her as she rammed my legs, her whole body wiggling. "Sorry!" he said, trying to pull her back. "She followed me from Beretania. It seems she remembers the bun."

"It's all right, Mr. Hart." The entire hunk of bread was snatched from my hand. "I don't think I'm as hungry as she is."

"Tantalus isn't as hungry as she is!"

I laughed. "Indeed. Welcome aboard. But what has brought you here?"

"Many thanks," he said, tipping his hat. "Well, I—*no!*"

He lunged for the dog, but she slipped his grasp. Slate had emerged from his cabin, followed by Kashmir, and Billie bounded across the deck to cozy up to them. The captain looked askance at the little beagle as she thumped his legs with her tail. "What is this?"

"Billie!" Blake snapped his fingers. She lifted her nose from Kashmir's shoes. Blake pointed sternly to the pier, and she trotted off the ship to wait by his horse. "That's

Billie. She took quite a liking to the young lady the other day."

"Did she?" Kashmir murmured, wiping his shoes with his silk handkerchief.

"Blake . . . Mr. Hart," I said. "Meet my father, Captain Slate."

"Ah! The captain himself. Just the man I wanted to see." He offered his hand heartily. I waited for it, the look back and forth between my father and me, but it didn't happen. "A fine man for a fine vessel."

"Blake Hart?" Slate took his hand. "The name is somewhat familiar."

"I don't think we've met, sir, I would recall, but it's a pleasure to do so now. And Mister . . . ?"

"Firas," Kashmir said, folding his handkerchief neatly and making a crisp bow.

Blake's brow furrowed as he took in the fine clothes. "A sailor?"

"Her tutor," Kashmir said smoothly.

Blake cocked his head. "You're much younger than any of my tutors."

"*Baleh*, I am wise beyond my years," Kashmir said. "And of course I have a natural inclination to it. My people did, after all, invent algebra. Including the zero." He was smiling too, but not with his eyes.

"Blake Hart!" Slate said then, snapping his fingers and pointing at Blake. "But you're too young."

Blake looked at him quizzically. "Too young for . . . ?"

"Maybe it was your father." Slate nodded to himself. He stood close enough now, I could see the signs; his eyes dark, his brow shining, his reactions a touch too slow. I cut in.

"What can I do for you?"

"Well," Blake said carefully. "Speaking of my father, I'm here at his request, to deliver an invitation." He pulled a white card, the color of bleached coral, out of the breast pocket of his jacket.

"An invitation?" From his father . . . who was hosting the ball. The brother of the mapmaker, then. I glanced at Kashmir, but he gave no sign of recognition—then it occurred to me he might be doing that on purpose. I pretended to have a sudden, keen interest in my fingernails.

"Yes. He asked me to say he'd be honored by your attendance at our little party. All of you." Blake grinned at me. "As would I."

"Oh, I'm certain you would," Kashmir said.

"Thanks," Slate said, fascinated with the card, tilting it

and letting the gilt writing catch the light. Then he shoved it into his pocket. "Okay. Let's go." I winced as Slate started walking down the gangplank; Kashmir followed, though more slowly.

Blake inclined his head, his expression still polite. "Good day, gentlemen." Then he offered me his arm. "Allow me?"

"To what?"

"To help you down the gangplank."

"Oh, I'm not going with them," I said, watching Kash and Slate cross the wharf toward town, just two fine gentlemen on a stroll. I sighed. "They're on business that doesn't involve me."

"Is that so?" Blake's raised his eyebrows. "Their loss." He put his hands in his pockets and glanced at the mast, the sails, the wheel. "You know, I've never been aboard a ship before." I couldn't help but grin when he jumped up and down a little on the deck. "I've been on canoes, the outriggers the Hawaiians favor, but nothing that could cross the Pacific. Mind giving me a tour?"

"Ah, unfortunately, I'd have to ask the captain—"

"Of course, of course." He tapped his finger on his lips, then he offered his arm again. "Well, if you're not otherwise occupied, allow me to make up for Billie's transgression against your breakfast? There's a café just up the street."

I hesitated a moment, wondering how proper it would seem to take Blake's offer, before throwing caution overboard and slipping my arm in his with a little thrill. Kash and Slate weren't the only ones who could reconnoiter. The map was hidden somewhere at Blake's house. If I could discover its hiding place, we might not need to wait for the ball.

CHAPTER
SIXTEEN

Arm in arm as we were, the gangplank—being only wide enough for one—took a bit of negotiating. I didn't need Blake's steadying hand as I stepped onto the pier, but I took it anyway, marveling at his calluses, where he must have held the pen . . . so different than mine. Blake looped his horse's reins around his free hand and we started up Fid Street, Billie leaping at our heels like a dolphin in our wake. My mind was racing: I wanted to ask about his father's map—where it was kept, if it was authentic, if an original even existed—but how? What would he know— and what was safe to say? I couldn't imagine Blake, with his honest, open face, being part of a cabal, but Mr. D had been clear about the risk if we made any mention of our meeting.

"I found Alexander Sutfin," Blake said, interrupting

my thoughts. "He's a drafter downtown, on Queen Street and Richards. Second floor." I blinked at him, and he smiled. "Well, I can't very well claim to be an expert if I can't answer your questions."

"I . . . thanks. Thank you." Although the information about Sutfin was useful, I was more concerned now with the other map. And now that he'd opened the topic—

"But I have one of my own," he continued before I could speak. "What's your name?"

I wondered, as always, whether to lie. But no, Mr. D already knew. "My name is Nix Song."

He cocked his head. "Nix? Interesting."

"Nix was a water sprite in Germanic myth," I said. "She lured men into the lake to drown."

"We have water spirits here too, although they're shaped like lizards."

"Harder for them to lure men, then."

"Depends on the man, I suppose," he said, making me laugh. Then he hung his head in mock regret. "Alas, I was only named after my uncle."

"The dead one?" I said, too quickly. His smile faltered, and my mouth went dry in the ensuing silence. "I—I beg your pardon. Clearly I've been too long at sea—"

"No, no," Blake said. "I never knew the man, although my mother tells me I take after him quite a bit."

The drunkard who mapped the opium dens? Thankfully I kept that thought behind my teeth. "How so?"

"I have his artistic bent. My father can't draw a square on a grid. But . . . how did you know about my uncle's death?"

I stumbled; he steadied my arm as I tried to think of an answer. "The . . . the newspaper, I think it was."

"Must have been a very old newspaper," he said, looking at me sideways.

"I . . . yes. It was . . ." I tried to think past all the curse words. "It wasn't the newspaper, I remember now. My father and yours are discussing a business venture, and he mentioned your uncle's misfortune."

"So you've met my father?"

"Well . . . no. It was a mutual friend who is making the introduction." Damn damn damn. "I don't know anything about their business," I added in an attempt to forestall any more questions.

"Something to do with the captain's excursion today, no doubt!"

"Difficult to say," I said weakly.

But he was smiling. "Well. That's good news, especially

if it means you'll be in Honolulu awhile. Ah, here we are."

He pulled me into Nolte's Coffee Saloon. Billie knew better than to follow; she wandered off after a departing patron holding a biscuit. Blake ordered coffee and scones, and we sat at one end of a long table occupied by a few other patrons: a young gentleman reading the paper, two sailors staring bleary-eyed into steaming cups, an old man warming his gnarled knuckles. Blake added enough cream to shade the brew the color of maple, while I took mine black and hot.

I blew over the cup and then stopped, reminded of my father, and tried to gather my thoughts for a new attempt. "So. Your uncle was an artist as well?"

"We have a great many of his paintings hung in the house. My mother admired his work. I can show you at the ball if you like."

"Oh, yes, I'd love to see!"

"Are you a connoisseur of the arts?"

I laughed a little, remembering what Kashmir had said at Christie's. "No, I am no expert." He gave me a quizzical look and I cringed internally; I should have lied. Why else would I have sounded so eager a moment before? "I mean, I like art," I stammered. "I just don't know much about it."

"Well," he said with mock resignation. "I suppose that explains your kindness about my sketchbook."

"Not at all!" I protested, hoping I wasn't blushing. "Your drawings really are lovely. Especially the maps. I know about maps." I ran my finger along the chipped edge of the saucer; I'd seen my opportunity come back again. "Did your uncle also draw maps? As you do?"

He stirred his coffee. "Not that I know of."

"Oh." I tried to keep the disappointment off my face. We both reached for our cups simultaneously; the silence felt long.

"You're very keen on maps," he said when he set his cup down.

"Well, of course I am," I said quickly. "They're useful to a sailor."

"To an explorer too." He gave me that secret smile again, and I couldn't help but return it.

"So . . . not only an artist?" I said, teasing. "Do you hope to follow in the footsteps of Dr. Livingstone?"

"And go to Africa? No. Hawaii has enough mystery to occupy a dozen Dr. Livingstones. At least for now," he added, his eyes darkening.

Nervous, I picked up my cup again. It clattered on

the saucer. "Times are changing?"

"That's one reason I record what I see. Things disappear otherwise."

Surprised, I looked up at him; my hands stilled. "I've noticed that very same thing."

"Have you?" He tilted his head, studying my face, but even under this scrutiny, I wasn't nervous anymore. "You must have seen a great many things in your travels, Miss Song, but having known nothing else, I can promise you this island is unique in all the world. And everything unique is worth preserving."

"And worth seeing!"

"Yes."

I stared at him, and the thoughts of reconnoitering fell away. What might I learn if I spent even a day on the island, instead of mining for information on this damned map? But my smile faded, and I swirled the gritty dregs in the bottom of my cup. "I never stay long enough to learn a place's secrets."

He sat back; his eyes seemed to reflect my sadness. Then he nodded, as though making a decision. "Finish your coffee and come with me."

I pushed the mug aside as he stood. "And where are we going?" I asked, following him out the door.

"Miss Song," he said, throwing a grin back over his shoulder, "I'm going to show you your country."

An answering smile crept unbidden across my face. It fell away, though, at his next question. "Can you ride?"

I stopped in my tracks. The horse seemed much more intimidating than she had an hour before. "I don't know."

He laughed. "Don't be nervous. I've named her Pilikia, but she's quite gentle."

"What's *pilikia* mean?"

"'Trouble.' More what we get into than what she gives me." He paused, looking at the saddle—Western, with the high pommel and the big stirrups with leather guards to protect the rider's feet when going through thick brush—and then back at me, or rather, at my skirt. "Will you be comfortable on the saddle? We can walk if you'd prefer."

"No," I said firmly. "We'll go farther on horseback."

He knelt, cupping his palms down near my knees. I stepped into his hands and sprang onto the saddle, sitting with my legs both over Pilikia's left side. I had a brief sensation of vertigo—the height was dizzying—but then Blake swung up behind me, steadying me with his arms on either side of my body.

"What would you like to see most?" he asked.

I considered all the places I'd been, most of them long gone. "Something I can only see here and now."

Blake glanced up at the sun; it was high in the sky. "All right. We just barely have time."

He put his heels to Pilikia's flanks, and we set off through town, traveling atop our shadow. It took me a few minutes to get used to the motion of the horse, so different from the rocking of the ship. As we passed by, Blake pointed out landmarks—here, the Kamehameha Post Office, Hawaii's only connection to the world beyond the shore; there, a grassy square where the king gave free concerts on nights of the full moon.

"He's even revived the hula, and they dance on the grass while the missionaries avert their eyes." His lips were just behind my ear, as though it was a secret, and I heard the amusement in his voice.

"What do you mean, revived?"

"It had been banned for many years before Kalakaua took power."

"Too licentious for past rulers?"

"It scandalized the foreigners, who only saw what they were looking for. The hula tells a story, but they weren't listening."

"You admire the king?"

"You're surprised?"

I bit my lip. Earlier, I had been nearly certain Mr. D had sent him to test me, but now I was not so sure. Unless, of course, it was just a ruse? Or perhaps this was only conversation, and my own involvement was making me paranoid.

"He has his faults," Blake continued. "But love of his own culture is not among them."

As we traveled south on King Street, a keening cry on the wind, like hungry gulls, resolved into the high, sobbing song of professional mourners. The smell of thousands of cut flowers was carried toward us on the humid breeze. "Iolani Palace," Blake said.

"I had guessed."

The palace was draped in swathes of black bunting that hung over the wide windows. Beneath the somber trappings, Iolani Palace was a grand structure: two tall stories with four corner turrets connected by wide verandas and lined with delicate columns.

"It's very European."

"The king toured Europe before he had Iolani built. Some foreigners expected a hovel, so he spared no expense. That was going to be the palace, over there," he said, pointing across the street to a smaller—though still lovely—building across the street. "The Ali'iolani Hale. But he put the government offices there instead."

"Ah." I licked my lips; my mouth was dry. "The treasury and so forth."

"Yes."

Beyond the palace, we passed rich town houses, including the black-draped windows of the home of the banker Mr. Bishop, Princess Pauahi's widower. "This is the wealthiest block on the island," Blake said. "Many of these families will be attending the ball, if you're interested in that sort of thing."

"What sort of thing?"

"The comings and goings of high society." I couldn't see his face, but in his voice—was it a hint of scorn?

"Oh. Not generally." Then I frowned. "Your father is . . . an important man?"

Blake paused before answering. "He has important friends."

Traveling north, away from the sea, we emerged into cooler air as we climbed out of the city. The shops gave way to the mansions and manicured gardens; the breeze shivered in the leaves of lush ferns by the side of the road. "This is Nu'uanu Valley," he said.

I sat up straighter. "My father once hoped to make a home here."

"Why did he decide against it?"

"My mother died before he could."

"Ah, is that why he took you to sea? If things had been but a little different, we would have been neighbors. That's our house, there, on the left."

I peered down a wide drive lined with chunks of coral that curved through an emerald-green lawn studded with flowering plants. Under a mantle of trailing vines rioting with flowers, I caught glimpses of a boxy white Victorian house with a deep veranda, in front of which was parked an empty calash and a delivery wagon hitched to a sleepy mule. It struck me then—I might be able to learn exactly where the map was kept. Pilikia leaned in toward the driveway, but Blake kept her on the road, pulling gently at the reins and, for a moment, bringing his arm close around my waist.

"Isn't your house included on this tour?"

"It's in a bit of a state, with the preparations for the party," he said apologetically. "You'll see it soon enough. Just a moment." He pulled the horse toward the opposite side of the road, where the trees drew in close. "There's a natural spring here," he said, dismounting and leading us into the trees.

It was only a dozen feet to the water, where Pilikia dropped her head and drank deep, but once inside the forest, the greenery wrapped around us like a soft embrace, and I could no longer see the road. "The island is peppered with them. There's one farther up in the valley that the chieftains used to bathe in. Back then, commoners weren't allowed to touch the water due to its mystic healing properties, on pain of decapitation."

My ears perked. "Is it true?"

"What part? The healing or the head chopping?" he teased. "They believed it. And that's what matters. I'm not going to risk it, anyway. Wouldn't that be the worst way to cure a head cold? I have tried this spring," he continued, nodding toward the water at our feet. "It won't heal so much as a paper cut, although the water's quite pure. Are you thirsty? Wait here."

He disappeared into the thicket in a direction I'd have assumed he'd picked at random but for the certainty with which he went. The sound of his footsteps, muffled by the damp humus that lay like a down blanket on the earth, quickly faded, and for a few minutes, Pilikia and I were alone in the forest. It was an odd feeling, the rich green life pressing close around me, hiding everything from view—so unlike the open sea. The burbling of the stream, the call of hidden birds, and the susurration of the wind in the tree-tops were no louder in my ears than the sound of my own breath.

Then, as suddenly as Blake had gone, he returned, holding handfuls of mottled yellow fruits, each the size of my fist. He took a small knife from the saddlebag and sliced one in half to reveal pink pulp studded with tiny yellow seeds.

"Oh, guavas!" I said. "I've only ever seen them green."

"Different species, I think." He crouched near the water and rinsed the pulp from the rind, which he then filled with clear water and handed to me as though it were a teacup. The water was cool and sweet.

After I drank my fill, he handed me another few guavas and I ate them whole, the rind giving way easily to the tart and tender flesh. Juice dripped down my chin, and he flicked out his handkerchief. "Mmm," I said, by way of thanks.

Blake scratched the horse's neck and fed her a guava. "They grow everywhere up here, along with several stands of excellent rose apples. Bananas and mangoes as well."

"Who planted them?"

"The birds. The breeze. The garden Hawaii resembles most is Eden."

"Ah." I handed back his handkerchief. "My father feels the same way."

He cocked his head. "But how do you feel?"

I hesitated. "I'm not sure yet."

"Oh? I must work harder to convince you. Here." He handed me the reins and swung himself up behind me. "We've got to hurry a bit, but I'll show you my favorite spot on the island."

"I'm not pressed for time."

"Ah, but I can't bring you there near to dusk!"

"Treacherous footing?"

"No, the Hu'akai Po."

I frowned. "That sounds like it means trouble, too."

"Of a very certain sort. Haven't you heard of the Night Marchers? The Hu'akai Po are the spirits of the ancient warriors of Hawaii. All the locals know the story." He leaned forward, his voice low in my ear. "Legend says they march all through this valley. When the warriors are walking, the first thing you hear is the sound of drums, far away, and someone blowing a conch shell. In the distance, you'll see their torches glowing in the dark. By the time you hear the sound of marching feet, you must throw yourself on the ground, facedown, to show respect, but also to shield your eyes, because if you look at them directly, they'll take you and you'll have to walk among them till the end of time."

His breath tingled on the back of my neck. I shivered, and he laughed, low in his throat. "Don't worry. I'll keep you safe."

We rode farther up into the rain forest of Nu'uanu, leaving the houses behind, and stepping onto a thin dirt track that wound through the tall rose-apple trees, studded here and there with enormous staghorn ferns, like fantastical brooches on the slender shoulders of society ladies. In the places where the path was steeper, he leaned forward to help Pilikia keep her footing. His chest was quite warm against my back.

"Have you ever seen them?" I said. "The Night Marchers?"

"I've never found myself facedown on the road surrounded by an army of ghosts, but . . . I have sometimes seen torchlight on the mountainside. Who can say?"

"Fascinating."

"Are you having fun with me?"

"Not at all! Myths reveal the history of a place. I mean, who are these warriors? What do they protect? Why do they wander? I know the Hawaiian chieftains never suffered commoners to look them in the eye—I read that once, but . . ." I stopped myself; I was gushing. "Well. I've never had a tour guide."

"I would gladly teach you all I know about the islands. I'd need some time, of course."

"A few weeks?"

"A few years!"

I laughed. "Maybe I should just look over your sketchbook."

"Oh, Miss Song. It's so much more than what you could read in a book."

A red bird flitted across our path, and the trees opened up into a clearing where flowers winked from the edges of the undergrowth. The sun warmed the grass beneath Pilikia's hooves, but the air was quite cool and as soft as a kiss. In the distance, rushing water whispered about where it had been.

"Is this it?" I asked.

"Oh, no, we're not there yet. This is . . . well. You can see the places where the grass is growing a bit thinner? That's because the earth was packed down under the *hale pili*—the grass houses. There was a village here when I was a small boy. The signs are faint, though."

"Where did they go?"

"They died."

I gasped. "How?"

"Foreign disease. The least dramatic type of slaughter."

The path continued on the other side of the sunny clearing, but it had grown narrower, and the trees lower; green and yellow guavas hung from lichen-gray branches that wove themselves together at a height just above our heads. Blake stopped Pilikia and swung down from her saddle. He offered me his hand.

"We have to continue on foot, but it's not much farther." I took his hand and slid from the saddle; my shoes sank into the loamy earth. Blake removed his own shoes and socks. He grinned when he saw me watching.

"How do you think I keep them clean?" He threw his jacket over the pommel of the saddle. "Come."

I followed him along a path no wider than my feet, lined with feathery ferns and drooping pink ginger. He pushed ahead of me, through the branches, bending them out of my way.

"What is this place?" I stepped under his arm as he held open a fall of vines like a curtain. The roar of water grew louder, and the fresh smell of crushed greenery filled my lungs.

"I told you before. It's a sacred place. A secret place, where the water comes out of the caves in a fall so powerful it turns to mist and drifts in clouds down into a healing pool. Please," he added with a grin. "Try not to lure me in and drown me."

I smiled back at him. "Don't you know how to swim?"

"Miss Song. Do you think I could have lived my life on an island and not learned how to swim?"

"Why is that a given? Do you want to escape?"

He laughed and reached for me, helping me across a rocky patch of the trail where orchids bloomed at my feet and my father's words resurfaced: "heaven in a wild flower." The path smoothed, but I didn't let go of Blake's hand. "My mother talks of sending me to England to complete my education," he said. "But no, I don't want to leave."

"Why not?" I asked, and then I stopped dead in my tracks. We had emerged from the exuberant undergrowth into a large clearing where, as Blake had said, a silver spray of water burst from the cliff face fifty feet above our heads, enveloping the mossy black rocks in clouds of mist as it fell to shatter the mirror of the black pool at our feet.

"Why not?" He turned to me, his face shining. "This is paradise, Miss Song," he said, gesturing at the roaring falls. "This is home."

CHAPTER

SEVENTEEN

Blake dropped me off at the ship near dinnertime. We hadn't had time to explore the caves above the falls, but Blake gave his word he'd show me some day. Neither of us set a date, though; we knew the promise was empty. Despite the guavas, I heard his stomach growling on the ride back, and I hoped it was loud enough to mask the sound of my own. This close to the ship, I smelled Rotgut cooking fish stew, and I hesitated on the dock. I might have invited Blake up for a bowl, if he were of another era and I'd had another upbringing.

Bee was there on the deck, watching us impassively. Blake raised his hand to hail her, and she nodded without saying a word. His eyes sparkled as he leaned in to whisper. "*She* is certainly a pirate."

"Not at all. She was a cattle herder."

"What? Like a *paniolo*? A cowboy?"

"Cowgirl."

"Like Annie Oakley!"

"She's better with a revolver than a rifle."

"Who cut her throat? Was it cattle rustlers?"

"A man jealous of her . . . her marriage, actually."

"How awful." Blake gazed at Bee. "It's hard to comprehend all the evil committed in the name of love."

"Or greed," I said, remembering Kashmir and Slate and the business I'd mostly forgotten all afternoon. I took a step back, toward the ship, suddenly anxious not to have Kashmir come up on deck and see us together. "Good night, Mr. Hart."

"Until the full moon, Miss Song." He tipped his hat to me, as though ready to leave, but he did not go. "I would like to ask," he said after a moment. "I would be honored . . . if you would attend as my personal guest."

"Oh? Oh! Oh, ah—I was attending with, uh . . . with my tutor, actually," I finished lamely. Puzzlement flickered across Blake's face; it was a terribly unbelievable story, for the time. "He is also my dancing instructor," I extemporized.

"Do you dance much on the ship, then?"

"Ah. Well. You must have heard that dancing is a cure for seasickness!"

"Odd," he said. "A sailor who gets seasick?"

I laughed a little. What else could I do?

"Well," he continued, dropping the point. "Perhaps he would prefer to have the evening off? There are many events in Honolulu that night."

"I . . . I know he is eager to attend the ball."

"Ah. Then I will be pleased to see the both of you there," he said, but he seemed less pleased than he had a moment before. He tipped his hat again. "Good night then, Miss Song." He turned Pilikia toward home. Her ears swiveled forward, and she broke into a trot with little urging.

I climbed up the gangplank; here, on the deck of the ship, I was once more on firm footing. I met Bee's eyes. "He doesn't have any cattle either," I told her, and she laughed.

Kashmir and Slate had not yet returned, so I needn't have worried about being seen, though I could have been worrying about where they were. But I was too hungry to worry. I ate so fast I barely tasted my dinner, outpacing even Rotgut, although that may have been because he was telling me about the rock lobsters he'd caught on the reef, while I was focused more single-mindedly on consuming them. It was only shortly after I finished my bowl that I heard Kash and Slate tramping across the deck above my head.

After a moment of consideration, I made up two conciliatory bowls of stew and carried them topside. I found them together, their heads close. The captain's face was drawn, and though they spoke in low tones, his gestures were emphatic, and he broke off abruptly when he saw me approach. Kashmir accepted the bowl gratefully, but Slate just shook his head.

It had been years since I'd last bothered trying to insist. I dug into the stew myself, more slowly this time. It was very good: huge chunks of white lobster in a broth rich with butter. Rotgut loved to eat well, and it showed in his cooking.

"So," I asked. "How did it go? On a scale of one to treason?"

Kashmir barked a laugh, but Slate waved a dismissive hand. I pursed my lips. "I was worried about you," I said to my father. He didn't respond. "Worried you'd get shot."

He folded his arms and glared off toward the blackness of the open sea. "We weren't shot."

"Yes, indeed, I see that now."

"Thank you for your concern," he said, stalking off to his room.

"You know we'd be stuck here if you died," I called after him.

He paused with his hand on the doorknob. "You wouldn't be stuck," he said, seeming to speak to the teak of the door. "You would find a way, Nixie. If you really wanted to escape."

He shut the door behind him, and Blake's words came back to me. "Why would I? This is home." I shook them out of my head and slid down to sit against the bulwark, setting my half-empty bowl on my knees, suddenly uncomfortably full. "Ugh."

"Today put him in a foul mood," Kashmir said.

"*I* put him in a foul mood," I corrected, leaving myself wide open, but Kash didn't even seem to notice.

"Then today made it worse." He tipped his own bowl and scraped the bottom with his spoon. Then he sat beside me and took my bowl from my hands.

"What happened?"

He made a face. "Do you really want to know?"

"Yeah. Shoot."

"Ha-ha. Well. We've encountered a few obstacles, the biggest one the weight of the gold. There's no way to carry it away without help. Or at least a couple of draft horses. There's also the Royal Hawaiian Guard to consider. It's only fifty local boys in nice uniforms, but all it takes is one lucky shot. Slate was talking about hiring mercenaries, but—"

"Ugh, not really?"

Kashmir shrugged. "He didn't seem happy about it."

"Where would he find them? The map ends a hundred miles out to sea. How would we get back here? And can you imagine having mercenaries aboard? Or, God, unleashing them here?"

"I don't know, *amira*. It's a last resort. He doesn't want any bloodshed."

"Well, then, he shouldn't be considering piracy."

"Do you have any better ideas?"

I scoffed. "If I did, I wouldn't share them with the captain."

"*Pourquoi pas?*" he said. "It will never actually happen. You and I will get the map first. But in the meantime, you could get back in his good graces if you would just promise to try to help him."

I made a face. "That's dishonest."

"Heaven forefend you lie so you can steal. He's thinking of giving you the evening watch on the night of the ball." My jaw dropped, and Kashmir shrugged. "I told you. He's in a foul mood."

"But I have to be there!"

"I'm sure I can manage without you, *amira*."

"No, I mean . . . I'm expected." It felt like a confession. "Mr. Hart asked me to come."

"He asked all of us to come."

"No, I mean, he asked again later. After the hike."

Kashmir's spoon stopped in midair. "After the what?"

"I was trying to reconnoiter, like you! Only I didn't have much success."

"You were trying . . ." His brow furrowed like he was trying to picture it. "*Amira* . . . what exactly did you say to him? Tell me you didn't tip our hand!"

"I don't think so. We did talk about maps, but it was a part of a previous conversation—"

"You mentioned the map? The map we want to steal? The map his father is using to barter for treason?"

"It wasn't like that! And he might not be on their side, at any rate. When we were at the waterfall, he was going on about paradise. . . ." I trailed off. Kashmir was shaking his head as though in awe. My cheeks went hot.

"Next time, *amira*," he said at last, "leave the reconnoitering to me."

"Understood." I dropped my chin, letting my hair fall over my face.

We were quiet for a while as he scraped the bottom of his bowl with the spoon. "You'd met the boy before."

"In Chinatown, yes."

"By luck or by design, do you think?"

"Oh, luck. Definitely."

He arched one eyebrow. "His or yours?"

I cocked my head at him. "Kashmir. Are you jealous?" I teased. He didn't laugh, though; his expression didn't change at all. An odd fluttering flew into my throat, and I swallowed it down. "What? Do you think he's in on the plot?"

"Oh, no, nothing so grand! But there's more than one reason to spy on a pretty girl." Kashmir stood up, taking the bowls, then he flashed me his teeth. "I told you you looked like a hussy."

"Takes one to know one," I called as he went below, but my heart wasn't in it. And that night when I changed clothes, I found myself staring into the mirror and wondering what Blake saw when he looked at me.

CHAPTER
EIGHTEEN

The next few days were busy.

The captain had accepted my offer of help with a huge grin and a bear hug, but it left a sour taste in my mouth—and not only because it went against what I had told him before. Ever since the hike, Mr. D's request had seemed particularly odious. But Slate and Kashmir were away from the ship for long hours of the day and night, and the captain didn't have time to ask me whether or not I'd made any progress on the challenges inherent in the theft.

I ended up having to pitch in on his watches, which we'd started keeping strictly since Mr. D's visit, but instead of studying the maps, I spent my time reading the paper. The majority of the articles were depressing items about Princess Pauahi evincing the Victorian obsession with death: her funeral was to be held on the second of

November, her husband was sick with grief. But alongside those morbid tidbits, other stories stood out.

The king had been busy of late. Aside from the funeral of his cousin, he'd been planning a jubilee to commemorate Hawaii's Independence Day, the anniversary of the day the Kingdom of Hawaii was recognized as a sovereign nation by the crowned heads of Europe. The celebration would begin on November 28 and continue through the weekend, and would feature performances of the scandalous hula and concerts by the Royal Hawaiian Band. There would also be a parade and fireworks "suitable for a nation twenty times the size of Hawaii," the paper noted, in what seemed to me like a sniffy tone.

Kalakaua was also dealing with a bill proposing to return to the practice of issuing opium licenses so proprietors might sell the drug. It was offered as a way to raise revenue, but the king declined in fear of the effect it might have on his beleaguered people, some of whom already struggled with alcohol. Auntie Joss might prefer the bill ratified, and Kalakaua might have to do it, were he to find the treasury in deficit.

But when I read two more mentions in the paper—one, the census reporting that, although the native population was in decline, the overall population of the islands was growing, and the other, an anonymous letter to the editor calling for "a closer alliance" with America—I saw the political land-scape come into view. Kalakaua's kingdom was being over-whelmed by foreign interests.

I gathered this intelligence, but I had no one to tell. Kashmir disappeared with Slate every morning to go into town and returned only late at night, spending the days before the ball preparing to give Mr. D his answer.

But I too had preparations to make, so on Thursday afternoon, I managed to finish my chores early and wheedle Bee into giving me a few hours of freedom so I could stop by to visit the Mercier sisters. They were pleased to see me, although perhaps less pleased than they might have been to see both me and Kashmir. Emily asked after him as she fussed with the bustle on the dress.

"He's in town. Doing . . . errands." I watched our reflec-tion in the long oval mirror; I did not look like myself.

"He's very dashing," Emily said. "And quite young. Is he really your tutor?" Nan's eyes cut to her sister; she made a small noise of protest at the question, but her mouth was full of pins.

"Yes," I said airily. "Did you know his people invented the zero?"

The jacket needed to be taken in at the waist, but the dress fit perfectly. I paid the remainder of the balance and asked that they have everything delivered to the ship when they were finished. In the rich silks and ribbons, would I pass for a society girl among Blake's father's important friends?

On the way back to the ship, I crossed Queen Street. Remembering the conversation I'd had with Blake, I took a detour south to Richards. I walked up and down the block twice before I saw it—there, on the second-floor windows of a white stucco building, the gold lettering on the glass: A. SUTFIN & CO, SINCE 1877.

The door was unlocked, so I showed myself in, up the narrow stairs, to a lived-in studio with a checked oak floor, well lit by southern windows and gas jets. The walls of this front room, obviously a converted parlor, were lined with wide, deep shelves, each holding a single sheet of paper: maps in their various stages of completion. There was a drafting desk by the windows where a man, perhaps thirty years old, although already starting to bald, sat drawing. I knocked on the half-open door, and he started at the sound, his gold-wire spectacles slipping down his nose. He thumbed them up in a peculiar gesture.

"Oh, hello, how do you do? Ah." He peered at me

closely. I was probably not one of his typical visitors. "How may I help you, miss?"

"Mr. Sutfin? You make maps?"

"Oh, yes," he said, gesturing toward the shelves on the wall, as if to prove it. "Yes, I do."

"I'm wondering about one in particular. A map of the island. You must have finished it very recently . . ." I frowned—what day had we arrived? "On October 24? But you dated it 1868."

"Oh, yes, those maps! What about them?"

"There was more than one?"

"Yes, I did three. The commission was for half a dozen maps, but the client canceled the last three a few days ago. And thank goodness," he added. "He wanted each one drawn by hand. I told him it would be faster to have an engraving made of the first, but he wouldn't hear of it. The whole affair was very time-consuming. If you are here to commission a map, I must tell you, it will be at least eight months before I can get to it."

"Your client. What was his name?"

"I— Miss, may I ask you why the questions?"

"We . . . my father purchased one of them, and I wondered why they were backdated."

"It was part of the commission. I'm sorry I can't say more. I'm not trying to be secretive, but I don't know why it was important, only that it was required. But I assure you, the map is accurate in all other respects!"

"Of course," I said, assuaging his concern for his reputation. "One more question—your other map of 1868. The one of downtown, that you signed as Blake Hart?"

"I'm sorry?"

"The one of the . . . ah . . . the bars?"

"Miss . . . I don't . . . May I—"

"Forgive my intrusion," I said quickly, seeing the truth on his face. It may have been too much to hope for, that the other map was as verifiably fake as the one that had brought us here. That would have been too easy. "Thank you for your time." I hurried down the stairs before he could start to ask *me* any questions.

Three copies. What had happened to the other two? Lost over time, I suppose. Or perhaps they would come up someday, at another auction. The one we'd bought was pristine; whoever had kept it must have had instructions to preserve it perfectly. At least I knew, now, if any of the other Sutfin maps ever turned up, we could write them off.

I paused on the street corner, and my hand went to

the pearl at my throat. Surely Mr. D had been the person to commission the maps, which meant he knew more about Navigation than I had imagined. In fact, he'd reached across more than a century to find us. The gall. He must have had Joss's help from the start. Was he waiting by the docks the day after Sutfin turned over each map? I yanked the pendant back and forth on its chain. I only had an hour left before Bee expected me back, so I hurried toward Chinatown.

Joss greeted me by name as I entered her shop. I don't know how she identified me without my having said a word, but I wasn't in the mood to ask. I didn't want to give her the satisfaction of seeming impressed.

I went all oars in the water, ramming speed. "Sutfin. Your idea or Mr. D's?"

"You needn't thank me," she said smoothly.

"I wasn't going to."

"Your father would." She leaned down to rummage under her counter. "How else would he be able to get the map he really wants?"

I frowned. "If that was your goal, you could have made sure it was as well preserved as the others."

"You arrived the day Mr. Sutfin finished his third map," she replied. "The first two were clearly lost. Good thing we could make more than one. How could we guarantee the safety of the other map, so rare and so valuable, across so much time?"

I ground my teeth, but she had a point.

She straightened up, and in her turmeric-stained hands was a pile of papers: a selection of maps. "But you might thank me for these," she said as she spread them on the rough wooden countertop. "If we can come to an arrangement for them."

My desire overcame my pride embarrassingly quickly, and I bent my head to sort through the maps. My irritation returned. Her collection contained some worthless pages cut from an atlas (the Cape of Good Hope, the Canary Islands, Eastern Europe), a torn Japanese whale migration chart from the 1750s, and a hymnal with all the pages ripped out but one. Only mildly curious as to which hymn had been left behind, I opened the cover and saw that the single page inside was loose, and that it was no hymn.

"What's this?" I said, barely above a whisper. The page, folded in quarters, was so delicate I was afraid a strong breath would cause it to disintegrate. The hymnal covers had been used to protect it.

"Very old, that map. Very valuable. It's from the Qin

dynasty. Shows the lost tomb of the first emperor. He was buried with all the riches of his empire, and his tomb is guarded by warriors of clay brought to life to watch over an eternity under the earth."

She spoke to me as though I were a gawking country girl—I wouldn't have been surprised if she'd thrown in a mummy's curse—but I'd heard of the tomb of Emperor Qin and his terra-cotta warriors. Sima Qian, the first Chinese historian, had written about the tomb, and a few of the warriors in one of the antechambers had been rediscovered in the 1970s by Chinese farmers, although the main portion of the fantastical tomb had not yet been opened.

Still.

"You're saying this map is nearly two thousand years old?" Skepticism practically dripped from each word; after all, she couldn't see my expression.

"That was when it was drawn," she said carefully. "But it does not seem to have aged two thousand years. Odd, isn't it?"

"Very. When did you acquire it?"

"Back when I could see. It came from a dying woman. She had no more need of it."

I chewed on my lip for another minute. It was highly

unlikely this map was authentic, but there was something compelling about it. "How much?"

She clasped her hands together eagerly. "Would you like some tea?"

I declined the tea, but I did end up with the map, and at one third her starting price, but four times my own. She was an excellent bargainer, but she seemed proud of my effort. In fact, if the map was genuine, she had let me off lightly.

As for the other map she'd brokered, I might as well ask, though I might not trust her answers. "The map my father wants," I said as I counted out the coins. "The one of the Happy House."

"Hapai Hale," she corrected. "What of it?"

"Was it actually inked in 1868?"

She lifted one shoulder. "Too bad Mr. Hart was drowned, or you could ask him yourself."

I cocked my head. "What do you mean, 'was drowned'?"

"In the bay," she said.

"What I mean is—"

"Very tragic," she said with a firm shake of her head. "A great loss. Blake Hart spent many hours entertaining us. He was a favorite of the ladies. He did indeed draw the map. If your mother was here, she could tell you. Of course, if she were still here, you wouldn't need his map."

I made a face, although she couldn't see it, and left the shop with the map she'd sold me and the bitter taste in my mouth she'd thrown in free.

As I hurried back to the ship, I thought of a question I hadn't asked. Just past the docks, the wharf rats were lounging on the Esplanade, and I stopped in front of one of the half-grown boys. "Want a nickel?"

He stood up straight and held out his hand. It was plump, and his fingernails were exceptionally clean. Half a world away in London, a street urchin his age would be black with soot or muck from head to toe from scraping a living picking rags. These boys might dive for pennies tossed into the Pacific, but the sea was full of fish and the mountains were full of fruit. I smiled at him. "What does *hapai* mean?"

His eyes got big, and the other boys tittered. He looked at them for help, and one of his compatriots stood, crossing his arms over his skinny chest. "It's delicate," he said, waggling his eyebrows, but I looked at him blankly. "You know," he continued, sauntering toward me. "Expecting? Swelling? *Poisoned?*" He held out his own hand.

I took a nickel from my bag and held it up so it caught the afternoon light. He opened his mouth, paused, then spoke the taboo word. "Pregnant!" He snatched the nickel and ran, ducking his head and laughing.

Victorians. The first boy was blushing so deeply I fished another nickel out of my bag for the poor thing, then beat it back up the dock, only a few minutes late to relieve Bee of the watch.

I sat in my hammock, facing the wharf. There wasn't much activity this late in the afternoon: a boatswain tarring the deck of the *Tropic Bird* three ships over, a couple of fishermen off-loading their catch, a lazy cat watching them from the shade of a piling. The sweet breeze strummed the rigging, and the waves rocked my hammock as gently as a cradle.

Hapai Hale. The very first hint of my existence was marked on the page. I was written into that map as a land-mark. Before I'd even known it, I'd been a part of this place, and it was increasingly hard to pretend that it wasn't a part of me. Something of it lived under my skin, indelible as a tattoo.

It was the home that might have been, and for the first time, I felt the loss of it—the world where my mother lived and my father stayed in Hawaii and I grew up within the boundaries formed by the golden line of sand encircling the island. But who would I have been in that version of reality? Me, or not me?

I felt close to my other self, and I dreaded meeting the conspirators against the crown. Treason felt like a personal betrayal, and I even avoided Kashmir when he returned at night after a day spent plotting. Although I was confined to the ship, I drank in the rhythm of life on the island as time's current drew the night of the ball closer.

On Saturday, the *Zealandia* came into port from San Francisco, bringing mail and news and goods and guests from the world beyond Oahu's shores. Her approach was announced by the semaphore at Telegraph Hill, and shortly thereafter by cannon fire and the ringing of the bells. Soon the dock was mobbed in a Boat Day celebration, the crowd at least triple the size of the one that had greeted our arrival. Local men and women swarmed aboard the ship, laughing, talking, some even serenading the small group of passengers who seemed dazed, like the unsuspecting dead awakening in Elysium.

The oily smell of the docks was erased by the honey-sweet scent of a thousand flowers strung on hundreds of leis, thrown over the visitors' heads and scattered like confetti on the waves. Locals greeted strangers like long-lost family, with smiles and kisses. Platters of fresh fruit were paraded by, tempting those long at sea; a covey of ladies, underdressed and over-rouged, did the same, calling out to the sailors from a corner of the pier. For a moment, I thought I saw Blake in the crowd, his head bent as he wrote something in a book, but then the man lifted his chin; he was twenty years older and thirty pounds heavier.

The mail was unloaded along with the sailors, and there was much drinking and gambling in town that night. Or perhaps it was brawling; it was so hard to tell the difference until you were much too close. Whatever it was, it petered out as morning dawned on Sunday, the day of Princess Pauahi's funeral. The contrast was sharp between the bright laughter of the carnival of Boat Day and the eerie, incessant wailing of mourning voices, drifting on the breeze like banshees through the streets.

A few of yesterday's leis came drifting back in on the afternoon tide, limp with salt, beside mangrove seeds and coconuts that had been floating who knows how long in search of a favorable shore on which to set down roots. The few locals in the streets were somber, burdened by a shared loss, respect for which quieted even us sailors in port. I contemplated it all from my hammock, apart from it, and not a part of it, as the sun rose and then fell, replaced by the moon waxing full.

CHAPTER
NINETEEN

The next day, true to his word, Mr. D sent a carriage to meet us—a barouche, to be specific, all polished black lacquer and rich scarlet velvet, topped with a rigid canopy, the sides left open to the breeze. Nevertheless, the seats gave off a musty smell; in the constant humidity of the Hawaiian Islands, velvet was never the rational choice. Mr. D, however, was nowhere to be seen; the driver told us he meant to meet us at the party.

The Merciers had sent their delivery on Saturday, and I'd chosen to wear the striped silk dress with the "modified bustle," which took the form of a giant pink bow below the small of my back. I had regarded it with great suspicion in the mirror, especially when I noticed Kashmir seemed to find it humorous.

"I feel gift wrapped," I had said to him.

"As long as we still have the receipt," he'd replied.

He nudged me now—as he had twice already—reminding me to sit forward in the carriage. I perched on the edge of my seat so as not to crush the taffeta. Kash had dressed impeccably, with a closely tailored sack coat, buttoned only at the top, the bottom open to display his vest and the gold chain of a pocket watch. He'd slicked down his thick black curls, and sitting this close to him, I caught a hint of some sort of cologne, like honey and leather and ambergris.

Slate had put on a frock coat and a stylish ribbon necktie, but his manic energy was barely hidden beneath his proper exterior; it welled up like the spring in the woods. He fidgeted uneasily as we crept through town, one knee bouncing madly as he peered out the window.

It had been nearly a week since I'd spend this much time with either of them, but the silence was thicker than the funk of the moldering velvet; I couldn't speak plainly to Kashmir in front of Slate, not about the map. Kash patted my leg then, gently but firmly; I'd been jigging it up and down in rhythm with my father.

I looked into Kashmir's eyes and found reassurance there. I gave him a grateful smile and let myself relax, then sat up quickly as I remembered about the bow.

The carriage had arrived at the *Temptation* about an hour after sundown, and it took us another half hour to get to the edge of town. Nu'uanu Street was even more crowded than usual, and the revelry did not end there. Once we moved beyond the laughter and shouting near the docks, the sound of brass music brightened the dusk—one of the concerts Blake had mentioned. Bee was likely there; Rotgut was on dog watch tonight, and Ayen had demanded a night out.

We rolled past late-night picnickers, groups heading toward the beach in their bathing costumes, young men and women on horseback enjoying a night ride, and a plein-air performance of what appeared to be a comedy (at least, the audience was laughing). The entire city had come alive to make merry under the silvery light of the full moon.

Nu'uanu Valley was no exception. Families sat on their lanais, playing music or cards, and farther back, in the darkness between the trees, torchlight writhed. The sound of a man singing and drumming, a distinctive rhythm—one, two, one-and-two—drifted out of the dark, making me shiver as I remembered the story of the Hu'akai Po.

The house I had glimpsed the other day had been transformed from a white box into a shining luminaria, and the coral drive was lined with lanterns at the edge of the lawn. All of the doors and the shutters were thrown open to the warm night air, allowing the guests to move in and out as freely as the breeze. The carriage pulled up to the door, where we were welcomed by a Hawaiian butler sporting stockings to display his well-turned calves.

He showed us into the foyer and announced our arrival to a delicate, exuberant blond woman in a rich gathered gown of sky-blue silk. Blake stood just behind her to her right, his hair perfectly parted, his scrubbed cheeks glowing, his hand over his silk waistcoat: the very picture of a fine young American gentleman, except for the garland of deep crimson blossoms hanging from his wrist.

Mrs. Kitty Hart, wide-eyed and giddy, was *so very pleased* to make our acquaintance, and I immediately saw the resemblance to her son, although Blake's eyes were much more sincere. "A ship's captain, how romantic!" she said to Slate, making a deep society courtesy, her ruffled skirts swishing above her tiny satin shoes. "It must be such an adventure, sailing the seven seas. How serendipitous the tides that brought you to my little party!"

"Indeed." My father made a perfunctory bow and waved his lips over her hand. "Very lucky."

"You don't know the half of it, sir! It was quite fortunate

the mourning ended yesterday! Why, can you imagine? If the princess had died but a day later, we would have missed the full moon and had to push our party off a whole month. It was bad enough with all that wailing. One could barely think for the clamor! Ah, and Miss Song." I waited for it—the flick of the eyes, to my face, to my father's, and back—and she did not disappoint, although she covered well. "So happy to make your acquaintance. My son speaks often of you."

Blake made a little bow, very formal. He lifted up the lei in both hands. "May I?"

"Ah . . . of course." I tilted my head, a bit self-conscious. The petals were cool as silk on my neck; I lifted them to my nose and breathed deep. "They're beautiful."

"The *ohia* blossoms are sacred to Pele," he said.

"The volcano goddess?

"The very same," he said. "Creator. Destroyer."

"I see," I said cautiously. "My thanks."

Mrs. Hart looked on. "One of the few charming customs the savages have shared with us," she said brightly. "And you, sir, welcome," she continued, moving to Kashmir, her eyes roving from his face, down his lean build all the way to his fine shoes. Her pink lips curved prettily. "Are you really an Arab?" The way she said it, the word rhymed with Ahab.

"My son tells me you teach mathematics and dance. What an unexpected combination."

Kashmir's careful expression barely faltered. "It is certainly unlikely!" he said, kissing her hand. Her cheeks glowed a delicate pink, as if on cue.

"Perhaps you can teach me a few steps later?" Mrs. Hart said. "Here on the islands, we've been dancing the same rounds for years. It's always exciting to have a fresh turn around the floor."

We were ushered into the grand central hall, which was filled with enough floral arrangements for a wedding . . . or a funeral. With one casual hand, Kashmir lifted the garland of flowers around my own neck, leaning in as if to smell them. "The young Mr. Hart suspects something," he whispered, then let the lei drop. "But I can't tell what." We continued through the hall, quiet for a moment. "Dancing and math?"

"It's a long story." I pretended to admire the decor, but I stopped long enough to give him a side eye. "Was she flirting with you?"

He winked at me. "The only thing that's gone well so far. But no matter. The night is young."

As we moved through the grand hall, I mapped the house in my head. From the outside, the house was a rectangle with the foyer we'd just entered facing east, to the sunrise. The grand hall behind the foyer was lined with three big mahogany doors to the south, one door to the north, and an open pair of wide double doors on the west wall, through which music and laughter rolled like a tide.

Which door hid our map—door number one? Door number three? But there was no telling from the outside, and I couldn't linger in the hall.

We stepped outside through the open double doors, and I gaped at the display. We stood under a golden cloud of Chinese lanterns on a stone patio that lay like a stage before a lush lawn silvered by the moon. At one side of the patio, an impossibly long table groaned with dishes that looked decidedly Continental: white-flour biscuits, puffed pastries with a savory onion filling, tiny triangle sandwiches with pale slices of cucumber, fillets of fish in a lemon sauce, roasted chicken with blackened skin, flaky crab cakes, puddings studded with raisins. The only things vaguely local were the halved coconuts, floating like skiffs in a tureen of ice and filled with chunks of fragrant tropical fruit, and the platter of pea-green cuts of cane.

At the other side of the lawn, a string quartet played on a raised platform draped with garlands. Guests danced on the grass: proud men in fine black suits with waxed mustaches, graceful ladies in dresses like bakery confections. What would Bee think of these women and their dancing?

"Why are you smiling, *amira*?"

"Because it's beautiful. Why are you smiling?"

"Because I want to dance." He held out his hand and whirled me into a waltz.

The steps were familiar; I'd done my best to learn the basic patterns of the most popular social dances of the last few centuries, and the waltz had enjoyed a great deal of popularity over the years. But I was not a natural dancer, not like Kashmir. He guided me, gliding across the crowded lawn, sweeping me in wide, graceful circles as though we were the only two dancing, and he did it all while seeming to see nothing else but my eyes.

"You're making me look better than I am," I murmured to him.

"It's not hard," he whispered. I laughed as he spun me out, brought me back.

We'd left Slate standing on the edge of the crowd. He was still there, his arms crossed, scanning for familiar faces. I sighed. "Do you see Mr. D?"

"Not yet. But Slate can handle that on his own. I'm more interested in the map."

I smiled tightly at him. "I didn't see it in the hall—"

"You wouldn't hang a map like a painting, *amira*. Especially not a map of unsavory locations, which you'd recently learned was very valuable. It would be tucked away somewhere."

"In a safe?"

"No. People who have safes rarely open them." He pursed his lips in thought as he moved us easily, absently, through the crowd. "Mr. D invited the captain to meet the members of the league, and to see the map. They will meet in a drawing room, or maybe a study. The map is likely kept there."

"And if we go in now, before Mr. D arrives . . . what?"

Kashmir was shaking his head. "If you'd been a thief, you would have been hanged a long time ago. If you hadn't starved first. If we go in *now*, and *then* Mr. D arrives—" He shrugged. "Best to wait till after."

"Then, after their meeting, we sneak in?"

"*We* do not sneak. I sneak, and you distract. The young Mr. Hart may be watching you closely," Kashmir said archly. "For more than one reason."

"This is important, Kashmir!"

He pulled me close, crushing the flowers of my lei

between us. "Exactly why you should trust me." I felt the curve of his lips as he breathed into my ear. "Please, *amira*."

"I do," I breathed back. "But I'm nervous. I've never—"

"Nonsense," he said, pulling back, his voice a touch louder. "The dress is lovely on you."

"What?" Then I noticed that Kashmir wasn't looking at me anymore, but over my shoulder.

"May I?"

Kashmir stepped back and bowed. "Aye, Captain."

I slipped my fingers into my father's palm. Slate danced almost as awkwardly as I did, but he closed his hand around mine tightly. "I'm glad to see you having fun. Kashmir's right, the dress is lovely."

"He practically designed it."

"The kid has good taste."

"You clean up nice too."

He guided me gently around another couple who waltzed by in a whirl of blue silk and blond curls; Mrs. Hart was on the floor. Slate's eyes were troubled. He took a deep breath, then let it out. "I'm sorry. About what I said about Kashmir."

I stiffened in his arms. "Of course you are. Now that you need him."

"It's not that." His expression was wistful. "I saw you dancing. You two are close."

"We're friends."

"Oh? Good friends, then. It reminds me of . . ." He trailed off.

"Of who?" I asked, though I knew the answer. He met my eyes, then dropped his own to his feet.

"Of better times," he said finally. "But things will get better again. Nixie—I'm sorry we fought. I hate fighting with you."

"Try agreeing with me instead."

That made him smile. "You have to know I'd never do anything to hurt you."

"Then don't do this," I said, surprising myself. I took a breath, and the scent of the blossoms around my neck was sweet on my tongue. "Leave the map. Tell them no."

He stopped moving at my words, and we stood still on the grass, the eye of a storm where wind and rain were laughter and music. "I thought you'd understand, now, why I can't do that."

"Why?" Then I realized. "Because of Kashmir? Dad, that's . . . insulting."

"Love is insulting?"

"It's not love!" I said, too loud; people beside us tittered, and my cheeks burned. I lowered my voice to a fierce whisper. "I'm not like you. I wouldn't sacrifice everything for some romance."

"I'm not sacrificing anything—"

"Oh, really? Well, even if you don't give a damn about *me*, this is a kingdom. An entire country. You called it paradise, and yet you'd—"

"Nixie!" He put his finger on my lips, and I did stop then, though it was a struggle. After a long moment, he took my hand, gathering it in both of his. The tattoos, black in the moonlight, peeked out from the edge of his cuffs: my name on one wrist, my mother's on the other.

"You have to understand," he said faintly. "Every day the options narrow. Chance becomes certainty and fate makes choices for us, but I cannot imagine a reality where . . ." He trailed off and was quiet as he stared fixedly at a point past my head.

"Where what?"

"Where the kingdom of Hawaii does not fall," he finished, although I didn't believe that was the sentence he started. I followed his gaze; Mr. D was raising a glass at him from across the lawn, where he stood near the champagne table with two other men, one young and barrel-chested, with the feverish eyes of a zealot, the other smaller and as quivery as a squirrel.

"Come, Nix," Slate said softly. "Let's meet our new friends."

CHAPTER
TWENTY

"**A**h, Captain!" Mr. D said as we approached. "What a pleasure to see you here. And young Miss Song."

He bowed. I bent my knees, but barely; the captain didn't bother with any pleasantries. "Which one of you is Mr. Hart?"

Mr. D laughed. "Our host is in his study, tragically far from the refreshment. Before we go in, may I offer you a drink?" Again he raised his glass of pale gold champagne, and I noticed it was still full, while the squirrelly man beside him tipped back his own glass, tossing the bubbly down his gullet. I regarded the rows of fine crystal glasses and the iced bottles with French labels. The drink alone must have cost a mint.

"Thank you, no," I said, and Slate half raised his hand, dismissing the proffered glass.

"A rare sight, a sailor who won't drink!" Mr. D joked, but the youngest man was nodding.

"A rare sight, *anyone* who won't drink, at least in Honolulu." The man's intense eyes were lit by a fire within. "The problem worsens by the year, ever since the Merrie Monarch repealed the prohibition against serving alcohol to the natives. They're worse than sailors."

"It's a problem common among aboriginals," said the squirrelly man as he picked up a fresh glass.

"But not exclusive to them," the younger man replied with a glare.

"Some men cannot control their appetites," Mr. D said pointedly. "Wouldn't you agree, Captain?"

Slate's spine had gone ramrod straight, but his face was blank while he chose his response. "Local issues are . . . of no interest to me."

Mr. D nodded sagely. "That is likely for the best. Let us to business, then. Come." He pointed toward the house with his still-full glass.

"A moment," Slate said, scanning the crowd. "There is a third member of our party. Do you see him, Nixie?"

I didn't, at first. Then I caught sight of him, in a swirl of sky-blue silk; Kashmir was dancing with Mrs. Hart.

"The tutor?" Mr. D said. His eyes twinkled. "He seems otherwise occupied."

"Don't worry, he's in artful hands," the squirrelly man said. "Mrs. Hart is a *very* capable host."

Although the third man was silent, he looked like he'd bitten a lemon. I kept my own face still.

"There should be no need for dance instruction at our meeting," Mr. D said, and he led us inside as the song ended. I didn't glance over my shoulder to see whether Kashmir and Mrs. Hart had parted.

We followed Mr. D into the grand hall. He knocked at the door closest to the front of the house and farthest from the party, but opened it without waiting for an answer.

The study was lit with gas lamps that threw gold light across a blond maple floor laid with a thick green rug. It had that library smell, like the map room did, but the undercurrent of brine was replaced by woodsmoke that must have come from the fireplace—a fireplace! In Hawaii! Not for warmth, but for wealth. There was even a small fire burning in it.

A huge window at the south of the room had been shuttered, and a small side door that must have led to the next room—door number two from the grand hall, likely a library or a drawing room—was also shut. I filed away that side door, an extra entrance to tell Kashmir about later.

The walls were a deep hunter green above the wainscot, and there was a large desk with bird's-eye grain, on which sat a cut-crystal decanter, a smooth round stone the size of a fist . . . and a black leather artist's portfolio tied with a red ribbon. The captain's eyes were drawn to it like iron to a lodestone.

The man behind the desk stood to greet us. He was flushed, or sunburned, and he had a dun-colored mustache of the sort that continued right past the corners of his thin lips, across his red cheeks, and connected up to the hairline in front of the ears. Those lips stretched in a smile that was almost a grimace.

"Captain," said Mr. D. "Meet Mr. Hart."

Mr. Hart shook the captain's hand, then took my hand in his and bowed over it. I resisted the urge to scrub my palm on my gown; his own had been unpleasantly moist. There was a thin sheen of sweat on his high forehead as well. Studying him, I had the incongruous thought that Blake had been lucky to get his mother's looks.

Mr. Hart was peering at me, though, a quizzical expression in his watery eyes, the color of weak tea. "Would the miss not prefer to be dancing?"

Slate raised his eyes from the portfolio for the first time since he'd entered the room. "No. She is more an expert than I am, with maps. She stays."

I tried to ignore the stares the gentlemen gave me, but Mr. D shrugged. "In such complex matters, the more expertise, the better." He clasped his hands. "Now that we are all gathered, let me make the introductions."

"Not full names, please!" said the nervous little man.

"He has *my* full name," Mr. Hart objected.

The little man scoffed. "Well! It is your house, sir, it could hardly be avoided!"

"As it is my house, I bear most of the risk here," Mr. Hart said. "Should we not share it more equally?"

"The captain has agreed to confidentiality," Mr. D said. "There is little risk."

"Then why don't we share it?" Mr. Hart asked again.

"One cannot be too careful," Mr. D said, not a bit ashamed that he was speaking out of both sides of his mouth at once.

Beside me, Slate shifted, impatient, but I put my hand on his arm. Of course their names did not matter—Slate would not risk the map in an attempt to blackmail the men, but I hoped they did not know how completely they had him in thrall. After all, if they did, we would be in no position to bargain.

"Have I not commanded you? Be strong and of good courage," quoted the youngest man, his brown eyes shining, but he tempered faith with prudence: "I am . . . Mr. T."

"And I'm Mr. D," said the squirrelly one.

"I've been introduced as Mr. D," Mr. D said.

"Then . . . call me Mr. M."

"Call him Milly, we all do," said Mr. Hart.

"Sir!"

"Can we move on?" Slate interrupted.

"Yes, let's," said Milly. "I am a very busy man." Having drained his champagne, he unstoppered the cut-crystal decanter and filled his glass. The sharp smell of brandy tickled my nose.

"First things first," Mr. D said. "Mr. Hart. The map."

Mr. Hart drew out the red satin ribbon and flipped open the portfolio. Slate crowded close and pulled me alongside him. He held his breath as he studied the map. He held my wrist too. Would he dare try to Navigate here and now? Was it even possible? Could he call up the fog in a stuffy room? I twisted my arm a bit; he wouldn't let go. I clutched the edge of the desk with my other hand.

The map was a sketch, really, without much by way of topographical elevation or contour, but the coastline was fairly accurate and the roads of downtown were inked in, along with, clearly marked, what appeared to be every saloon, brothel, and opium den in town. I saw it then: Hapai Hale. Pregnant House. Quaint, indeed. That was where my mother was supposed to be.

The ink was dry and faded, and the paper smelled old. I released the wood of the desk and stretched out my hand; I didn't touch the page, but I was close enough to feel the heat of my palm trapped between my skin and the paper.

I drew my hand back. "The maker was your brother?"

Mr. Hart's eyes jerked toward me. "He was."

"And . . . he frequented these places? He knew them well?"

His thin mouth twisted. "Yes. Yes, he did. He had an artist's temperament and was familiar with much he would better have left alone."

Milly snickered, and Mr. Hart blinked rapidly. It may have been a trick of the firelight, but for the barest instant, his eyes seemed filled with pure rage.

But the captain chuckled. "Hart. Blake, yes. I remember the man." Was he remembering old days—old friends? "He died?"

"He drowned," Mr. Hart said. His eyes flickered over to

Mr. D, who did not exchange his glance.

"A tragic accident," Mr. D added simply.

The sweat shone on Mr. Hart's brow. My own eyes narrowed. On the surface, this map didn't seem like a fake, no matter how much I had hoped otherwise. But why was Mr. Hart so nervous? Was I being overcautious? After all, he was hosting traitors in his home. I scanned the map again. There was nothing I could hang a doubt on, at any rate, if I'd been inclined to lie.

I nodded, grudgingly; the captain relaxed, taking a deep breath through his teeth. He released my arm, and we both stood back.

"I should very much like to . . . to come to an arrangement for this map," the captain said.

There were sighs of relief, and tight smiles behind beards, but Mr. D was still gazing at Slate intently. "So we are agreed on the terms?"

But Slate hesitated, glancing at me, then back to Mr. D. "Actually, gentlemen, now we're together—all together, here—and before we get into a dangerous situation, I want to . . . to extend to you a counteroffer."

My eyes cut to the captain. A counteroffer? He hadn't mentioned that to me. But when his words sank in, Mr. Hart flipped the portfolio closed and put his hand to his waist; under his jacket, did I see the glint of a metal barrel? "I am already in a dangerous situation, sir!"

"Now, now," Mr. D murmured, but Mr. Hart ignored him.

"You are in my home, you know my name! I hope you can appreciate the delicate position I am in!"

The captain held up his hand. "I appreciate it, sure. And my offer is a lot safer. The map for a million dollars of my own money."

Mr. D's nostrils flared, and his voice was colder than the champagne. "I believe we already discussed this, sir."

"You and I did. But *we* didn't," Slate said, gesturing to the other men. Their faces went as still and pale as wax; they must have been mirrors of my own.

I saw the question in their eyes—how did a ship's captain attain such wealth? But I knew better. He hadn't had more than a few hundred in the bank.

"Think about it," Slate urged. "There would be no risk to any of you. You could spend the money however you want, as soon as you want, without worrying that anyone might put two and two together."

How on earth could he manage that sum without

robbing the treasury in the first place? I would bet double that amount he had no plan. That would be like him: promise something impossible and expect me to come up with his solution.

Still. It was a more honorable option, and it was heartening to know Slate had given it thought. Maybe he'd even been swayed by me. This time, I was the one holding my breath.

For a while there was silence. Even Mr. D had no pithy response, but then Mr. T shook his head vehemently.

"No. No, sir! Do you not see the issue at hand? This is not about the paltry sum of a million dollars," he said, his voice breaking in his scorn.

"Not so paltry, surely," Mr. Hart said. His face had broken out in a fresh glow, and he had dropped his hand from his holster. My heart beat faster at the look in his eyes; he was going to take Slate's offer.

"Do not be swayed by mere riches, sir," said Mr. T. "This is about the very future of the islands."

"Yes," Milly said. "And we stand to make much more if all goes to plan."

"The rest of you do," Mr. Hart said. "I am not so well positioned."

"You may always continue borrowing from us." Milly raised his bushy brows. "Under the new government, we should have enough to suit even your wife's prodigious appetite. At least, for money," he added snidely.

Mr. Hart looked as though he was being strangled by invisible hands, and I waited for him to burst, to shout, to push back, but Mr. D stepped in firmly. "Gentlemen, let us put this topic aside, please." He leaned in to Slate with a self-satisfied air. "I told you, sir, we seek stronger leadership. Money is not our aim."

"Not our only aim," Milly said. He made a move toward the brandy decanter, but Mr. Hart took it himself and set it down out of reach before taking a folded square of linen from his pocket and dabbing his forehead. Still, he said nothing more.

"We may all have different motives," Mr. D said. "But we have a common purpose. We are not brigands, Captain. We are visionaries. Your money will not be sufficient."

My father sighed. "Then," he said, and my heart sank, "I have no choice but to agree."

CHAPTER
TWENTY-ONE

Back out on the lawn, the night air made me shiver. I hadn't realized how hot the study had been.

The meeting had dispersed shortly after Slate had acquiesced. Mr. T had been eager to discuss the plan then and there, but Mr. Hart refused to have the discussion in his own home, and besides, Milly was entirely drunk. Mr. D promised we'd meet again midweek to talk through the particulars in a place offering more privacy.

Mr. D escorted us back to the party, where the dancers still reeled as though nothing had changed. I gathered my thoughts. I had to find Kashmir and tell him where the map was. Putting what I hoped was a blithe look on my face, I asked Slate if we could stay.

He didn't answer right away. We stood at the edge of the grass, beneath the cloud of lanterns, as numerous and brilliant as if the fixed stars had dropped to earth.

"This is a good map, Nixie," he said at last. "This is the one. I can tell."

I sighed. "Dad—"

"I know it. This is the last one. I promise you that." Something in his voice made me look up into his restless eyes, and when I saw his expression, I very nearly believed him. Gooseflesh rose on the back of my shoulders, but then he grinned. "Enjoy the party."

The captain made his way back toward the house, stopping to talk to Mr. Hart on the patio. I scrubbed my hands on my skirt and scanned the crowd—where was Kashmir?— but instead, there was Blake, trying to catch my eye.

"Miss Song," he called as he approached, folding his arm in front of his waistcoat and making a neat bow. The color was high in his cheeks. "May I have this dance?"

I hesitated, but it was the height of rudeness in the era to refuse when asked. How could I do so without further arousing his suspicion?

So we danced, his right hand warm and gentle at the small of my back, just above the pink bow. At first, I was stiff in his arms, but he was smiling at me and his eyes were the blue of the open water, so for a moment I let myself imagine we were simply two young people whose entire purpose tonight was to dance on the grass under a hundred paper stars.

Then the moment passed and the song ended, so I prepared my excuses. But rather than removing his hand to clap for the musicians, Blake pulled me closer, his cheek next to mine, his lips brushing my ear, and whispered, "Don't do it."

Suddenly the polite applause of the crowd seemed to roar like crashing waves. My first instinct was to run, to forget the map, to simply escape, but I couldn't even catch my breath. "I don't know what you're talking about," I said, sounding much calmer than I felt.

"You don't? Let me explain." The next number began. He held me firmly as the dance started—a two-step. "The men you met with. All members of the Hawaiian League, which supports annexation by America. Interestingly, not a single Hawaiian among them. Now," he said as we spun across the grass, Blake advancing as fast as I could retreat. "I'm not one to claim that *haoles* can never have the interests of the natives at heart, but I will insist it's the truth about these *haoles* in particular. So whatever the business is between your father and those men, don't let him do it."

"Sugar," I said quickly. "Your father needs someone to carry his cargo to California."

Blake lowered his chin and sighed, almost regretfully. "My father is not a plantation owner."

I was hot and dizzy, my feet like anchors, and the music of the band like the shrieking of the wind in a gale. The more I spoke, the worse it got. "Excuse me," I said, pushing away from him. "I need to powder my nose."

"I'll escort you," he said, still at my side.

"Don't bother." I quickened my steps.

"No bother at all," he replied, still behind me.

I glared over my shoulder, but before I could object further, I ran directly into a man's broad back. He turned and looked down at me with those weak-tea eyes. I swallowed. "Excuse me, Mr. Hart."

"Pardon me, I'm sure," he muttered. Behind him, my father raised his eyebrows.

I practically fled across the patio, but Blake dogged me all the way to the great hall. "Miss Song—" He caught my arm and I rounded on him.

"How dare you accost me?" I mustered all the outrage I could. "Remove your hand!"

He did so, lifting it, palm open, his eyes wide. "Now *that* was very nearly convincing. Very nearly." He stepped closer, his voice dropping to a whisper. "It's your crewmate, isn't it? What is he? An assassin?"

"A *what*?"

"Certainly he is no tutor! Please," he said, taking my hand, his eyes softening. "I don't want to have to bring him to the attention of the authorities, but if you go forward with whatever you are planning—"

"And what will you report?" I ripped my hand away. "That we came to a rather dull party?"

"I'm certain I could come up with something better than that. It doesn't have to be true. It only has to be worth investigating."

I glared at him. Was he bluffing? But as frustrating as Blake's questions were, I was more furious at myself. A fine job I'd done of distracting, leading him right into the hall! "I'll tell you everything," I said, desperate to get rid of him. "But not here. They might see us. Meet me in the garden in ten minutes."

He stared at me, and I tried as hard as I could to look truthful. "I have another idea," he said. "In here." Then he put his hand on the door to the study.

"Mr. Hart," I began, but I was spared coming up with

another excuse when we heard a little gasp, followed by shushing. We both turned; the door to the next room was cracked open. I caught, in the shadows, the glint of blue silk on a bodice and the curve of a man's black coat sleeve. Mrs. Hart was in the drawing room, and she wasn't alone.

And Mr. Hart was still speaking to the captain on the lawn.

Blake was red to the roots of his hair. I stared him down, and he looked away. Then I tossed my hair and left; he did not follow me this time.

I rounded the corner and stopped, pressing myself against the wall. As I did so, I heard a light, trilling laugh in the hall. "Oh! Blake, dear, what are you doing so far from the party?"

"I might ask you the same question," he said.

Mrs. Hart's reply was immediate. "If you must know, I was enjoying a moment of solitude. You know how exhausting guests can be. But now I'm ready to dance some more. Come, dear, escort your mother back to the lawn." The sound of their footsteps receded.

I peeked out around the corner. The hall was clear.

My God. Now I understood the sly eyes, Mr. Hart's embarrassment, Milly's little joke. "Capable host" indeed.

Scratch the surface, and you'd find Victorians were nearly as obsessed with sex as they were with death.

But who was in the drawing room with her?

I shouldn't have done it, but I crept toward the door, which she'd shut firmly behind her. As I reached out for the knob, it twisted. I stepped back softly, softly, as the door cracked open and a man peeked out. He was facing in the other direction, but I recognized the slicked black curls, and my jaw dropped. "Kashmir?"

He startled, seeing me, his eyes widening. I stumbled away, my fingers cold, my face hot. He came toward me, one hand out; not stopping to think, I ran into the study and pulled the door closed, leaning against it so he couldn't follow.

Kashmir and Mrs. Hart! What a disgusting flirt—the both of them! All this time I'd been fending off Blake, and there he'd been, with her and her blond curls and her tiny shoes and her faux-charming mispronunciation of "Arab," while we were supposed to be concentrating on the map!

The map.

I shoved Kashmir out of my mind. He'd found a completely different distraction. There was no time for me to do the same.

The portfolio was on the desk where we'd left it. I took it up with shaking hands just as the floorboards creaked in the hall. Kashmir coming in? No . . . there were two men's voices, speaking low, right outside the door. I darted left a step, then right, but there was no place to hide.

A latch clicked—the hinge creaked—my heart stopped—

"Amira!"

I whirled around. The side door was open, and Kashmir beckoned me from the next room.

I ran through, pulling the door shut just as the men entered the study. I leaned on the heavy mahogany door, my blood pounding in my ears, willing my heart to slow down.

"What were you doing in the hall?" Kashmir whispered fiercely, but before I replied, he put his hand over my mouth. The men were speaking behind the door.

"Sir," Mr. Hart said, "I am in debt to every single one of them! If I comply, they forgive the sum, but if I do not, they will ruin me!"

"You would be far away, and more than rich enough, besides." That was the captain's voice. "You could pay the debt twice over if you chose!"

"I could," Mr. Hart said slowly. "But if I were to betray them, we would have to leave immediately. Mr. D, he—he would contact the authorities . . . with lies, to be sure, but you must understand, though my brother was a scoundrel, he was quite well liked—"

"We could sail this evening."

"And where would we go?"

"Anywhere you like."

"Anywhere?"

My back was pressed against the door, and Kashmir was pressed against me, the portfolio sandwiched between us, one of its corners jabbing my thigh. Slowly he lifted his hand away from my mouth. There was frustration in his eyes, and it made me furious. I responded by lifting the portfolio and raising my brows, but he only shook his head. Then he stepped back from me on quiet cat feet and picked up a roll of paper leaning against the side of a blue upholstered chaise, giving it a little shake.

The map.

I ground my teeth and leaned the empty portfolio against the wall. "When did you—"

He put his finger to his lips. Then he beckoned me to step away from the door, but I took one step and his hand flew up again. He pointed down near my feet.

The hem of my new dress was caught in the door.

I grabbed a handful of the fabric to pull, but Kashmir's frantic gestures stopped me. He handed me the map and reached up over his shoulder, drawing a short knife out from under his collar.

Mr. Hart was speaking again. "But there is one more thing you must do for me."

"If I can," the captain said.

"If you cannot, there is no hope elsewhere."

"What is it? Well?" Slate's impatience was palpable.

"They say . . . you and your crew have access to . . . all manner of strange and mystical items. And it is . . . I am not proud to say it, but I—I require . . ." The pause was so long I wondered if they'd left the room, but finally Mr. Hart continued. "I require a love potion."

So Mr. Hart knew too. Not only about our ship, but about Mrs. Hart. What would Slate say? I had asked him about love potions once, and he'd scoffed at the notion, disgusted by the very idea of forcing someone to fall in love. Still, mythology is rife with potions, powders, Cupid's arrows. Love as something taken, rather than something given.

I pressed my lips together. Kashmir was still flushed with anger . . . or was it shame? He avoided my eyes; his knife whispered through the silk.

"It would mean the world to me, sir," Mr. Hart continued. "You understand? You told me why you want the map. You know what a man will do for love."

"Fine," Slate said at last. "Yes. I . . . as I've said, I am not the expert. But my . . . Nix will find one. She can find anything."

"Ah, excellent! Excellent!"

Kash stepped back; I was free of the door. I handed him the map and made a shooing motion, but he looked at me quizzically. *"The captain,"* I mouthed, nodding back toward the door.

My plan was simple: barge in, tell the captain I had a message from Bee to return to the ship immediately, and whisk him out of the room before Mr. Hart could object. But I couldn't explain it all to Kashmir, who shook his head and gestured for me to follow him.

"I can be found at the dock as soon as you're ready to leave," Slate was saying. "The sooner the better. I would hate for your colleagues to have time to suspect anything. Perhaps even tonight, after the ball?"

"I will need time to pack and to put my affairs in order. Oh, what am I saying?" Mr. Hart's voice was elated, thrumming with impending freedom. "It's a new life. I needn't bring a thing!"

"Except for the map," Slate said.

"Yes, the map. The map . . ."

I met Kashmir's wide eyes. "Go," I whispered, but he put his finger to my lips. Then he took me by the wrist and pulled me toward the door. It opened as we approached; there, silhouetted in the light from the hall, stood Blake.

We froze, all of us, as he took in the scene: Kashmir hauling on my arm, my torn dress. Everything was still, for one long, dreadful moment.

And then Blake rushed toward us, shoving Kashmir. "Release her!"

Kashmir stumbled against the chaise, dropping the map, which I grabbed up reflexively, pulling it away from Blake's trampling feet. I flung out my hand between them as Kashmir bounced back upright. "Blake, it's not what—"

But Blake bulled forward, half enraged, half disbelieving. "Is that all you are? A common cad?"

"Just what are you implying, boy?"

"Stop it, both of you!"

And then the door behind me flew open. "By God, Nix, what the hell are you doing?"

I turned to meet my father's wrath and Mr. Hart's panic. The man's eyes were as round as coins on a face pale as death.

"What is this?" he whispered, and his eyes lit upon the map in my hand. He rounded on Slate. "Thievery?"

Blake pointed a furious finger at Kashmir. "I don't know what your game is, but—"

"Blake, *get out!*" Mr. Hart shouted. Kashmir took Blake by the shoulders and pushed him out into the hall, slamming the door shut behind him.

Slate's face was inches from mine. *"What were you thinking?"* He wasted no more time on me, though. Instead, he took the map out of my hands, and his own hands trembled to touch it. He held it so delicately, as though it was the most precious thing in the world to him, and he seemed hardly to breathe.

Then Mr. Hart plucked it right out of his hands and dashed away to the fireplace.

"No!" Slate reached toward him, hands high, palms out. Mr. Hart stood on the hearth, towering over the captain, his feet apart and his face a mask of wrath, a Colossus of Barletta, and in that moment, I could not imagine ever seeing weakness in his maddened eyes. He raised his hand as though to strike the captain across the face, and his arm shook with the effort of holding back the blow. But then anger cooled to cruelty, and instead he dipped the map toward the flames.

"Please." Slate clasped his hands in supplication, and Mr. Hart stopped, the paper a handspan above the hungry blaze. I held my own breath to see this spectacle, to watch my father beg. Maybe it was the last map, just as my father had said, and if Mr. Hart would only lower his hand, my worries would burn with the paper into smoke and fire, heat and light.

"Please, believe me," Slate said, imploring. "This was not my plan." Mr. Hart did not move, and sudden rage rose in my father's eyes. "Burn the map, and lose your chance of erasing your debts."

"Debt is the least of my worry if he catches me double-dealing." Mr. Hart's voice was a frosty contrast to the fire.

"Not a word." Slate wrung his hands; all the fight had fled. "I won't breathe a word to him, I swear. Let me honor our agreement. Please."

Mr. Hart pulled the map back slightly, but he shook his head. "You will. You will honor the *original* agreement of the evening."

"Whatever you say."

But Mr. Hart twisted as if in agony, reconsidering his own demands, weighing riches to ruin, and his own fury ebbed in the struggle. Finally he spoke again, almost pleading. "You must understand, I cannot risk it!"

"I do, I understand," Slate said, his voice soft as mercy.

"Yes," Mr. Hart said, as though agreeing with him. "Yes. And not a word about our little . . . *discussion* to the others, or—"

"Not a word!"

Mr. Hart lifted the map away from the flame, and my own wild hope turned to ashes on my tongue.

CHAPTER
TWENTY-TWO

Mr. Hart shut the door between the study and the drawing room, and after a long silence, Slate turned to Kashmir.

"Get the coach."

Without a word, Kash opened the door to the hall, where he found himself face-to-face with Blake. Neither spoke, but Kashmir took the opportunity to brush past him with a stiff shoulder.

Blake's eyes were on me as the captain took my arm, gripping my wrist like he gripped the wheel in bad weather, but I avoided Blake's gaze. Humiliation flamed on my cheeks.

Slate barged through the hall and down the stairs. I practically had to run to keep up, red petals from my lei falling in our wake. I heard the startled murmurs of the crowd, felt the stares like spiders on my shoulders, and prayed Kashmir would be quick. My prayers were answered; as we got to the front steps, the carriage was pulling up to the drive.

But Blake wasn't far behind. "Wait!" he said as Slate climbed in. Kash reached down to help me up, staring coldly at Blake all the while. "Miss Song!"

But I willed myself not to react. The captain pounded on the canopy, the driver put the whip to the horses, and we rolled away, leaving Blake on the steps.

We reached the road, and the captain slammed his open palm down on the velvet, his face white with rage. "What the hell were you thinking? Did you want him to destroy the map?"

"That would solve my problems," I said, but Slate had already rounded on Kashmir.

"And you! How could you double-cross me like this? You're lucky that map is safe, or your worthless carcass might not be."

Fury boiled in my breast as Kashmir paled. "Captain, I'm sorry—"

"It wasn't him, Slate!"

"Oh, sure, I believe that," he retorted. "The professional

thief had nothing to do with the heist!"

"A professional thief wouldn't have botched it," I snapped back. "It was completely my idea."

"And he went along with it?" Slate jabbed a finger into Kashmir's chest. "You better get your loyalties straightened out quick, kid. If I didn't need you on this job, you'd be swimming to your next destination."

I stared at my father. "Slate. You can't honestly be planning to go through with the theft."

"I can do whatever I damn well choose!"

"Blake knows something's up."

"Who?"

"The boy we just left on the steps! He's suspicious, and he'll report you before you can get near the treasury."

"Hart's son? Why would he do that?"

"Because he doesn't want his father to destroy something important," I said pointedly.

Slate's eyes widened. "Did *you* tell him what was going on? Nixie." He took me roughly by the shoulders, his nose inches from mine. *"Did you tell him?"*

"No." My voice was calm and I did not flinch; he leaned back, eased up. "But I should."

"Don't you *dare*."

"Why not? I could even make the report myself. The king will arrest the Hawaiian League. The kingdom will be safe. You won't have to worry about the money, and I won't have to worry about the map."

Slate raised his finger, pointing it at me in a silent accusation. Then he curled his hand into a fist and brought it to his mouth, as though to keep himself from speaking, and the hollow rhythm of the horse's hooves seemed very loud in the night. Finally he spoke, though I did not hear what he said.

"What?"

"I'll teach you," he repeated, a hoarse whisper. "Help me and I'll teach you how to Navigate."

I scoffed. "You're lying."

"No," he said quickly. "I swear."

I looked into his eyes, and I believed him. But rather than the triumph I expected, I was filled with a cold fear, squirming in the pit of my stomach. "You must really believe this map is the one."

"I know it is."

I wet my lips. "If you're so sure, why should I risk it?"

"Is it such a risk?" he said, his voice faltering. "Would a life here be so terrible?"

Out of the corner of my eye, I saw Kashmir turn his face. I clenched my jaw, but Slate pressed forward.

"Or the life you want, then—the escape you've got planned," he said desperately. My mouth fell open; I never thought he'd acknowledge it so openly. Suddenly, irrationally, I wished I'd let Joss tell me my fortune.

Slate plowed on. "Not a risk, then, Nixie. A gamble. And think of the reward." He took my hand, and his was so hot—mine so cold—I pulled away. "Sometimes a person has to let go of something to take hold of something else. You always have to choose what's more important."

"Oh?" I swallowed, curling my fingers on my lap, holding fistfuls of silk. "And what is more important to you, Captain? Lin or me?"

He stared at me for a long time, but he didn't answer my question. Then he put his forehead against the canopy support and stared at the trees. When Slate spoke again, his voice was changed, the tone simple, the passion gone. "I have to try, Nix. If I don't, what am I? I love her. Do you understand? I can't just let her go. And maybe—even if it does change everything—maybe you'd be happier too. Did you ever think of that? If none of this had happened? If I'd never disappointed you? If I could do it all over again. I could have been the best father. I still could."

We rode the rest of the way to the docks in a vast and airy silence. I felt empty, my body cold and light as the night breeze, and Kashmir's face was still as stone. Once back aboard, the captain went back to his cabin and paused outside the door. "Think about it, Nixie." Then, as though ashamed of his words, he opened the door swiftly and disappeared behind it.

I gripped the rail and stared at the mountains; they were steely as knives under the moon. The sound of laughter and music still drifted from town, and it grated on my ears. Kashmir came to stand beside me, putting his hand close enough to mine that I could feel the warmth of him. I folded my arms across my chest. "What should I do?" I said softly. "I don't want to turn him in, but I don't think he'll stop otherwise."

"I don't think he'll stop either way." Kashmir shrugged one shoulder. "Why not help him?"

"What?"

"It's very altruistic to try to save the kingdom, but this is not a fairy tale. He's offering what you'd always wanted. Why not take it?"

"Kashmir." Did he really not understand? "If the map

works and . . . if I'd had a different life, we never would have met. You would have been cornered on that dock in Vaadi Al-Maas."

He waved my words away, trying to look nonchalant; if I didn't know him so well, I might have been fooled. "You shouldn't worry about me, *amira*. You shouldn't worry at all."

"Why not?"

"Well. If we'd never met, neither you nor I would have known it could have been different. But even if the captain rewrites his own history, how could it affect your reality? I'm from a place you call a fairy tale, and I'm still here."

"But . . . the Vaadi Al-Maas was real once. People believed in it."

"I believe in you. Simple enough, right?" His smile was heartbreaking.

I pulled the pins out of my hair, letting it fall down in coils on my shoulders. Of course it wasn't that simple, but I didn't want to argue against his point. "Why should I take the risk?"

"He'll take it for you, either way."

"You're not even angry," I said with wonder. "How can you forgive him?"

"How can you hold it against him?" Kashmir returned. He shrugged off his jacket and folded it over his arm. "Love makes fools of us all. He has to believe it will work, because he's in love." He ran his hand through his hair, mussing the gel, and leaned against the railing, watching the full moon shimmer on the water. "And I have to believe it will not."

I tried to read his face, but his eyes were a mystery. I pulled my shawl tighter around my shoulders. The silence was unbearable. "At least it seems like you had fun at the party," I said finally.

He laughed a little. "Ah, yes. I did enjoy the dancing."

"Mrs. Hart is quite a good dancer, I hear."

Kashmir scoffed. "That woman. I've been chased by *policemen* with less tenacity. I tried to shake her on the lawn, but she found me coming out of the study. She very nearly dragged me into the drawing room by the collar. Thank all the gods she didn't notice I was holding the map."

"You certainly found a clever way to distract her."

"It was necessity, I assure you. Nix," Kashmir said, a smile creeping into his voice. "Are you jealous?"

"No!" Suddenly the whole dock seemed very quiet, the sound of many ears listening. Unasked for—and unappreciated—my brain reminded me of an Arab proverb: *Jealousy is nothing but a fear of being abandoned.* I lowered my voice, flustered. "I'm not jealous. I just don't . . . I'm not jealous."

"Oh. Good." Kash bit his lip, but the ghost of his smile lingered. "I'd hate for you to be a fool, as well."

We stayed there a long time, then, the only sound the water lapping on the pilings. Kashmir seemed to be waiting for me to say something, but I didn't—I couldn't. Finally he took a deep breath. "Good night, *amira*."

For a while after he left, my eyes wandered across the sky as though the answers were there. Then I dropped my shawl on the deck, kicked off my shoes, and gently removed the crimson lei from my neck. I hung it from the bar at the top of my hammock, then I lay down hard. The full moon swam like its own reflection in my vision.

Had I been too selfish? I had never known my mother, but I knew my life as it had been without her: the ship, the sea, the myths, the maps . . . and, yes, Kashmir. The pain I felt at the thought of losing him—the same pain that kept me at arm's length—gave me a hint of my father's own struggle.

But what if I could Navigate? I could forget about my

father and his search and finally be free to do—and to feel—whatever I wanted. And all that it would cost was a king's ransom.

I buried my head in my pillow. Kashmir had been right about one thing. This wasn't a fairy tale.

CHAPTER
TWENTY-THREE

The morning watch was mine, but I only half-registered the sound of the caladrius crowing for her biscuit, and I was definitely sleeping when Rotgut came on deck to relieve me at eight. It was a relief too. I'd been having a nightmare: standing before a mirror, gazing into a pair of eyes that weren't brown like mine, but as black as the abyss, and they were gazing back into me. After Rotgut woke me, I fell back into a light doze, twitching at every sound. The sun pried my eyes open sometime after noon, so I rolled out of bed and put my foot on something cold and slimy.

"Ugh!"

On the deck, in the shadow of my hammock, lay a striped silver fish about the length of my hand. Its eyes were still clear and its scales hadn't yet lost their opalescent sheen: no more than an hour old. The only marks it bore—aside from a flattened area in the shape of my heel—were twin puncture wounds right behind the eyes. Swag had left me a present.

Rotgut glanced over his shoulder at the sound of my voice; he was standing on the quarterdeck, casting his bait into the blue water. "It's you and me today," he said. "Hey, nice dress."

I reached behind me; the huge pink bow had been crushed as I slept, and the hem was a ruin. "You and me? Double watch?"

Rotgut looked embarrassed. "The captain actually asked me to watch you. He doesn't want you leaving the ship."

"I see. And what are you supposed to do if I try?"

"He didn't say. Just don't do it. Unless you want him mad at me."

I sighed, but I hadn't been planning on leaving anyway. At least not yet. I nodded out at the ocean. "Any luck?"

"Oh, lots," he said, grinning. I checked the bucket beside his feet; the only thing in it was seawater. "All of it bad."

"I know how that feels. Here," I said, slipping the dead fish into the pail. "It's only a little mangled."

"Wow. Thanks." Rotgut pulled up his line to check the

bait; the hook was empty. He put on a fresh piece of squid. "I ran away from home once," he added, almost cheerfully.

"What?"

"I suppose technically I'm still running, since I never went back. That's why you want to learn to Navigate, isn't it?" He cast his line. "So you can leave us."

I leaned on the rail. "Don't try to guilt me."

"I'm not." He was quiet for a while, both of us watching the painted wooden bobber. "Even though we'd never, ever see you again."

I pursed my lips. "You just said you've done the very same thing."

"Doesn't mean I don't regret it. Of course, that's what life is. Gathering regrets to mope about in your old age."

"Is that what they taught you in your monastery?"

"Nah, I didn't learn that till after I left. Trouble is, once you leave it's too late. You can't come back. You particularly." He checked his hook again: nothing. "So I would just figure out first if you're running away, or running to."

"Running to what?"

He snorted. "I guess that's your answer."

"You know, I haven't made any decisions yet," I said, annoyed.

"Okay. When you do, give me a chance to say good-bye before you go." Rotgut dropped the line back into the bay.

The afternoon sunlight was heavy on my shoulders, so I went below to change. The air was stuffy in my cabin, and I was grateful to swap the silk dress for my shirt and trousers.

Back above, I watched the surfers out past the reefs, lithe and tan, flying effortlessly ahead of their white wakes. The sun was harsh in the sky, and it scattered on the water like shards of broken glass. Unbidden, my mind revisited the events of last night and then skittered away from the embarrassment of it all, then of course back again, like a shark to a carcass. What a mess. I pulled the pendant of my necklace back and forth on the chain, and my eyes went to the lei. It had fallen in the night and now lay in a heap on the deck, wilted and withering.

The choice before me was no clearer in the light of day. Although if Blake made good on his threat to turn us in, perhaps the choice had already been made. In a way, it would have been a relief not to have the option. And yet . . .

I couldn't deny the temptation. In fact, it was easy to make excuses; I'd read the history. The monarchy was already in decline. Much of the island was owned by foreign interests. Even Blake had said it: the kingdom of Hawaii was already disappearing. Perhaps we were even meant to take the money—perhaps that history had already been written somewhere. And if it was supposed to happen, who could blame me?

The red flowers, sacred to Pele, lay at my feet. Creator, destroyer. I knew exactly who would blame me.

And then, as though summoned, came the voice from the pier. "Miss Song?"

Blake was standing at the bottom of the gangplank, holding his hat in his hands. He'd replaced the black mourning ribbon on the band with a blue that matched his eyes. "May I come aboard?"

My pulse quickened, but I had to know what brought him. Back at the stern, Rotgut was still fishing. It wasn't as though I was leaving the ship. I beckoned Blake up the gangplank.

"You look well," he said to me.

"Did you come to check after my well-being?"

He pursed his lips. "After the behavior of your 'tutor'. . ."

I blushed; I couldn't help it. "You have the wrong idea."

"I know." He ran his hands along the hat brim, smoothing the ribbon. "But what's the right one? I was convinced you were conspiring with the league, but it appears you were in fact conspiring against them. Thievery, my father said. What did you want with that old map?"

I swallowed. Denying it would be foolish at this point, but I couldn't tell him the truth. At least, not all of it. "I . . . my father needs the map. Your father is willing to sell it if the league forgives his debts."

It was his turn to blush, but he did not lower his gaze. "And what is the price?"

"It is . . . quite high."

"Must be, to outstrip my father's debts. And every penny they get, they'll use to further their goals." He rubbed his chin with one ink-stained finger. "So you were trying to steal the map instead. I'm sorry I interfered. If I'd known, I would have helped you."

"You hate your father so much?"

Blake hesitated. "I cannot condone his actions."

Hope rose in my throat. I took Blake's arm and pulled him close enough to whisper. "You can still help. I'd be willing to pay you to—"

"Please, Miss Song. I would need no pay if only I could find the map. I looked this morning." He shifted on his feet, still playing with the brim of his hat. "I have no right to ask, especially after my accusations, but if you could see your way to appeal to your father . . . ?" My laugh was bitter, and he nodded sadly. "I deserved that."

"That's not it," I said. "I've tried to speak to him many times, but he will not be swayed."

Blake's slapped his hat against his thigh. "Why on *earth* is that map so valuable to him? I could do one similar in half an hour."

"Similar, but not the same," I said carefully. "The original is a . . . connection to my mother. It was drawn while she was still alive."

He looked at me closely, his eyes the hard blue of sea ice. "Quite a lot of money to spend for something of sentimental value."

Why was he so damnably observant? I shrugged, trying to seem nonchalant. "They say love makes fools of us all."

His gaze was like a harpoon; I couldn't look away. "They do say that." He was quiet for a moment as I glanced from his face, to the sea, then back, and away again. "Miss Song," he said finally. "There is some mystery here."

"I can't think what it might be," I said breezily.

"I can't either." He cocked his head, studying me. The late afternoon sunlight shone in his hair like a crown. Suddenly he smiled. "But it's very intriguing."

I blinked. "Oh?"

"And it has been from the very first day you arrived. Under other circumstances, Miss Song, I may have come to the ship to make a very different appeal to your father."

My eyes widened, and there was a feeling in my stomach then, like small fish leaping. These were uncharted waters, treacherous and strangely tempting. "Mr. Hart—" Then out of the corner of my eye, I saw a familiar pair returning to the ship. "You shouldn't be here."

He stiffened, chagrined. "I apologize for my boldness."

"No, I mean—you really shouldn't be here."

I grabbed his arm and pulled him down to crouch behind the bulwark so Slate and Kashmir wouldn't see him. I caught Rotgut's glance; he had a hand over his mouth, and his expression was somewhere between amusement and alarm. I put my finger to my lips and a question in my eyes. He spread his hands, but he nodded once and waved us toward the hatch.

CHAPTER
TWENTY-FOUR

I took a moment to throw my silk dress over Swag's bucket before I pulled Blake into my room and shut the door.

"What's happening?"

"Keep your voice down!"

"Why?" he whispered.

"I don't want him to know you're here!"

"Who? The captain? Or Mr. Firas?"

I put my hands on my hips. "Your insinuations are not very gentlemanly!"

The corner of his mouth quirked up. "Neither is your tutor."

I opened my mouth to respond but fell silent at the sound of footsteps on the deck above and voices as they passed overhead.

"Come, Captain. How and where would we find so many we could trust?"

"Perhaps in one of these back valleys . . ."

I cleared my throat more noisily than I had to, but thankfully their conversation faded quickly to murmurs, and for once it seemed like Blake was not listening closely. His eyes were flitting around the room, never resting long on one spot, and he shifted on his feet. "Mr. Hart," I said, crossing my arms and making a show of studying him. "This may be the first time I've seen you at a loss."

He laughed a little, but he was spinning his hat nervously in his hands. He glanced at the triangular corner of my room, the part behind the bow, which was bare but for some pillows and the tattered quilt Slate had wrapped me in when he'd taken me from the opium den. "Is this where you live?"

I shook my head. "It's only where I keep my things."

He stretched out his arms; standing where he was, his fingertips brushed the sides of the ship. "There isn't much space."

"I have the rest of the world."

"Hmm." He dropped his arms to his sides. "Have you ever considered a life elsewhere?"

"Oh, many times," I said lightly. "And many places."

"Spoken like a true adventurer." Blake turned in a slow circle, and his eyes fell on my scattered books. He knelt to pick them up, but I crouched beside him, taking his hand in mine.

"Leave them be," I said. "I'll clean later." Then I tilted my head. "Are you blushing?"

He pulled his hand back as though stung. Then he laughed ruefully. "It appears I am not so at ease in your territory as I am in my own."

"I'll keep that in mind," I said, feeling bold. "The next time you try to impress me, I'll press-gang you instead. We could use an extra deckhand."

He grinned. "I'd rather find a way to draw you back ashore. Tell me, Miss Song," he said, taking my hand this time, running his thumb gently over my skin. "Have you ever considered staying in Honolulu? I promise you, on this island, you will find a lifetime of adventure without ever having to raise a sail."

I opened my mouth, partly in surprise, partly to speak, but I was interrupted by a knock at my door.

"Amira?"

For a moment, we were both still. The silence was stifling. "Yes?"

"Can I . . . I wanted to talk to you. About last night."

If I hadn't been nearly nose to nose with Blake, I wouldn't have seen it, the tightening around his eyes. "I . . ." I cleared my throat, trying to keep my voice light. "There's nothing to talk about, Kash."

He was quiet so long I thought maybe he'd gone. "As you say," he said, finally. I didn't hear his footsteps as he left, but I did hear his door open and close.

I sighed, and Blake dropped my hands and stood, taking a step back, suddenly quite formal. "Perhaps rather than—" He cleared his throat. "Perhaps I might indeed take a moment to speak with the captain."

"What for?"

He straightened his shoulders. "*I* am no scoundrel."

I pressed my lips together and took a step back myself. "I don't think that's wise."

"Have I flattered myself to think you've enjoyed the time we've spent? I am not asking for a promise. Only an opportunity."

An opportunity—and an escape, although not the one I'd planned. I imagined it then, not just another week, but another year, another decade—a lifetime here in the place of my birth. Learning more than what I could in books, in paradise before the fall.

Although fall it would.

Knowing what I knew, the choice should have been clearer, but looking into Blake's eyes, I couldn't find the words to give him a real answer. Instead, I resorted to cowardice. "My father would likely refuse."

"Perhaps he's never considered that a ship is not the best place for a lady."

"I'm not a *lady*, Blake. I'm a sailor."

"But so nearly a local. You may consider extending your stay—just for a time? A year? Two? We could explore the hidden trails and the secret caverns and live on fish and fruit. I could even teach you to surf if you miss the rhythm of the water." He took my hand again and stared into my eyes. His own were the color of the open sea. "We could map every hidden spot on the island."

"Blake." My mouth was dry. All I could add was "Please."

He clenched his jaw, locking all the objections he wanted to make behind his teeth. Blake was indeed a gentleman. He stood the next few minutes in excruciating silence, his hands clasped and his head bowed, before I crept out of the room to check the hall.

The coast was clear, and quietly, we went above. Rotgut didn't look at us, but he did raise one hand in a salute.

I walked Blake to the gangplank, where he stopped. "Come, Mr. Hart," I said.

He opened his mouth to speak, but he didn't say anything for a long moment. Then his eyes fell on the red lei lying on the deck, and he sighed. "Do you know, it's customary for people leaving the islands to toss leis from the boats, in the hopes that they, like the flowers, will return someday to Hawaii's shores?" He put his hat back on his head. "Good-bye, Miss Song. It's been quite an adventure."

I didn't want to watch him go, but it was difficult to turn away. Once he was out of sight, I picked up the lei and let it fall onto the waves, where it floated like blood in the water. Would I ever reconsider? One day, might I grow old seeking a map of this place and time?

The thought terrified me.

I had promised myself years ago I'd never make my father's mistake. I was not meant to drop anchor or seek harbor.

I went below, out of the island sun and away from the sight of the town, to hide in the bosom of ship, but she was like a sleeping beast. I didn't know whether I was safe under her protection or caught in her claws.

My room felt claustrophobic when it never had before,

so I made a halfhearted attempt at clearing the floor, piling my clothes against the trunk, and stacking the books Blake had so nearly taken up. Half of them had been printed in the next century, although they covered the last few millennia. *The Gods of Egypt*, the Prose Edda, and here, *Beowulf* in the original Old English, the story of a hero who saved his people by killing a monster. Of course, if you consider Grendel's mother, Beowulf was the monster who murdered her son. I closed the book and placed it atop a book of fairy tales: the old ones, the Grimm ones, the ones without happy endings. The ones that had been real.

Why did the stories I knew best never end well?

But why too did I feel at home among them?

I could never give up the myths, the maps, the ship that had shaped me. Blake's home might be paradise, but my home was the *Temptation*.

The last book in the pile wasn't a book at all, but the covers of the hymnal that protected the map Joss had sold me. I sucked in a breath. I knew then how to get my father what he needed. I took the map with me as I went above and, with a new sense of purpose, knocked on Slate's door. "Captain?"

It was a moment before he responded. "Yes."

He was sitting cross-legged on the floor with his elbows on his knees, his palms open toward the sky, his jacket flung over the chair. By his mussed hair and flushed cheeks, he must have just lifted his head from his hands, but when he saw the look on my face, he scrambled to his feet. "You found something."

I met his gaze. "You'll teach me."

"Yes."

"Then this is the last map I help you with."

"I promise," he said quickly, but I shook my head.

"I'm not asking you," I said. "I'm telling you. This is the last time."

He caught his breath, then let it out, something softer than a sigh. "I always knew you'd abandon me once you knew how."

"I'm not abandoning you," I said. "I'm letting you go."

"I don't want you to leave."

"But you want the map, and you need my help." My claim sat in the air between us, and he did not contest it. "You said it yourself, Slate. Sometimes a person has to let go of something to make room for something more important. You have to choose."

He was quiet for so long, I began to fear he'd made

the offer without thinking I'd accept, but as I watched, his expression cycled from sorrow to resignation and then to something like relief. "You're right, Nixie," he said at last. "I'll let you go too."

I bit my lip to keep it from trembling; he'd let me go a long time ago. After all, you can only hold one person tight if you're holding on with both hands.

CHAPTER
TWENTY-FIVE

As promised, a note came from Mr. D midweek, setting the time and the place for our next meeting: *10 p.m., at the business of our mutual friend.*

We arrived late at Joss's apothecary. The captain had lingered over dinner and dithered when he was dressing, and as we were leaving the ship, he stopped dead just off the gangplank and wouldn't move for half a minute. Then he started walking again, but slowly, and he hesitated once more on the street outside the shuttered apothecary. Slate didn't want to go in.

I shared his reluctance, although my reasons were different. But we were committed to the scheme, and it was unwise to loiter outside. Although curfew was only for native citizens, we didn't want to call attention to ourselves just now. Kash pushed on the door to the Happy House;

it swung open easily. A candle flame shivered in the gloom.

"Come on, Captain," I said, with more confidence than I felt. I took Slate's arm and pulled him along.

That same peculiar odor hit my nose, of dust and leaves and bitter tinctures, but in Auntie Joss's place behind the counter, there stood a behemoth of a man, with knuckles like walnuts and eyes as narrow and impassive as gaps in window blinds. His presence confirmed my suspicions even before I smelled the smoke. We were not meeting in an apothecary.

He moved his chin almost imperceptibly toward the crooked stairs behind the piles of crates at the back of the shop. I led the way, grasping the rickety rail with one moist hand. Stepping down, I was nearly blind in the dark, following the sweet reek in the air with my other hand in front of me. When I touched velvet fabric, I pawed at the curtains to reveal a bleary light.

The room was wide, larger than the footprint of the apothecary above. The ceiling was low, and the blue smoke gathered along it like storm clouds. Some parts of the wall were plaster, some rough wood; there was a section with peeling wallpaper, as well as a portion of unfinished stone, but along all of the walls were bunks with thin mattresses, some occupied, at least physically, by dreamers. On a chair in the corner, a bored woman, nude to the waist, plucked the strings of a *guhzeng*.

Guided by another woman with a pocked face and downcast eyes, Auntie Joss approached. She wore a rich silk robe and carmine on her wrinkled lips, which cracked into a courtesan's smile as she greeted us.

"It's been so long, Captain," she said. "Pity your friends are waiting, or we could talk about the past."

"I have no friends here," Slate muttered.

She laughed lightly, as though he'd made a witty joke, then turned her unseeing eyes on me. "And Nix, welcome back. If we had more time, we could talk about the future."

"Joss. Didn't you know that selling opium is illegal these days? Although I suppose it's hard to make ends meet, selling our secrets." I started to follow Slate and Kashmir, who had gone with the young woman off into the smoke, but Joss grabbed my arm and leaned in close.

"Why, Nix," she said, her cloudy eyes wide. "They are not yours alone. I wasn't always blind. I used to be able to read maps too. Perhaps another time, I can tell you my own secrets. For a price." She released my arm, but I was rooted to the floor. The temptation to ask her then and there was formidable, but I had brought nothing to barter with.

I caught up to Kashmir and Slate as they reached a large rug, surrounded by piles of flat, tattered pillows, where the four members of the Hawaiian League were sitting.

"Captain! Miss Song," Mr. D said as we joined them on the floor. "And the math tutor." His expression was careful and even. "Or was it the dancing instructor?"

Kashmir inclined his head and gave them his charming smile.

Of all the conspirators, only Mr. D seemed comfortable here. Mr. Hart was glaring at Kashmir, and Milly's legs were folded awkwardly, all angles, like a colt lying in a field. Mr. T was staring with an outraged expression at the musician's bare breasts. "Forgive him," Mr. D said with a conciliatory gesture. "We are well outside his usual social circles. It was an effort to get him to attend at all."

Mr. T turned his face, but not his eyes, toward the captain, and whispered through his sneer. "It's not your forgiveness that concerns me."

"Come now, Mr. T, we are not in church," Milly said. "We are here so we may speak plainly, without fear of being overheard."

"Indeed, there is no fear of that, sir, for God himself would shun this place!" Then Mr. T drew back as a woman in an embroidered red dress brought tea, kneeling down to place the tray on the rug and pour each cup. Her fingers were stained brown. Had my own mother held me with tar-stained hands?

The men were silent as she poured, and Slate in particular stared at his cup like she'd filled it with poison. Although the basement room was cool, his brow was covered with sweat.

Mr. D raised his own teacup. "A toast to the success of our venture?" The others lifted their cups, but when I reached for mine, Kash touched my arm. I started.

"Poppy tea," he said under his breath.

I curled my fingers back into a fist. I should have guessed. Slate was still staring at his cup, and Mr. D was watching him. He must have chosen this place specifically to get to the captain, and it was working. Had Mr. Hart told Mr. D what had happened the night of the ball, or had Mr. D guessed?

The smell of the tea was bitter in the back of my throat. I took Slate's cup and raised it. "Cheers," I said, before dumping it out on the rug.

Mr. D's smile didn't falter, and he inclined his head. "Let's move forward with the plan, then. Captain?"

Slate blinked, and he refocused, not on the men seated

across from him, but on the teapot in the center of the rug. "Yes. The plan. Over the last few weeks, we've—Kashmir and I—have been checking out the layout of the palace and the grounds and so forth. Well. We've found the treasury is guarded at all times by . . ." He looked at Kashmir for confirmation. "Four members of the Royal Hawaiian Guard?"

"Indeed," Kashmir said, taking over smoothly. "But when the king hosts events, only the youngest guards are left at the treasury across the street. The most experienced guards are nearest the king, to impress the guests and so forth, and the rest are in the barracks on the palace grounds. So our excursion is best planned for a night when the king is throwing a party."

"Shouldn't be difficult," Milly said, laughing through his nose. "He's always throwing a party."

"Fine," Kashmir said. "Next consideration. The Honolulu Rifle Club. Thirty-two armed men, mostly American, by all reports excellent shots. The only force on the island aside from the Royal Hawaiian Guard, and they have better training and nicer guns. Mr. T. You have a connection there."

Mr. T's eyes widened. "How did you learn that?"

Kashmir gave him a withering look. "From what I've

discovered of their political sympathies, it would seem an easy matter for the Honolulu Rifles to be encouraged to avoid the fray."

Mr. T paused for a moment. "That . . . can be arranged."

"Good. I'd rather you do it than I," Kashmir said. His eyes flicked to me then. It was almost my turn. I sat up straighter and surreptitiously wiped my sweaty palms on the legs of my trousers. "Next item," he went on. "The vault in the treasury holds an estimated—"

"I know the keys to the vault are held by a Mr. Frank Pratt," Milly said, interrupting. "A jumped-up little man, married well—"

"Mr. Franklin Seaver Pratt, the registrar of public accounts," Kashmir said crisply. "Recently appointed, though he served on the staff of Kamehameha the Fifth. Mr. Pratt, who resides on Beretania Street with his wife, Elizabeth Keka'aniau Pratt; Mrs. Pratt, who is grand-niece and blood heir of Kamehameha the Third. Mr. Pratt calls her Lizzie, I'm told. Yes, I'm aware of who holds the keys." I couldn't help but stare at him, and he smiled with only his lips. "Now, I estimate the weight of the treasure at a ton and a half. Could be over two, depending on how much of it is in silver."

"I must remind you," Mr. D said. "Our agreement regarding confidentiality is of utmost importance, should you decide to hire any ruffians to help you carry the weight. I trust this will not be a problem?"

"It will not," I said, hoping my voice wouldn't quaver, but then I tried not to laugh when heads whipped around, as though they'd forgotten I was there. The weight of the gold had been the easiest problem to solve. "And we won't be hiring any ruffians."

"You have a crew of five. How else will you manage this feat of strength? Or protect yourselves from the Royal Hawaiian Guard?" Mr. D said with unconcealed interest.

I met Mr. D's eyes, unwilling to even hint at the answer. "Unfortunately, confidentiality is of utmost importance."

His expression stayed pleasant, but barely. "Indeed."

"We can deliver your payment wherever you like, but we'll need to know in advance where that is," I said. "Unless you're coming with us that night?"

Mr. D sighed. "I believe I'd prefer an evening in. But we will send one representative. We have to be sure the job is done, after all, and done correctly."

Milly had gone pale. "And how will we decide on that representative?" he asked. "I cannot volunteer, sir, and I hope we're not doing anything so low class as drawing straws!"

"I will not be available that night, I assure you," Mr. T agreed. He thought for a moment. "Whatever night it may be."

"No," Mr. D said. "But I thought Mr. Hart would like the chance."

"Me?" Mr. Hart half stood, upsetting his teacup. The *guhzeng* music paused, and in the sudden, shocked silence, the dreamers stirred in their beds. He settled back down at a gesture from Mr. D, but the furious gleam was back in his eyes. "I see," he hissed through his beard. "I see how it is. The map is not enough for you. My shame is not enough for you. You would bleed me dry."

"The map is a doodle on a bit of paper, Hart," Milly said with a sneer. "Admittedly, so is a banknote, but the values are nowhere near the same."

"It was valuable enough to you when you all came to me with this scheme—"

"Gentlemen," Mr. D said, perhaps to remind them. "Mr. Hart, we need a member of our party to represent our interests, and you will do nicely. You are, after all, the bravest of our group, at least as judged by willingness to take risk." He brought his teacup to his lips, although he only pretended to drink.

"And will Mr. Hart bring the map at that time?" Slate said, his voice a touch too loud.

"I think that is unwise. What if it were to be damaged in the scrum?" Mr. D asked. "We will meet again after the event, at which time we will trade the map for the location of the treasure."

"What do you mean, the location?"

"In case there is an investigation, Captain. You cannot expect us to hide two tons of gold and silver in our gardens! Once the uproar dies down, we will retrieve it from its hiding place."

Slate clenched his fists. "When exactly do I get the map?

Mr. D spread his hands, palms up. "We can meet within a week. Perhaps two. Longer, if you are suspected of the theft. Patience is a high virtue, Captain."

Slate ground his teeth. I waited for the captain to refuse, to change his mind, but he said nothing more, so I did. "We cannot accept your proposal."

"Excuse me?"

"Nixie—"

I held up my hand, silencing my father, but I kept my eyes on Mr. D. "Since Mr. Hart will be coming with us for the theft, he might easily learn the location of the gold. This does not affect you—one man cannot carry it away, at least not without our special abilities. But it does affect *us*. If he tells you the hiding place, you have no reason to give us the map."

Mr. D looked at the captain, a hint of scorn in the curve of his mouth. "I didn't know you let your daughter make your deals."

Slate's face was stony. "I've told you before. She's more of an expert than me."

Mr. D wet his lips. "I don't suppose you'd accept my word of honor? Fine," he said when I laughed. "Hart will hand the map over after the gold is hidden."

"After it's stolen," I countered. "Or we'll leave it on the palace steps."

Behind his beard, Mr. D clenched his teeth. "It doesn't matter to me," he said, all appearances to the contrary. "After it's stolen, then. How long will it take for you to make your preparations?"

Kashmir and Slate both looked to me for the answer, and despite the circumstances, I felt the glow of pride. "It won't seem long to you," I said. "All we need to get started is a map. One of here and now, so we can return after we fetch what we need. I trust you can commission another from Mr. Sutfin."

Slate glanced at me, and then at Mr. D; I hadn't had the

chance to tell him about the map. But Mr. D didn't even bat an eye. "Why not use the one you have?"

I shook my head. "It has to be inked now, after we've made all our arrangements."

"But it takes the man half a year at least!" Milly said.

I shrugged. "I've heard patience is a virtue."

Mr. D's veneer of civility was thinning quickly. "The longer we wait for the theft," he growled, "the longer you wait for the map."

The captain glared at him. "If you think six months is a long time, try waiting sixteen years!"

Mr. Hart sat forward, catching Mr. D's eye. "I know someone who can draw," he said hurriedly, perhaps trying to defuse the tension. "He made the copy you showed the captain. He's not busy."

Mr. D nodded. In my chest—a sinking feeling.

"Good," Slate said. "Send him to the ship tomorrow. We'll all cross our fingers he can work fast. I won't be sorry to weigh anchor on this port."

And finally Slate gave in and reached out for a cup of tea—not his, which was empty, but mine. He downed the lot in one gulp.

CHAPTER
TWENTY-SIX

The next dawn, when the caladrius alighted on the rail, I was ready with a biscuit in a box.

The bird considered my proposal long and hard before deciding that hopping into the crate—which I'd found in the hold and emptied of penicillin—was an acceptable trade for a bit of bread. But when she did, I closed the box gently and set out for Chinatown.

I had to wait for Joss to open the shop, but she didn't seem surprised to find me on her doorstep. "You have money?"

"Better."

She laughed. "What is better than money?"

"A cure." I opened the box, and the caladrius tilted her head up toward her face and stared for several heartbeats. I watched the film spread like a caul over the pebble-black eyes. The bird ruffled her feathers, then shot straight up out of the box and toward the sun to burn away the blindness.

I regarded Joss. Her eyes were as wide and clear as a cloudless night sky.

"Ah," she said, after a very long moment, still staring at the empty box. She blinked twice, and on her wrinkled lips, the hint of a genuine smile. Her eyes roved over my face. "You do look like her. Your cheeks. Your chin. But . . ." The smile faded.

"You do not have her confidence. You are adrift, like your father. You are his daughter more than hers." She turned away. "Come inside," she said, leading me into the shop.

I set down the empty crate inside the door. I didn't mince words. "You know how to Navigate."

"I traveled in my youth, yes," she said. Her voice was soft, distracted, as she peered around the shop she must not have seen clearly for years. "Your father is special, but he is not unique."

"How many others are there?"

"I have only ever met two I recognized as such. Other than myself." She walked down the length of the store, drawing me behind her like a ship after a tug.

"Who?"

"You know them well." She ran her hand over the top of a glass jar and grimaced at the dust on her fingertips.

I narrowed my eyes. "Then my father is one . . . but who is the other?" She gave me a disappointed look, but I had already come to the answer. "*Me?* But that's . . . how can you know for sure?"

"I told you. I have seen your future."

I gnawed my thumbnail, unsure whether or not I believed her. "What did you see, exactly?"

"You told me you didn't want to know."

I made a face. "I should have known better than to pay in advance." I reached into my pocket and fished for coins. "If you want your half-dollar—"

"That's no longer the price."

"Well, that's all I'm willing to pay."

We stared each other down, and to my surprise, she broke first, her eyes sparkling as she laughed. It made her look very young. "I was wrong. You are like her." She reached out and touched my cheek; her hand was soft and cool. Then she drew back and tottered to her spot behind the counter. "I saw you at the helm of the black ship. You took hope to a barren shore and gave a woman a new life."

"That's sufficiently vague."

"It will come to pass by the time the week is out. Afterward, you may regret not asking further into the future."

"I don't care who I'll marry, and I don't want to know how I die."

"I don't see why not. I myself will never marry, and I will die in the Great Fire in 1886."

Suddenly the room seemed to narrow, and my heart squeezed in my chest. How did she know? "The Chinatown fire?"

"Where else would I be?"

"You can really see the future."

"Can't we all? I just have clearer eyes than most. Especially now. A favor to ask," she said then.

"For a price?" I countered.

Joss laughed again. "Certainly. In exchange I will give you hope." She slid a cylindrical leather case out from under the counter and put it in my hands, moving confidently now. "I will keep this box," she said, picking up the crate I'd brought the caladrius in. "As part of your payment to me."

I opened the case and slid out the map: Chinatown in 1886, in the aftermath of the fire. "Ah." A thick black line demarcated the outline of the destruction of the blaze, and near the center, someone had inked an X in red. "Where did you get this?"

"From your father, fifteen years ago. He asked me to tell his fortune. This map was his payment."

"What does the X mark?"

"X marks buried treasure." She went back to the counter, dragging the box behind her. "A note. An elixir for my condition. Money. A map of 1841. Everything I'll need for a new life."

Hope, she'd said, and a barren shore. "You'll come here in 1886 . . . after the fire you died in?"

"I *came* here in 1886, which was after the fire I *will* die in. I was a young woman at the time I arrived, and poisoned besides, but with the payment from Mr. D, I was able to make my way."

"Poisoned? You—" I put my hand to my temple, trying to piece it all together. "You came here in 1886, dug up this box, and went back to 1841. I give *you* a new life?"

She only smiled, but the importance of that had come to me. "And you introduced my parents."

No answer. She took out a sheet of rice paper and a brush, drawing choppy characters in short, quick strokes.

"If you know you'll die in the fire, why stay here now? If you know your fate, why wait for it?"

She paused then, her expression almost puzzled. "Because it is mine," she said, as though it was obvious. "Everything must come to an end, Nix. Your father would be happier if he could accept that." She glanced over the letter she was writing, finding her place. "Besides," she murmured, "there is always a sacrifice. If I was already there, I never could have come."

"You can't come to a map where you already exist?" She didn't answer my question; rather, she already had. My hand crept up to my necklace. "New York, 1981. That's why it didn't work."

"Didn't you ever wonder why all the maps he's collected failed?"

"Of course I did. But he wasn't here in 1868."

"No," she said. "You were."

I put my palms down on the counter to steady myself. "So this whole plan is pointless? The map Mr. D is selling is a dead ender?"

"As long as he tries to take you with him." She paused in her brushstrokes. "Of course, as long as you stay with him, you know you are safe," she said.

"So it's possible? He could erase my past?"

"That I cannot say," she said, and her regret nearly seemed real.

"Because you don't know? Or because there's nothing else you want in exchange for the information?"

"Because it would only be what *I* believe, and that is not what matters when you are traveling through the fog. But I do believe that some things are meant to be." She blotted the letter, then rolled it and tucked it into the leather case. Then she sighed. "Leave it on the shore, don't forget. I was close to him, you see, because I was his favorite."

"Whose favorite?"

"Do you still have the numbers I gave you? Remember them well," she said, ushering me out the door. "Good-bye, Nix. I don't think I will see you again in the time I have left. Although you may see me."

I returned to the ship, walking slowly. She had known what I was planning. Of course she did. She'd seen it years ago. She'd even sold me the map.

But she'd given me this one. The map she needed to escape, and a note to tell herself how. The leather case was heavy across my back.

What would happen if I threw it overboard and let it sink to the bottom of the bay?

I took the case in my hands as I reached the dock, the hungry sea rolling at my feet. Something wild inside dared me; I might discover, in an instant, for a moment, what was truly possible.

But I couldn't do it.

CHAPTER
TWENTY-SEVEN

I was still standing on the dock when the mapmaker arrived.

"Miss Song?"

I gripped the leather case in my hands like a talisman. Blake was carrying a black portfolio under his arm and a box of pens. "If I am to draw you a map," he said, "you must first promise me that you'll not become sentimental over it."

A smile began to creep unbidden across my lips; I bit them hard to chase it away. "I suppose you'd best come up."

Hearing our voices, Kashmir looked over the rail and laughed. "Ah, Mr. Hart. If I'd known to expect you, I'd have gotten a lei, though I suppose I could still dredge up a handful of seaweed."

"I'm sorry we got off on the wrong foot, Mr. Firas," Blake said blandly. "I can see now that your propriety is matched only by your good manners."

Kashmir grinned as he sauntered off to knock on the captain's door. Slate met us on the deck, his eyes bleary and flat. "You."

Blake didn't flinch under his unrelenting stare, but the captain was studying him as though he was a new species.

"What are you, an amateur cartographer?" Slate said finally.

"Even worse, sir. An amateur artist."

Slate scoffed, waving a vague hand in my face. "You're . . . taking care of this?"

"Aye, Captain."

"Good," he said, peering at Blake again. "There's a drafting table in my cabin. But don't lay a finger on anything else."

"I assure you, Captain," Blake said. "My intentions are honorable."

Slate cocked his head; understanding dawned on his face. "I meant don't touch my stuff." He rolled his eyes. "I need some coffee." Then he strode off toward the hatch without a backward glance.

But Kashmir was watching, his arms folded, standing against the door to the captain's cabin. As we approached, he smiled thinly. "Don't they say the road to hell is paved with honorable intentions?"

"That's *good* intentions," I said, making a face.

"Ah, yes. Of course." He turned the knob and opened the door with a flourish. "But perhaps Mr. Hart can go to hell anyway." I stepped inside easily, but Kashmir forced Blake to squeeze past him. I put my hand on the door, but he lingered in the doorway.

"Thank you, Kashmir," I said.

"I can come in to protect you from his intentions if you like."

"I can handle it." I shut the door firmly, with him on the other side of it.

The air in the cabin was cool, and Blake's expression was chillier still. "I think your father does you a disservice, letting him near you."

I folded my arms. "He's my best friend."

"You don't exactly seem spoiled for choice." But he held up his hand. "I apologize, Miss Song. I will not further impugn your crewmate." His eyes moved past mine to the shelves lining the walls. "You have so many maps," he said

then, moving around the room. He inhabited the space differently than I did; he was tentative, considerate, as though
everything was delicate and of great value. He laid his pens
and his hat on the drafting table and reached toward the
shelves—I took a breath—but his fingertips stopped inches
away from a touch. "Where are you going for the money?"

"What?"

"My father said you need a map so you may return, and
it would seem you haven't yet purchased his map, since he
is still in debt. You must be sailing to retrieve the payment.
Where are you going?"

"New York," I said; it was the first thing that came to
mind. "My father has his accounts there."

"Such a long journey. Couldn't he have the funds wired
to California?"

I wasn't about to get mired in more lies; instead, I went
on the offensive. "Do you want to tell my father how to manage his finances?"

It worked. "Forgive me," he said. "It's just that part of
me hadn't been expecting something so . . . prosaic. I was
imagining treasure maps and gold doubloons," he said, gesturing at the cupboards. Then he sighed. "And when do you
sail?"

"As soon as you're done with the map."

"Is that so? No wonder my father was so eager. It might be satisfying to delay," he said, raising one eyebrow. "And not only to spite the league."

I tried to look stern. "Mr. Hart—"

"I'm eager to spite your tutor."

I did laugh then, and his smile bloomed. Then he opened the portfolio and removed a wide sheet of vellum; it floated like a petal in his hands. He smoothed it onto the table, his inky fingers in sharp contrast to the pure cream of the page. "Instruct me, Miss Song. What am I to draw for you?"

"Here," I said, opening one of the cupboards and selecting a map. "Let me show you what we need." I unrolled the paper. "Here's the map we used to get here."

"Ah." His eyes roamed over the page, and after a moment, he raised his eyes to mine. "Sutfin, 1868? But he's only been in business since 1877. It's painted right there on his window."

"He misdated the map," I said.

"What an odd thing to do."

"Indeed." I sensed his questions coming, like a swelling wave, but there was nothing for it. "Now, we'll need a current map of Oahu to return."

"But . . ." Blake scanned the page. "This seems . . . but for the date—"

"Yes, it's a very good map," I said. "But we still need a new one. You may use the Sutfin as a template," I continued hurriedly. "But don't copy it exactly. Anything you know has changed recently on the island, you should make the change on the page."

His brow furrowed. "Changes in the harbor? Or on the island itself?"

"Either."

He laughed. "You can't be worried about running aground on Princess Pauahi's mausoleum."

"If it has changed since Sutfin did his map, please just draw it."

"What happens if I don't?"

"If you don't . . ." I hesitated, but in this case, perhaps the truth could indeed set me free. "If you don't, we will not be coming back once we go. The map must be accurate, or we cannot return."

He looked at me sideways and, perhaps seeing my expression, for once he did not ask why. Instead he gave me that half smile. "The mystery deepens, Miss Song."

His eyes were so inviting that for a moment, everything

in me wanted to reveal this part of myself, as though the truth was a butterfly, wings fluttering, green and gold and quivering to be free. I was a closed book, a rolled map, a dark territory, uncharted; I was surprised by my urgency, but after all, to be known was to exist.

A knock at the door interrupted my thoughts. Kashmir didn't wait for an answer; he breezed into the room juggling a lantern, a pair of buckets, and a piece of flat glass.

"I thought you could use this." He upended the buckets on the floor, put the lantern between them, and balanced the glass over the whole assembly. "You can backlight the original and mark off the measurements," he said. "Should make it all go faster, and the faster the better."

"Thank you," Blake said. "Did your people invent this too?"

"Get to work, Mr. Hart." Then he propped the door open and went back outside, leaving a long silence in his wake.

I sighed. "Do you have any more questions about the map?"

Blake didn't answer immediately; he was tapping one finger absently on the table, and his eyes were far away. "I believe you've implied," he said slowly, "that your payment to the Hawaiian League depends on the accuracy of my work."

"Have I?" My eyes went to the open door, but he had kept his voice low. "You should strive for . . . integrity," I said. "But if the map is inaccurate, the captain won't know until it's too late."

Blake worked for days. He spent half his time practicing in his sketchbook, sitting on the floor, his back against the wall, his knees bent like an easel with the book propped upon them. Once his techniques were perfected, he'd turn to the map, hunching over the drafting table with intense focus.

He took pains with the path of each meandering stream, careful with the curves of the scalloped shorelines, and traced the lacy edges of bays and inlets with a slow, steady hand. He wrote the names of each region and city with even block letters. He smudged ink into the valleys and shaded the elevation of the mountains using a technique I would have called pointillism, if I could have remembered whether the term was in wide use yet. Instead, I settled on admiring the details in the work.

"Sutfin should have done better. See here." He swept

his pens and inks to one side of the table and unrolled the old map side by side with his version. "On his, you see this structure marked 'Old Ruin'? It's the foundation of Kamehameha III's summer home, Kaniakapupu." He pointed. "I've put that in. And here, where his map shows nothing, there's actually another ruin of a *heiau*. And of course the waterfall I showed you, and lots of villages Sutfin missed. I hope it's not too much?"

"You *are* an expert. You did all this from memory?"

"Ah, well." He grinned at me. "When you like something well enough, certain details become . . . unforgettable."

I couldn't help it; I laughed, delighted.

"I can start over, if you'd like? Try again? With the map, I mean."

"The map. Of course. No," I said. "I love seeing the islands through your eyes." My gaze fell on his sketchbook on the corner of the table, and I reached for it. "In fact, the maps you—"

His hand darted out under mine to cover the book. I froze; his face had gone serious—no, trepidatious. But after a long moment, he removed his hand and turned back to the map. "Go ahead," he said, almost brusquely, picking up one of his pens to refill the ink in the reservoir.

I took the sketchbook. Suddenly I was nervous, too. But my curiosity overcame my hesitation. I opened the book and found what I'd hoped, what I'd feared. "I thought you'd been practicing drawing the map," I said softly as I flipped through the pages.

"I never thought I'd find a more compelling subject than the islands," he said, still pretending to focus on the pen. Then he looked up through his lashes. "I wanted to capture you before you are gone."

My lips parted, but not to speak. Warmth crept into my stomach like sunlight through deep water, but I turned my head, confused, and immediately regretted it.

It took another half day to place the last flourishes. He added a tiny square to represent Princess Pauahi's new tomb at Mauna 'Ala, as well as a detailed, decorative compass rose. He did seem to be dawdling as he worked, taking his time at meals, and breaks for fresh air, though he no longer spent time sketching. Eventually, though, despite the distractions and delays, there was nothing left to add but his name, and the map was complete.

It was a work of art, rich in details only he knew. Had he drawn accurately, or had he added something in, something imperceptible to me, to keep us from returning and prevent the Hawaiian League from collecting its payment? I couldn't tell, and I wouldn't ask.

Blake chewed his lip as Slate studied the paper, spread across the drafting table. The captain gave it his highest praise, considering he was in one of his darker moods: a nod and a hint of a grim smile. He showed Blake and me to the door. "Make ready!" he called to the crew. Then he shut the door hard behind us.

Blake raised his eyebrow. "You're leaving so soon?"

"Before the day ends." I led him off the ship, dodging around the sudden flurry of activity, and we both stood on the dock, at the base of the gangplank, reluctant to say good-bye.

"I should have worked more slowly."

I thought of Joss then, gazing clear-eyed at her future. "Why hold off the inevitable?"

"Why, for the sake of the ephemeral, Miss Song," he said. "And in the hope of making it last."

My paths diverged, and for a moment I imagined I, too, could see the future, but two versions, the ship and the shore. I stood frozen for what seemed like an hour—an eternity.

Was I more like my father than I thought? No. The beauty of the ephemeral was in its impermanence; I couldn't have let myself feel for Blake had I not known there would be an end. And I could admit it now: I did feel for him. There was safety here, at the end of our short story, and it made me bold. Though my heart shook like a luffing sail, I would not leave the moment with only my regrets, so I rose up on my tiptoes and kissed him before I could think twice.

It was strange and stomach churning and over too soon; still, his pale cheeks went even paler, and then the bright pink spots reappeared, deep as the blush on a ripe apricot. "You have changed me," he breathed. "I never thought I would look longingly out to sea."

I gathered my own longings in my fists, clenched by my sides. "Good-bye, Blake."

The seconds stretched, but then he tipped his hat. "Nix."

When he rode away, he did not look back. I knew because I watched until he was out of sight.

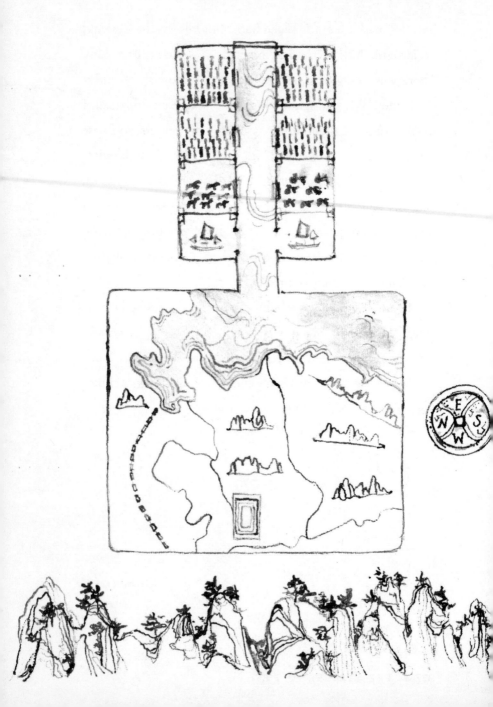

CHAPTER
TWENTY-EIGHT

We clipped along under our unfurled sails, their bellies full with the breeze, and soon the city of Honolulu was just a dark smudge on the thin gold band of the shoreline. Then I realized Slate and I were both watching the shore as it receded, so I turned to face the sea, and the sight of the open horizon was as heady as the salt wind.

After Blake had gone, I had placed the map we'd be using—the map Joss had sold me, the ancient, crumbling piece of paper, probably among the very first pieces of paper ever made—on the wide drafting table. I'd unfolded it carefully, teasing it apart; it was stamped in faded red at the bottom and brushed with quick, bold strokes of ink in choppy handwriting.

As Joss had promised, the map did indeed depict the tomb of Emperor Qin, who had died in the second century B.C. The Chinese historian Sima Qian had described it in his historical opus, the *Shiji*.

After his death, and just before all he built had crumbled, Emperor Qin had been buried in a massive underground complex underneath Mount Li in Xianyang. He rested in a representation of his palace placed in the center of a scale model of China itself, with rolling hills cast of bronze, mountains assembled out of fine cut stone, and rivers and seas of mercury. Along with the rich clothes, fine jewels, and masterly weapons with which most prestigious persons were buried during that era, Emperor Qin was guarded in death by some eight thousand terra-cotta warriors. They were what had caught my interest.

As Joss had mentioned, the legend said that in the lofty vault of the tomb, these warriors had sprung to attention to serve the emperor in his afterlife, along with the various terra-cotta acrobats, jugglers, musicians, and concubines. This clay court was rounded out by a coterie of living attendants who'd been sealed up with the emperor as a reward for being his most favored.

I gazed at the familiar handwriting. When Joss had sold me this map, she'd said it had come from a dying woman. Suddenly I was appalled that I'd considered throwing the leather case into the sea.

After I laid the old map down on the table, I covered it

with a sheet of glass to protect it from the sea air, or from coffee spills. Then, following my internal script, I cleared the cabin of cups and plates and put away all the books on the shelves, secure behind their rails. But most importantly, Slate and I sat together, he in the attitude of a Buddha, cross-legged, and I with my knees drawn up to my chin. This wasn't our typical exchange, however, where I told him all I'd learned about the legend and era we were visiting and he listened. Instead, it was my father teaching me.

He was, as usual, an abysmal teacher, and soon enough I found myself shaking my head. "What do you mean, you just let go?"

"Once you know where you're going, and you're sure it's there, you have to let go of where you're from. You look straight forward, you keep the land ahead in sight, and you don't look back."

"Literally or metaphorically?"

"Both. Once you sight your shore, you keep an eye on it. But you'll never see it if you're still in port."

"Running away and running to."

"Sort of, yeah."

I frowned at him, but he seemed in earnest. Furthermore, he had no reason to lie; I'd shown him the map and he'd admitted he had no chance of Navigating there. My father knew almost nothing about ancient China; he had never read the *Shiji*. "How did you learn?" I said then. "Who taught you?"

"I . . . no one." He sounded surprised at the question. "I taught myself."

"How?"

He ran his hand through his dark blond hair, and for a moment, I saw lines of blue ink on his scalp. "I . . . tripped."

I made a face. "I should have known."

"No. I really—I fell. I was on the stairs. Maybe it was a little of both. I was at the library."

"New York Public?"

"With the lions, yeah. I used to go there when my—Christ, it was ages ago—when my own parents . . . they hated each other. Fought all the time. I would go to the library and . . . It was different back then. 1981. The librarians didn't watch too close." His jaw worked as he searched for words, but I stayed quiet, waiting—he spoke so rarely about his past.

"I found an old—it was in a storage room—an old map, one of those architect drawings of the library from when it was being built, 1903, I think. There were photos too. I must have been staring at it for hours. It was very real in my head. When I was leaving, I fell down the stairs, and there was a moment I could see the picture of Fifth Avenue—no concrete—and when I landed it was facedown in the mud. It was an accident, that first time. All I really wanted was to be somewhere else."

His eyes were faraway, as though he could see that elsewhere from where he sat. In the silence I heard the gentle lapping of the water against the hull. "If you can go on foot . . . why did you build a ship?"

"It's a safe space, no matter where I go. And I can bring everyone I need with me." He sighed. "It was easier back then. Nowadays . . . I don't know where I'd go without you."

"Without me, you'd already be where you want to go, Captain."

"No. Without you I wouldn't be anywhere at all." He dropped his gaze, and I was at least as uncomfortable as he was. I didn't know what to say—or rather, how to say it. I had imagined leaving so many times, but the excitement I'd anticipated had not rushed in. I felt hollow.

He could have everything he wanted, but only without me, and I hesitated to leave—why? Was it the fear I might be unmade? Or was it because when I was free to go, I could remember all the reasons I had to stay?

"Let's look at the map again, shall we?" he suggested then, and I sprang to my feet too eagerly.

It was a challenging first trip, to put it mildly. Fairy-tale maps were always the most difficult, and living terra-cotta warriors were certainly a fairy tale. But I was confident; the captain said I had to be. And Joss had said she'd seen me at the helm.

We were to use all possible precautions for the journey. Kashmir had his long knife hung on his belt, and I'd watched Bee check the bullets in her revolver. Slate had a long piece of oak, a length of an old yardarm, and Rotgut, having carefully considered the strengths and weaknesses of a terra-cotta army, had picked up a hammer.

I was the only one uncomfortable with a weapon. Fighting wasn't my strength. I wasn't even certain we'd need to. The warriors were there to protect the emperor; we didn't plan to threaten him, but it was always best to be prepared, especially when traveling so far. After all, what else might we encounter in a place where clay soldiers came to life? What else did the mapmaker believe?

As Slate took the helm and pointed us away from shore, I didn't wait for Bee to tell me to start hauling in the sails. Kashmir and I worked side by side in silence, clearing the deck (including my hammock and the washing rope), battening the hatches, securing the halyard, cleaning the drains and the scuppers, and tying off lines. It was as easy as the waltz we'd shared; we slipped past each other through tight spots without having to push, hauled lines together that neither of us could haul alone, and knew what the other needed without having to be told.

And yet . . . there was a quality in our silence that had never existed before, almost imperceptible from the outside, but such a difference, like salty water instead of sweet. It was the same feeling I'd had the night of the ball, as we'd stood on the deck. I'd been unable to speak then. I'd been unable to speak for years. I steeled myself. "Kashmir?"

He was stringing the jack line and he didn't look up, but by his face, I knew he'd heard me.

"Kash."

His shoulders rose and fell in a sigh, but he met my eyes. *"Amira—"*

"I just wanted to say—"

"You don't have to," he said quickly. "It was my mistake. The other night I thought—" He shook his head and laughed a little. "Well. Will you forgive me? I only hope it hasn't hurt what we have."

My hand went to my pendant; the pearl was warm and smooth on my skin. "And what is it we have?" I asked softly.

"Our friendship," he said. "As you've said many times." He searched my face. "Yes?"

I hesitated, but only for a moment. "Yes."

He nodded, and after a moment, he opened his arms. *"Viens."*

I stepped into his embrace, and he wrapped his arms around me . . . only to clip the jack line to my belt, giving it a yank. I gave him a shove in return, then I reached back and unclipped my line. "I don't get one this time, remember? I've got the helm."

"Oh, aye, Captain," he said, grinning. "Why do you think the rest of us are roped in?"

I stuck my tongue out at him. Tying in was standard for any difficult journey, where the rough seas in the Margins might climb over the deck to clutch at our feet. Of course, no one but the captain had ever Navigated the *Temptation*, so none of us really knew what we might face when I took the helm. Would the fog rise for me?

On deck, Kashmir would have to ride out whatever I steered us into. As soon as I attempted to Navigate, the ship—my home—and the crew—my family—became my responsibility, and fear wrapped cold claws around my spine as I walked to the map room and shut the door behind me.

I'd known for years how to use a compass and read the stars. But now, as I stood alone in front of the drafting table where the two maps lay side by side—on my left, where we were; on my right, where we were going—I didn't know up from down, much less east from west. My eyes slid from one map to the next: from the blue Pacific under the open sky, to the silver sea deep beneath a man-made mountain. Right off the edge of paradise and into the afterlife, as long as I didn't steer us into some kind of purgatory.

I took a deep breath, then another, trying to calm my nerves. The smell of the maps and the books—the ink and the paper—helped me relax, and my hand went to the pearl at my throat. I bent my head and studied the map of the emperor's tomb, turning the lines on the page into a shoreline in my head, the shore I would expect to see through the fog.

"It will be there," Slate had said to me. "And sort of . . . not there. Do you understand?"

"Yes," I'd replied. "And no."

"Smart ass." And he had reached out to ruffle my hair, like he used to when I was little.

But the memory of our conversation, that rare closeness,

was cold comfort. I shivered then; the air actually was colder. I had to get to the helm. I took one last look at the two maps and left the cabin, but I paused in the open door.

The sky that had been so blue not an hour before had faded to a tea-stained gray, and the sunlight, once golden, had the aged tint you see before a thunderstorm. The margins were coming up fast.

I threw a glance back over the stern, at the little island disappearing. Would I see her shores again? If Blake had chosen to thwart the Hawaiian League, I might never return. Against the biting chill of the stiff breeze, I wrapped myself in the memory of our kiss—my first—and walked toward the helm.

Slate watched me warily as I approached, and it was several moments before he stood aside and let me take the wheel. My palms were slippery on the brass, which was still warm from his grip. I wiped my hands on my trousers and grasped the wheel again. Almost immediately, wisps of fog drifted up like steam from the steely water, the air thickening like churned cream.

I heard Slate catch his breath. Goose bumps skittered across my forearms as I kept our course steady into the mist until it swallowed us completely. Would it lift again, or would we join the other ships—the *Flying Dutchman* or the *Mary Celeste*—and journey without end, ghosts in the fog?

The wind dropped, then gusted, then dropped again for a long minute. Suddenly it was back, whipping through my hair and lashing it against my cheeks. I couldn't see more than thirty feet ahead in the swirling fog, but the sea was calm, almost eerily so. I squinted as light flickered far away in the clouds, followed, half a minute later, by sullen, distant thunder and the taste of metal on my tongue. The wind snapped in the jib, and I tensed. Then my father put his hand on my shoulder and squeezed.

I gritted my teeth and tightened my grip on the wheel, still staring into the pearly mist off the bow. As my eyes slid across the insubstantial gray horizon, I became aware of an odd unspooling in the center of my chest, an incongruous, lighthearted feeling that made me want to laugh. At first it was gentle, a tug and a flutter, upward like the rope on the kite I'd flown those years ago, and my body trembled as would the needle of a compass seeking north. Was this the draw of the faraway shore? Then came the counterpoint, a nauseating sinking in my gut, down like a fish on a line, and as we sailed farther into the margins, the drag deepened like the haul of the anchor on its chain. But still something drew me forward, and in the center, I stretched like the sails in a gale wind.

Sweat broke out on my forehead, and I swallowed bile. The muscles in my back grew taut and my spine creaked as I tried to catch my breath; the pain in my chest was unbearable, and I thought I would start to fray like a rope. What was holding me back? I knew the answer before the question had finished forming, and I pushed the thought of Blake from my mind, letting that anchor drop away, down, down, until there was nothing behind me and I was unmoored in the current pulling me onward as steadily as time.

"Can't see a thing!" Rotgut called from the lookout, but suddenly I could. Through a break in the fog, a shoreline, vague but there, as though I were seeing a picture beneath a sheet of vellum. I blinked twice, and my eyes refocused. It was like that optical illusion where you hold a tube against the side of your hand and you can see a hole right through your palm, clear as day and yet impossible at the same time.

I gave the wheel a quarter turn, and the ship creaked and dipped. "Do you see it?" I called, my heart pounding faster.

"Nothing yet!" Rotgut said. His voice sounded very distant; I could no longer see him in the fog.

A few drops of rain hit my cheeks. The sun dimmed in

the sky, and the deck seesawed. Lights flickered at the edge of my vision, and I thought I heard the far-off groan of a mast under full sail. Out of the corner of my eye I saw Kash working alone to trim our main, hauling down on the hawser, straining against the swelling sheet. Bee was somewhere up near the bow, invisible in the fog. "Slate—"

"I'm going."

He left my side and went to Kashmir, but I had lost my concentration, and the hint of the shoreline vanished. I put the crew out of my mind as my eyes swept the horizon. I knew it was there—

Yes, *there*. Clearer now. Darker. Just off the prow.

The wind turned icy, and it carried a foul smell, like sour musk. My skin was clammy against my jacket, but I did not take my eyes off the shore. We pitched upward on a swell, down on its back, and up again on the next. The rain intensified, small wind-driven drops that stung my face and lashed in bands across the black water, but I did not take my eyes off the shore. The sky darkened to charcoal and the fog swallowed Kash and Slate, but I could still see the shore as clear as a mirror.

Then the ship seemed to leap upward under my feet, and I fell to my knees as the wind and the rain simply stopped.

Suddenly everything was still, and the cold darkness was absolute.

My heart throbbed in my throat. Had I been struck blind? Blind *and* deaf; the silence was overwhelming. Then again, so was the smell, that cloying musky odor I'd noticed on the wind. There was movement too, an odd swaying of the ship. Then I heard Slate's laugh: wordless, delighted. Had he seen it too—our distant shore, the same shore I had seen?

The fog was gone. As my eyes adjusted, I made out the glimmer of starlight above us and the silvery moonlit shine of the glassy water below, although I saw no moon in the sky. Then Rotgut swore. He lifted the lamp at the top of the mast. It wasn't the sky I was seeing.

A hundred feet above our heads, the light of our lanterns was glittering back at us from a ceiling studded with diamonds. In this cavern, the sky was a bowl with stars stuck on it. I recognized the constellations . . . Orion, or—in China— the face of the White Tiger of the West. And Hydrus, the Snake's tail.

I hadn't seen moonlight on the calm sea; rather, we floated on a rippling pool of mercury, just as Sima Qian had said. Where the waves of quicksilver lapped the shore, our light shone on the skeletons of dying trees looming over piles of shriveled leaves on browning blades of grass. Far off, at the edge of the light, the gleam of red lacquer and bronze: the sarcophagus of Emperor Qin in the center of the blasted, barren terrain. We'd done it.

I'd done it.

I was so proud of myself, it took me three heartbeats to realize the ship was listing.

CHAPTER
TWENTY-NINE

The deck tilted starboard in slow motion; as the rudder twisted, the wheel spun. I grabbed for it, but it wrenched itself out of my hands. I clutched the base of the wheel and tried to haul myself to my feet.

"What's happening?" Slate said, stumbling toward the mast and gripping it in both hands.

"The mercury!"

"What about it?"

"It's denser than water!"

Bee had slipped down nearly to the rail, but she was arrested by her harness. Kashmir was the only one still on his feet. He sprang past me to pull himself against the port rail on the high side, but it was too little, too late. Creaking, the ship continued to tip.

I looked up at Rotgut in alarm. He was wrapped

around the mast; even in the dim light I could see the whites of his eyes. The glow from the lantern he held brightened as the crow's nest swung toward the wall and, with a crunch and a jolt, slammed into the stone. Rotgut cried out as the *Temptation* stopped there, the deck at a forty-five-degree angle. "My leg!"

I pulled myself up with the wheel; it didn't budge in my hands. The top of the mast had snapped, and Rotgut's knee was pinned between the platform of the crow's nest and the rough stone wall. He was gripping the flesh of his thigh in pain, but he wasn't moving, and I could see why. The slightest motion would send him scraping down the wall as the ship capsized.

"No one move," I said, nearly afraid to breathe. "We need ballast."

Slate closed his eyes. "I wish you'd thought of that before we got here."

"Me too."

"Is it poisonous?" Bee whispered, staring down at the silvery pool five feet below her. Her voice echoed oddly in the tomb.

"I . . . I don't know. Qin believed it was an elixir, but—never mind," I said. "Just let me . . ." I half-turned toward the hatch as the thought occurred, and even that slight motion made the ship slip sideways. Rotgut's scream echoed in the tomb.

"Kashmir?"

"*Amira?*"

"The bag."

"What bag?"

"The bag on the nail, the one I use to bail the bilge. Can you go down and empty it?"

He didn't bother answering; he unclipped his jack line and moved along the rail, hand over hand, until he was in line with the hatch. Then he let go and slid down, catching the opening with his fingertips and swinging inside. Rotgut screamed again as he slid another foot down the wall.

We waited on deck, keeping our positions as though a gorgon had flown through. My palms were slick on the wheel, but I did not adjust my hands. I did not move a muscle but to tighten my grip until my arms shook. Rotgut sighed then, and after what felt like an eon, the ship began to tilt back aright.

As soon as I could let go of the wheel, I scrambled over to the mast. Slate was already loosening the halyard. I shimmied up toward Rotgut, slowly at first, but the ship was more and more stable. I grimaced as I came eye to eye with the side of his shin; it had been skinned from knee to ankle, and blood dripped down his leg and off his toes. He screwed his face into the semblance of a smile.

"It's not broken. Looks worse than it is." He wiggled his toes and then hissed through his teeth. "But it feels worse than it looks."

The crow's nest was smashed, but the pulley below it was intact. I clipped Rotgut's harness to the halyard, and Bee and Slate lowered him to the deck. I climbed down after him, and by the time I'd arrived, Slate was using his shirt to staunch the blood. He looked up at me. "It's like road rash."

"You know I've never ridden a bike." I wrinkled my nose at the sight of the wound; when daubed clear of blood, the scrape was the pale pink of the bottom of a rose petal. "There's a first-aid kit in the cupboard under the desk."

Slate put Rotgut's arm around his shoulders and helped him stagger to his feet. "Come on. I've got some painkillers." Rotgut laughed, and I made a face as they hobbled off toward the map room.

I found Kashmir downstairs, sluicing water from his bare arms. I picked up his shirt—he'd tossed it in a wet linen puddle on the floor—and wrung it out into the open hatch of the bilge. "Good job," I said to him, tossing him the shirt.

"Quick thinking," he replied, clapping me on the shoulder. Then he smelled his shirt and wrinkled his nose. "I think there was a dead whale in that bag. A small one, but still."

I laughed. "Change, then. I know you have plenty of clothes."

I went into my own cabin then, to get Joss's map, but I stopped when I stepped in a puddle. The porthole was shut—the water had come from Swag's bucket, upended on the floor by the starboard side. I grabbed it and swore; the little dragon was nowhere to be seen. I pawed through my things, but he wasn't under my quilt or in my jewelry box.

My hands stilled, and I chewed the inside of my cheek. There was nothing else I could do. He knew where the pearls were when he wanted to come back. I threw a couple of dresses over the puddle to soak up the water and grabbed the map case, slinging it over my shoulder.

I joined the others back above deck. When I saw Kashmir, I shook my head, impressed. I was still bedraggled from the rain during our journey, but he'd even combed his hair.

I stood beside him at the rail. The air was chilly in the

tomb, and it soaked into my wet clothes and curled next to my skin. Together, we peered into the dim gloom. Waves from our sudden appearance still rippled against the sculpted shore to portside, the representation of the coast of China, where the emperor rested in the central place of honor. His servants would be elsewhere.

All except one. His favorite.

"It's very quiet," Kashmir said.

"It is." The sound of the water, the ship, our voices, all were swallowed by the darkness, and nothing came back out of it. Beyond the circle of light from the ship, there was no sign of life. The only movement here was our own.

Kash sighed and shrugged one shoulder. "Better than the alternative, I suppose."

My head was still light from the thrill—or from exhaustion—but I could still clearly recall the map I'd used to bring us here. "The terra-cotta armies would be in a side chamber," I said, crossing carefully to the bow. The sea of mercury was bordered by the stone wall; was that deep shadow halfway down its length a doorway? "We'll need to row over there."

Together with Kashmir, Slate and I stared at the dinghy.

"It'll tip without ballast," Slate said.

"I know." I wrinkled my nose. "It won't be pleasant rowing in a tub of bilge water."

"Tell me about it," Kash said, shaking back his wet curls. "The bag is empty anyway. You don't have a magic pocket full of lead, do you?"

"This might be the only time you'll find me regretting giving up that aboriginal water toad." I folded my arms and sighed, trying to think. "We need something very heavy."

"Or a different boat," Slate said. "Something flat, with more surface area. Like a really big tray. Something stable."

Kashmir tapped his chin. "Could we take the doors off the hinges downstairs and nail them together?"

"We need an outrigger," I said. Kash and Slate looked at me. "Like the Hawaiians used on their sailing canoes. Or a catamaran."

Working together, we fashioned a crude outrigger out of the repair kit we kept in the hold. Laying one beam parallel to the dinghy, we attached it with two perpendicular crosspieces, one at the bow and one at the stern, and lashed the whole contraption together with sisal rope. Then we lowered the boat to the mirrored surface; it sat there as light as a leaf on a pond.

"Let's be quick," Bee said. "Ayen says it's crowded here. The air is thick with spirits."

I sucked air through my teeth. "Are they dangerous?"

She took a moment to answer. "No . . . they only miss the light."

I shivered as a drop of cold water from my damp hair trickled down my neck and ran down my spine. Slate laid his hand on my arm, his face serious. "Kashmir and I can go. Rest if you're tired."

"Rest?" I couldn't keep the disbelief off my face. "And miss this?"

The captain squeezed my shoulder. Then his brow furrowed. "What is that, there?" he said, tapping the leather case on my shoulder.

I hesitated. "A map."

"Of what?"

"It's 1886. Joss gave it to me."

His eyes narrowed. "Chinatown? The Great Fire?"

"She asked me to bring it here."

He dropped his hand to his side, tapping his fingers on his thigh, his eyes distant. "I always wondered how she knew."

"Knew what?"

"Knew I had a map like that. I hadn't remembered it myself. But she asked for it specifically. Gave her fortune-telling a bit of credibility. I wonder if she really saw everything she predicted."

"Maybe I *should* have asked her about my future."

"I'm glad you didn't," he said, his face grim once again as he stared out into the shadows on the bronze shore.

CHAPTER
THIRTY

Kashmir climbed down into the dinghy, and I followed after him. The rowboat bobbed a little when I settled in, but the modifications made it very steady. I was put in mind of those pond striders, the water-walking bugs. I let Kashmir man the oars. He shipped one, laying it in the bottom of the dinghy, and pulled the other out of the oarlock to use like a paddle, with two hands, leaning in and pushing through the mercury first on one side, then the other.

We sculled along toward the massive stone wall, and I closed my eyes to better see my memory. "According to the map, this central part of the tomb is rectangular, with canals leading out in each cardinal direction. Along either side of the canals are the rooms where the warriors are."

"Why are you whispering?"

I opened my eyes and kicked him. The boat bobbed, and I froze for a moment. Kash had the decency to stifle his laugh. "The soldiers seem quiet so far, but I don't want to press our luck," I said, my voice low. "The story is, they guard Qin's riches and his actual . . . person."

"So, his decaying body?"

"Yes. Don't touch it."

"Wasn't going to."

"And don't take anything."

"You're no fun."

There was indeed an arched doorway, twenty feet high, midway along the wall. Kash turned the boat toward it, and as we approached, the light from our lantern illuminated the damp stone, which was marred at even intervals by sooty black streaks above the burned-out oil lamps. But the lamps could not have been dark long. I smelled the scent of sweet oil and bitter flame, cutting through the sour odor that seemed to permeate my very skin.

"There's something wrong."

Kashmir froze in midstroke, beaded droplets of quicksilver dripping from the oar. "Care to elaborate?"

"In the legend, Sima wrote the lamps would burn forever, and they're out."

"It makes sense, *amira*. There is not enough oil in all the world to burn forever."

"No, I know, but in the myth, they're supposed to last. So were the trees, but they're dying too. Then again . . ." I bit my lip. "Sima didn't draw the map."

"Who did?"

I was, nervous, for some reason, to say it aloud. "I think it was Joss."

"Ah." We sculled along for a moment in silence. "So. Do you suppose she believed the soldiers would come to life? Or that they were no more than fancy pottery?"

"But why would she have sent us if . . . ugh, that's a stupid question."

"We're here now. We might as well check."

Our little boat passed between two huge archways that opened onto rooms where matching junks were moored, their beautiful red lacquer sides studded with gold coin-shaped reliefs. The masts were rigged with silken sails, ready for the terra-cotta sailors who manned her ebony deck.

"That's lucky," I murmured.

"Hmm?"

"If this works, we can tow one of the junks back with us

and use it to get into Honolulu Harbor," I explained. "The *Temptation* is pretty recognizable."

Beyond those chambers, there was another opening, this one smaller and set above the waterline with stone steps leading up. Kashmir pulled us near enough for our light to crawl inside; painted pottery horses stood, hitched to chariots cast in bronze. They were absolutely immobile.

"Wait," I said as he dipped the oars. I lifted the lantern higher, inspecting the shadows at the corner of the doorway, and then I flinched.

"What?"

I pointed. Starkly lit and edged in shadow, I could make out a bloated hand, reaching through the doorway toward us, as though in supplication. That was the source of the smell. We were breathing in the dead.

"A grave robber?" Kashmir pushed us off from the bottom step.

"No . . . Qin had the artisans who built the tomb buried with him, along with his chief officials and . . . and his favorite concubines." I took a shallow breath; the air was heavy, suffocating. "The exits were sealed with tons of earth."

"But Joss escaped."

"Yes." I took another breath, the strap of the leather case tight across my chest.

Kashmir and I continued down the waterway, passing a space made up like a stable, with more horses and foals tended by terra-cotta grooms. Next we saw a room filled with replica officials holding clay tablets and scrolls to tally up the emperor's riches, then a chamber of clay concubines, every delicate face cast in an everlasting smile . . . a smile that seemed familiar to me. In the lap of one kneeling form lay the head of a dead artisan, as though he'd laid down to rest.

In the dim light, I could just make out two huge bronze doors at the end of the quicksilver canal, cast with reliefs of dragons ascending to heaven. Debris was piled high at the base of the doors, the mercury pooling and seeping through the rubble—no . . . not rubble. As I stared, I recognized the shapes of heads and hands, arms and legs. Bile rose in my throat. The masons and artists, the tile setters and painters, the sculptors and plaster workers and carpenters and gardeners who had used the best of their skills for the glory of their emperor had found their way here, to die before the bronze gates cutting them off forever from the country they had re-created in this necropolis.

My heartbeat was fluttery, irregular. Was Joss really here

somewhere, holding on? Should I look for her?

What was she eating?

Then I gasped and pointed.

Immediately, Kash raised the oar like a club. "What is it?"

"Something's moving!"

"Where?"

"Look, the ripples!"

Both of us stared at the surface of the mercury; the rocking of our own boat had marred the patterns, but after a moment he saw it too—a trembling V, something small swimming toward us.

"Wait . . . is that . . ." Kashmir lowered the oar, and a moment later, Swag's reptilian head popped over the edge of the boat, quicksilver beading on his gold scales.

"How did you get out here?" I said, my voice hoarse with relief. He didn't look to have suffered from his swim, and the mercury slid right off. Still, I reached out to him gingerly, and he clambered up my arm to settle on my neck. "Stay," I said, hoping he would obey.

"I see soldiers," Kash said then, pointing toward the last doorway on our right. I stroked Swag's smooth scales, hot against my skin, as we bumped against the steps.

Kashmir lifted his lantern. The light threw crazy shadows,

but everything else was still: the taller generals, the kneeling archers, the straight-backed spearmen. My legs shook as I climbed out of the dinghy, careful not to touch the mercury.

"Hello?" I said, my voice swallowed by the closing dark, my breath purling in the air. *"Ni hao?"* No sound returned but the dripping, far away, of a trickle of water. The silence of the dead was the sound of despair. I reached for Kashmir's hand and stepped through the door.

Although they all stood in straight rows, no two warriors were alike. Every face was different: fierce determination, boredom, pride. Their uniforms varied as well, painted in greens and blues, pinks and lilacs, bright colors with no single soldier the same as the next. They held real weapons, fine swords, spears with bright bronze tips, graceful wooden bows. All were still, but every stony gaze was almost lifelike. Almost.

I stood face-to-face with an imposing general, his armor washed with Han purple, his hair pulled into a high knot. The lamplight gleamed dully in the painted orbs of his terra-cotta eyes. I moved on to an infantryman and rapped my knuckles on his hollow chest. It sounded just like a flower pot. None of these statues displayed the slightest interest or inclination in waking up and walking about.

"Well," Kashmir said. "You came very close."

"Shh." Joss was slick, but would she go so far as to sell me a worthless map? I racked my memory. The warriors were supposed to have come to life in the tomb; clearly that hadn't happened. Yet. How could I get a bunch of clay men to come to life?

Clay men that came to life . . . various gods and goddesses often breathed life into clay men and women, including the goddess Nuwa, in Chinese mythology, but she was apparently declining to make an appearance. Golems were made of clay and given life when a person wrote the magic word on their foreheads, but golems were a Jewish myth.

I decided to try it. I believed in golems, didn't I? I just had to remember the magic word. I shut my eyes to concentrate. "It's Hebrew for truth," I said.

"Quoi?"

"I'm thinking. The Hebrew word for truth brings them to life. What's the word?"

"I don't speak Hebrew."

"Quiet!" I pressed the bridge of my nose. "Truth. Truth. But the trick of it is when you erase the first letter, the golem stops because the word spells . . . spells death. *Emet!* The word is *emet*." I squeezed the last bit of water from my hair into my cupped palm. Then I dipped my finger and wrote EMET on the general's broad forehead.

The thirsty clay absorbed the water, and the letters faded. Nothing else happened.

"Damn."

"Maybe they don't speak Hebrew either."

"No," I said slowly. "They wouldn't." A thought kept buzzing by, like a mosquito in my ear.

"You have any other magic words?"

Something about Chinese tradition and numbers . . . and Joss the day we first met. "Four," I said. "Four is death." Swag raised his head from my chest and hissed. "Shh. Five is *wu* and it sounds like 'me' but also 'not.' Me and not me. So fifty-four would be . . ."

"Me, dead?"

"And not dead." I dipped my finger in the water again, and the shadow of my hand passed over the general's eyes. I wrote the characters in Chinese, as Auntie Joss had written them for me on the chart she'd sold me—my number, and my mother's, the numbers that would control my fate. The marks shone wetly on the clay forehead, and for a moment, everything was still as I held my breath.

The numbers started to fade, and I dropped my hands

by my sides, the water in my palm dripping down my fingers. Swag shifted on my shoulders. "Nothing."

"It was a good try."

"Maybe Slate has some ideas? We can go back to the ship and . . ."

"And what? *Amira?*"

Part of me was aware he was speaking, but I didn't answer. I was too mesmerized by the eyes of the general, no longer blank, but glowing with scarlet light.

It faded as the letters faded, but I turned to Kash, flushed with triumph. Swag was still hissing in my ear, and Kashmir's eyes shone with wonder in the glow of the lamp.

Then the light was ripped away, like a sheet pulled off a painting, as a dark shape screeched out of the shadows and leaped at his throat.

CHAPTER

THIRTY-ONE

Glass smashed, and the sky herring scattered to the corners of the room. A black form crouched on Kashmir's chest, growling; the thing was almost the size of a man, but it smelled of rot, and the sound it made was inhuman.

Kash's knife was pinned under his hip. His hands were pressed up under the creature's jaw as it twisted, wet teeth snapping as it shrieked in fury. With every cry, the herring darted, throwing shadows behind them. Kashmir's eyes widened, white in the dark: the thing had its claws around his neck.

I drummed the beast with useless fists, but it didn't even feel the blows. I whirled and yanked the bronze sword out of the general's grasp, swinging wildly—the flat of the blade connected, but the sword bounced out of my hands. It clanged like a bell on the stone as the thing howled and arched backward. Kashmir finally threw it off, but it rolled to its feet and turned to me.

I stumbled back and fell under an onslaught of gray teeth. My shoulder hit the unforgiving stone, followed by the back of my head. For a moment the world was bright with pain. Then the shadows in my vision blurred with sudden tears, and all I could see clearly were two bloodshot eyes.

I tried to push the beast away, but it clung tight, all bone and sinew under my hands, though the weight of it crushed the air out of me. The creature screamed, and so did I, until its hands closed around my throat. I scrabbled at the bony fingers as my lungs burned and my ears rang; weakening, I stared, face-to-face with the thing. It wasn't a thing at all.

Then Swag leaped—a gleam of gold in the wavering light. The wild eyes widened and the hands loosened their grip; I was coughing and curling up and reaching out as my attacker fell away and hit the stone with a wet crack. Kashmir loomed over the prone form, raising his knife. In the shadowy light, Kash's own face looked like a skull.

"No," I said, wheezing, my breath stuck high in my throat. "No!" I waved my hand like a flag of surrender. "It's a person. Oh, God, it's a person."

Kashmir lowered his hand, then sheathed his knife. Our

attacker lay sickeningly still. I crawled over to push back the stringy hair with shaking hands. Lifeless eyes stared out of sunken wells. My heart thundered in my ears, but even accounting for starvation, those eyes were unfamiliar to me. "It's not her." I choked on my relief; I could breathe again, but the air was so sour. "It's not her."

Swag was wrapped around the skinny throat like a golden collar, teeth deep in the loose flesh, blood dripping through his coils and spreading in a black pool on the floor below. My palms were wet with it. I wiped my fingers on my trousers and cupped the man's wasted face in my hands, my shoulders heaving. "I killed him, Kashmir."

"No, *amira*, it's all right—"

"It's not all right. If not for me, he'd be alive!"

"No," he said, shaking his head. "Not for long." Kash knelt beside me and put his hands on my arms; they were searingly hot.

"But I could have helped him if—if—" But I couldn't think of the end of the sentence.

"*Amira,*" he said again, rubbing my skin, warming me. I let go of the dead artisan, and Kash pulled me against his chest. "Shh," he said, patting my back as I shook. My head was ringing like a struck bell, and just as empty. "It was going to happen. His fate was sealed the day the tomb was. There's nothing you can do."

With my eyes shut against the shadows and the scent of clove filling my nose, my heart started to slow to the rhythm his was beating. He stroked my hair, and it was hypnotic; my arms were so heavy and his, so warm. I didn't know how long we sat close together in the tomb—an hour? An eternity? But then something sharp pricked my leg, and I jumped.

It was only Swag, peering up at me and testing the air with his tongue. Abruptly, I straightened up and wiped my face on my damp sleeve. Then I took a deep, shuddering breath, picked up the dragon, and put him back on my shoulders. "Let's get the soldiers and get out of here."

The sky herring were schooling in a corner, and Kashmir used his shirt as a net while I scraped soot from the walls above the burned-out lamps. He took the other lamp off the bow of the dinghy and tipped the fish inside. Then he brought the light to where I stood before the general with black and bloody hands.

We marked the foreheads of fifty-four warriors; it seemed like an auspicious number. Their eyes began to glow and their bodies move. Each soldier stood differently: some slouched, some favored one leg. One scratched his thigh as he waited. What patience, what artistry it must have taken to create eight thousand individual warriors from a changing mold. How many of the artists had pounded their skilled hands on the thick bronze doors at the end of the hall?

Was the man I'd killed one of them?

I shook off the thought. Kashmir was right. There was nothing I could do; it had already been done, hundreds of years before I was born. But I forced myself to take one long look at the artisan lying dead in the corner. I had no magic words to bring him back to life.

Then, with fifty-four pairs of eyes watching, Kash and I stood on the steps leading to our little dinghy and waved the soldiers after us. "Follow me!" I shouted. Thank all the gods, they did.

Kashmir steered us back down the canal, using the oar as a rudder. We were pushed on a swell of mercury created by the contingent as they marched behind us, waist deep in quicksilver. We stopped before the archways, in the last room on the right. I marked the sailors with soot and scribed a name on the prow of the junk: the *54*. As I led my army toward the *Temptation*, Slate's face was as pale as the moon above us, and in the sharp shadows of the lantern light, I couldn't tell if his expression was pride or fear.

The soldiers swarmed aboard, and Bee and Slate made fast the junk, throwing ropes between the *54* and the *Temptation* and winding them tight around our cleats. Meanwhile, I took the leather case in my hands and pointed Kashmir toward the bronze beach.

He drew up close to the edge, where liquid met solid metal, near a withered pomegranate tree, the red fruit hanging shriveled on the branch. Careful not to touch the shore and risk angering the emperor, I threw the map up above the line of the mercury, just as Joss had asked. Should I call to her? What would I say? Would she even know me? But she was waiting in the dark, and sick. Poisoned. I closed my eyes and put my thumb on the spot between them.

"Are you all right?" Kash said.

"I'm thinking again," I said irritably, but the thought was gone, and my shoulder was throbbing where I'd fallen. I had done what she'd requested, and the fact she'd been there to ask me to do her this favor was proof it worked. She hadn't asked for anything more. It was enough.

No. Maybe for her, but not for me. Gingerly, so as not to capsize us, I crawled up toward the tip of the dinghy and unhooked the lantern from the bow.

"Closer, Kash," I said, but he had already dipped the oar, bringing our skiff near enough for me to lean out, my arm shaking, and set the lamp ashore beside the map.

I watched the lonely pool of light as we rowed back to the *Temptation*, the last lantern to shine on Qin's final realm. It must have been beautiful when he'd been laid to rest—an underground Eden, full of the fresh scent of fruit and flowers, the jeweled stars glimmering above. Qin thought he'd rest forever in a heavenly afterlife, but the effigy of his empire had faded faster than his crumbling kingdom above. Joss had said it herself. Everything must come to an end. In every myth, paradise is meant to be lost.

Slate helped us raise the dinghy, but he gasped when he helped me over the rail. "What happened?" He reached toward my face.

I pulled away from his hands, not wanting to be touched. "Just . . . fate." I wiped my sleeve across my cheek—blood, thick and tacky. "It's not mine." I clenched my fists, suddenly angry. "What's the use?" I shouted into the dark, my voice echoing in the cold stars. "Why do we bother if all we do is what was written a thousand years ago? What's the point if we can't try to change things?"

"Oh, Nixie." My father reached out again and I let him; my rage had burned too hot and flamed out quickly. He stroked my cheek with the back of one finger. "I always knew one day you'd understand."

CHAPTER
THIRTY-TWO

Before we left the tomb, I emptied out a wine bottle and dipped the mouth carefully into the quicksilver. I knew mercury as a poison, but Qin had believed it was a cure-all, so I tucked the bottle away in my room, just in case I was ever brave enough—or desperate enough—to test it. I left Swag in his dry bucket and sent Kash back to the bilge to wait with the bottomless bag.

Then I took the helm.

The return passage was as gentle as a blessing. The foul air of the city of the dead was pushed aside by the fresh trade winds of the tropics. The still silver sea melted into moonlit waves, and the unchanging diamond ceiling lifted away to reveal the deep black velvet of the starry night. Here we were, back in paradise; Blake's map had worked after all.

I sighed. Then I licked my teeth and spat. The miasma of rot had left a film all over my skin. *Et in Arcadia, ego.*

Slate stood beside me on the quarterdeck as we sailed, his face to the wind, his expression inscrutable. He had said nothing for hours: no instruction, no conversation . . . no praise. Finally I spoke. "Trouble, Captain?"

"What? No." He clasped his hands behind his back and walked toward the rail to stare at the sea. "No trouble at all. But I wonder . . ." He turned and came slowly back. "I wonder if you really needed that map." He cocked his head, studying me. "This may be your native time."

Out of the corner of my eye, I noticed Kashmir shift on his feet. I blinked. "My what?"

"You were born in . . . well, sixteen years ago or so. You belong in Hawaii. In 1884."

"I belong here, Captain," I said quickly. "Aboard the *Temptation.*" The response was almost automatic, and for the first time, something about it rang false in my ears.

"Nevertheless," he said. "This may be what you find past the edge of every map. The place you return to again and again. This may be your home, whether you like it or not." He watched me, as though waiting for me to say something, but I had nothing to say. I only stared out over the prow at the island as we approached. She waited for me, as patient as a mother.

We'd sighted a bay to the south of our position, and we pulled close enough to shore to drop an anchor. The north side of Oahu was lit by nothing but moonlight; if there were people living along the shore or in the deep valleys, they had long since put out their fires.

Somewhere, on the other side of the mountains, Blake was in his bed, his hands still stained with ink from the map he'd drawn. Was it only hours ago that I'd seen him? It felt like centuries.

After the ships were made secure, I stripped down to my underclothes and dove from the bow into the cool blue sea. The waves were silvered by the moon, but so different from the quicksilver sea of Qin's dead kingdom. Diving in and out of the water, I felt entirely renewed.

Well, almost entirely. I couldn't shake the sense there was something I'd missed in the tomb, a thought I'd almost had, a question I'd almost answered. I hated this feeling; my mind kept casting about and pulling up other thoughts in the process, and they swarmed around my head like flies.

I filled my lungs with air and rolled into a dead man's float, my eyes closed, my ears below the waterline, trying to clear the distractions. I hadn't seen Joss in the tomb, but she'd told me she had seen us. In 1866, when Slate first came to Honolulu, she must have recognized the ship, perhaps even before Slate came to her shop to sell his cargo . . . and to meet my mother. In 1884, Joss would soon be burying the crate, stuffed with the money she'd gotten from Mr. D, so she could uncover it in her youth. That, and a map of 1841. And an elixir as well, for her "condition." She said she'd been poisoned; was it weeks of exposure to the mercury? Or had she lost hope just before our arrival?

Poisoned.

I remembered then the wharf rat I'd embarrassed by asking the meaning of *hapai*. Bubbles streamed slowly through my lips and up along my cheek.

Lin had been in her mid-twenties when she met Slate. She'd have been born in 1841, or thereabouts.

I lifted my head, the breeze cold on my face. Salt dripped into my eyes as I treaded water for a long, still moment. Then I plunged below the surface, twisting in the cool clean water, holding my breath until it hurt, until my lungs clenched like fists, until I could not concentrate on anything else.

I burst into the night air and took a painful breath that cleansed like fire. Then I heard a short laugh from above. I blinked away the saltwater; there was Kash at the rail. "You were under so long I thought you'd drowned!"

"No such luck!" I called back.

"I'm beginning to think I'll never inherit that hammock."

I climbed up the ladder at the stern. The night breeze gave me gooseflesh after the warmth of the water. Kashmir met me on the quarterdeck with a thick towel. His own hair was still damp, and he'd changed into a fresh shirt. He started to wrap the towel around me, then he winced.

"Your shoulder."

I glanced at the ugly purple bruise and made a face. "You know, you shouldn't spy on a lady bathing."

"Reconnoiter is a better word," he replied easily. "Besides, it's not a bath unless you use soap. You should try it."

"I thought I smelled something strange." I sniffed him; he smelled of bitter almond. Then I squeezed my hair into the towel. "Maybe someday," I said, starting toward the hatch, but as I stepped away, Kashmir caught my arm.

"*Amira—*"

"Yes?"

"Are you really all right? You seem . . . distant."

When the answer came to me, it was not a lie. "I'm fine."

His eyes searched mine. "I . . . you did very well at the helm. I am—amazed."

Pride, like a mouthful of sweet wine. "Thank you, Kash."

"The captain was wrong," he called after me. "You belong on a ship." But it very nearly sounded like a question.

I went downstairs to find fresh clothes. As I pawed through the trunk, I caught sight of the map of Carthage, waiting for me. I pushed a jacket over it. Then I dressed and took a moment to look at myself in the mirror. My own eyes stared back.

It was only when I was leaving the room that I noticed Swag was not in his bucket.

I refilled the pail with fresh water and put out another dish of pearls, but he did not return that evening, and at dawn the next day, I emptied the bucket back into the sea.

At sunrise, we sailed into Hana'uma Bay, escorted by a pod of dolphins, and we dropped anchor in the still, protected waters while they played tag between the hulls. Honolulu Harbor wasn't an option; if we were inspected, I could not think of a single way to explain the silent terracotta warriors or the ancient junk to the harbormaster, or to anyone else.

Hana'uma Bay was thankfully deserted. Someday Elvis

Presley would stand there on the beach in the movie *Blue Hawaii,* but in 1884, the entire bay was still part of the estate of Princess Pauahi, and no one dared to swim or fish on the royal beach without permission. The water was pristine; peering over the rail, I could see the bright colors of the fish shimmering in the coral twenty feet down.

Slate had risen early in the morning with his disgusting coffee and a distracted air. "It's going to be a long hike to Honolulu," he said to me.

"Yeah." I sighed, pushing away from the rail. I knew what was coming.

"I want you and Kashmir to make final preparations, so we can set a day to . . . to conclude the transaction."

"Right." I watched him blow the steam off his coffee. "Any preferences?"

"Mr. D and Kashmir can work the schedule out between them. Oh, and find a place to hide the treasure. Not on the beach like some cut-rate pirate story. The erosion will expose it too quickly."

I licked my lips. Since my outburst in the tomb, I had been considering where we'd leave the gold. "I already know a place."

"Really?"

"I promised to help, didn't I?"

He nodded. "Okay. Good. The trip to Honolulu is twelve miles or so, and the terrain's not easy. It may take you a whole day. Bring supplies, and enough money for lodging and so forth. You'll need to stay in town until you hear from Mr. D."

"Aye, Captain." I started downstairs to make ready, but he called me back. "Yes?"

He was quiet for long enough I almost turned again to leave, but then he smiled at me. "You did good, Nixie."

Something in my chest came loose like a knot slipping, and I smiled back, so wide it hurt. "Thanks, Dad."

He leaned close, as though he were about to tell me a secret. "I always find—for me—knowing I have a . . . an escape . . . makes a situation less difficult. I am hoping, now you know you have an alternative, we might keep course together awhile longer."

I regarded him for a moment, and the words formed and reformed themselves in my head, but I was too much of a coward to tell him what Joss had told me—that he would never reach 1868 with me aboard. "As long as we can, Captain," I said finally.

He blinked at me. "Well. That's more than I hoped for."

Then he grinned and came at me low, wrapping me up in a hug as he had back outside of Christie's, before we'd come to this place. I locked my own arms around his neck, and I didn't let go until after he did.

CHAPTER

THIRTY-THREE

Slate himself rowed us to shore, beating the water vigorously with the oars, as though he were trying to best it. When we reached the beach and stepped out into the warm water and the soft, shell-studded sand, Slate saluted us before he pulled away.

"He's in high spirits," Kashmir said.

"He's happy it's nearly over."

"Aren't you happy, *amira*?" Kashmir said.

"Sure," I said, and I tried to mean it. Slate was right; I had an alternative. I could set out on my own if I liked. This was what I'd always wanted . . . only now I understood the meaning behind the old curse, "May your every wish be granted."

I pushed the thoughts from my mind as I rolled down the cuffs of my trousers. I'd eschewed a dress for our hike, and packed simply: a change of clothes, a handful of coins, and a letter that I'd written in private, in haste, and shoved in the bottom of my bag.

Hana'uma had been formed by a volcanic cone, and it was a long, steep climb up a winding trail from the beach to the lip of the crater. We walked in silence, the path too steep to speak easily, but we listened to birds serenade from the scraggly trees that shaded the track. At the top of the dead volcano, we stopped to rest and drink. Below us, the water lay like a sapphire cabochon in a partial capture of the shore, marred only by the ships like flaws on the stone.

I sighed, and Kash quirked up an eyebrow. "It's so beautiful," I said, in answer to his unspoken question.

"This?" Kashmir shrugged. "It reminds me of Bengal."

"It's unique," I insisted.

"Unique like everything else you've ever seen."

I took another mouthful of water to consider my response. Then I reached out to grab Kashmir's arm. "Look!" I pointed at a small black bird sitting on a branch above our heads.

Kash stared dubiously. "Does it heal things?"

"Wait till it flies away," I said. "There are yellow feathers under each wing. The Hawaiian chieftains used them to make their golden cloaks."

The bird called out, and Kashmir cocked his head. "Pretty melody, at least."

"Fifty years from now, the last one will sing his final song somewhere on Mauna Loa."

"Ah."

We watched the bird fly. "Doesn't that make you sad?" I asked, exasperated.

"Why? It's here now, *amira*."

We walked in silence almost directly west, over the black volcanic pumice of the crater's edge, and down toward the water and the inlet of Maunalua Bay, where we passed a fish pond and a native village beside a stream where Hawaiians were shrimping with woven baskets. I stopped for a moment to watch, and a man offered us some shrimp. They were about the length of one of the joints in my finger, translucent pink, and still living as he crushed them between his white teeth. I took him up on his offer; they were salty-sweet and bitter, all at once.

We continued for a while along the shore, giving wide berth to basking sea turtles and startling a small gray monk seal. We crossed a flat of tide pools where tiny red crabs scrambled in and out of the pocked holes formed by ancient bubbles in the superheated liquid stone, and I made Kashmir stop to watch as a woman and her daughter pried opihi off the mossy rocks with dull flat blades. We passed a thicket of Kona oranges and pulled fruit from the trees, filling my bag near to bursting. Kashmir offered to carry it, and I handed it over gratefully. Finally we turned inland to avoid hiking up Diamond Head—or Leahi, Blake's map had labeled it— jumping over streamlets and tramping down tall grass.

The sun followed behind for a while and then overtook us, leading us along like a beacon as we approached Waikiki, where white peacocks walked at a stately pace under the tall trees. I led Kash onto the sand to walk along the water's edge. I knew it was the longer route, but I felt an odd reluctance, a push and a pull, running away and running to. I shied away from the natural end to our journey, and I gave in to the draw of seeing all I could in the time I had left. My native time.

Kashmir must have noticed me dragging my feet. The last few miles he'd been quiet, his usual humor fading with the afternoon, but he hadn't made any effort to hurry me. The sun dipped into the ocean as we caught sight, in the distance, of the black forest of masts in Honolulu Harbor, and it was just a slip of molten red above the horizon by the time we reached the last stretch of beach before the blasted coral of the esplanade.

I stopped on the sand. Kashmir continued a few steps, then turned around.

"Maybe we can stay on the beach?" I said. "Tonight, I mean. It's very late to try to find lodging at a hotel."

Kashmir held my gaze for a long time before answering. "As you will." Then he dropped the bag and flung himself down beside it.

I tried to smile. "What, Kashmir?" I gestured out across the ocean, taking in the fiery sunset, the soft sand, the nodding palms. "You don't like the accommodations?"

He didn't answer at first, but his green eyes shone in the dying light. Then he slipped his hand into his pocket and drew out a folded piece of paper, holding it up between his first two fingers. My heart sank and I snatched the letter from his hands, but his expression didn't change. "'Dearest Mr. Hart,'" he recited, still watching my face. "'I have little time to write, and even less to visit, so instead—'"

"Kashmir—"

"'So instead, I have left something for you in the place

you promised one day you'd show me, the day we went on the hike. I cannot say more except to ask your forgiveness. Nix.'"

"You don't understand." I shoved the letter back into my pocket.

"I thought I did, the other day. When you kissed him."

I blushed, deeply, but I didn't drop my gaze, although Kash didn't make it easy. Finally he broke, looking down to pull an orange out of my bag, and I was grateful for the small mercy.

"But then I wondered," he went on. "What on earth could you be leaving for him?"

I folded my arms and watched the waves advancing, receding. "He wasn't supposed to make a map that worked. I practically spelled it out for him."

Kashmir laughed softly. "You expected him to let you go so easily?" He dropped the orange peel all in one piece beside him and sectioned the orange. "Not everyone has your skill for it. I will admit, I was relieved to read that you would not see him. Although I did notice you didn't say good-bye."

"It's implied. Like I said in the letter, I didn't have much time."

"If the captain has his way, you could have your whole life." He offered me a slice of orange, but I stared at it. He shrugged and ate it himself. "I know you've considered it."

"Kashmir . . ." I fumbled for the words. What could I say to him, this boy who knew me so well? The truth, of course; he knew already. "It's compelling. I can feel it now, the pull my father feels toward a place and time. This is where I would have grown up. This is the life I would have had. The friends and . . . the family." I took up a handful of sand and let it pour through my fingers. "And maybe— maybe if I'd never known another life, it's a life I could've loved. But that's not what happened. I won't be staying. The *Temptation* is my home." I reached over and took his hand. We were quiet for a while. The sun was gone, and only a slender belt of gold along the horizon remained. "At least, for now."

He squeezed my fingers. "Until when?"

I put my other hand to my throat. "Do you remember that night in New York? When you gave me my necklace? Remember we talked about jumping ship?"

"I do."

"Now that I can Navigate . . . if I did leave the ship—I'm not saying I will. But if I did. Would you come with me?"

His answer was immediate. "You know I would."

I let my breath out all at once. Then I grinned at him. "We could get our own boat."

"I've never stolen a boat before."

"You've stolen enough we could buy a boat," I said, thinking of the pile of jewelry he'd given me over the years. All the treasure I hadn't cared for at the time. I might not even need the map of Carthage.

"Who would be captain?" he said.

"Uh, I would."

"Oh, no, no no. Guess again."

"You can't mutiny, we don't have a ship yet."

"I'm planning ahead."

I grinned at him, suddenly feeling free—expansive—like full sails and an open horizon. "If you could go anywhere, where would you want to go?"

"Could we find a map of someplace perfect?"

"Like paradise?" I asked, teasing.

"Here? No." He stared upward, the first stars shining in his eyes. "A better place. Someplace where nothing goes wrong. There must be a myth like that somewhere."

I bit my lip; my shoulders fell. "Navigation involves the beliefs of the Navigator and the mapmaker. And I don't think I've ever met anyone who truly believes in a world without suffering."

"Ah."

I dragged my fingers through the soft sand. "You know, Slate was right. This place is dying. If I'd grown up here, I would be seeing it firsthand, like Blake is."

"And you wouldn't have met me, which is the main thing, of course!"

I laughed. "Of course." I let go of his hand, and then, a moment later, I wished I hadn't. "I will admit though. It was fun."

He sat up, cross-legged, facing me. "Being in Hawaii?"

"Flirting with a stranger." I ducked my chin, suddenly shy. "I can see why you like it."

"You should have taken my word for it and not wasted your time testing the theory."

"It wasn't a waste of time," I said.

His mouth opened a little, closed again, and the muscles of his throat worked. But all he said was "Oh?"

"Don't judge me," I said, exasperated. "You and Bee and Slate and Rotgut, you all had lives, you all have stories and memories. You're worldly and experienced." I wrapped my hands around my knees and watched the rising moon lay a path of silver on the sea. "I've never had anything or anyone outside the ship."

He reached into the bag for another orange, turning it over and over in his hands. "Why does it have to be someone outside the ship?"

I tensed, cautious—suddenly sensing the reefs only inches below the surface, but I couldn't go back. I had to keep my eye on the horizon ahead. "Knowing something has an ending . . . makes it easier to begin," I said carefully. "I never want to be stuck missing something I didn't expect to lose."

"*Baleh*, I understand."

"You do?" I checked to see if he was making fun, but his face was earnest.

"Of course." Kashmir started to peel the orange; the smell of citrus perfumed the air. "When I was young, I learned to expect loss. Every time you slept, something disappeared. Whenever you woke up, someone else was gone. But . . . I also learned that every day, you created everything anew. And whatever you had, you enjoyed as long as it lasted. Spend money when it's in your pocket." He took my hand and put the orange in it. "Eat fruit while it's ripe." His other hand found my cheek, his thumb brushing the corner of my mouth. "Paradise is a promise no god bothers to keep. There's only now, and tomorrow nothing will be the same, whether we like it or not."

I bit my lip and tasted oranges; the juice was very sweet. "Is that really true?"

His smile was bright in the moonlight. "I promise."

"Then I suppose . . . just tonight—"

This time I did not turn away, and so I discovered that his lips were even sweeter than the orange.

CHAPTER
THIRTY-FOUR

I woke naturally before dawn and went to stand watch at the water's edge. The sky lightened from the color of stone to the soft purple of lavender blossoms, then to the rich blue and orange of a gas flame, all reflected in the mirror of the morning sea. As the sun began to glow gold, Kashmir came to stand beside me, very close but not touching, giving me space. Flecks of foam washed our feet. Words came to mind and then melted away like spun sugar on my tongue. Last night, there had been so much to say, but tomorrow had become today, and everything was different.

I turned from the sea and kicked sand over the coals of our little fire. Kashmir washed his hands and face in the Pacific. In silence, we gathered our things. Finally I spoke. "Breakfast?"

"Absolutely."

We found a saloon that was serving eggs and hash to patrons who looked like they'd had a liquid supper. After we'd had our fill, we hired horses and bought shovels and torches from the general store downtown. Then I led Kashmir up into the mountains.

We took Nu'uanu Road, past the little stream, by the boxy white house, onto the track in the woods, through the empty clearing where we tied our horses, and up to the waterfall Blake had shown me.

"He told me there were caves above the falls," I said.

Kashmir put his hands on his hips and assessed the craggy mountainside, a wall of orchids and bromeliads and wet, mossy stone. "Did he tell you how to get up there?"

"There's an old trail somewhere," I said, walking along the edge of the greenery. "But it may be hard to find. The Hawaiians used to keep the bones of their kings in caves along the ridge, and the locations were very secret because the bones had great power. Ah." I pushed aside a tangle of ferns to reveal a slippery trail, little more than a path for runoff. "Let's try this."

We explored the mountainside, ducking into caves and crevices, finding the occasional petroglyph but, thankfully, no graves. We settled on a narrow cleft near the stream with a loamy floor where we dug a deep trench, working side by side in companionable silence. It only took an hour, but better now than the night of the theft.

When we finished, we left the supplies there and climbed gingerly, slowly down out of the mountains. I made sure to map the location in my head, the twists and turns of the narrow track that led us back to the ghost village where our horses grazed in the slanting afternoon sun.

We arrived at the Royal Hawaiian Hotel covered with mud to the knees and endured the tight-lipped disapproval of the concierge, but Kashmir put on a show and pulled out a heavy handful of coins, and suddenly rooms became available. We lingered in the lobby that night, being seen, and the next morning there was a message waiting for us at the front desk.

Dinner at the Palace, December 1. Will you be able to attend? —D

"December first?" I glanced at the newspaper on the counter. "So, ten days from now. That should be . . . just after full moon. A Monday night?"

Kashmir laughed. "Why are you asking me?"

"No, I know, it is," I said, remembering an article I'd

read. I made a face. "It's the Monday after the Independence Day celebration."

Kash raised his eyebrow. "Tacky. Very tacky."

"Hmm. It should also be . . ." I plucked a newspaper from the desk and flipped through it to the schedule of the mail ships. "Ah," I said, finding the spot. "Tacky but clever."

"The most annoying combination," Kashmir said, reading over my shoulder. The *Alameda* was scheduled to leave Honolulu on the morning of December first. We could slip right into her empty berth.

He sent back a message before we left Honolulu:

Arrival at 10 p.m. Send H to meet us at the dock.

I left a message as well—the note I'd written to Blake—giving strict instructions that it be delivered on December second.

We retraced our steps to the ship, and although it was out of character for him not to needle me mercilessly at every opportunity, Kash never said a word about the last conversation we'd had on this journey. I was quietly grateful, although it was only a promise kept.

Back aboard the *Temptation*, snags had developed in our absence. They'd had time to repair the crow's nest and the mast, and Rotgut was healing well, but once I'd left, the clay soldiers had stood motionless on the deck of the *54*, their eyes dimming like banked embers. Not even Rotgut could make them budge, no matter how he shouted in his native Chinese. But he told me he'd known I was returning when scarlet fire had flared again in the general's eyes.

The general tracked my movements as I came to stand before him, and when I spoke, he seemed to listen. I explained the army's part in the theft—it mostly involved silent and stoic marching, which they were good at—and he put his fist to his chest and bowed, although he never said a word. The emperor had not given his warriors tongues.

Rotgut watched me with wonder in his eyes. "How did you do that?"

I licked my lips. "I don't know," I said, which was technically true, although I had a guess.

"It must be because you woke them," he said, after a moment's thought.

"Must be." And I left it at that.

We gave each soldier a torch to carry, the old-fashioned kind, made with branches hewn from the trees above the bay, their ends wrapped in oil-soaked sailcloth. The warriors performed admirably; their brooding silence and red eyes were frightening enough by day, and I imagined how terrifying they would appear by firelight, especially to the locals. And the locals were the only ones we had to worry about. The Honolulu Rifles sided against the monarchy.

When I had explained the plan to Slate before we sailed to Qin's tomb, he'd looked doubtful. "Very impressive and everything, but how will we actually carry the gold?"

His expression had changed when I'd handed him the bottomless bag. "I couldn't do any of this without you, Nixie."

I shrugged. After all, it was because of me that he still had to.

So it was on December first we stood on the deck of the *54* and watched the *Alameda* leave for San Francisco. Once it was a misty speck on the horizon, we pointed our prow toward Honolulu Harbor. The wind filled the red sails of the junk and snapped the black flag flying above our heads: it was really one of the curtains from the alcove where Slate slept, but after all, we were only pretending to be pirates.

We had gone over the plan dozens of times, and we did so again as we approached the harbor. Our faces hidden by bandannas, and Slate sporting the reddish-blond beard he'd been letting grow, we would hail poor Colonel Iaukea and take the harbormaster prisoner when he came aboard. We would tie up at the pier and presumably meet Mr. Hart on the dock—that is, if he decided to show up. Part of me wondered if he would turn on Mr. D instead, or even turn him in—but no. Self-preservation would win out over revenge.

That late on a Monday night, the streets would be quiet. Once ashore, Slate and Kashmir would lead the column of warriors to the treasury at Ali'iolani Hale. I had taught the general the simple one, two, one-and-two rhythm on the ceremonial *ipu* drum, and the army would be carrying their lighted torches, doing their best imitation of the Night Marchers. Kashmir would even be blowing a conch shell as best he could; so far he'd managed less of a haunting call from beyond the grave than the squashed *blat* of a disappointed goat, but hopefully it would be enough to cause the members of the Royal Hawaiian Guard to throw themselves on the ground and cover their eyes, where they would be easily tied.

None of us wanted bloodshed—as Sun Tzu had said, the supreme art of war was to subdue the enemy without fighting. But if the ruse didn't work, the warriors still had their swords. I had impressed upon the general not to harm a living person, except to protect Slate or Kashmir.

Once at the treasury, Kashmir would open the vault, and

the gold would be loaded into the bottomless bag. As soon as the vault was cleared out, Mr. Hart would hand over the map and leave, able to confirm to the others that the job was done, and Slate and Kash would bring the bag to Nu'uanu to bury the money. When the treasure was hidden, they would return to the 54 and sail to Hana'uma Bay to meet the *Temptation* and leave this place behind for good.

Rotgut would be guarding the junk while it was docked in the harbor, standing watch at the helm with a contingent of warriors in case any of the Royal Hawaiian Guard escaped. "And my job?" I asked Slate as the lights of Honolulu came into view.

"You're staying behind."

"What?"

"This isn't one of your myths, Nixie," Slate said, checking the revolver he'd borrowed from Bee. He wore half gloves, hiding the tattoos on his hands. "We don't know what might happen. I won't have you getting hurt."

"You said there wasn't going to be any fighting."

"I said we weren't going to attack anyone. Just because we don't start a fight doesn't mean they won't fight back!"

"We've got fifty soldiers—"

"You wouldn't be coming if we had armored trucks!"

"You normally let me do all kinds of dangerous things."

He clenched his jaw. "I know. I've been regretting that since the tomb."

As the memory of the dead artisan resurfaced, suddenly my protests caught in my throat.

Kashmir led me away. "Don't worry so much, *amira*. We'll be fine."

I took his arms in my hands, gripping so tight the muscles slipped under his skin like fish. "I just—" He had darkened the area around his eyes and under his cheekbones with soot to obscure his features. I suppressed a shudder. "I don't want you getting hurt."

He grinned and put a gentle hand on the back of my neck, pulling my forehead to his. I followed his gaze down through the gap at the front of his shirt; underneath his white button-up, he wore a Kevlar vest.

I pulled free. "I didn't know we had those."

"Just the one. The captain insisted I take it," he added when my face fell.

"Did he?" I looked back at my father, who turned away quickly, as though he hadn't been watching us.

Kashmir brushed my forehead with a gentle hand; a smear of soot had found its way from his skin to mine.

"Don't worry. I'll throw my worthless carcass in front of him should anything happen."

"Kashmir—"

"Stop, or you'll make *me* nervous. You can do us both a bit of good if you would trust me."

"You're right. I'm sorry. I do." I stared into his granite-green eyes. "I do." He touched my chin with his thumb.

And so it was, as night fell and the *Alameda* steamed east toward America, the 54 slid toward her spot in the harbor. The harbormaster was tied safely belowdecks; he'd given in without a fight when he came muzzle-to-mustache with Bee's revolver.

As Slate and Kashmir led the warriors in two solid columns onto the dock, sailors and fishermen fled the wharf, but from the shadows, a single man approached, wearing a battered hat pulled low and a kerchief knotted around his face. Mr. Hart had come after all.

Slate and Hart stood before each other, but neither reached out to shake the other's hand, and for a moment, all was still and quiet as a hundred red eyes glowed like embers in the night. Then Kashmir blew the conch, and the low, hollow wail of the empty shell floated over the bay like a lost soul. He had been practicing.

The general began to beat the *ipu* in the rhythm he'd learned—one, two, one-and-two—and the men marched away into the darkened streets of Honolulu, leaving me behind, sitting against the bulwark, guarding the ship with Rotgut and a small contingent of terra-cotta men.

An hour passed, or more, the stars wheeling overhead. Once the sound of marching feet had faded, a hush fell over the town, especially near the harbor. News must have spread, and all of the townspeople were huddled in their beds—the locals out of fear, the foreigners out of indifference. Every so often, the faint sounds of the harbormaster struggling against his bonds would drift up from the hold—less frequently as the man exhausted himself.

I was beginning to grow impatient. They still had to hide the loot, but they must have been nearly done at the treasury; Kashmir had said it wouldn't take more than an hour to load the gold. Rotgut had a good view down Nu'uanu Avenue from the crow's nest, and he'd be able to see the column of torches as soon as they began their march into the valley. I waited for him to sing out a sighting, but none came.

Then hoofbeats broke the silence in the street: a single rider approaching. A lone, brave guardsman? A reckless reporter?

Rotgut and I shared a glance. He shook his head ruefully, and my skin went cold before I even peeked over the rail.

"No," I whispered, and I dropped back down to the deck, trying pointlessly—foolishly—to hide as hooves thudded on the wooden planks of the pier.

"You there, lad!" Blake's voice rang over harbor. "I saw you. Stand up!"

I slapped my palm down on the deck, but there was nothing for it: the damage was done. No. I had done the damage. Slate told me often enough: he couldn't have done this without me.

I pulled off the cap that was hiding my hair and stood to face Blake. Then my eyes widened. "Don't shoot!"

He stared at me from over the barrel of a small double derringer. Then he blinked and lowered his gun. "Miss Song? What are you doing here? It's not safe. I heard there were . . . pirates in Honolulu."

Realization crept across his face like a tide, and he raised the gun again.

CHAPTER
THIRTY-FIVE

The gun gleamed in Blake's grasp. The four warriors I'd stationed on the quarterdeck were quiet, their eyes like dying coals. He could take one shot before they reached him, and all it took was one. But would he?

"Mystery indeed," Blake said bitterly. He scanned the ship, his eyes gray as flint in the moonlight. "Where is your father?"

"With yours at the treasury," I shot back.

"That doesn't shock me. I know the depths to which *he'd* stoop."

The scorn in his voice bit like an eel. "I was going to return the gold."

He laughed. "Of course you were!"

"I wrote you a letter giving you the location." I lifted my chin. "It will be delivered tomorrow."

"Is that so?" he said sarcastically. "Perhaps I should go home then, and wait for it."

"Or just shoot me and find out later I was telling the truth."

He stared at me, incredulous. "Have you ever once told me the truth?"

"Many times," I said. "Most notably when I told you how to prevent us from returning."

"Don't try to make me responsible, Miss Song. I knew it was about money, but I didn't think your return would lead to *this*." Pilikia danced beneath him, but he kept the gun steady. His eyes, though, were less certain, and behind them I recognized it—not anger, but pain.

"What did you think it would lead to?" He didn't answer, but the heartless moon illuminated every expression— regret, shame, longing. I cocked my head. "You're not going to shoot me."

He ground his teeth. "No," he said with new resolve. "I'm going to take you prisoner so your father will return what he's stolen."

"He won't," I said, certain now. "And you still won't shoot me."

Blake's eyes narrowed, and he stared at me for so long,

I began to doubt. But then he lowered his gun, shoving it in the holster. Then both of us looked up at the sudden sound, a few blocks away, of the tinkle of smashed glass and a scream. Suddenly Blake slammed his open hand down on his thigh; Pilikia reared back, but he kept his seat. "*Why?* Of all the places you might go to loot, why this one? *Why mine?*"

"Blake . . . it's inevitable," I said, repeating the words I'd learned. "You've seen it on the horizon. You know what's coming. Paradise is always lost."

"That's a convenient turn of phrase," he said. "But paradise is never lost. Only destroyed." My cheeks burned with shame, but he continued, merciless. "But for what, Miss Song? Not money, I wouldn't believe that of *you*. What is the map really for?"

"You know what it's like," I said, desperate, not for clemency, now, but for understanding. "To try to hold on to something as it disappears."

He shook his head as Pilikia pawed the deck; he pulled the reins sharply, turning her in a tight circle, keeping his eyes on my face. "There is more to this story. Something you're still hiding. No one does something like this for a memory."

I bit my lip, the answer on the tip of my tongue, but why shouldn't I tell him? "He needs it to save a life. To save my mother," I said at last. "My reasons are less altruistic," I added with difficulty, but I owed him the truth. "I'm doing this to save myself."

"To save yourself? Who threatened you? And how does the captain—"

Then the sound of shouting and a high, manic laugh from the town made him turn his head. "That's my father." Blake's voice was distant, as though he was listening to a song I couldn't hear.

Another smashing sound, like furniture being overturned. "What are they doing?"

Blake's shoulders sagged like an empty sail. "I would imagine he'd find it difficult to stop at the treasury."

"Why?"

"There are some men in town who . . . who have . . . wronged him. He's been at the edge for quite some time. It would not take much to push him over."

I felt uneasy then, as though the deck were rolling beneath my feet; but no, we were in harbor. "You should go home. Wait for my letter and rescue the kingdom. You'll be a hero."

"It isn't heroic simply to do what's right."

"Then do what's right, but wait till tomorrow. Tomorrow

this will be over and we'll be gone and . . . everything will be different."

Then we both jumped to hear a shot ring out over the town.

And another.

Before the echoes died away, I was running down the gangplank and Blake was reaching for my hand. He hauled me up in front of him on the horse. Rotgut called after me as we clattered down the dock, but his voice was drowned out by the pounding of Pilikia's hooves and my own heart.

We took King Street toward the palace, and though the streets were empty and lights extinguished and shutters closed against the thieves in the night, I felt eyes peering out from behind curtains. I listened past the sound of Blake breathing, ragged in my ear, but there were no more shots.

At last we reached the area near the palace, and I saw the orange glow of the torches two blocks north—the wealthiest block on the island. I gasped as we rode by bodies in the street, but there was no blood; they were guardsmen, still lying flat on their faces, their hands tied behind their backs. They didn't open their eyes as we passed them by.

Then Blake swore and pulled Pilikia up short. She neighed, high and panicked. "What in hell?"

There, in the pool of torchlight, the terra-cotta men stood, still and silent, single file in the street. Their backs were straight as ever, though the general had been draped in a yellow feather cloak and a long string of pearls.

"It's not them," I said, breathless. "It's not the Night Marchers."

"Then what are they?"

"No time, Blake—"

"Miss Song, wait!"

But I had already slid from the horse and hit the ground running.

Beretania Street was a mess: doors hanging open on the fine homes, windows smashed, glass glittering in the torchlight, banknotes tumbling in the breeze of our passing. I smelled brandy spilled from broken bottles and heard the sound of a woman crying, a man's hushed voice, furniture being pushed against doors. The destruction made a trail from the treasury. Blake had been right. That was only the start of it.

I couldn't see Slate or Kashmir anywhere.

"Kash?" I stopped in the middle of the street, unsure where to go. "Dad?"

"*Amira?*"

I whirled around to find Kashmir trotting toward me from behind the nearest house. He took me by the arm and pulled me along until we were in the shadow of a garden wall. He appeared well and whole, but I couldn't stop myself from reaching out, running my hand over his shoulder and down his arm. "Are you all right?" Then my heart sank. "Slate?"

"He's fine, *in shaa' Allah*," Kashmir said. Then he glanced at Blake, who had ridden up behind us. "He's looking for Hart. We've had a bit of trouble."

"You've faked the Hu'akai Po?"

I ignored Blake's outrage. "Did you shoot him?"

"He shot at us! Someone recognized him—mocked him to his face—and he snapped. Hart beat the man and went down the street smashing things. The captain tried to reason with him, but he just ran off with the bag. And the map."

Blake clenched his fists, and Pilikia danced under the tight rein. "You expected honor among thieves?"

"It's more common than honor among gentlemen!" Kash retorted.

"We don't have time for this," I said. "Where did they go?"

"Come on," Kashmir said, taking my hand. Then he pointed at Blake. "Not. You."

"I might be unwilling to shoot you, Miss Song, but I have no such compunctions about your *friend*."

"Blake," I said firmly. "Your father may be heading home with the gold. You have a horse. If you want to help, you could stop him."

"Or I could find the guards and have you all arrested."

I met his eyes. "Do what you think is right," I said finally.

Behind Blake's eyes, he struggled, but after a moment, he cantered off down the street, toward Nu'uanu Avenue— and away from the garrison at Iolani Palace.

Kashmir glared after him. "I almost wish he'd gone to the barracks."

"Why?"

"He could have spent the night trying to unchain the doors." His head whipped around at the sound of voices from the houses down the street, and he swore. "They would still be in their beds if Hart hadn't looted their houses." He took my arm. "Let's go."

Kashmir led me one block north along the trail of destruction that ended where Beretania met the Cathedral of St. Andrew. The soldiers followed at a swift march, their torches trembling in the night air, and Kash and I listened for more shots and called out for the captain. My heart had climbed into my throat by the time we found him, crouching in the shadow of a tulip tree on the cathedral grounds, but he was unhurt, and he held his revolver cocked in his hands. He swore as we ran to the shelter of the trunk, the soldiers stopping in formation on the grass nearby. "What are you doing here, Nixie?"

I narrowed my eyes, trying to catch my breath as my heart slowed. "Nothing's going as planned tonight, is it?"

Slate frowned, shifting his grip on the gun. "Hart has his own addictions. Go back to the ship. It's not safe here."

"No, Dad. I'm not leaving you."

The captain turned his haggard face to me and smiled like a sunrise.

"So, Captain?" Kashmir scanned the street beyond the grounds and the wide lawn ahead. The shadows were sharp as knives under the spotlight of the moon. "Where did he go?"

"I lost him," Slate said. "But he dropped the gold." The captain jerked his chin toward the center of the lawn; there, stark in the light of the moon, perhaps two ships' lengths away from where we stood, was the bottomless bag.

I sucked air through my teeth. Where was Mr. Hart hiding? In the shadow of the low stone wall? Under the dark crowd of hedges across the way? Or perhaps in the deep coves behind the limestone columns of the side of the cathedral? I searched, but I saw no one. "It's a trap," I said, my blood pounding in my ears—or was that the sound of pursuers, closing in? "He's waiting for us to go for the bag so he can pick us off."

"Yeah, well," the captain said. "If we wait here, someone else will shoot us!"

"Let's all go back to the ship, Dad." I plucked at his sleeve. "Please."

"And leave the map?"

Kashmir turned sharply at a sound I had not heard. "Captain—"

"Hart has the map, Dad, and I don't think he's bringing it back!"

"They want the gold," he said stubbornly. "They'll make him give up the map to get it."

"Not if he kills you first!"

"We'll send one of the soldiers—"

"We have to *move*, Captain," Kashmir said urgently.

Slate rounded on him. "Not without the bag!"

Kashmir hesitated only a second before he sped out from the shadow of the tree.

I grabbed at his sleeve but missed; I called after him, but he paid me no mind as he ran across the moonlit grass, ducking, dodging, zigzagging back and forth. He rolled past the bag and came up with it in his hands as the report of a rifle crashed in my ear.

I screamed—something stung my cheek—and one of the clay soldiers beside me exploded into potsherds. But Kashmir was already coming back, and he threw the bag to Slate and barreled into me, pushing me to the other side of the tree and shielding my body with his, pressed close. He had run hard, but I was the one panting. He cupped my face in his hand, his thumb brushing my cheek gently. "Shh. It's all right."

Slate grabbed the bag and crouched beside us, his eyes darting about like fish. "Where did that come from?" He pointed his gun this way and that.

Without taking his eyes off mine, Kashmir nodded upward, toward one of the looted houses across the street—just visible through the trees that lined the grounds. "Top floor. Third window."

The glass had been smashed, and the shutter hung at a crazy angle, wreathed in a pall of gun smoke. I pulled away from Kash and squinted, but all I could see was a deeper shadow, and the long barrel of a rifle glinting in the moon-light. "Is it Hart?"

"I can't tell."

"Either way . . ." The captain fired three shots off toward the house—they went wide, but the barrel withdrew behind the shutter. "Let's go."

He set off at a run, and Kash followed, pulling me along beside him, keeping the tree and his body between me and the shooter. The soldiers formed up behind us, offering additional protection.

We marched north then, and east, out of the city at a quick pace. The soldier's feet, rising and falling in rhythm with the drum the general beat, and the sonorous tone of the conch shell were the only sounds in the nearby streets—although far off behind us, the night air jangled with the racket of raised voices, shouted orders, someone wailing. And ahead, the murmur of fear, the soft click of locks, the clatter of shutters closing.

Blake was well out of it, although I could only imagine the row that would ensue when Mr. Hart got home. Although perhaps neither Blake nor his father would speak a word of it. Blake had known of his father's involvement for a while now. Perhaps they would keep pretending.

Soon we left the city behind and entered the dark roads of the valley. We passed the beautiful estates of the wealthy, which gave way, higher up, to the little grass houses, their cook fires still smoking. We only saw one rider, already facedown on the ground, his horse stamping nearby and whickering gently. The light we carried was the only light on earth, although above us, the brightness of the moon shamed the stars.

We left the road and found the winding path where Blake had shown me his idea of paradise. The smell of ancient loam rose up beneath our tramping feet. It was darker under the trees, and sinister; the path more treacherous, with fallen trees trying to trip us, vines winding around our ankles, and branches ripping at our sleeves. Once, something rustled in the undergrowth, and my heart jumped in my chest, but it was only a rat eating guavas.

As the path narrowed, the warriors began to crush the undergrowth, and I called a halt in the clearing where the village had once stood. "We should leave them here," I said. "They'll leave a trail a mile wide if we bring them to the cave. Put out their torches." Kashmir sprang to, taking the torch from the general and extinguishing it. Eerily, the other warriors followed suit, all at once, and stood in silence, their red eyes glowing in the night like scattered coals from a dying fire.

Slate's face was pale in the moonlight. "How much farther?"

"Not far, Captain," I said. "But from now on we're climbing."

We pushed into the forest, taking the path hand over foot at times, it was so steep. It hadn't rained today, at least not near the sea, but the undergrowth was wet here, and the leaves glistened where the moon shone through the trees. It was easy to lose sight of one another in the thicket, and I slowed, not wanting to get lost in the dark. We passed the waterfall, the mist writhing through the rocks like ghosts among headstones, and continued upward with muddy hands and knees.

"Are you sure we're going the right way?" Kashmir said.

"Almost positive."

Slate barked in laughter, violating the dark. "Confidence! Now that's the mark of a good Navigator!"

I paused, throwing back my hand. "Wait!"

"What?"

I listened. My breathing was even louder in my ears than the sound of the rushing water. "I thought . . ." I paused again. "I thought I heard something."

"Oh, that." Kashmir stepped closer, lowering his voice. "Yes, *amira*. Someone's following us."

"Probably Hart," Slate muttered. "Just keep going. We can't take a stand here. The money isn't our business. We only need the map."

"Dad. Do you honestly think he still plans to give us the map?"

Slate was quiet. "He has to answer to Mr. D," he said, but he sounded uncertain.

"What a cock-up," Kashmir said. "I should have gone back to his house and taken the damn thing."

"On our way down?" Slate said.

"Perhaps," Kash said. "If we make it down."

We continued up—the cave would offer more cover in a fight—and mercifully soon, the path widened and leveled, leading us through the twisted trees along a windy ridge. I recognized the ledge up ahead, or at least, I thought I recognized it. Steely in the moonlight and slashed with deeper shadows, everything seen by the light of day was always slightly foreign in the dark.

As we entered the cleft in the rock, I found the torches we'd laid by the opening. I lit one gratefully, throwing light over the pit we'd dug and the shovels we'd used to dig it. I leaned out of the cave then, peering into the dark, but it was even harder to see with the light in my eyes, and the only sound was the soft question of a white owl.

I stabbed the torch into the soft sand in the back of the cave and rubbed the mud from my palms while Slate flung the bag down by the hole. "You deal with the gold." Then he drew and cocked his pistol, leaning against the wall at the mouth of the cave, facing the trail. "I'll wait for Hart."

"Let's bury it," Kashmir said, tossing the bag down by the trench. "Grab a shovel?"

I picked up one of the spades and hefted it. It was reassuringly solid in my hands—but no match for a gun. I peeked over my father's shoulder and into the dark outside. It might not have been Hart in that second-floor window—it could have been one of the men whose houses he had looted. Yet it had to be him; he would not have left the gold behind unguarded. Of course he would have followed us, but here in the cave, we had the advantage. How had he gotten hold of a rifle? Unless . . .

"Stop!" I whirled around, too late. Kashmir dropped the ties; the leather flap twitched, and out of the bag climbed Mr. Hart.

CHAPTER
THIRTY SIX

Hart still wore his hat, but he'd pulled the kerchief down around his neck. He gave us a humorless smile and leveled a revolver at me. His hand was much steadier than his son's.

Kashmir's hand had gone to his knife, but he dropped his arm. My father lowered his own gun, and when Hart gestured at me, I threw the shovel aside.

"An unexpected pleasure, Mr. Hart," Slate said.

"The pleasure is all mine, Captain. And ah, the charming dancing instructor is still unscathed." Kashmir's jaw clenched. "Do pardon my behavior earlier." Mr. Hart waved his gun. "The heat of the moment, you understand."

"That's all behind us." Slate held out palm in a placating gesture, the hand holding the gun low against his thigh. "We're just here to bury the gold, like I said we would. But if you want to change the deal with the league, it's not my business. My only business is with the map." Slate paused, but Mr. Hart's smirk hadn't budged. Slate's eyes roved from Hart's face, down his arm to the gun, to me, and then back to the revolver. He took a shallow breath. "I don't suppose you've brought me the map."

"No, Captain." Mr. Hart stepped away from the limp bag. Gold coins rolled away under his feet as he walked toward me. The dark center of the steel barrel was like a black hole, pulling me in. "The map would do you little good anyway."

"What do you mean?" Slate said.

Mr. Hart's thin lips hinted at the tips of his white teeth. "Do you know, at the very beginning, I was simply grateful to have my debts forgiven? The others would stand to make their fortunes, while I would barely remain afloat." He reached down and picked up the bag, laughing in delight.

"I would have offered more if I'd known you needed so much."

"You don't know how that woman can spend. Spending is one of two things that make her happy. You may guess the other, sir." He glanced at Kashmir with eyes as hard as coffin nails. "You, and half the men in their fine houses downtown.

She wasn't always like this. It was living here, on this rock, with these heathens; it has changed her. I blame my brother. He was the first. She couldn't have made it more obvious, naming the boy after him."

My breath hissed in my teeth, but Blake had told me himself—he had his uncle's artistic bent.

"Take the money, Hart," Slate said. "I don't care what you do with it. What is wrong with the map?"

"Why, nothing, sir," Mr. Hart said. "But you would find it little use without your ship."

"My . . . ship?"

"I've told you, sir, I cannot stay. By tomorrow the whole island will know what I've done. Besides, this climate is too . . . hot for my wife's temperament. No, she and I will be leaving aboard the *Temptation*."

"Fine, yes." Slate ground his teeth, and Kashmir's face had gone pale. "We'll take you away. We'll start a new life for you, somewhere else."

"Alas, sir, it is long past time I take my fate in my own hands. *I* will be starting my new life elsewhere. You will be staying here."

"You can't sail the *Temptation*."

"I won't have to. The girl is the expert, you said it

yourself." He hefted the bag and threw me an appraising glance.

"No," my father said, his voice low. "No, no, no. Take the ship then, take the money, leave her. Just go. We'll stay here. Come, Nixie, come here." Slate opened his arms, but Mr. Hart jerked the gun toward the captain.

"Stay where you are," he said to me. "He wouldn't be the first man I've killed, and shooting is a lot easier than drowning."

I swallowed, but my mouth was so dry. Kashmir had the vest, but the revolver was pointed at my father's face.

Slate did not quail. "Don't do this," he said, his face pale with rage. "Don't take her from me, because I will kill you if you do. I will hunt you past Good Hope and round the Horn and to hell itself before I give her up."

"Captain!" Kashmir said, but Mr. Hart only smiled.

"So you do understand," he said. "Why a man would kill for love." Mr. Hart cocked the revolver.

"Wait!" My voice broke, but I'd found it again. "Wait, please." Mr. Hart half turned his head, though his eyes—and his aim—stayed on Slate. "I'll take you wherever you want. Just don't shoot. Whatever you need." I racked my brain. "Diamonds. In Arabia. And, uh, gold." The gun dipped a little, and his eyes flicked to me then. "Gold from the Cibola. El Dorado, you know El Dorado?"

"It's real?"

"I can take you there. Or Carthage. In Carthage they pay gold for salt." Tears stung my eyes and I knew, then, just what my father felt: I would do whatever it took. "I can take you anywhere. Anything you want. Only let them live. Please."

Mr. Hart stared at me for a long moment, then he nodded once. "Throw down your weapons."

"No!"

"Dad!"

Mr. Hart shrugged, as if in regret. He raised his gun again, but I was out of ideas.

Kashmir wasn't. His hand flew to his knife, and Mr. Hart whirled around—a shot rang like a bell in the cave and I smelled cordite and iron—but it was not Kashmir who stumbled back. It was Mr. Hart.

He clutched his right shoulder with his left hand, but he did not drop the gun as he stared, as we all did, at Blake standing at the mouth of the grotto. The boy stepped forward heavily, into the circle of our torchlight, as though his own feet were made of clay.

"I followed you." Blake was breathing hard, but his gun was still high in his trembling hand. "I heard it all. Let her go."

Mr. Hart glared at him while red blood bloomed like a boutonniere on the shoulder of his linen jacket, but then he swung his own hand back up and pointed the gun at Blake. "Put it down, boy."

"You first."

Neither moved, and then Mr. Hart smiled again, as bitter as truth. "Just like your father," he said, and he fired.

Blake fell back into the dark, and I leaped on Mr. Hart's back, wrapping my arms around his throat. He swung me around as Kashmir came toward him and my legs connected, knocking Kashmir against Slate as I tumbled to the ground.

Mr. Hart pulled up his arm and fired at Kashmir, square in the chest, and I rose, grabbing for Hart's wounded shoulder and squeezing as hard as I could. He cried out and dropped the gun, but he managed to reach up with his other hand and twist his fingers in my hair until tears stood in my eyes and my own hand opened. Then he grabbed the bag and ran, dragging me along behind him.

We stumbled over Blake's prone form on the path; he was still moving, reaching out, clutching at Hart's leg. Mr. Hart yanked out of Blake's grasp, but I heard the boy's words, soft and raspy: *"Get down."* I tried, but Mr. Hart still had me by the hair. He pushed me into the forest along the narrow path.

"Move!"

Behind us, feet slid through the loam—it must have been Slate—but then came the sound of something ahead: snapping branches and the conch shell and the feet, marching. Our warriors . . . had we brought them this close? But Kashmir had fallen in the cave, so who was sounding the conch? Torchlight shimmered between the trees, blurring in my teary eyes, and I understood what Blake was saying.

"Get down," I wheezed, sucking in air. "Get down!" Slate heard me, and his footsteps stopped, but Mr. Hart wouldn't listen.

I closed my eyes and covered them with my hands, blind as he shoved me forward. And then he stopped.

There was a chill and a stillness; then Mr. Hart released my hair. I sagged to my knees and pushed myself down to the earth, among the loam and the leaves. My palm was sticky against my face, and I smelled the tang of blood and something else, a whiff of cold earth and damp stone and dry moss, but I did not look, I did not dare. Blake had warned me about the Hu'akai Po. The silence stretched, but it wasn't silence; it was the sound of a hundred souls holding their breath.

And I could no longer hear Mr. Hart.

I reached out blindly, tentatively, groping through the empty space beside me where he had just been, but I found nothing. I was relieved; I was appalled. I closed my fingers around a handful of dead leaves and crushed them in my fist to stop my hand from shaking.

I lay there shivering, water seeping up from the soil and into my clothes, along my forearms and elbows and knees as I pressed myself into the ground, until the mournful conch sounded once more, until I felt the rhythm of two hundred feet passing me by and fading away, until the Hu'akai Po vanished beyond all hearing and the only sound was my heart beating in my throat.

And my father's voice.

"Nixie?"

I crawled over to him, staying low, finding my way with my hands, too scared to open my eyes. I touched his hand and he grabbed my fingers, crushing them in his own. "Are you all right?" I whispered, afraid to speak too loud, and he wrapped me in his arms.

"Oh, God, Nixie." His breath was hot on my neck as he

clutched me tight. "I thought I'd lost you."

"I'm still here," I said, half to convince myself.

"And Hart?"

"Gone. They took him, Dad. The Night Marchers. They—" I couldn't finish the sentence; Slate had tightened his embrace, squeezing the air from my lungs. But there was nothing more for me to say.

"Good," he murmured. "He's lucky it wasn't me."

I heard footsteps then, and I couldn't help myself, my eyes flew open. It was Kashmir, and he was propping up Blake, who had blood seeping through his coat. I scrambled to my feet. "Are . . . is he—" I started, but when Kashmir stopped, Blake slumped to his knees, and I didn't wait for an answer to the question I couldn't bear to ask. I pulled off Blake's jacket and groaned at the sight of the blood soaking his side.

Kashmir handed Blake over to Slate, wincing through his own pain, but he shrugged me off when I reached for the big powder burn on his stomach. "Yes, yes, my shirt will never recover," he said, pushing my hands away and holding his side like he had a stitch. "Come, we've got to get him to the ship. See if we've got something to help him. Where's the gold?"

I glanced back at the ground—the hollow where I'd huddled beside Mr. Hart—but the bag had disappeared too.

Slate propped Blake up with his shoulder, and I wadded his jacket and held it to his wound as we stumbled and slid down the mountain. I kept an eye out for torchlight along the way, half afraid the Night Marchers would return, but they had disappeared completely. We moved as quickly as possible, but by the time we reached the waterfall, Blake was pale as bone in the white moonlight, and despite my efforts to staunch the blood, his shirtfront was soaked with a slick like black ink. He wouldn't make it to the ship; he wouldn't make it down the hill. And even if he could, I had no idea if the mercury would kill him or save him.

Why had I let the caladrius go? I couldn't take my eyes off Blake's face, and I remembered how he'd blushed, his cheeks bright pink, when he'd first shown me this spot, this sacred place he loved so well. My heart pounded above the sound of the waterfall, roaring in my ears.

"Wait," I said. "Stop. We have to stop." Slate stumbled to a halt, and Blake fell to the ground. I gazed up through the pearly clouds of silver spray drifting down to the round mirror of the pool. The healing pool. "Here," I said, desperate for hope. It had to work. There was no other option. "Bring him here. Lay him in the water."

Slate lifted Blake and staggered to the bank. He didn't

ask the questions that were in his eyes—he was breathing too hard to speak—as he knelt down to lower Blake gently into the pond.

The white of Blake's shirt seemed to glow in the reflected moonlight, but soon his blood clouded the pool. My heart sank. I reached in—the pond was frigid, and I pawed at the water, at his shirt, at the blood as it drifted like mist. I found the ragged hole in the cloth and reached in, gingerly, fearfully, but the skin beneath was smooth and whole.

I started laughing, crying—joyful, hysterical—and I pulled Blake from the water and clutched him close, soaking the front of my shirt. Then Kashmir's hand, warm on my shoulder; I reached up to grab his fingers. "Come, *amira*. We have to go."

We met our warriors back at the clearing, and they fell in line behind us. Blake was still unconscious, but with Slate and me supporting him, we managed to make our way through the city to the boat. We were joined halfway back by Billie, who nipped at my ankles hard enough to draw blood before Kashmir picked her up, whining and wriggling, and carried her clamped under his arm.

A few brave souls were peering out their windows as we passed through town, so I pulled Blake's gun from his jacket pocket and fired it into the air; shutters and doors slammed as the sound of the shot echoed in the street. As we boarded the junk, I heard shouted commands from the vicinity of the palace. Had the Royal Hawaiian Guard managed to escape their barracks? We cast off as quick as we could, dumping Colonel Iaukea unceremoniously on the pier—but even under full sail, we seemed to inch toward Hana'uma as dawn began to paint the sky pink. Still there was no pursuit from the American warships in the harbor, and I wasn't surprised. Mr. D and his friends were well connected.

I clenched my fists as I watched the city grow smaller and smaller behind us. The league had won, though they hadn't gotten the money. Of course the annexation of Hawaii had never been in doubt—but now I was complicit in the monarchy's downfall. I would be reminded of that every time I had to bail the bilge.

Blake was still so pale. I checked his breathing, although Billie, who lay pressed against his body, growled when I came close. His chest rose and fell, the motion shallow but steady. Beneath the rags of his shirt, there wasn't even a bruise.

Kashmir approached, walking gingerly. He'd stripped bare to the waist, and he was still holding his side. Peeking out beneath his fingers was an ugly weal, red and purple.

"Oh, Kashmir—" I reached toward him; I couldn't help it.

"Ah ah ah!" He shied away from my hands, but then he smiled wryly. "I'll be fine. My worthless carcass will recover."

"Don't, please." I put my hand to my mouth, then down to the pendant at my throat. "Don't joke about that. Not right now."

His smile softened. "Of course, *amira*. I'll be fine," he said again. Then he turned his gaze to Blake and raised an eyebrow. "Damn. He looks better off than me."

"Yes, you were both very brave," I said, suddenly angry at the memory of my fear. "And very stupid!"

"Not as stupid as he was. I had a vest on."

"It's not a competition!"

"What's not a competition?" Blake said, his voice soft and slurred. I swallowed the bitter taste on my tongue. Billie half stood, then sat again, then stood, her tail vibrating.

I knelt down beside him. "Nothing. How do you feel?"

He tried to sit up, but I pushed him down gently. His hand crept up along his ribs. "How . . ." He cleared his throat and tried again. "I thought I was . . ."

"The healing spring," I said. "The one you showed me."

"The spring? It works?"

"It does. On your map, at least."

"On . . . my map?"

"Yes. The one you drew . . ." My voice trailed off. Did the healing spring exist before Blake drew it? Had he brought the Night Marchers into being? Was this version of Hawaii the real one, or only a fairy tale he'd told? "I don't know, really. Just rest now."

He nodded vaguely. "I'm cold," he said.

"Here." I picked up his stained jacket from the decking and shook it out, pulling it up to his chin. Then I saw it, in the pocket where he'd always kept his sketchbook: a tightly folded piece of paper, one corner brown with blood.

"I took it from the fireplace," he said. "It was atop a pile of kindling." I unfolded it gently. It was creased, but it was whole. HAPAI HALE, BLAKE HART, 1868. The map of my mother, and I, the anchor. The page trembled in my hands. It was so fragile; I could destroy it in an instant. Kashmir met my eyes, a question in his own, but I wasn't ready to answer. I folded the map carefully and slipped it into my own pocket.

"Where are you taking me?" Blake asked then.

I hesitated. "We'll make sure you get home."

"Home?" he said. "Where is that?"

CHAPTER
THIRTY-SEVEN

After what seemed like hours, we arrived at Hana'uma Bay and came alongside the *Temptation*. Bee threw a line over the bollard and leaped over the gap, taking me by the shoulders and inspecting me closely. Once she was satisfied I was unhurt, she wrapped her arms around me and pulled me close. Then she pushed back to arm's length, clapped me on the back, and went to help Slate bring Blake over. Kashmir climbed after them, leaving Rotgut and me standing there on the deck of the junk beside the general. I surveyed the contingent with regret.

"I'm sorry I can't bring them home."

"Maybe it's better that way," Rotgut said.

"How so?"

"Well, in their case, home is a tomb. Given the choice, I know I'd prefer to stay under the infinite stars."

"Maybe so."

Side by side, we sailed the two ships into the indigo waters past the bay, where the coral skirt ringing the island ended and the lava shelf dropped off and the seafloor plunged away a mile and more. When we reached a likely spot, I stood before the general, hesitating.

When I had envisioned this scheme, the warriors had been an abstract, faceless force to stand behind me for backup, or between me and trouble. But, as was so often the case, the reality was different from what I'd imagined. In doing their duty, they had created a debt in me. I wanted to thank them, to honor their journey, but would it mean anything to the soldiers? They were only made of clay. Then again, perhaps the same could be said of all of us.

"Thank you," I said finally, because it felt right, and the general saluted, putting his fist to his chest. I did the same. "You can rest now." He inclined his head, bringing the mark on his forehead to the level of my eyes. I used my thumb to remove the five. As I turned the "me/not" into a smear of soot, the light went out in his eyes.

Then, simultaneously, the fifty-three remaining warriors reached up to drag their hands down their own foreheads, and their lights went out forever.

Then we set about smashing the warriors to potsherds while Kashmir went to work on the hull with an ax. It wasn't long before we climbed back aboard the *Temptation* to watch the remains of the *54* sink beneath the blue waves. Would someone find it someday and wonder what had happened? The sea was wide and we were over deep water, but there were no guarantees.

Rotgut laughed a little. "Such a sigh!"

"Well, it was nice while it lasted."

"The power?"

"The loyalty." I swallowed a lump in my throat. "I need to speak to my father."

He was there in his room, sitting with Billie on the floor beside the bed. Blake slept behind the single remaining curtain; I'd forgotten to take down the flag before we'd scuttled the junk. Slate looked up with wide eyes when I came in. I almost went back out when I saw he'd pulled his box out from under the bed, but he stopped me with a question.

"What's that?"

I blinked, surprised; I'd pulled the map from my pocket. I turned it over and over in my hands, gently, like an egg about to hatch. Then I held it out, thrusting it toward him.

"This is it. This is your next map." He took it but did not unfold the paper. "Before you go, I . . ." I trailed off, not wanting to finish the sentence, but I took a breath and opened my mouth, willing myself to speak, although when I did, I didn't say what I'd meant to. "We'll need to get him back to Nu'uanu, first."

"No," the captain said, but his voice cracked. "No. The boy asked to stay."

"And you said yes?"

Slate twitched one shoulder in a half shrug. "He saved your life. How could I send him away?"

He still hadn't unfolded the map, so I took it back and unfolded it myself. I opened my mouth again, but it took several long moments before the air would leave my lungs. "This one won't work any better than the others," I said at last. He took a breath, as if about to speak, and I hurried on before my cowardice caught up with me. "At least . . . at least not as long as I'm on the ship. I'm already there."

I went to the table. It was easier to talk when I couldn't see his face. "You can't go to a place where you exist. Joss told me. It's something about Navigating. That's likely why none of the others worked. For you to go back, we need to part ways." I laid the old map down over the new map of

Hawaii, the father's over the son's. "She wouldn't tell me whether or not you'd be able to change the past. So I suppose my leaving is a gamble for both of us." Slate whispered something. I turned back to him. "What?"

He cleared his throat and spoke again. "I said, don't go."

"Slate." I ran my hands through my hair, then dropped them to my sides; it was a gesture I'd picked up from him. "You're not listening."

"I am, Nixie. I wasn't before, but I am now. I don't want to lose you."

"You have to, Slate. You have to choose. You can't have both."

"I—I am choosing. I can't . . . I don't want to—I am choosing you."

"I don't believe you. You say that now, but in a few days—"

"No, I swear to you—"

"Slate!" He snapped his mouth shut, and Billie startled too, her ears perked, suspicious. I paid her no mind; I unclenched my fists, trying to breathe, and gestured to the box on the floor. It was battered now, the lid askew, one hinge bent. "I know you, Captain. I know about inevitability. This is an addiction. You won't stop."

"Everything comes to an end," he said softly, in an echo of what Joss had told me weeks before.

"Yes. We were nearly killed, Slate."

"Nixie, I would never—"

"But you did. We were all nearly killed, and if it wasn't for your obsession, none of us would have been there in the first place. In fact, if it weren't for your obsession . . ." My voice trailed off. He wasn't meeting my eyes, but there was a look on his face, and my mind was racing again. Everything comes to an end, it was true . . . Joss had said so much that day.

There is always a sacrifice. Slate had told me much the same thing in the carriage; sometimes you have to let something go to take hold of something else. I had thought he was talking about me.

Joss's sacrifice, I knew. It was like the myth of the phoenix; if not for her fiery death in 1886, she never could have risen from the ashes and gone back to 1841, to start a life, to have her daughter—my mother—to introduce Lin to the captain.

But to escape Qin's tomb, she had needed us to deliver the map of the aftermath of the fire. My father could never have made that trip; he hadn't grown up steeped in the mythologies that made it possible for me to bring us to the emperor's mausoleum. Besides, I had done it—had already done it, Joss had said.

Of course, if we hadn't needed the soldiers to help with the robbery, I'd never have taken us to the tomb. If I hadn't gone to the tomb, Joss would never have escaped. If she'd never escaped . . . I stared at the map. "If not for your obsession," I said to my father, "I wouldn't be here at all."

He gave me a pained smile, more like a grimace than a grin. Then he put his hand on the map and traced the bloodstain at the edge. It cut right through the name at the corner. The silence between us was infinitely deep. "It does work, you know," he said then. "Eventually."

"What does?"

"This map, 1868."

"Dad—"

"At least, Joss thinks so." I must have looked surprised, because he laughed, short and bitter. "It was years ago. She told me my future. My fate. I didn't really take her seriously until—well." His eyes were far away, but he tapped his finger on the map. "She says I'll spend my last months there."

"Your last months?"

"In the time before I . . . arrived. To take you aboard

the ship. She said I die of an overdose, believe it or not." He laughed again, like it was funny.

"Do you believe it?"

His smile twisted. "Sometimes."

I swallowed a sudden lump in my throat; everything Joss had told me about my future, she had seen in her past. We were both quiet for a moment. It was nearly impossible to force myself to speak, but I had promised to let him go. "Do you want to try it?"

His face paled. "Try . . . this map?"

"I wish we hadn't scuttled the junk," I said. "But if you leave me ashore, I can find my way. I'd like to stop in New York first, but if you can't wait, I understand. And I'd like to take some of the other maps, if you won't need them any longer. Although if Joss is right, you won't need anything but this, really." I nudged the box with my foot. "As usual."

"Nixie, please—"

"Don't deny it, Slate. This is what you want."

"It's not all I want!" Slate kept his voice low, but it was fierce, and Blake stirred on the bed. "If we part ways, we will never see each other again."

"I can live with it if you can," I said, jutting out my chin as though it was a dare; it was all I could do to pretend that his response would not matter.

"Don't give me this choice, Nixie."

"I don't think I am, Captain." At my words, he raised his eyes to mine, and I did smile then, because I saw the truth in them now. "Sometimes fate makes choices for us."

I went out on deck into the light, shutting the door behind me and leaning on the warm wood. I took a deep breath. Then another. Kashmir was there on my hammock, Bee was at the helm, Rotgut was fishing. Topside, everything seemed just as it always was. "He'll be wanting to cast off again soon," I said at last.

Kashmir sat up straight and met my eyes. "Where are we going?"

I shrugged, feeling whimsical. "How about somewhere perfect?"

He slid out of the hammock and came to stand beside me. "But no one believes in such a place."

"You're a good liar, Kashmir." I grinned. "Maybe you can convince me."

"And . . . when do we leave?"

"Whenever the captain's ready," I said, but the door to the cabin had opened again.

"Well, I'm not ready," Slate said. "Not yet."

"No?" Then I noticed that he held his wooden box, filled with all his precious things.

"No." He paced the deck slowly, tipping the box back and forth between his hands. "I haven't got a good map," he said, his brows drawing together as he peered over the rail. Then he rubbed a streak of green verdigris on the copper.

"I need you, Nixie," he said firmly. "Go in the cabin and find me one, would you? Maybe something where we can make some honest cash this time? But you'll figure something out, you always do." He squared his shoulders. Then he hefted the box in his hands once, twice, leaned back, and flung it, spinning, tumbling, into the deep blue sea.

There was quiet on deck for a long time, and I was acutely aware of the sound of the waves brushing the hull, the wind trembling in the sails, my heart drumming against my ribs. Then Slate smiled at me, one of his brilliant smiles, as though nothing was wrong, or ever had been. "I've made my choice, Nixie."

I sought out Kashmir. There was a question in his eyes, but he found the answer in mine, and he nodded a little. My home had always been the *Temptation*.

That evening, we left 1884 behind us for good. Blake

came out on deck to watch the island grow smaller in our sight until it was a gray smudge on the horizon, and even after. Billie, standing beside him, howled once—"Rooooooooooo!"—and then trotted toward the bow to face the open sea. The sun arced overhead; the sea turned from cobalt to sapphire as the light made the deep water glow. The sails snapped in the breeze as we clipped along, heading away from the island, but toward what?

When I checked the captain's cabin, the wide drafting table was empty. I came back out on deck, and Slate was at the helm, his strong hands on the wheel, looking for all the world as though he intended to remain there. He called out to me.

"Well, Nixie? Where are we going next?"

AUTHOR'S
NOTE

In a book like this, there is a fair bit of reality to help ground the fantasy. Certainly the Kingdom of Hawaii existed; almost certainly a time-traveling pirate ship does not. Between the two poles, what is fact and what is fiction?

THE HISTORY

On December 1, 1884, fifty pirates sacked Honolulu, looting the treasury and the homes of the wealthy, making off with $3 million in coin and plate without firing a single shot. This daring theft was only mentioned in a single newspaper article, in the *Daily Alta California*, which reported that over the course of nine hours, no attempt was made at resistance. Indeed, the locals were said to have "thrown down their weapons without waiting for the opposing force to fire a single shot." On the night in question, the Honolulu Rifles, a militia controlled by the Hawaiian League, was very fortuitously out of ammunition.

The pirates were led by a tall man who seemed to know his way around the island, although no one claimed to recognize him, and by morning, they had disappeared without a trace. Where they disappeared to, no one seems to know.

The article emphasized how helpless Hawaii was, at the mercy of any band of determined men, which was a rather pointed insinuation about the inability of the king to protect his citizens. Indeed, not a decade later, U.S. soldiers helped the Hawaiian League to overthrow the monarchy for the same reason—to protect the citizens—this time, from the queen, in whose garden the league had planted a cache of rifles.

The Hawaiian League (also known as the Committee of Safety or, in quieter tones, the Annexation Club) was a secret society, so official records were not kept, but the group's constitution was drafted by the prudish Mr. Lorrin Thurston. Mr. Sanford Dole, businessman and lawyer, was also a member of the group, and later he became the president of the Republic of Hawaii. Mr. Samuel Mills Damon, who had ingratiated himself to parties on both sides, helped to negotiate a peaceful resolution to the overthrow, whereby

Queen Lili'uokalani surrendered under protest.

From first contact between Europeans and Hawaiians— in 1778, during Captain James Cook's third voyage—to the overthrow of the Hawaiian monarchy 115 years later, foreigners coveted Hawaii's paradisiacal bounty, first in the form of victuals, later in sugar and pineapples. Of course, Cook's attempt to capture a Hawaiian monarch ended in Cook's death, while the Hawaiian League's final attempt was clearly much more successful.

THE FAIRY TALES

HEALING SPRINGS AND HU'AKAI PO

Almost any hike in Nu'uanu Valley will lead to a beautiful waterfall, and there are several legends concerning healing springs in Hawaii, including Kunawai, at the base of the valley, and many springs throughout the island that were *kapu*, or forbidden to commoners. If you go in search of Blake's sacred spot, watch out for the Hu'akai Po; the legend of the Night Marchers was a tale I was often told growing up. Only the young and the foolish seek out the warriors, and I have been both. Several nights, while visiting a boy who lived in Manoa Valley, we saw torchlight wavering on a mountainside too steep to climb. We spent many days hiking together but never found the source.

MYTHS AND MAGIC

The mythological items mentioned in the book are all inspired by real legends. The sky herring that light the lamps are a reference to the ancient Swedish name for the aurora: *sillblixt*, meaning "herring flash." Fishermen thought the lights were the reflections of huge shoals of fish.

The bottomless bag is from the Welsh epic *Y Mabinogi* and can never be filled unless a person steps inside. The golem is a Jewish myth wherein a figure of clay can be brought to life and made to toil, although their great tragedy is that they cannot speak.

There is a lovely illustration of the caladrius curing a king in the Aberdeen Bestiary. And of course, Katz's pastrami and Di Fara's pizza have attained mythological status but are decidedly, deliciously real.

THE EMPEROR'S TOMB

As yet largely unexcavated, the description of Qin's tomb is based on the *Shiji*, as mentioned in the book, as well as on speculations by archaeologists who have used ground imaging technology—sonar and the like—to map out the sprawling necropolis. Unusually high amounts of mercury in the surrounding soil give credence to Sima Qian's account of underground rivers and seas; perhaps one day, if exploration continues, we'll learn just how accurate he was.

Any imperial dragon depicted in the tomb would likely have five claws; the more proletarian dragons make do with three.

THE BLACK SHIP

The *Temptation* is based on a ship called the *Notorious*, a replica caravel built by Graeme and Felicity Wylie after the legend of the Mahogany Ship, an Australian shipwreck. The *Temptation*'s keel, a huge bone carved in runes, is a reference to the myth of Ullr's bone; apparently, the Norse wizard Ullr used "a certain bone, which he had marked with awful spells, wherewith to cross the seas, instead of a vessel; and that by this bone he passed over the waters that barred his way as quickly as by rowing." That quote is from Saxo Grammaticus's twelfth-century work *Gesta Danorum*.

The *Temptation*'s figurehead is fashioned after the first girl Slate ever kissed. Slate is a terrible romantic.

SAILORS' SUPERSTITIONS

Sailors have a great many omens and superstitions about being at sea, some of them contradictory. Women aboard were usually considered bad luck, although they were thought of as the very best navigators. In addition, the sight of a woman's breasts was thought to shame the storm right out of a rough sea; to this end, most figureheads are bare-breasted women.

Sailors also considered the sight of an albatross to be a good omen, although in "Rime of the Ancient Mariner," a sailor who kills an albatross brings hardship and misfortune to his ship. Albatross are very long lived and typically mate for life, spending months—sometimes years—apart but always reuniting, parting only in death.

KASHMIR'S BACKGROUND

In 1704 or thereabouts, Antoine Galland translated *One Thousand and One Nights* into French, adding some stories that were not in the original Syrian text. The work became very popular in Europe over the next century, with people publishing their own versions and translations, some more fanciful than others. Thus, Kashmir hails from the Vaadi Al-Maas, or Diamond Valley, which is a reference to the story of Sinbad and the Rocs. He shares other characteristics with some characters in the stories attributed to Scheherazade, which of course Nix had read. He speaks Persian, Arabic, English, and French, befitting a man from a fairy-tale version of "Arabia" as seen through the eyes of an eighteenth-century French cartographer.

Yalla! (Arabic): Let's go!

Vite! (French): Quickly!

Ya sidi (Arabic): Sir.

Khahesh mikonam (Persian): You're welcome.

Khodaye man! (Persian): My God!

Negaran nabash (Persian): Don't worry.

Cher (French): Dear.

Baleh (Farsi): Yes.

Pourquoi pas? (French): Why not?

Viens (French): Come.

In shaa' Allah (Arabic): God willing.

ACKNOWLEDGMENTS

Many myths include quests, and many quests include helpers without whom the hero would fail. Writing a book is not heroic, but those who have helped me along the way have been.

My keepers of knowledge, Rebecca C. Brown on maps, Duncan Stephenson and Gordon Young on ships and sailing, Matteen Mokalla for Persian, and Haatem Reda for Arabic, who gave me as much information as any good god of wisdom, without too many of the demands for worship, thank you.

Those who encouraged me when I first needed it— Diane Drotleff, Michelle Elliott, Rob Hartmann, Karen Henderson, Lisa Sindorf, Lori Steinberg, Sana Hamelin, and particularly Robert St. John—I owe you all drinks. Where did I put that bottomless pitcher of wine? I am also grateful to Zack Fornaca, for his willing sacrifice, and to my shaman, Curtis Zimmerman. And to the philosophers, Anthony Gregory and Tommaso Sciortino, thank you for holding up your lamps.

I am so lucky for my first readers, Sharon Rader, Bruce Lamon, Thekla Hansen-Young—I put my heart in your hands and you didn't feed it to Amut. To my first fan—ever, not just of this book—Diana Hansen-Young, thank you. I love your work.

My incredible agent, Molly Ker Hawn—like Hermes, intercessor between me and the gods—you are definitely the answer to a prayer. My amazing editor, Martha Mihalick, all-seeing, all-knowing goddess of Greenwillow: I worship you just a little bit. And to the team at Hotkey, Sara O'Connor and Naomi Colthurst—thank you for smiling on this author.

And finally, to Felix, little egg that hatched a dragon, and to Bret, like Hephaestus, hammering out the plot on your forge, it's always been true: I need you.